BURIED HEROES

Age of Azuria Book One

BETH BALL

rove
GUARDIAN
PRESS

Published by Grove Guardian Press

Edited by The Blue Garret

Cover design by 17 Studio Book Design

ISBN 978-1-952609-01-5

Hardback ISBN 978-1-952609-02-2

Ebook ISBN 978-1-952609-00-8

groveguardianpress.com

To Jonathan
Thank you for traveling to Azuria with me

ALSO BY BETH BALL

Age of Azuria (in chronological order)

Aurora: An Age of Azuria Novella

Song of Parting: An Age of Azuria Novella (preorder before release
February 9th, 2021)

Buried Heroes: Age of Azuria Book One

Story Magic: An Age of Azuria Novella (forthcoming 2021)

Hadvarian Heist: Age of Azuria Book Two

Forest Deep: Age of Azuria Book Three (forthcoming 2021)

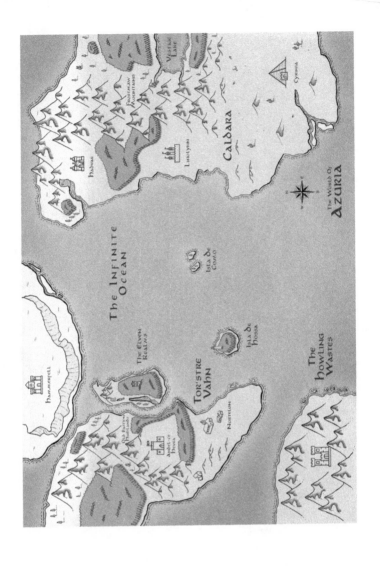

PROLOGUE

The sharp ends of tree branches tore at Yvayne's face and hair as she darted through the forest. Her breaths came quickly, her heart pumping adrenaline into her veins to maximize the fleeting seconds she might have before Lucien captured his prey.

Yvayne discarded the flashes of regret behind her flying footsteps. After she saved Fhaona, she could apologize for dismissing her. She only needed to ensure the survival of one more druid in the world. They were each necessary to the others.

Fhaona's role had to be more complex than sacrifice.

A scream flickered through the trees ahead, and Yvayne groaned, pushing herself harder. What had happened? Had he caught the elf already?

She called on the latent fae energy buried deep within. Green ripples of vitality ricocheted off nearby branches and joined her magical aura. Only used as a last resort, this gathering of natural power would serve as a beacon, declaring her position to the dark forces that sought to destroy her and her allies. But in this moment, she had to see what transpired, despite the loss of anonymity.

Yvayne's vision narrowed; her eyes burned, molten gold, as nearby spirits surrounded her. They blotted out any details she didn't need to see, freed her focus to the two souls ahead. Ancient lines of sacred trees, rooted through centuries of upheaval elsewhere in the world, crashed into one another in the corners of her eyes as the spirits swarmed around them, dimming their visual presence. They would be there, waiting for her after the confrontation was over. Fhaona might not be.

A wing of possibility caught on the wind. Fhaona fled, and the forest grew behind her feet to protect her—perhaps Lucien might be stopped this time.

But she was already too late.

A few thousand feet ahead of Yvayne's pounding footsteps, at the edge of her heightened senses, the attack unfolded.

Fhaona fell, exhausted, at the base of a towering silver tree. The scarlet canopy of the autumnwood above her trembled, and the leaves recoiled as evil stalked closer to the elven druid, one of their protectors against the greedy ravages of the outside world. Even from a great distance, Yvayne could feel the tree's desire to catch Fhaona in its branches, but something held it fast.

A tall, cloaked figure glided closer to the woman's shaking form. As Lucien's fungus-ridden cape caressed the earth, the young grasses and freshly fallen tree petals became perfumed with the stench of death.

"Fhaona," his voice sighed out, half from his mouth, half from his decaying throat. The elf screamed in terror as her eyes lit upon his face. "You are perhaps the most interesting of those I've tracked. The greatest challenge, we'll say, if that's of any comfort."

The druid tried to pick herself up from the ground, but Lucien withdrew a thin, gray-green arm from beneath his robe and, with a simple twirl of his long, delicate fingers, her body grew rigid, and she collapsed back to the forest floor.

Yvayne ran faster, trying desperately to arrive before he was able to finish his task, but already, the silver-tinged glow faded from the elven woman's face.

With a cry that originated from her very core, Fhaona arched her back against the magic holding her and clutched at the moon-shaped charm around her neck. Yvayne felt the despair as her own when the druid was unable to shape-shift, a special ability enabled by the crescent pendant. A low sob escaped from Fhaona's throat as she grabbed on to a root with her other hand and pulled herself forward. Surely in this moment, the forest would be able to protect her.

She could sense Fhaona willing an explosion of vines into existence. Again the forest's desire pulsed in Yvayne's heart, but no vines appeared. Fhaona's labored breathing pressed on her ears, urgent, and Yvayne shuddered at the heavy, wet breaths of the pursuer. Beneath each of their exhalations of life and death, the burnished oak and her fellows groaned; no matter the power of the spell or their own wishes, they could do nothing to aid Fhaona.

"*Tsk, tsk, tsk,* my dear." A gray-green hand reached down toward the druid's walnut-brown hair and selected a set of lightly curled strands. She looked up at him in horror as each breath grew more strained in her chest cavity. "You won't be able to perform any of your tricks in my presence." Lucien withdrew his other bony, half-decomposed hand from beneath his robes to show her the large black ring that clung to his rotting finger.

"It took quite a long while to discover these, hidden away within the Shadowlands. But I succeeded nonetheless. I have an excess of time now, as you and your kind once did." He smiled. "But, my, how things change. Darkstones were designed to restrict other magical energies, particularly nature-based magics as"—he inhaled deeply over her head—"yours most certainly seems to be."

Yvayne leapt over a fallen tree. She would be upon them in a moment. Spectral faery wings sprouted from her shoulders, and another breath of hope entered her lungs. *Stay strong, Fhaona.*

"Relax, and this will all be over soon," Lucien purred. He twirled Fhaona's hair in his hand. Yvayne choked on bile at the sight. If she could catch him and rescue Fhaona, they could bring an end to this particular aspect of their greater enemy. Alessandra wouldn't expect to lose one of her servants so soon.

Fhaona's hand darted out and struck Lucien's throat. The elven woman was more powerful than he had reckoned, and the darkstone didn't render her immobile as it did many of the others. The contact with his skin covered the back of Fhaona's hand in pus and spores. She screamed as the poison began to do its work, nearly all her energy sapped by the necrotic ring.

Lucien clutched his hand to his neck and growled. His fingers dug in and reformed the injured areas in a fresh layer of fungus. "Enough. I grow tired of this." He snapped his fingers, and the earth around Fhaona roiled. Two narrow sets of feline shoulders emerged from the soil, and warm dirt cascaded to the ground.

"No!" Yvayne shouted. If she could distract him with more promising prey, perhaps she could save Fhaona.

"Madeline, Micaela, show our guest below." Lucien's cold, dead eyes searched the clearing until he found Yvayne's speeding form closing the distance between them. The corners of his mouth lifted.

Shadows continued to rise from beneath the earth and took the shape of two hulking tigers made of smoke and darkness. Their entry left open an abyss that led directly to the Shadowlands.

"I'll send my regards to your mother then, shall I?" Lucien called out to Yvayne.

Fhaona opened her mouth to scream, but the dark maws that had emerged from the depths claimed her body and dragged her below.

"Fhaona!" Yvayne cried. Her wings, finally ready, lifted her into the air and propelled her the remaining distance to the clearing as the druid slipped beneath the surface. At the edge of the darkstone's sphere of influence, twenty feet off the ground, the magic pulsing inside her stopped, and her wings vanished. She didn't need her special vision to see Lucien's smirk as she plummeted to the earth below. Her momentum dragged her along the forest floor, and she collided with the base of one of the grove's oldest trees. Her breath burst from her body.

Lucien stood over her panting frame. "I have been expecting you, Yvayne. I am pleased you did not miss your cue. We shall meet again soon." The lich's foul form floated into the portal he had summoned between the planes and disappeared deep into the realm of shadow.

Yvayne lay motionless on the ground, unable to pick herself up. When her breath finally returned, she scrambled forward to where Fhaona had lain only moments before. The druid's crescent-moon necklace rested against the leaves and scattered dirt. The gold charm was cold even though it had recently rested so close to the heart of its keeper.

Had Fhaona left it behind on purpose, knowing her successor was coming soon?

"Please, I only need a few days," Fhaona had said after she arrived outside Yvayne's secluded home high in the Frostmaw Mountains.

"It's too dangerous for us to be so close together. He'll sense it."

"Yvayne, he already has. He's following me."

"So you decided to lead him here?" She shut her eyes against the memory. If Fhaona had known to come find her then, just on the edge of their waiting's end, it would only be a matter of time before Lucien made moves of his own if he hadn't already. She needed to act, now.

Yvayne ran her fingers over the dry leaves that had last touched the druid, their life suddenly sucked away as Fhaona's would soon be inside Lucien's lair. She pulled their corpses into her chest as she sobbed. There was one less soul in their conclave. Fhaona was gone. She had failed again.

A breeze of cool night air roused her from the ground. Whispers darted through the trees, vying for her attention. The spirits knew another was coming, someone returned, yet new. The ancient mountain site was only a few days' travel to the south. She had time to prepare. Yvayne's cheeks lifted against her dried tears as she smiled. For the first time, they would have the upper hand.

CHAPTER 1

Iellieth trailed her fingers lightly across the tall wildflowers trapped inside their designated plot in the castle gardens. She breathed in their shy, hopeful aromas as she passed. A memory trickled by from when she had been only as tall as they, running through the fields outside of Aurora, ready to show off her newest discovery. The flowers' faces seemed to turn toward her as she walked; they alone would bear witness to the tears that gathered in her eyes. She would be forced to leave them behind, like everything else that had grown in her years here. But however hopeless the situation appeared, she was determined to have a say in her ultimate destination.

She and Katarina had arranged to meet in her favorite spot in the gardens, just at the edge of the arboretum. Many others had claimed it as a cherished location since Iellieth started tending it a few years before. She felt more at peace than she had in days as the blush-flowering trees poked their arms above the other greenery and beckoned her forward to their petaled embrace.

When she first told Mathilde, the gardener, what she

wanted to plant in the formerly overgrown bed, the woman had scoffed. The Lady surely had her head in the clouds if she believed the spring-blossoming trees would grow beneath the shelter of the carefully groomed forest. They wouldn't receive enough sun, and if they did grow, they would cast too long a shadow over the collections of crimson and ivory flowers Iellieth wanted to cultivate beneath them.

"Breathtaking as always, Lady Amastacia." Katarina feigned a short curtsy from beneath the stone archway. Iellieth grinned and hurried forward.

"Did you catch sight of yourself in a mirror, or are you waxing poetic about the flowers?"

Katarina laughed at Iellieth's teasing. She extricated herself from the raptures of the climbing roses and embraced her friend. "How are you?" she asked as she leaned away to look at her face.

"I am as alright as you would guess." It seemed they were alone in the gardens, but the fresh growth obscured the far bends too fully to be sure.

"I cannot believe it's finally here."

"Nor can I."

"And there's no way they can be talked out of it?"

Iellieth sighed. "No, dear Katarina, not that I have found."

"Well, I find it truly abominable—"

"Wait, please. We cannot all be free-roaming Celestial scholars, and I would choose for . . ."—her voice grew husky as the tears gripped her throat once more—"for our final chat to be of something more high-minded than my stepfather's scheming. One last story, before I go." Katarina loved telling stories and would never be able to resist such a request, especially under the circumstances. "A new one."

Katarina grinned at her as a tear fell from her dark eyes and carved a path across her warm brown skin. "Very well." She pulled Iellieth's arm through her own, and they began their final walk together around the gardens.

"There was once a beautiful oread, one of the dryads of the mountains, who would disguise herself as a human and tell her tales to curious travelers making their way from one land to the next. Eramis, that was her name. What Eramis valued, as most oreads do, was a mingling between cultures so that all lands might be joined, especially through their stories, one to the other.

"The type of traveler Eramis encountered determined the story she told. Those who left their small villages seeking adventure learned of distant, exotic lands where even their wildest dreams for what life might contain would be surpassed. Those who returned home from a long journey heard of incredible transformations or revelations that others had experienced after an extended time alone on the road, engaging with the sanctity of the land around them.

"But Eramis's favorite story to tell was that of Hugh and Lilia, two great heroes of old. He was the leader of the lycan people, the first humans to emerge on the surface of the prime plane, protected by the wolf god Fenrir in their journey across the lands. One day as he ventured through the forest, he heard a heartbreakingly gorgeous song that danced its way between the trees to nuzzle against his ears.

"Oreads are beautiful mistresses of song, as you recall I'm sure, so this part of the story is somewhat suspect. It's possible that Eramis inserted herself in some ways into the role of Lilia in the romance, which is of course up to her to do as the storyteller, but it bears noting all the same.

"Hugh tore through the forest in search of the singer, sure that his life would be forever darker if he could not find the being behind the song. And there ahead of him, with her pale hand pressed against the firm body of an oak tree, was Lilia.

"She looked rather like you if the stories are to be believed. Deep red hair that cascaded all the way to her waist and mystical green eyes starred through with gold.

"The lycan alpha was caught off guard by the embodiment of loveliness before him, and he stopped, frozen in his tracks. Lilia's bright eyes turned slowly at the disturbance she felt in the woods. In the space of a heartbeat, she withdrew a deep green bow and notched an arrow. 'Who dares disturb our morning ritual, between the woods and I?' she demanded. Hugh stumbled back, surprised by the aggression from what he had previously seen as pristine beauty.

"By this point in the story, Eramis would have walked for some time with the traveler and would know which part of the legendary love between the two they might most need to hear. And, in that tradition, thinking of our friendship, I'll leave you with the end.

"A great tragedy overtook the world and drove apart what had previously been woven together by the natures of magic and time. Hugh and Lilia faced a choice: to abandon their peoples or to be divided from one another. They each chose the latter, though it was the hardest thing they'd ever done. He remained with the humans on the prime plane. She retreated with the other fae to the Brightlands, a realm of wild beauty and mischievous magic well suited to their empathetic, curious natures.

"Enid called the soul of her daughter into the heavens after a time, and Fenrir brought his warrior to a place of peace. Through the ages, they would long for one another, as we long for those we are separated from, either through space, time, death, or other machinations. Some believe that this longing proves that we are alive. Others, that it marks the path forward."

"What do you think it means?" Iellieth asked, knowing Katarina was fond of burying lessons inside ancient tales.

"I believe the answer is somewhere in between the two. Many emotions remind us of the life pulsing through our veins. Many forces conspire together to illuminate the roads ahead. We live, learn, and love by both."

"I shall dearly miss your stories, Katarina." Their moments together were among her few bright memories of life in the castle.

"And I shall dearly miss you, Iellieth. In my heart, I want to tell you that things may turn out better than they seem, but I don't wish to make your journey any heavier than it is already."

"Thank you." Iellieth turned to go before the parting became more difficult, but Katarina caught hold of her arm.

"Are you sure that telling your mother about Lord Stravinske's behavior would do nothing to change her mind?"

Iellieth shook her head and suppressed the shudder in the middle of her spine. "She and the duke know exactly what sort of man he is. Nothing of that sort could possibly be a surprise. I already tried to tell her before, and she did nothing."

"But he—"

"He may have his wedding ceremony, and a night or

two at most if I can do nothing to prevent it. But I'll not endure longer than that. What the duke means to be a cage, I mean to be a step, however unwelcome, to freedom. I'll find someone who doesn't know who I am, book passage across the ocean, and make my way to the Realms."

"Are you hoping to seek out Teodric, after you find your father?"

"It has been years, Katarina. I haven't heard from him since we tried to escape, and his aid to me brought about the ruin of his family. He doesn't want to see me. I'm sure he has only painful memories of our past now."

"I wish there were more that I could do, Iellieth."

The sob she had struggled to hold back leapt from her chest, and Iellieth threw her arms around her friend. "You've given me access to worlds I could never have otherwise known, to languages and literatures extending beyond these lands and back through time. I would never have been able to endure all of this, to find a way to survive, without the tools you placed in my hands."

Katarina's tears mingled in her hair as she was sure her own were doing in her friend's twisted locks. *"Kev'rei mau, adeli lei,"* she whispered into Iellieth's neck. *I'll never forget you*, in the language of the Celestial realm, their favorite to translate together. Katarina kissed the pointed tip of Iellieth's ear and stepped back. "I'll be there to see you off at the Lyceum. Take care."

She squeezed Katarina's hand. "Until then." Iellieth turned toward the garden's side entrance. In a trick of the early morning light, the beds of flowers appeared brighter, more vivid than they had only a few minutes before. Hadvar, where she and her family would transmigrate later that morning, was too far to the north to have open-air gardens. They kept them only in glass houses, trapped and forced to stare through panes to capture the life-giving rays of the sun.

ॐ

Iellieth stepped into the enclosure of the castle hallways. Linolynn's additions to the ancient fortress of Io Keep were primarily large windows, pale stone walkways, and beautifully crafted turrets. From the foundation of a time of violence, Katarina liked to say, arose a testament to light and beauty. Iellieth wouldn't be so lucky in her new home in Hadvar, though luck was the wrong word for it; she had no desire to stay here either.

She hurried down the castle corridors toward the Amastacia wing. On most days at this time, her family would be blessedly absent but, this year, they were all traveling to the Festival of Renewal together. It was unlikely that she could make it through the receiving area without either the duke or her mother catching sight of her.

Her boots echoed on the cool gray stone as she walked in and out of rays of sunlight to her family's rooms. When the castle was full and bustling, Iellieth tried to choose lesser-traveled routes, where she stuck to the carpets in the middle of the halls to muffle the sound of her footsteps. She preferred to go unnoticed and, whenever possible, to blend into the world around her.

Iellieth paused at one of the multistory windows. The Infinite Ocean gleamed in the distance, sparkling like a beacon of freedom. On moments like this, it felt as though the waves called to her as they had when she was a child, asking her to step in and join her being to the water.

As she grew older, her connection to the ocean

changed. It crashed against the cliffs below the castle, day and night, reminding her of those she was separated from: her father, whom she had never met, and Teodric, who had been sent away across the waters.

But water also brings together, by its very nature. When she lay awake at night, she would imagine the sea spray below as having come from the distant Elven Realms, where her father might have walked along the shore with trouser legs rolled up, scrunching his toes in the sand. Or when the wind whistled against the cliffs, crafting a unique melody each night to sing her to sleep, she heard again the songs Teodric used to write and play, created just for her.

Reluctantly, she pulled herself away from the view and hurried on again. Her stepfather would be irritated that she had left in the early morning hours on such an important day, but she loved to feel the dew against her ankles and watch the petals greet the sun.

Iellieth twirled her amulet in her fingers as she tiptoed to the castle's northern reaches and her family's generous wing. The amulet was the only trace of her father that she possessed—she didn't even know his name. He had left the amulet with the young duchess when he and the other elven diplomats were sent back across the Infinite Ocean. They were expelled from the kingdom of Linolynn, the weeks spent forging trade partnerships and alliances undone by the revelation of an affair between one of the ambassadors and a beautiful young noblewoman, her mother, who was married to the powerful Duke Calderon Amastacia.

Soon after the affair was uncovered, a terrible illness began circulating across Linolynn, affecting young and old of all classes, and the duchess took her young son by

Calderon away to live by the sea, in Aurora, to escape the illness. Emelyee had left with the revelation that she was expecting her second child, one not fathered by her husband but by the elven diplomat. She refused to give in to Calderon or her parents' urgings to get rid of the child, and she returned to Aurora, where her tiny daughter had been conceived.

Calderon stayed away, angry and sulking, for the first year of Iellieth's life, but when the sickness crept beneath the door of the Amastacia household, claiming the lives of Emelyee's parents, he found his way to making peace with his wife. Their second child, Lucinda, was born a year later.

Iellieth loved living by the seashore, and she constantly brought Emelyee magical shells and flowers she found. The young girl had insisted that she could see the flowers growing before her eyes, but her mother had explained the illusion and that she merely saw them blowing in the wind.

After the Autumn of Rebirth blew healing winds across the lands, Calderon convinced Emelyee to leave behind her peaceful life by the seashore and return to Linolynn proper, to the castle and the court.

Iellieth had watched as the servants loaded all the trunks and ushered Bruden, Lucinda, and their keepers into the coaches for the day-long trek back to Io Keep. She didn't want to go. *Mamaun* had said that the new castle was too tall on the rocks for them to play in the ocean, and there was no forest nearby, only a small park. Why would they leave their home? There was only one thing to do. She'd take the ocean with her.

Marie saw her on her way and asked if she might accompany the young lady to the sea. Iellieth said yes so long as she helped carry the shells. She could only hold a few, and there was no way for her to contain the immensity of the sea. Dirt and sand coated her new white dress. Mamaun would be cross with her and would make her go to the cold castle. "What should we do?" her heart asked the ocean. It cried in reply, and Iellieth did as well. It didn't know.

Her beautiful mother appeared and found her as she spoke with the sea. A few blades of the long grasses clung to her skirt, and Mamaun's hair had fallen into loose, flowing strands just like hers.

"What is it, my darling?" her mother asked. She knelt down so they could be at eye level and smiled at Iellieth's armful of shells and shiny rocks from the beach.

"I don't want to go. He'll never be able to find us. The duke won't let him." Saying this out loud was more than she could bear. Iellieth pitched forward into Emelyee's open arms. The sandy collection was cold and wet against her skin, and she shivered.

"Are you talking about your father?"

Iellieth nodded her head, and her mother wiped the tears free from her cheeks.

"I think you're old enough now for me to give you something very important. But you must be careful with it, like a good lady. Would you like to see?"

Iellieth sniffled and straightened. "Yes, Mamaun."

Her mother removed a small wooden box from her pocket. "Your father told me that this box is made from different types of oak, each of which tells us a long story. It was made by one of the finest woodworkers in the elven capital of Thyles Thamor. Do you remember learning about the elves in our books?"

She nodded. The box was too beautiful for her to speak, and the ocean called for her attention as well. She wanted to touch it, but Mamaun did not like that. It was important to wait.

Her mother opened the box and revealed the amulet inside. The center of the necklace featured a deep-red ruby, held in delicate, twisting strands of gold that crossed the gem in a curving hourglass design interrupted by a diamond shape at the intersection point.

"Your father gave this to me before we parted," Mamaun said, tears glistening in her own eyes. "I think he would have wanted you to have it." Her mother reached behind her neck and unclasped a thin gold chain. She threaded it through the top of the amulet.

"Turn around," she said, and Iellieth dutifully obeyed. The necklace reached to the center of her torso after Mamaun clasped it around her neck and gently pulled her hair out of the way. "What do you think?"

Iellieth gazed in wonder at her gift. The ocean and the shells had answered her. They were going to help her father find her and them too. Iellieth's eyes brimmed over once again as she smiled. She sprang forward and hugged her mother, her hips thrust back so as not to crush her new treasure. "I love it, Mamaun," Iellieth whispered in her ear.

"I am so glad, my sweetheart. Do you think you're ready to go to the castle now?"

"Do we have to?"

The duchess nodded. Iellieth glanced at the seashells and rocks scattered around her feet. She placed one in her mother's hand and one in each of her pockets. She looked once more at the ocean. The waves crashed their good-bye. Her hand opened and closed to answer them. She wrapped her fingers around her amulet and placed the other hand in Mamaun's, ready to be shown to their carriage.

On the journey to Io Keep, Iellieth was quiet. She stared at the amulet, turning it over and over again in the sunlight that twinkled through the coach's windows.

Iellieth wore her most prized possession always. When she was still quite small, she tucked it carefully under her shirts and dresses so no one would try to take it from her. As she perfected the art of blending into her surroundings —vanishing into the movement of a room during a social event or shrinking away from the gaze of her peers and their parents, having learned that the circumstances of her birth made her an outsider in Linolynn—she was more willing to wear it outside her garments. For a few years in her early adolescence, as her relationship with her mother worsened and she became more isolated than ever, Iellieth wore it openly. She relished the aggravation her one small rebellion caused the duke.

And in the days before her wedding, she couldn't help but return to the childhood state of trying to call to her father through the necklace that, she was sure, was somehow imbued with magic. If only she could cry out to him loudly enough, if only he could somehow hear her need, she knew he would come for her. He wouldn't have let someone like Lord Stravinske occupy the same room as his precious daughter, let alone betroth her to him. Of that, Iellieth was certain.

Lost in this reverie of trying to access her father, wherever he was in Azuria, and begging him to come find her, Iellieth rounded a corner and found herself back at her family's wing more quickly than she'd meant to be. The heavy wooden door bearing the Amastacia crest—an intricate shield bedecked with black roses cast in silver, steel, and onyx—bore down on her, absorbing the shadows nearby.

Iellieth had inherited her great-grandmother's family ring, the one her mother had worn as a girl. She always found it to be a fitting complement to her amulet. Tendrils of golden ivy stretched from the base to the tip of her left ring finger. Along the ring's spine, silver-stemmed black roses grew from bud to bloom and back, each blossoming out of the other, and the two fully extended roses kissed at a tiny hinge above her knuckle.

Tradition held that the oldest woman in a lineage was the head of her family until she passed the honor down to her next female descendant. The duchess's ring, a heavy gold signet worn on the middle finger of her left hand, proclaimed her station. And because Iellieth was older than Lucinda and recognized by her mother—she was, after all, an Amastacia, as the surname passed through the matrilineal line—her ring signaled that she held the second-highest position in the family and would be next in line to lead.

However, Hadvarian society was patriarchal. Before her wedding ceremony, she would have to turn her ring over to her half-sister as part of her abdication of her place in the Amastacia line. Iellieth glared at the shield and imagined Lucinda's haughty demeanor in that moment of victory over her despised "bastard" sister. She seized the metal handle and leaned back, shifting its weight with her own till it creaked open, and slipped inside.

Iellieth walked through the entryway and receiving room, intent on reaching the one sanctuary she could, at least most often, call entirely her own.

"I would say it's well past time that you arrived, but it

would be a waste of breath to express surprise on the matter."

Iellieth jumped at the nasal sound of her stepfather's droning voice. She was still upset following her conversation with Katarina and looked at the floor until she could compose herself to face Duke Amastacia.

"Where have you been?"

Iellieth took a deep breath. "On a walk." She saw her mother standing behind Calderon, bathed in sunlight. The duchess rearranged the flowers on one of the many side tables in the elegantly appointed room, but Iellieth knew she was listening closely to the conversation.

"To the gardens no doubt. I told you she would be there," he called over his shoulder. "We all have enough to deal with at the moment. I trust you will be punctual and attentive during the Festival, particularly to Lord Stravinske."

"I would hate to burden you with undue worry. I can assure you that I will be neither, particularly when it comes to Lord Stravinske." She spun on her heel to go.

"I'd stop there if I were you." The note of warning, though spoken with quiet control, dripped with threat all the same.

"Would you?" Iellieth turned back toward him, fury blazing from her eyes. She should have known it would be pointless to try to resist his goading on this day so near to his triumph. "I certainly wish you would. You can both turn a blind eye all you want, but your senses will need to be deadened beyond violence to delude yourselves into believing that I will not fight you every step of the way to this ceremony that I have neither welcomed nor consented to."

"Now, that is—"

"Do you expect me to grovel in thanks for a marriage to a disgusting man who assaulted me two years ago? Am I to forget about being shoved into a column outside the ballroom and forcibly kissed the moment your back was turned?"

The duke's lips were two thin lines of anger, and his expression narrowed in malice. Iellieth was afraid to look at her mother. She couldn't bear the thought of her mamaun willingly sacrificing her to this, and she refused to see if the expression on her mother's face was the apathy she feared.

"You and I both know that nothing of the kind happened. I spoke with Lord Stravinske myself shortly after your 'encounter,' and we settled any element of misunderstanding."

"That sounds terribly expensive. How much did it cost you, Calderon?" She spat out his name.

"I will be damned before I brook another instance of disrespect from you. Were you not already betrothed, I would throw you out for such insolence. You will—"

"But you have no right to throw me out, do you?" Iellieth twisted her lips into a small smirk to hide the terror coursing through her veins. She had nearly succeeded in angering the duke to the point of banishment before; perhaps she could manage it this time? But he would never allow the public disgrace those actions would provoke, however much he wished to be rid of her. And his way was crueler.

"That is more than enough, both of you." The duchess stepped toward her husband. Why was she stopping him? This was Iellieth's last chance. Frustration coursed through her, the anger so intense she could feel it spark between her fingertips, waiting to explode outward. She wanted to scream.

Thwack.

Her mother leapt back as the pot she'd been tending burst. A tumble of vines poured across the table. Her step-father clutched his chest, surprised. "Bridget, come here please," the duchess called, gazing at the tangled greenery.

Staring at the pot, Iellieth wondered why she herself had not been startled by the sudden noise. Had she known that the pot couldn't take any more and all the life contained within had to be released? Had she willed that to happen?

Emelyee stepped carefully over the shattered pieces and glanced at the wild profusion of fresh-cut flowers spread around the room. "Something strange has happened, to be sure." The other bouquets were suddenly overgrown and unseemly. The sprigs used to enhance the decor had sprouted new growths and run off the tabletops. They reached out, collided. Like the call of the ocean when they left Aurora.

The duchess wrapped her hand around her husband's elbow. "Now, Calderon, why don't you see about Bruden's preparations for the Festival. I worry that he hasn't packed his warmer finery appropriately." Before he could object, she added, "And I am well aware that Sir James has assisted him. I'm sure Layne has done his part as well. Please?"

"Yes, dear," he said. He patted her hand and, with a final glare at Iellieth, skulked away to their son's room.

"Iellieth," the duchess began.

"Are you going to tell me that I don't have to go through with it?"

"Well . . ."

"Then you have nothing to say to me."

CHAPTER 2

Iellieth felt the tears coming fast and knew she couldn't withstand her mother's response, whether it was an offer of compassion or a harsh correction. She spun away and strode past the doorways of her half-siblings' rooms. Hers had been beside theirs originally, when the four of them returned to live at court years ago. The duchess took pity on her heartbroken daughter and allowed her to move to what should have been a guest room. It was situated at the end of the family wing, but Iellieth couldn't sleep without the sounds of the seaside that had been their home. From the isolated part of the hall, Iellieth could hear the Infinite Ocean pounding against the rocky coast beneath the castle, wave upon wave throwing itself against the cliffs.

As was only fitting for the nation's richest and oldest still-surviving family, the Amastacias possessed a beautiful section of Io Keep, second only to the halls of the king and his family. Their portion stretched along the north-western reaches of the cliffside, rounding out in the beautiful circular room, made almost entirely of windows, that

Iellieth called her own. She didn't have the en suite bath, separate visiting room, or dining quarters that the legitimate Amastacia offspring did in their suites. Despite what might otherwise be considered shortcomings in elegance and status, Iellieth's room offered her, as unendingly as it could manage, a picture of the outside world.

The 270-degree circle of windows looked out on the coastline and the Infinite Ocean beyond, wrapping around to include vistas of the castle gardens. But if she climbed over her wooden desk—careful not to disturb the pages of notes and open books from her translations with Katarina —Iellieth could see ships pulling all the way in to port.

It had been several years since she regularly studied these arrivals, hoping for a sign of Teodric's return with his parents or, even less likely, a delegation of elves making a tour of the Caldaran coast. Her hopes for a chance of escape or a new life dwindled slowly as time passed. She still enjoyed the exercise occasionally and was fascinated by the intricacies of the rigging and crews that she had read about but never been able to investigate in person. Almost everything in her home kingdom revolved around them, but she was forbidden from going to the docks.

Today, however, she would only be able to visit her windows and books briefly before she had to leave them behind forever, and she hurried down the hallway, eager to reach a sanctuary that wouldn't be hers for much longer. Even if she were able to return to Linolynn when it was their turn to host the Festival of Renewal every other year, she would stay, she recalled with a shudder, in the guest suites reserved for foreigners and dignitaries.

Her door, bleached by the sunlight that caressed it each day, seemed more alive and welcoming than the polished, dark doorways of the other family bedchambers.

Iellieth glanced over her shoulder before she turned the large iron handle, and the hinges swung open effortlessly to the airy expanse of her chamber. After a row, the duke liked to send the family guard to supervise her activity, and she was sure that one of his private soldiers would be along at any moment.

She gasped as the open door revealed a tall, gangly figure sitting on her desk, swinging his legs while consuming an apple. "Scad, what are you doing here? They're quite serious about a punishment if you're caught again."

Scad's easy, cocksure smile answered her concerns as he sprang off the desk. "And miss the chance to tell you good-bye? Hang their punishments and pronouncements—I couldn't just let you go now, could I?"

"Shh," Iellieth said as she checked that the door was shut behind her and carefully turned the lock. The emotions that had been building during her time with Katarina and her rage at the duke threatened again to overwhelm her in her friend's presence. She rushed forward to Scad's embrace and buried her face in his thin linen shirt. The warm scent of wood chips and the crisp whiff of an apple danced into her nostrils. "You know that I'm relieved to see you, right?"

Scad patted the back of her hair before he released her. "I wouldn't have known that exactly, given your alarm."

"I can't bear the thought of something happening to you on my account, especially as I won't be here to try and help."

"No offense, Ellie, but in the past, your help has made things worse, not better."

She felt a stab of pain at that reminder. Following her and Teodric's attempted escape, Scad was implicated as an accomplice to the fallen nobleman's schemes. After a week, when Iellieth was finally allowed to leave her room, she found out that Scad had faced a similar punishment, having been relegated to the servants' quarters and threatened with imprisonment but given a heavy fine instead. When Iellieth tried to speak to the guard on his behalf, their suspicions of his involvement were confirmed, and they locked him away for several more days.

Katarina had helped, in that time of heartbreak. Many of the guards were smitten with her, so she used that leverage to check on Iellieth's friend and bring him small treats from the kitchens. Iellieth had snuck the money for the fine to Scad's mother, Celia. The Delarios were incredibly hard working, but they didn't need unexpected expenses, especially ones that were no fault of their own.

"I am awfully sorry about that," Iellieth said. "But, Scad, someone's going to be down here any moment to fetch me for the Lyceum."

"Alright, alright. Will you be needing"—he glanced around the room—"this in your new abode?" He cleared his throat and held up an alabaster wolf figurine that Iellieth kept on her dresser. She'd stumbled upon it when she was young on the grounds at Aurora and had kept it ever since. Something about the freedom of wolves spoke to her and, as a child, it had felt like destiny for her to find a pretty trinket that made her think of them and the closeness of their packs.

She blinked to clear her eyes before she answered him. "I would love for you to have it, Scad."

"It's not that I'm worried about forgetting you or anything. I just wanted a way to keep you nearby. This is the best I've come up with besides more involved schemes like we attempted before."

The finality of their time together, the end of Scad's forbidden visits to cheer her up or bring her news from around the castle, weighed down Iellieth's heart and threatened to rip it from her chest. Living in a cage was difficult enough, but at least in this glass enclosure, there were people who loved her. "I . . . Scad, I don't know what else to say. I'll miss you so much."

"I know you don't believe me right now, but I think you'll figure something out. There's more for you than what they've planned, Ellie. You'll see."

She sniffed and looked up at him. "I hope you're right, Scad. I'll write to you as I can. Katarina will let you know how I am too. She's already promised."

"Now, that I wouldn't mind at all," Scad said with a wink. "As I've failed to win you over, perhaps in your absence, your scholar friend will fall for me."

"Perhaps she will." Iellieth smiled. She felt a light breeze of relief across her jagged internal landscape before the urgency of their present moment returned to her. She shook her head quickly. "Alright, now it's really time." She closed his fingers over the alabaster wolf.

"I have a parting gift for you too, Ellie."

"You do?"

"I made this, to go with your dagger." He nodded at her bag, well aware that it held the blade he'd brought to her room the night she and Teodric tried to escape. He withdrew a thin, angular piece of wood from his pocket. A sheath, cut in a botanical lace pattern and tied with two thin strips of leather. "These can weave through on the sides so you can wear it underneath a dress or keep in your boot. I was thinking about you, and I remembered a story Teodric told me of a woman who lived with a pack of wolves, and that was what she did just in case she lost them somehow and had to survive on her own."

Iellieth traced a finger across the pattern of inter-twined vines, marveling at the delicacy Scad had managed to achieve in the inflexible wood. "Scad, it's beautiful, thank you. It's so intricate. I don't know how you kept it from falling apart." She blinked back tears and smiled at him sadly. "That story was one of my favorites growing up, from those books. *Lady of Canis* was the title of the first one, I think. The girl's name was Daphne."

"He always had a better memory for those sorts of things than me," Scad said, "but yes, I think I remember now."

Iellieth pulled the dagger from her bag. The top of the blade resembled a root structure that grew into the Adhemar crest at the hilt, a sprawling golden oak tree with silver leaves.

Scad waited breathlessly as Iellieth slipped the dagger into its sheath. He sighed as it slid home. "Phew, I'm relieved that fit. I didn't want you to think someone had stolen it, so I couldn't come in and take it to measure and bring it back." He grinned at her. "You really do like it, Ellie?"

"I love it, Scad." It must have taken him ages to make in his little free time.

"Does it work with what you have on?"

Iellieth sat on the end of her bed and unlaced her boot before she tied the dagger's hilt around her calf. The straps were long and thin; it would fit easily over her thigh as well. She retied the boot and stood for inspection. "What do you think?"

A glint of gold winked at her from the top of her boot. She tucked her sock over the exposed hilt tip.

Scad grinned. "It's perfect."

Heavy boots walked down the hall toward her room. "You have to go," Iellieth whispered. She propelled Scad to the servants' door hidden in the wainscoting. "I love you. Don't forget me, and know that I'll be thinking of you."

He took her hand before they parted. "I love you too, Ellie. Be careful, now, and take care of yourself."

Her lips pressed together and turned in a sad smile that mirrored his. "I will, and you too." Scad nodded and ducked into the small opening.

Iellieth walked a slow circle around her room, running her fingers over the grainy surface of her wooden desk and taking in the velvet fur of the patterns on the couches. Halfway to the line of bookshelves that rounded out the circle otherwise made of windows, a solid knock banged against her door.

"Lady Amastacia," the muffled voice of either Welton or Roswell called, "it's time."

Iellieth picked up her bag from the bench at the foot of her bed and draped her fur cloak over her arm. Since Hadvar was located so far to the north, she had the excuse of traveling in the leather breeches and corset Henri had made specifically for her. The designer had taken great care in the pressed pattern of moonshade flowers and ivy that trickled delicately over the set of ladies' armor. Iellieth had a jacket that matched as well, but she'd stashed it in her bag along with a few days' supply of food and most of her gold coins. If the smallest opportunity of slipping away from her family and Lord Stravinske arose, she planned to take it.

Sir Welton, one of the family guard, waited at her doorway and followed as she joined her mother, half-siblings, and stepfather in the receiving room. "I believe we're all accounted for, then," said Sir Merud, the family steward, nodding to the duke. With his liege's permission, he strode forward and opened the main door to begin the procession down to the Lyceum. He peered out for a moment and scowled.

"Are you really going to let her go like that, Mother?" Lucinda complained to the duchess with a snide look at Iellieth's polished leather boots. "She makes us look quite common."

"Lucinda, I don't think it would be possible for anyone in *our* family to look common," Bruden answered. Iellieth pretended not to hear them.

"I believe you're both aware that it's not unusual for women in Hadvar to clothe themselves in a wide variety of ways on account of the climate," the duchess replied. She didn't look at any of her children but kept observing Merud's vigil.

"So it's to impress her new husband then?" Lucinda gloated. Iellieth clenched her jaw, determined not to respond.

"That will do, both of you," the duke snapped from beside his wife. "His Majesty's guard will be here any moment, and I would have you represent the dignity of this family."

The sound of marching feet rising and falling punctuated the duke's proclamation and hushed any retort from his offspring. Iellieth knew better than to think the duke was coming to her aid, but she noticed, as the royal guard approached, that he seemed unusually fidgety. Calderon had become the right hand of the king thanks to his conniving nature and cool demeanor. He was anxious about something, which was far outside the norm.

The sight of the armor-clad dwarf proudly leading his troops interrupted Iellieth's reflections. Stormguard Basha, the head of Linolynn's military and the king's security, strutted proudly in the center of the two lines. He raised a hand and called down the hallway, first to Sir Merud and second to the duke.

Their Graces Amastacia stepped forward once he arrived. Basha gave a short bow to the duke and bent to kiss the duchess's proffered hand. "It is our great honor to escort your family to the Lyceum for your transmigration to the Festival of Renewal this fine morning," Basha said with a smile.

"You bestow upon us great honor," the duchess replied.

"Would you be so kind as to walk with me?" Calderon asked the stormguard.

"I'd be happy to, sir. If you'll allow me just one moment. Troops," he said with a glance to his front ranks, "proceed." Basha waited at the doorway for the family to begin filing out. "Ellie, so good to see you," he said as Iellieth stepped up beside him. They walked together out of the Amastacia hall. Basha was only a few inches shorter than she, and he held out his elbow gallantly for her to take hold of for the procession.

"Are you doing alright, miss?" He kept his voice low so as not to be overheard by the rest of her family. Basha was less than skilled at whispering, but the clanking of boots against the stone floors helped to mask their conversation.

"That's so kind of you, Basha, thank you. I . . . I'm alright."

"I asked the king for this assignment personally so you might have some friendly faces seeing you off."

Iellieth grinned. "Well, that certainly makes me feel better. You're very thoughtful. It's one of the things I shall dearly miss."

"Aye, and I shall miss you as well. The lads always did better in their training on days when you came to visit."

"I am not sure about that, but I'll take the compliment all the same." She lowered her voice. "Thank you for all of your help. I'll do my best to put it to use as I can."

"See that you do," Basha said with a wink. He patted her hand and stomped forward to catch up with her stepfather.

The duke's nervousness didn't seem to have eased with the stormguard's arrival, and Iellieth watched the twitches of his shoulders as he and Basha spoke. She could only overhear pieces of their conversation at first, but as they reached the larger halls that descended into the old keep, she caught more.

"This change in His Majesty is . . . nothing to do with my station . . . Lord Nassarq is still so little informed of the larger . . . in the kingdom. He's only recently returned from Nocturne . . . why has he advised that troops be made ready before we've even spoken to our allies?"

Basha's voice was less subdued. "You heard his report on the regiments amassing outside the Jorgan's northern estate, same as I did," Basha answered. "That's within Linolynn's regional borders. The king cannot simply sit by."

"I only wish to suggest that we look into it further. These disappearances in the mountains, whole villages slaughtered, there could be . . . they're not monsters."

"I do as the king orders, Your Grace. My men are looking into it, and whatever evidence they find, they'll be sure to send back."

"Yes, very well," the duke said. "Thank you, Storm-guard." Calderon stepped ahead to take his wife's arm.

Iellieth couldn't make sense of what she had overheard. The duke had been on edge since Lord Nassarq's return a few weeks before. Was he suddenly out of favor with King Arontis, who had trusted him beyond reason for years? Surely he couldn't be afraid of someone doing to him what he had done to Frederick Adhemar, Teodric's father? Sending him against his wishes across the Infinite Ocean, never to be heard from again?

Groups of guards paraded about the castle center. They patrolled the keep's ancient hallways as though they still operated in the time of war the stronghold must have been constructed for. On the lowest level above the dungeons, an elite group supervised the goings and comings of the transmigration circle. There were very few instances of this powerful ancient magic still functioning in Azuria. A century ago, Hadvar's mages had been able to restore the function of their own circle. Linolynn's was used only rarely and had yet to succumb to the unworkings of time.

No records remained of how the circle had been made or how, given enough of a magical charge and a precise inscribing of runes, it could transport a group of people from one place to another almost instantaneously. Several millennia ago, an advanced civilization had created the transmigration circle, one of many, it seemed, that allowed twenty people or more at a time to travel to the linked locations. Linolynn's scholars, through careful study, had discovered how one might reach Hadvar from its southern neighbor, negating the need for a week's travel across the cold roads that wove in and out of the Stormside Forest.

The Transmigration Guard, set apart by their pale-blue

doublets emblazoned with a magic circle, found little to occupy themselves during the vast majority of a solar year, but the Festival of Renewal provided ample opportunity for vigilance and a show of their capabilities. In addition to bestowing honor upon Linolynn's nobles, the only people allowed to utilize the transmigration circles, the military tasked these guards with protecting the castle from any unknown entities that might make their way into the castle through the ancient portal.

Katarina and a few of the other high-ranking castle residents stood waiting at the entrance to the ancient chamber that held the transmigration circle. Iellieth saw her friend's eyes alight once they met hers, and Katarina waited until the first of the royal guard had passed before joining Iellieth to travel into the Lyceum.

The two linked elbows and stepped together through the large, arched doorway to begin their descent. The Lyceum was one of the grandest rooms in Linolynn and possibly all of Caldara. The ancients had carved the room from the cliffside bedrock, a feat made more impressive by the space's enormous size. The ceiling extended more than seventy feet overhead in a series of interconnecting, pointed arches that met above the center of the transmigration circle.

On the far side of the chamber, elderly scholars in long robes flitted back and forth between the thick tomes of crackling parchment that explained how the circle might be manipulated to reach different destinations. "In the records," Katarina said as she noticed Iellieth studying their movements, "there are references to dozens of other circles, only a few of which we understand. But it has to be true, as I saw inklings of in some of my older research, that at one time, the world was much closer, as well as, I believe, more populated, than we have any conception of it being today."

"And why is it that you turned your attention elsewhere?" Iellieth asked. "We haven't worked together on anything of the kind."

"It's true, we haven't. I did this work before I moved to Io Keep. Most of the records I found were incomplete. I believe Aravar is still searching. Lost and destroyed tales of the past are a special interest of his."

"Yes, I recall," Iellieth said. It had been several years since Katarina's brother had visited Linolynn, but he always had interesting news to report when he arrived.

"He may travel this way soon. His most recent excavations have him just south of Penshaw. He'll be very sorry to have missed you." Katarina's brows knit together as she looked at Iellieth.

"Please let him know that I regret not being able to hear about his latest journeys. I hope the two of you enjoy your time together. It will be nice for you to have some company." Iellieth cleared her throat and fluttered her eyelids to compose herself.

"That it shall. But come, let us have one final lesson before you go." They stood together outside the circle and looked at the runes carved into the stone floor. "Do you recognize this script at all?"

"It's one of the Arcane scripts, but I don't believe it's of Elvish origin." Iellieth scrutinized the ancient symbols. "These here," she said, pointing at the succession of glyphs in one of the smaller circles to their right, "they are the elements, are they not? Fire, water, air—"

"Light, darkness, and earth, very good. Now, why do you think they're positioned inside the circle in this way?"

"Equally spaced from one another?"

"Yes, or why in this circle and its interlocking position with the larger one?"

"Iellieth," the duchess called, "they are nearly ready for us."

She tightened her grip on Katarina's arm. "We also need to ask why a circle," Iellieth added quickly. "Or I think that's what you would say."

Katarina nodded.

Iellieth squinted up at the tiled ceiling and its sweeping arches. "There's something about these circles, this room, that meant direction, or at least where one wanted to go." The pale-blue runes along the outer edges began to glow. "We often think that the straight path is the one of progress, but circles represent completion and restoration. Maybe the ancients would see it as a different way forward that we too readily ignore or dismiss."

"I think you are right about that," Katarina said. The tears in her eyes danced in the runes' pulsing light. "Take care, my friend. Write to me."

"I will." Iellieth couldn't let herself say anything more, so she hugged Katarina a final time and went to stand beside her mother at the end of their family line. They faced the row of soldiers overseeing the sendoff. Iellieth glanced over her shoulder at her friend and felt the amulet's warm glow against her chest. In moments like this, when her heart was racing, it seemed like the metal and gemstone absorbed some of her energy and sent it back to her.

But in this instance, it continued to grow warmer, almost uncomfortably so on her bare skin. Iellieth reached beneath her tunic and withdrew it. "Hold still, please," one of the guards called from beyond the circle's limits. The woman's voice sounded as though she were shouting through water.

The duchess glanced down at Iellieth, a reprimand on the edge of her lips, but her mother's eyes widened instead as she looked at the amulet. Iellieth turned from the red glow on her mother's face to find its source at her fingertips, burning. Rays of light stretched glittering fingers out of the ruby, and the metal grew too hot for her to hold any longer.

She let go, and the necklace floated in front of her, raising parallel with her chest. "Wait," Iellieth heard, impossibly elongated, tinged with worry and fear, drifting toward her from her mother. How did she sound so far away? The golden bands began to spin; the additional diamond in the center of the hourglass blinked in and out of existence as Iellieth stared, transfixed.

The runes on the stone floor around them throbbed in the same instant that a bright red flash erupted from her necklace. Iellieth's ears filled with a disembodied, horrified scream. All the world around her turned black, and the intense compression of transmigration began.

CHAPTER 3

For the second time in as many months, Teodric found himself sailing away from a scene of destruction, the choking odor of ash and smoke clinging to his nasal cavity long after he'd left the fires behind. The unmistakable stench of burning hair and flesh mingled with wood and hay as they crackled beneath purifying flames.

Attacking unruly orc settlements was an unusual activity for Syleste and her band of pirates, but the orcs posed a threat to her shipments, and the admiral wouldn't stand for a competing terror on the Infinite Ocean. She'd been looking for a lost artifact, something magical, along the coast for months now, constantly agitated that she couldn't locate it, though Syleste refused to say what precisely they were searching for. A recent interrogation after one of her crews assaulted a merchant vessel revealed that the orcs might have it. Teodric had been part of a special regiment that would take care of ridding the coast of the marauding tribe while others searched the ruins beyond the camp for what they had stolen.

Memories of the previous night blended in and out of shadows. The scent of sage, lemongrass, lavender—the protective herbs. His sword cutting through flesh, cries and screams, bright red blood, even though orcs' blood was dark blue. Underneath it all, a low-level panic and determination. He had to be here. No one else could ensure that his mother was provided for. No one else would be able to find his father. Finally, after falling out of Syleste's initial favor, he was rising in the ranks again.

"Lost in thought this victorious morning, Teodric?" Kriega, Syleste's first mate and personal guard, leaned against the ship's railing and studied him closely. "Are you not pleased with our evening's handiwork? I was prepared to speak to our fair admiral about your prowess yesterday, but I will withhold my compliments if you regret your actions for some incomprehensible reason."

Kriega, a half-orc, was one of Syleste's most prized pets. When he had first set foot aboard the *Dominion*, Syleste brought Teodric into her intimate circle. The first mate had not taken this well, and she harbored resentment toward Teodric until Syleste grew tired of him and her former appetites returned.

A sigh of sea spray caressed his bare cheek and the edges of his stubble. The ocean was choppy, restless. He gazed at the pale gray horizon and let Kriega's question float on the air between them.

"I was running back over a few details from the evening is all. Are you on early watch today?"

"That I am. The admiral likes to take the mornings in after our journeys ashore to run her eyes over the new cargo."

"Did we take something valuable aboard? What would they have had?"

"Something?" Kriega chuckled, revealing the full length of her protruding lower tusks. "No, sweet Teodric. I believe you mean some*one*." She shrugged. "Run down to the hold and see for yourself."

Wordlessly, he nodded to Kriega and crossed the deck to one of the stair flights below.

TEODRIC WAITED FOR HIS VISION TO ADJUST TO THE tepid darkness of the ship's second deck. Syleste kept two holding areas for prisoners. One here, between the crews' sleeping quarters, and one for more serious offenders deep in the ship's bowels. No sound escaped the *Dominion*'s lower dungeons.

Since they were only a few weeks out of Isla de Hossa, the island Syleste had claimed for herself at some distant time in the past, the prison hold was uncharacteristically empty. Soon enough a ship would cross their path and catch her eye, and in most of those cases, a few prisoners survived the encounter and were brought aboard.

There was only a single woman, a human, in her early middle years.

"Who's there?" the woman called out. She had a soft, scratchy voice, her fear encased in vibrato.

"No one of any importance," Teodric answered. He stepped into the lantern's low glow. "I'm not here to hurt you."

"Is that what you said to them last night too, lad? I'm not here to hurt you?" She mocked his voice, dropping hers an octave and enunciating between the syllables to mimic his Caldaran accent. He had long resisted the drawl and slur of Tor'stre Vahn's coastal regions and quickly stood out as a foreigner.

"I'm surprised the raid last night would be of much consequence to you," he said. "Were you a captive of theirs then?"

"A captive?" The woman eyed him carefully, her expression torn between rage and confusion. "That was my home."

"Oh." He looked down and straightened his vest. "I didn't realize. Most human captives are trapped with orcs against their will. That's one of the reasons we intervened."

The woman stood and slowly approached him. She stopped a few inches from the edge of her cell. "Look in my eyes." Her voice shifted again, low and thick in the back of her throat. The woman's plain brown hair was matted at the ends, a few clumps sticky with blood, but she seemed in good health beyond a few cuts and scrapes and dark circles under her eyes.

Eyes that pulled him in. Eyes that turned from brown to black to deep-sea blue as he stared into them. Eyes that opened wide and overwhelmed the entirety of his vision.

The sensation of falling forward. He landed hard on his feet, caught by the soft sand of a beach at high tide. It was night, and the moonlight glinted on his rapier blade.

A quaint village glowed on the other side of a row of dunes, the two dozen wooden houses lit by small fires in their hearths. The shipmates beside him crept forward, their bodies blending in and out of the wind-piled sand. It was time.

One faction broke off to infiltrate the far side of the village. They were to search out the largest hut and pillage it. Somewhere nearby, Syleste had been sure, was a powerful magical artifact. They should stop at nothing to retrieve it. Better yet, wipe them all out.

Teodric and Lars leaned against the wooden beams on either side of a window. A family sat together inside, unaware of the doom lurking just out of sight. A human girl played with a doll near the fire. Her brother giggled in their mother's lap.

The mother turned and met his eye. Time surged forward as the same woman begged Teodric to spare the life of herself and her child. The screams he had been unable to suppress all morning. She had brown hair like the woman in the cell, worn slightly shorter, and her son had his father's sandy brown locks, much like Teodric's own when he was that age, lightened by the sun.

He drew his sword across the woman's throat, and her cries stopped. A strangled cry pulled him back, his own scream, that prevented the vision of him murdering the little boy. He crashed backward into the solid wood wall across from the cells, and the lantern swung on its hook.

Teodric stared at the woman, mouth agape. "What have you done to me?"

"Only reminded you of a small part of the horror that you and your kind have done to me," she growled. The woman spit at his feet, her upper lip curled, and crawled into the distant corner of her cell, arms wrapped around herself for the small protection they could give.

His breaths came quickly, and he pressed himself against the solid hallway walls. It was important not to provoke mind mages as they were capable of all sorts of tricks and games.

"Teodric?" The admiral's voice greeted him like the tinkling of chimes in the wind. "My, this morning is full of surprises. Have you been getting to know our guest?"

Syleste sauntered up the half-stair that led to the cell block. Her full hips slid to and fro, accentuating her ample curves. No one was coming down the stairs he'd descended a short time before. Syleste brushed her thick black hair off her shoulder; her blood-red lips twisted to the side.

In whispered tones along the coast, they spoke of the Scarlet Harbinger. She had told him this, delighted with herself, after their first evening together. It was a mood she saved only for her lovers. With the rest, her vanity took on other, more aggressive forms.

He cleared his throat, but the visions remained seared onto his mind. "Yes, Admiral. Kriega mentioned we had brought someone aboard. I hadn't remembered taking captives and came to see for myself."

"We take on prisoners often, do we not?"

"Of course, Admiral. I had simply not understood that as part of our purview last night."

"I see." Syleste pursed her lips. The woman in the cage glared at her freely. "We had an unfortunate turn to our work last night, dear Teodric, at the hands of the witch you see before you." Syleste's golden-orange eyes flashed dangerously.

The admiral slid closer to him and traced her fingernail up his arm, across his shoulder, and brought the tip of her red nail to rest beneath his chin. She tuned his face to hers.

"You know I don't like it when people stand between me and what I want, don't you, Teodric?" she sighed into his ear.

He should have stayed above decks. Nothing good could come from this shift in her mood. "I do."

"You remember what happened when you were in her shoes?" A dark memory flew forward from the back of his mind, its black wings outstretched to obscure his present surroundings. Syleste sneered above him as his body contorted in pain. His neck snapped back as Kriega yanked the gnarled rope. His blood splattered onto the deck. *"The most distressing news from Linolynn about your little sweetheart,"* Syleste had crowed in delight. *"I'm sure she'll wish for death before too long and, lucky for her, she'll receive it."* Again the terrible grin. *"Eventually."*

"Tell me," the admiral's harsh whisper brought him back, "has our prisoner been filling your head with visions?"

"She has, Syleste." Teodric's heart pounded in his ears, *get out, get out*. His voice burned in spite of his desire to control his emotions. It would be so simple for her to harm his mother in retribution. She was only a few days' sail away, and Syleste had several spies stationed in Nortelon who could dispatch her will even faster.

Her eyes narrowed at him. She raised her hand and clenched it into a fist held at shoulder height. His breath stopped. The pirate queen took slow steps forward to accentuate her words, hips swaying in rhythmic confidence. "She's undone my hard work, I see."

Teodric fell to his knees, hands clutching his throat.

"You'll pay for that as well," Syleste hissed to the caged woman. "However"—the admiral glanced at the sunlight filtering down the stairs to the lower deck before she turned back to the woman—"with your magic added to mine, I've no fear of it happening again. The process will demand your life, of course. But that was bound to happen sooner or later." Her white teeth flashed, and she withdrew her emerald-encrusted sword.

"I'm afraid the exchange may be inappropriate for you to witness, Teodric." The admiral turned her eyes to him.

"Our guest has upset you enough already." Before he could speak, Syleste whipped around and, like a bolt of lightning, slammed the hilt into his head.

୬୬

"TEODRIC." AMBROSE'S SCRATCHY VOICE PULLED HIM into consciousness. Where was he? Dim light, dank air. His stack of books and a short candle rested on the shelf beside him. A wool blanket from home across his legs. He exhaled slowly, relieved. Anywhere was better than the cells on her island.

What had happened to the woman he was speaking to? The one who showed him that it wasn't orcs they'd attacked on the beach after all. And if it wasn't orcs, then that woman, the child—

"Teodric!" Ambrose's tone grew more insistent. "Come on, lad, this is the first chance I've had to get away. What happened?"

"I . . . Syleste . . . I'm not sure. There was a woman held prisoner. She showed me a vision. I keep hoping it isn't true, but, Ambrose"—Teodric placed a fist against his heart—"I can feel that it is."

"What did she show you?"

"I was back on the beach, where we were last night. Except we weren't there to kill orcs. I was just below the window of a home, like I had been in the moments before we attacked, but it was a human woman inside. With her family. Not someone responsible for the death and slaughter of many, like Syleste and Kriega'd said."

Ambrose studied his face. The older man's dark eyes shone against his tanned skin and then looked away from him. "What do you mean? Why would that be true?"

He was holding something back. Even after all this time sailing under Syleste, people still wanted to protect him, still hoped to shield him from her. Ambrose ran his tongue over his upper lip, a habit for when he was deep in thought.

"I know you don't want to, but you need to forget what you saw on the beach." He held up a hand to stop Teodric's protest. "She'll send you back to the island, mate, if you don't give her cause not to. I doubt she'll let you out of there again."

The door at the end of the narrow passage squeaked open slowly. Heeled boots descended the stairs one by one.

"How nice of you to check on our dear musician, Ambrose. I was just coming to call on him myself." Syleste's voice rang out around them; her higher, airy pitch warned of a short temper. "You know, there are days when I question bringing you aboard. Though your magic has its uses." Syleste stood framed in the doorway, hands resting on her hips, sword swung artfully behind her.

Teodric had seen Ambrose face the sudden arrival of bloodthirsty sea creatures without the slightest reaction, but Syleste's presence made the blood drain from his face.

"I have a proposal for you, then, seeing as you're fond of meddling. You can aid me as I test out something I've just acquired or find yourself new employment, immediately off-board." Her lips curled upward in amusement. "I really don't want to lose my bard, and he doesn't want to lose dear Aurelia, does he?" Her eyes glimmered, and she tugged gently at the ends of her black gloves.

Teodric's jaw clenched at the threat to his mother, and he leapt to his feet. "Syleste," he said, swaying. The sudden rush to his head made his senses swim like he'd lost his sea legs. "There's been a mistake. I did nothing more than talk to that woman."

"Ah, but she allowed you to see, and that's what I cannot tolerate, my sweet. You'll never serve me as well on my own terms—you haven't the stomach for it."

"But she didn't show me—"

"I know what you saw." Her voice was cold, each word enunciated slowly. "But fear not. By the time I'm through, that new mother and her darling tot will be forever stripped from your mind. I'm only trying to do what's best for you." Her eyebrows twitched. "Ambrose"—she turned her attention back to the older man—"are you ready? It will be better for him if you assist me. We'd hate for him to forget who he is, wouldn't we?"

Teodric's mouth went dry. He turned from one to the next. Ambrose wouldn't do this. He'd stop her somehow. Teodric had rescued him when they found him, floating and starving, in the middle of the sea. He was the one who had convinced Syleste to let Ambrose stay on board.

"On the count of three," Syleste said. She pulled her pocket compass from her belt, its gold chain tinkling softly as it sought to rebalance itself. "This is your final warning, Teodric."

He watched as her dark ginger eyes swirled into sickly, bright green orbs.

Her voice deepened. "I don't think you'd survive another memory adjustment."

The space between himself and the two humanoid shapes in his cabin lengthened and compressed to the point that he nearly fell, but he couldn't take his eyes from the monstrous spinning circles. They pulled away from him and invited him closer. To look away would be to lose himself. But to stay, to not resist would be to—

A slow, satisfied sigh. Someone was in his mind. The outside world was gone. Only the other presence. Here. Inside. And they wanted . . .

"Relax." A soft voice dwelled on the end of the word, hissing through their breath. "Release." The snake slithered, searching. It encircled his arms, licked his neck, and breathed into his ears.

"Who are you?"

"Syleste," the serpent wheezed. The spinning green orbs merged, and the circles engulfed him.

CHAPTER 4

Freezing wind and hard, icy snow struck Iellieth's exposed face and neck. She cried out in surprise, clutching her still-warm necklace to her chest, looking for something familiar in the surrounding blizzard. They had clearly missed their target location, arriving somewhere in the wilds beyond the splendid Hadvarian palace rather than safely inside. She wrapped her arms around herself and yelled for her mother, wanting to assure her that she was nearby.

As Iellieth stepped forward, she felt the ground shift beneath her foot and threw herself backward. The ledge of snow she had been standing on gave way, tumbling out of sight into the swirling white below. She gasped as snow reached her skin through a gap in her leathers at the base of her spine. Iellieth backed a few paces away from the cliff and pushed damp strands of hair out of her face. If she could only find a landmark she recognized, she could get her bearings. The wind's insistent howl drowned out all other sounds, which had never happened on any of her previous trips to the sprawling northern city. Between gusts, a rocky outcropping flared in and out of existence ahead of her. It might provide some protection from the storm, at least long enough for her to don her fur cloak.

Iellieth called out for her mother again, desperate to raise her voice above the winds. She had never been sent to the wrong place while transmigrating before. When the magic worked correctly, those being sent always arrived precisely in the same formation they had been in when they left. Though it was rare, it wasn't unheard of for someone to be slightly off the mark and land a short distance away from their fellow travelers. Rumors spoke of people disappearing entirely when the circles' magic went awry, but Katarina had told her that each of those cases, in actuality, were instances of other, human forces at work against an enemy, using the convenient excuse of a scarcely used form of transportation.

She staggered toward the collection of boulders to lean into the sloping stone. From behind this slight cover, she peered out at the hazy whiteness and the premature twilight hour. The wall of fallen rocks gave her a respite from the wind, and she drew the fur cloak out of her pack and around her shoulders. The wind picked up as though it was furious at her presence, but the gaps between the drifts revealed the jagged crest of a mountain in the distance. Up above, the rough stone wall beside her stretched far into the sky. It towered over the rival peak, separated by a chasm that gaped between the opposite ridge and where she now stood. Rows of pine trees crosscut her line of sight and obscured the bluff's lower elevations.

Iellieth struggled to make sense of what she was seeing. Hadvar had been carved into a plateau. Its founders were anxious to ensure a sturdy foundation under which to mine precious gems and metals for untold generations. She was somewhere else entirely. A single mountain range stretched along the spine of Caldara, the Frostmaw Mountains. The tallest mountain, located just beyond Linolynn's northern borders, was Torg's Peak. The mountaintop arched far out of sight, so that could be where she was. But if she had been thrown so off track, where was her mother? And the rest of her family? Was Mamaun the one who had screamed?

Even with her cloak, the cold was unbearable. She needed to find more substantial shelter or her body would slowly stop. After she found cover, she could search the area for her mother. If she had been sent here too, though, she would have been close to Iellieth. More likely, Iellieth was lost here alone.

Iellieth ran her fingers over the lines of her amulet. In *Celestial Maps*, one of her favorite novels, Diana would carefully observe her environment in case she had missed something at first. That's what she would do.

She took a deep breath and surveyed the scene in front of her, noticing an aberration in the rock pattern ahead. A perfectly smooth line ran into the sky, interrupted twenty or thirty feet in the air by a crossbeam. Iellieth pressed into the mountain and trod carefully toward the structure.

It took several minutes to move through the deep snowbanks and avoid the edges in case there was more loose powder, but she eventually reached an enormous stone pillar, at least ten feet across in diameter. The massive cylinder emerged from the mountain itself, which made navigating around it difficult, but there was an abscess on its other side, possibly a doorway. That would be her best chance at avoiding frostbite.

She hugged the pillar and dug her arms and feet as far

into the accumulation as possible. The cold burned the side of her cheek and the tip of her ear, but it would be worth it if she could find a respite from the elements. After several minutes of achingly slow progress, she finally reached the other side of the pillar.

Her cheek throbbed from the ice and tiny scratches, but the recess was covered and partially dry. Its tall stone ceiling allowed snow to gather along the mountain's edge, but, further in, she would be safe from all but the strongest gusts. From inside, the pillar seemed to be part of a doorway, though the other half of it, the pillar's twin, had toppled over into a chamber hidden inside the mountain.

The fallen column was nearly horizontal, but it was only lightly covered in frost, unlike its saturated surroundings, which suggested a recent fall. As she ran her hands over it, her intuition coaxed her back to the entryway between the two columns. She'd missed something. Her eyes adjusted to the shelter's shade, and a set of carvings emerged from the stone. The runes were in an ancient form of Elvish that she couldn't translate perfectly, but from the script that wasn't frosted over, she read THE LONELY HOLD and THE SIGN.

Reaching forward, almost as in a dream, Iellieth brushed the snow and frost away from the door. The piercing cold had fused the wintery elements to the stone, but as she broke off a chunk of the coating, she saw etchings beneath. Iellieth pulled her hand deeper into her sleeve and used the leather armor to scratch at the frozen surface.

The out-of-body sensation continued through her newly awakened, mystical muscle memory as she carved away the frost. Part of her knew already what she would find, though her conscious mind couldn't place it. After a few cold, determined minutes, she stood before a symbol she knew well: an hourglass shape intersecting in a diamond, identical to the one she wore always.

Iellieth traced the familiar shape and felt the warmth against her chest return as her own amulet responded. She removed the necklace from beneath her armor with her other hand and held it out toward the door.

There was a great cracking sound, and the stone in front of her parted along a central seam. It slowly swung open into a receiving room that looked as if it were centuries, if not millennia, old.

❧❧❧

IELLIETH GLANCED BACK TO ENSURE THAT NO OTHER figure had mysteriously appeared behind her before she stepped into the large antechamber. Tendrils of white from the piercing cold stretched across the smooth stone beneath her feet, and the wind howled into the room from above.

The ceiling in the first part of the rectangular chamber was twenty feet high and grew taller toward the center. The floor, like the ceiling, had split when the pillar crashed through, dividing the room in two. Part of the pillar leaned against the far wall, and the rest must have fallen below. It left a wide gap between where she stood and the rest of the receiving room.

Fading, intricate frescoes drew Iellieth to a nearby wall. The paintings depicted a great war, with combatants bathed in light, their faces stretched in grimaces of pain and fear, on the run from dark, oppressive hordes. The fleeing figures glanced over their shoulders; their expressions betrayed the cold knowledge that they would be overtaken.

She ran her hands over the textured surface to admire the detail and craftsmanship. Some of the paint contained precious metals. The armor of the heroes and villains alike shone in the snow strewn about the chamber, glinting against the reaches of frost.

Among the various groups of humanoids and creatures, black dragons fought alongside demons and strange, monstrous forms she had never before seen. Opposing them, desperately outnumbered, humans, elves, fae, celestial beings, and dwarves made their last stand. The battle looked ancient, epic, and yet she did not know if or when it had occurred. Its tales must have been long since lost to legend, absorbed into indistinct lore. Surely Katarina would have told her about this if she had known? But it looked too tragic to be only from the world of story.

Iellieth walked away from the images to investigate where the pillar had landed and better understand her surroundings. At least three times the distance between where she currently stood and the ceiling above, she perceived the column's outline below, resting amid scattered debris in a carved stone cavern. There wasn't anything on this side of the divide that could span the gap to the other side.

A cold silver shape gleamed amid the sparkling marble: a grappling hook, embedded in the broken floor, holding a length of rope that reached nearly to the bottom. If someone had left the rope here, it must have been strong enough to hold them on their way down. Maybe they were still there, and they could help her, or at least tell her where she was. Besides, the lower chamber would offer shelter while she decided what to do next.

There was an alcove on the far side of the receiving room that disappeared into what could only be a set of stairs. If she went down the rope, she could find her way back up, a feat that seemed more promising than being able to span the twenty-foot distance to reach the other side of the chasm in the middle of the room.

Before she descended, Iellieth tested her weight against the rope. She lay on the floor and tugged to see that it stayed fast. Her heartbeat pounded against the confines of her chest as she sat on the edge. She risked certain death if she was wrong about the hook's security and plunged into the stone floor.

The end of the rope dangled about ten feet from the floor below, but it seemed near enough that she could safely jump the rest of the way down. After she found the entrance to the stairs on the lower floor, she could climb out of the hole in the ceiling on the opposite end.

Whenever soldiers were preparing for a practice duel, Basha told them to inhale deeply and exhale slowly to force a sense of ease. Her own nerves were unconvinced by this tactic, and the pounding migrated to her ears. She reached down to wrap the rope around her wrist, clutched it tightly, and brought her left hand just beneath. On the third audible exhale, she transferred her body weight to her hands and slid her legs and hips over the edge.

Hand under hand, she descended. Her arms held her weight; her legs squeezed against a fall. After the first twenty feet, her arms began to flag. Iellieth tightened her hold with her legs and stopped her descent. She released her right hand, shook out the tension, and did the same with the left. They wouldn't continue to bear her weight. She'd need to rely on her legs and slide the rest of the way down.

She gritted her teeth and ignored the heat against her breeches. The palms of her hands burned, but she didn't have much farther to go. She could bear it—her stomach flew into her throat as her legs broke free. Her skin screamed as she caught herself and hugged the rope, dangling freely fifteen feet from the ground.

Iellieth panted, and her arms shook with fatigue and panic. She only had a few seconds before her body would decide what to do next. No alternative presented itself, and there was a relatively clear spot just below her. She let go of the rope.

CHAPTER 5

Iellieth executed the rolling landing she'd seen others perform nearly perfectly, thwarted at the last moment by an unseen, fist-sized rock that pressed into her right shin when she spun over it. A short gasp of pain escaped her, but she caught herself before she crashed into the stone floor. Her eyes cast around, following her own echoes. If there was anything unsavory nearby, it was surely aware of her presence now.

She carefully slid over to a place against the wall where the stone jutted out and created a sliver of shadow. Iellieth hid in the narrow column of darkness, sheltered by the fallen column to her left. The stairway that let out on the floor above would have to lie in the opposite direction.

Katarina, while they got ready for a particularly important gala, had explained that an affected air of confidence might inspire the actual feeling. She wanted to see Iellieth enjoy herself instead of "floating" by the exits. Stepping away from the wall and continuing down the passage, Iellieth hoped that she would have an easier time applying this lesson in an abandoned cavern than she had in a ballroom. The top of her boot glinted gold as it caught the light from above. There couldn't be any harm in having Teodric's dagger out at the ready as she walked. The blade whispered as she unsheathed it from the covering Scad had made her. She could almost hear their voices, *be careful*, as she tiptoed ahead.

Iellieth jumped at each of the hallway's long shadows in turn. The patterns of darkness increased the chance of something catching her unawares. The light filtering off the fallen column faded behind her, and she stepped into the shroud of the dimly lit hallway, beyond the boundaries of the column's plummeting destruction. Her boots clicked, *heel*, *toe*, *heel*, and her breath rattled in her ears.

Then, ice grated against a hard surface. Confused, she stopped and turned in the direction of the sound. A being made of jagged ice, with the suggestion of a head, torso, arms, and legs, rushed toward her out of the darkness. Iellieth leapt out of the way and extended her dagger behind her. Her shoulder wrenched to the side as she caught the creature's midsection.

Its strange glassy eyes scowled at her with cold fury from only a few feet away. It emitted a terrible screech from a slit that opened sideways above its crooked jaw. The creature rushed forward again, icy claws extended. Iellieth stumbled backward and threw her arm up to defend her side as it attempted to pierce her internal organs. The bladed fingers stabbed the muscles of her forearm instead. Instinct took over as she fought for her life for the first time. She screamed as it gnashed at her in its fury and plunged the dagger deep into its chest.

Her blood pooled over its hands, and the ice began to melt. Iellieth pulled her arm free, desperate to get away from the creature, and yanked the dagger from its chest.

The icy being wavered on its feet and collapsed to the ground. Her breath was rapid, almost hyperventilating. Survival instincts urged her to make sure the being was truly dead, but the horror of its shrinking, sharp hand embedded into her arm made her recoil. Before she could decide, the elemental being made the choice for her.

Its icy body shook on the floor and exploded, spewing sharp shards in all directions. Iellieth threw her arms over her face and ducked to avoid the flying blades of ice. One sliced through the right shoulder of her leather jacket, but the freezing wound barely registered over the throbbing of her punctured arm.

Heaving, her mind a roiling storm of panic, Iellieth backed into the solidness of the cold stone wall, and her knees slowly slid beneath her. Shaking, she struggled to withdraw a spare tunic from her bag. She would have to stop the blood if she wanted to stay conscious. Dark stars danced at the edges of her vision, and her stomach lurched when she looked at her sodden arm, an ominous red in the shadowy environs.

She rolled the tunic with her uninjured arm and dabbed at the cuts. The slivers of blackness covered her eyes completely, and her head drifted sideways. The sharp spring of her neck returned her to her senses. Best not to do anything besides cover it and stop the bleeding. She wrapped the tunic around her arm and pulled the knot tight with her teeth. Surely there would be somewhere to rest at the end of the hallway, or another chamber, but she couldn't stay out here in the open where more ice creatures might be waiting for her.

The passage came to an end ahead of her, at a stone door carved to resemble a face. When she was nearly within arm's reach, looking for a handle that didn't seem to exist, the skull-sized eyes above her opened.

She jumped back, sure she had triggered a deadly trap. The eyes focused on her, and the mouth twisted into a smile.

"Hello," the door proclaimed, making no effort to keep its voice low.

Iellieth retreated further. "Hello, door."

"What are you doing here?"

"Well, I was hoping I might be able to get through." It was possible that the ice monster had poisoned her and was now causing her to hallucinate. But seeing as she was already talking to an enchanted door, there didn't seem to be any need for subterfuge.

"Ah, yes"—the door sighed and looked up to the ceiling before it fixed its gaze back on her—"that is often the desire of those approaching doors, isn't it?"

"I suppose." Iellieth wasn't sure if it was trying to ask her a riddle or not. As she glanced about, she saw, inscribed above the door in an antiquated but legible form of Elvish, OPEN SAYS ME.

"I hope it's obvious that I would let you inside if I could."

"That's quite kind of you."

"I am very nice—I've been told before."

"It is always encouraging to hear ourselves praised."

"I don't know if they meant it as a compliment or not," the door said. "They were not thrilled to leave me down here to guard the great evil."

"Great evil?"

"Yes, of course. I have never seen it. Do you have eyes in the back of your head?"

Her years of noblewoman training should have better

equipped her to guide the conversation back in a helpful direction. "No, I'm afraid I don't."

"Neither do I." The door smiled at this commonality between the two of them.

"You said that you were placed here to stand guard? Who put you down here?"

"Why, the victors did, of the great battle. They left me here some time ago."

"Have you been lonely?"

"I am not sure."

"Oh, well then, that's probably a good sign at least. Is that what the frescoes are on the upper floor?"

"The great war, yes. They were very happy with the outcome."

"Were they evil?" The dark forces depicted above were a stark reversal from most of the illustrations she'd seen in novels and fae tales.

"They said that what is behind me is evil, but they did scowl a lot."

"And they never told you how you might open?"

❧

AT HER LAST WORD, THE DOOR'S EYES GREW WIDE AND its face split down the middle. The round shape of its mouth bifurcated as Iellieth voiced its password. The expression lasted only a moment before the two sides flew into the smooth walls of the underground hallway.

On the other side, Iellieth couldn't see anything but shadows and curved stone walls. She walked over the magical door's threshold, afraid it might slide shut and trap her in the darkness.

This space was warmer than the hall had been, the cold

unable to penetrate beyond the enchanted door. The hallway, hung with unlit torches, narrowed into a short set of stairs that descended into a circular chamber shrouded in darkness. Iellieth removed a torch and took a match from her pack to light it. As she did, lectures she'd overheard from Basha echoed through her memory. *Keep your head up. Listen for movement. Trust your instincts.* Before, these instructions appeared to be advice for combat with people. Surely Linolynn's soldiers weren't encountering ice creatures or infiltrating chambers guarded by talking doors.

She stepped onto the first stair, and the torch sputtered. A low wind whistled out of the chamber and pushed against her, holding her back. The darkness clutched at her heart; it hurt to stand still, let alone move forward. There was a tangible force at work against her; it didn't want her to proceed. Iellieth steeled herself and leaned forward, the torch at her side. After the first few difficult inches, the force began to abate.

She stepped down, her footfall a dull thud. The wind slowed. She stepped again and gritted her teeth. Her hair fell back against her neck. At the bottom stair, stillness returned, and the torchlight flared to full, blazing strength. What appeared at first as a shiny, frozen expanse on the far side of the room took shape as she proceeded in, the echoes of her boots lost in the vastness of the hidden chamber. As though a folk tale stretched off the page and took on flesh, the figure of an ice giant, frozen against time, emerged from the chamber's far wall. Iellieth hurried forward, amazed at the craftsmanship and scale of the massive form.

The underground chamber was the size of the three grand Hadvarian ballrooms put together. There, on the far side beneath a shadowy archway, stood the base of the stairs she had seen on her way in. That part of the room could wait until after she investigated the statue.

A flash of red distracted her from the sparkling iciness of the giant's body. From a distance, she had mistaken it for discarded rubble, but as she approached, a second, much smaller figure appeared from the murkiness of her surroundings. The warm, bright red of the humanoid statue provided a striking contrast against the imposing creature behind. The smaller figure arched away from the giant, its shield raised to stave off the massive, outstretched hand that threatened to crush the defiant being.

The smaller statue, though identical in level of detail, almost lifelike, was only half-carved. At the bottom, the red crystal was rocky and rough, the lower half of the figure hidden, locked away in the artists' imagination. But the top half was fully finished, the hard red crystal contoured to reveal a strikingly handsome countenance. The figure's rounded ears and strong jawline attested that he was human. But what made him seem almost alive was the intensity of his gaze. The piercing eyes were accompanied by an aquiline nose and full lips pulled down ever so slightly at the corners. The upraised shield lent a powerful resolve, the focus all the more impressive for the twinge of pain behind his eyes and strain in the tightened ligaments of his neck. His broad shoulders and chest pivoted away from the giant, and the flickering of her torchlight made it seem as though he also struggled against the bonds that held him below.

Enraptured, she moved closer, and the glimmer from her torch began to mirror light back to her from runes carved into the floor. They surrounded the man, like a personal transmigration circle. As she drew nearer, motes of firelight from her torch broke free. They glided over and embedded themselves into the runes. Stroke by stroke, the script surrounding the statue glowed. New runes she hadn't perceived alighted and crawled toward him, illuminating winding paths from the circle to the base of the statue. The fire they absorbed continued to burn and move inside them, and their dancing light appeared to breathe in and out of the sculpted warrior as, one by one, the runes shone against his skin, branding the statue in intersecting, glistening patterns of text from his feet all the way up to his neck.

The glyphs grew brighter as the circle filled in. Iellieth stepped over the runes' border, careful to avoid placing her foot on one of the flaming symbols, her torch all but extinguished. The statue absorbed the light and began to shine from within as she drew nearer. She closed the distance between herself and it and watched as the final spark from her torch plunged into the last rune.

Iellieth reached out to feel the smooth crystal skin, warm beneath her touch. She gazed, mesmerized, into the dancing glow of his eyes, pools of pale blue topaz that strove against their ruby surroundings. In that moment, the runes on the floor flashed, their reflections on the statue blazing brighter before they extinguished. The burning imprints sank deeper into the crystal figure, swirling toward his inner light. The two sets of fire collided and, with a second flash, plunged the cavern into total darkness.

The sound of ice cracking and a rumble across the floor muted Iellieth's gasp. A large chunk of rock fell against her thigh, and she nearly fell over a heap of rock on the previously bare floor as she lurched away in the blackness. More stones crumbled around the statue, and she pawed through her bag for a match.

Rocks and ice shifted with the whisper of sharp metal gliding against another surface. A line of flame erupted from a longsword wreathed in fire. Iellieth threw up her arms to protect herself and shield her eyes from the light, but she froze. A human man held the sword back away from her and reached out with his shield-bearing arm.

His dark eyebrows knit together in worry, and light danced off the early spring blue of his eyes, accentuated further by his olive complexion. He blinked, confused, and stretched further to take hold of her hand.

Iellieth fumbled for words as she tried to understand the muscular, bare-chested man standing across from her. The runes she'd seen embed themselves in the statue shone out beneath the covering of his skin, raised marks that glowed like pale white scars. "Wh-who are you?"

He blinked slowly again, somehow surprised by her voice. "Marcon. Marcon Colabra, lady. And who are you?"

His voice was low, gravely, and earnest. It resonated in the center of her being. "My name is Iellieth Amastacia." She let him take her hand and pull her up. "How is this possible? You were a statue a moment ago."

Marcon stared back at her. A muscle in his jaw clenched when he released her hand. His eyes flashed down to the blood-soaked cloth wrapped around her arm. "You're hurt. How many of them stayed? Did you see the —" He turned over his shoulder to the towering figure above.

It looked brighter than it had a few moments before.

"Run."

Marcon's command snapped Iellieth's instincts back into control.

He held his shield up between her and the waking giant. "Run!"

The other archway was closer than the short stairway where she'd entered the chamber. Her boot slid on the debris scattered across the stone floor, but she retained her balance and sprinted for the full flight of stairs.

A deafening crack echoed through the cavern as the ice giant roared to life. It reared back, and its eyes flared open. Its hand darted forward, coiling reflexively around where Marcon's statue form had been. She could hear Marcon's pounding footsteps behind her, but they slowed as the creature bellowed. Iellieth glanced over her shoulder where the stalwart figure of the awakened warrior squared off against the hulking, tower-sized body of the giant that was dragging a great club in its wake.

She turned away with a shuddering breath. After they were away from the monster, she could thank him for risking his life for her. The floor beneath her feet shook with each of the giant's steps, and she heard Marcon's yell of defiance, meant to distract it from her escape. She heard the sound of a massive chunk of ice sliding across the cavern, a hiss of doom. The base of the stairs ahead beckoned. They curved, a beautiful marble that matched the floor above. The stairs spiraled up out of the chamber, though she would have to navigate several turns before she reached the floor above.

The skid of ice whistled faster against the stone, and the creature roared at its captive. A stomach-churning moment of silence flew past Iellieth as she reached the bottom of the stairs, and then a sickening crunch rang out as the club smashed into the ground. The firelight behind her was suddenly extinguished, but the snowy light from the chamber above guided her up the stair's winding circles. Earthquake footsteps resumed, and Iellieth slipped and hit her knee as she tried to take the stairs two at a time. The creature was too tall to use this way up. Perhaps she could make it.

Iellieth emerged into the frescoed antechamber, opposite the side she had been on before. The hole in the ceiling from the column was the only escape on this side. Halfway there, the ice giant's fist exploded through the floor beneath her and sent her tumbling toward the wall. The flying pieces of marble collided with the pillar's remains, and Iellieth scrambled up the pile, away from the new hole in the floor. The giant roared in frustration, its cold white eyes glaring at her as she clambered toward the shattered ceiling. Sensing no other option, Iellieth leapt forward and clung to the top of the broken wall. With all her might, she pulled herself up and out of the chamber into the snowstorm raging outside.

She was on a different part of the mountain than where she'd arrived. The snow was several feet deep, and she struggled but failed to climb up the heavy banks. Each slow step took the effort of ten. Another great crash resounded from lower down the icy bank as the giant erupted from the mountainside prison. It cast its eyes around and found her, a helpless creature caught in a predator's trap. Iellieth froze as it barreled toward her. With a sob, she clutched her amulet and held it out toward the giant. It was supposed to protect her but had sent her here instead. She never would be able to tell her father what having this small connection to him had meant to her.

As if in answer to her heart's anguish, Marcon appeared from out of thin air in the snow ahead, between Iellieth and the giant. He stared back at her in amazement, but

Iellieth couldn't take her eyes away from the rapidly approaching form. Marcon followed her gaze, let out a cry, and once again raised his shield to stand between her and it.

The creature shouted when it noticed Marcon's return. It reared back, drew its club overhead, and brought it down over the two tiny figures. The giant misjudged its reach, however, and embedded its club in a sheaf of ice in front of Marcon instead of crushing its targets. The force of the impact disrupted the mountainside and sent Marcon and Iellieth flying backward. The mass of snow and ice tossed Iellieth into the air and slid her across the frozen ground.

Faint from blood loss and the cold, Iellieth could make sense of little else in the environment beyond a great rumble of ice. Black spots obscured the edges of her vision, and the mountain embankment slid away ahead of her, coating everything in its path in misty white. Her amulet released a brief pulse of heat before the darkness overwhelmed her.

CHAPTER 6

"**W**e can't find her anywhere, *Varra*."

Yvayne turned her searching gaze from the mountainside to Erolina, one of the saudad rangers, in front of her. "That's not possible. Keep looking. Have Cassian and his people come back from inside the Hold?"

"Not yet."

"Send someone to uncover what they've found." Erolina nodded and strode away through the snow. Any number of disasters could have befallen Iellieth after her arrival here, but Lucien couldn't have adapted so quickly to the half-elf's surprise relocation, especially as his servants were ready and waiting for her in Hadvar. The cold wind whipped at her ears, and Yvayne drew the black-furred collar tighter around her neck.

"Varra Yvayne, Varra." A heavily accented voice alighted on the wind and glided toward her. Down the mountain, Persephonie, one of the youngest members of the scouting party rushed up the steep slope, a blur of amethyst and sapphire.

"Persephonie!" a familiar voice cried from the recently excavated entrance. Tall and broad-shouldered, Cassian, the saudad leader, cast a dark silhouette against the mountain. He waded through the snow to Yvayne's side as his daughter scrambled up Torg's Peak to meet them. The bright-eyed young woman sprang forward and grabbed hold of Yvayne's hand in her excitement. "I saw it, just over there."

"You saw what, Sephie?" Cassian's smile shone against his bronze skin.

"The giant. He is buried in the snow." Persephonie pointed down the mountain after her trail of footprints. The howling winds kicked up drifts of snow that decreased visibility and prevented Yvayne from seeing the hulking form's silhouette below.

If the amulet had woken the ice giant, it must have awoken the warrior as well. And since the giant had been felled, and there was so far no trace of the warrior or the girl, this was something to pin their hopes on at least. "And no sign of Iellieth?"

"No, Mistress Yvayne, but the giant, he was lying like this." She raised an arm over her head and clutched her fingers into a fist. "He was holding a large club that was stuck in the ice. And he made a terrible face"—she screwed her striking features into a snarl—"so he probably was angry, maybe at Iellieth."

"That would be a welcome turn of fate."

"I will pray for Cassandra's guidance and keep looking, *Datha*." Persephonie grinned at Cassian and bounded away through the snow.

"Please forgive, Yvayne. Sephie is . . ." His voice trailed off as he watched her rise and fall in the undulating snow drifts. "She has a gift. The eye of Cassandra, to see the future, like her mother." The pride writ plainly across his face accentuated the saudad's handsome features. Cassandra, their most treasured goddess, bestowed the gifts of foresight and divination on her followers.

"That's how you knew to come and find me?"

"Among other senses, yes." He gave her a characteristic saudad smirk and returned his attention to Persephonie's progress.

Strangling cold fingers of terror had gripped Yvayne's heart when she realized she could no longer sense Iellieth's whereabouts, but now, one by one, they loosened their hold. The saudad people created an aura of calm in spite of the fact that they often faced what was darkest in Azuria. They had served as Yvayne's eyes and ears through the ages, and she would continue to trust them now.

"Yvayne! Datha!" Persephonie called to them. Her dark hair and gem-colored clothing glimmered brightly against the shining white environs. The girl bent down and pulled something out of the snow, tendrils of flowing garnet caught on the wind.

"By the ravens, she's found her," Cassian whispered, but Yvayne was already rushing ahead. His longer stride matched hers after a few moments, and he passed her, laughing as he kicked up snow behind him in his wake.

Tiny blades of ice lashed Yvayne's skin as she ran against the wind, but no amount of hostile weather could tear her eyes from the frozen half-elf Persephonie carefully extracted from the snow. The mountain, cursed long ago to hold in his heart a Champion of Fire, was furious that they'd arrived and extracted his secrets.

Cassian slid to a stop beside Persephonie, and Yvayne arrived just behind him. Her leather boots crunched through the compact snow. She collapsed to her knees next to the young woman, anxious to provide a second shield for Iellieth. Cassian had a similar idea and wrapped his arms around Persephonie and her charge.

"She's breathing." Persephonie looked into Yvayne's eyes, her own glistening from happiness and the biting cold.

The pent-up tension in Yvayne's shoulders and chest released in a deep sigh, and she laid a black-gloved hand against the back of Iellieth's head. *"Elenai, Ambrosea,"* Yvayne murmured. The life-giving incantation of the druidic faith melted the frost around Iellieth's lips and eyes, and the half-elf's breath deepened alongside Yvayne's. It was too dangerous for her to exert her power over the natural world to cause the storm to cease, but this was delicate enough to remain beneath their enemy's notice.

"She will be alright now, Varra Yvayne? Oh! She will stay with us and join the saudad?" Excitement glittered across Persephonie's expression as she looked from Yvayne to her father and back before she returned her gaze to the young woman she'd found beneath the snow.

Cassian's eyes were compassionate, touched by his daughter's sentiment, and a flicker of hope at the turn in their fortunes thawed a sliver of the frozen doubt Yvayne kept insulated within. No one had looked at her with that degree of warmth for some time, but the glance's balmy halo sparked an idea. "For now, Persephonie, we will take her to a place of shelter, and she can decide where she would like to go next."

Persephonie bit her lip but nodded. The enthusiasm that had flared so quickly faded from her expression.

Lucien and his followers would be here in a few days, among other places in Caldara. He would have been alerted the moment Iellieth didn't arrive in Hadvar with her family. They needed to relocate her to a place of at least temporary protection. It had been some time since she'd called on the Caldaran druids.

"However," Yvayne said, and the girl's eyes grew wide, "she will need a friend in the Vagarveil Wood. How might you feel about helping her?"

✦

A WORLD OF COLD DARKNESS GAVE WAY TO PRICKLING warmth. Iellieth's eyes fluttered beneath their lids and, slowly, she returned to herself. To a dull but extensive, engulfing pain. Her entire body ached, and a great weight pressed on her. She blinked to clear her vision and pressed against the restraining force before she collapsed back. A hazy shape separated itself from its surroundings and hurried toward her, accompanied by the tinkling sound of light wooden bangles clinking against one another.

"Easy now," a low, lyrical voice said over her. "You've been out a few days. No need to hurry yourself just when you're waking."

The unfamiliar face slowly came into focus. The woman's dark brown skin was warm like the walnut trees in the arboretum, and her eyes were even darker than Scad's, but lit from within by shimmering flecks of copper. Plump mauve lips curved upward on the ends as she studied Iellieth. She pulled her gaze from the woman's dramatic features to her immediate surroundings. The mist clouding her sight cleared enough to solve the mystery of the weight. A pile of heavy furs and blankets pinned her to the ground.

"My name is Mara. You're safe here." Mara sat beside her and laid her arm delicately on the stacked fabrics.

"Where am I?" Iellieth craned her neck again. The wooden wall directly beside her was the only unadorned surface in the cramped round room. Across from her, an aged, olive-green cabinet held countless jars and leather-bound tomes stacked precariously beside crystals, feathers, and wooden bowls. A low table bridged the distance between the cabinet and a small kitchen organized around a large fireplace, engorged with blazing logs and glowing embers. A few feet behind Mara, an etched silver room divider hid the circular hut's remaining contents, but Iellieth assumed she kept a dressing area behind the intricately crafted decoration.

"Here, let me assist you." Mara placed a warm palm on Iellieth's back and gently helped her sit up. She peered at Iellieth for longer than was polite before she gave another warm smile, pulled a dark green shawl from the end of the pile of furs and blankets, and wrapped it around her shoulders. "That color suits you well," Mara said. "I've just put the kettle on for tea, so we will be quite cozy in a moment. But first, to answer your question, Lady Amastacia, you are in the northern reaches of the Stormside Forest, in the Vagarveil Wood, near the foothills of the Frostmaw Mountains."

Iellieth drew back from the stranger. "How do you know my name?"

"We know many things about you, but don't be alarmed. We're here to help."

"How many of you are there?" No one else was in the hut, which meant they could be waiting for her on the other side of the animal-skin door. If she ran and made it beyond the entrance, how far might she get before they caught her, and then what would they do? A wave of nausea coursed up her throat at the thought of her stepfather negotiating the terms of her release.

"Iellieth." Mara laid a few fingers lightly on her shoulder, and she flinched away. Distress flickered across Mara's expression, and she withdrew her hand. "I promise that no harm will come to you while you are in my care. Can you trust me?"

She should say yes regardless. A low whistle began by the fireplace, and Mara glanced at the teakettle. But wait, it couldn't be. Elongated tips of sharply pointed ears emerged between her curling black locks. "You're an elf," she said. "I thought there were none left in Caldara save the few who live in Hadvar."

"That I am. And I am not the only one either. But before you ask, no, dear, I am afraid I do not know your father."

How did this person know so much about her when she hadn't even known there were elves living in the Stormside Forest?

Mara mistook her doubt for disappointment and lowered her eyes. "Let me see about that tea I promised you."

Iellieth sat up straighter in her absence and looked for her clothes. Besides the evergreen shawl, she was wearing only a thin shift and her undergarments, but she couldn't spy her satchel among the scattered piles of Mara's collections. The metal kettle kissed the tops of the ceramic mugs with a soft clink, and the sudden dryness of Iellieth's throat threatened to choke her.

"I believe I've taken a presumptive tactic that was unwise," Mara said. She turned with two cups and saucers and picked her way across the cramped hut to return to

Iellieth's side. "There is much for you to know, but perhaps it would make you feel more comfortable to tell me your understanding of what happened. What is the last thing you remember?"

"Why should I answer? You still haven't said how you know who I am."

"I don't wish to be rude, but how many choices do you have at this exact moment? Set aside the litany of things you've undoubtedly been told might happen to a noble-woman out in the world and tell me this: What does your intuition say about your present circumstances?"

Her mother's warnings faded, as did her half-sister's wild fantasies that glorified her own importance, as though anyone would wish to kidnap her. If Mara had wanted to harm her, she likely would have already. Why wait till she woke up? She cast back and tried to recall how long she had been unconscious, but the time floated in opaque storm clouds around her. There was no reason to not be wary, but she could try to trust Mara and remain alert at the same time.

"It says that if you wished to hurt me, you would have. Or that you would poison my tea."

Mara's laugh brightened her dimly lit dwelling. "Very well, very well, we will make our peace with that for now. I can assure you that your tea is not poisoned and that it will help revive your circulation after your tenure beneath the mountain's snows." She took a sip from her own cup and nodded encouragingly to Iellieth. "But I am most curious, at present, about how you came to be on Torg's Peak. The mountain can be treacherous at any time of year. He doesn't recognize seasons like the rest of us."

"You found me underneath the snow?"

"Some of my dear friends did, and they brought you to

me. I promise that you will meet everyone in good time. There's a beautiful young saudad woman desperate to make your acquaintance."

"The saudad? Really?"

"Your arrival has created a great deal of excitement among my community and our more exotic allies. But your recovery is of the utmost importance. So, the mountain, do you remember anything?"

"I remember all of it." Iellieth recounted her mother's scream and the mis-transmigration. She told Mara of the intricate murals and the great battle they depicted. She felt again the ice creature's piercing of her skin when she reached that part of the story and, when she raised her arm as proof, found the wound half the size it had been. Surely this was more than a week's worth of healing in only a few days' time.

"I have been carefully attending to your arm to ward off infection," Mara said when Iellieth paused to stare at her forearm. "We will wrap it again soon."

Iellieth grew more cautious after her story self walked through the magical door into the hidden chamber and approached the statue of Marcon. "He saved me from the frozen giant," she told Mara. "But then he disappeared. It chased me out of the underground room. I climbed out of an opening in the wall on the far side, but it found another way out too and saw me again. I . . . I was holding out my amulet. Scared. Wishing for"—she wouldn't tell this stranger, however kind, about the connection she had long hoped the amulet possessed to her father—"well, wishing for help. And he appeared again, in front of me. There was nothing, and then he was there.

"He tried to protect me as he had in the large chamber, but the giant swung at us. It missed, and we both flew through the air. The mountainside slid away. I think there may have been an avalanche? I don't remember anything else."

"This statue man, did you speak to him?"

"I did."

"Did he tell you his name?"

"Yes." Perhaps it had been unwise to recount this story in such detail. Mara's eyes looked hungry, almost desperate. But if she wanted the elven woman to think she trusted her, she should give her this information at least. "Marcon Colabra."

Mara inhaled sharply, the curiosity in her eyes more than sated. "My gods, *vrail'sai mehn*. I can't believe it."

"Someone found him too, didn't they? Whoever located me on the mountainside, did they find him too?" Dread clutched her stomach and pulled her insides toward the earth.

"No one saw him, Iellieth."

The earth tones that filled her vision swam before her, and Iellieth fell back. Through a dark chasm, Mara's muffled cry reached her. The clash and jangle of something breaking. A warm splash against her chest. Thin arms around her shoulders, and a soft clasp at the back of her head.

A rapid heartbeat thumped a soothing rhythm. She shook her head and blew stray strands of hair away from her eyes. Iellieth ignored Mara's protestations and sat back up. She rested her chilled fingers on the back of her neck and, with her other hand, picked her amulet up off her breastbone and stared into the ruby's center. Brown liquid dripped from the bottom of the hourglass. Mara leaned on her wrists in front of her and looked from the amulet into Iellieth's eyes. Her concern melted away with her smile.

"That's right," Mara said. "You nearly have it. Do you remember what you did before?"

"How do you . . ." What harm was there in confessing this last withheld secret in the ordeal if there was a small chance it could help them save Marcon? "I was trying to call my father." Iellieth's voice was soft. She had only confessed this to Teodric before. He was the one person she knew would understand.

The sides of Mara's eyes crinkled in sadness. "I am impressed that you sensed what it does. Did this start at a young age?"

The knot in Iellieth's throat blocked speech. She tried to mouth the words, but her lips wouldn't stop trembling. She nodded to indicate that yes, it had. Was Mara saying she truly could call her father through the amulet?

"I sense that you will be everything we've hoped for and more, Iellieth Amastacia. But allow me to ease your mind first. Try what you did before, as closely as you can, but think of summoning the man you met instead of your father."

"But how would—"

"This is one of those moments where I will ask you to trust me, and we will save questions for later. Calm your fears for the time being. Try to call him."

Iellieth closed her eyes and took herself back to the swirling turmoil of those final moments on the mountain. An agent of death charging toward her, her wish for her father, and the rune-covered warrior's appearance instead.

She fluttered her eyelids open. Nothing happened. She glanced at Mara, who smiled encouragingly. "Go on, keep trying."

This time, Iellieth spoke. She owed Marcon that much. He had saved her twice, without question. "Marcon," she whispered, "please come if you can hear me. I am sorry about what happened, but I want to know that you're alright. We are . . ." She overturned stacks of words in her mind, hurriedly searching for what he might respond to. "We're safe here."

When she said the final words, Iellieth believed them. Not necessarily because of Mara's assurances, but if she knew how the amulet worked and what it did, the rest could be true as well.

The center of her amulet glowed. Pale, brilliant rays shot from its center, and the man from the mountain appeared again in the space in front of her, between Mara and the door. Marcon saw the crouching woman first and stepped back, muscles taut, prepared to defend himself.

CHAPTER 7

"**M**arcon," Iellieth called out, and his piercing eyes settled on her. Relief coursed through her. He wasn't gone after all.

"Iellieth." His shoulders relaxed, but he maintained his defensive posture and turned back to Mara. "Who were those others you spoke of?" He had lost none of his commanding presence from the mountain.

Mara raised open palms toward him and lowered them slightly, a gesture of ease. "My conclave, the other druids who live in the Vagarveil, and a few visitors from afar." She stared at Marcon in amazement as though she couldn't believe he was really standing there.

Marcon looked at Iellieth and waited for her signal. "I think we are alright here, at least for the time being. She's trying to help us." Iellieth glanced down at her amulet, its inner glow diminished, replaced by the rune-covered man before her.

A trick of the light when he appeared made the runes glow as they had when he first awoke, but as the amulet's brightness faded away, the runes turned to pale tattoos, a few shades darker than his own skin. Some raised slightly from the surface, others drifted beneath it.

He glared at Mara for a moment longer before he lowered his shield and sword. "Do you mind if I rest these here?" He indicated the wall across from Iellieth, where collections of herbs and colorful paintings gathered together in small communities.

"Not at all." Mara still looked surprised and was short of breath, but she composed herself as she watched Marcon stash his gear and begin to acquaint himself with her home. "I'll make everyone a fresh cup of tea momentarily." She handed Iellieth a small towel to dry herself off with.

"Thank you, Mara." Iellieth smiled at Marcon, who stood uneasily on the far side of the room. "Would you like to sit with me while Mara tells us about her druid friends?" She patted the pile of furs and scooted to the side to make space. "I've never met any druids before," she said to the two of them, "though I have long been curious about them." She had been waiting to encounter druids since she had first read tales of their wondrous magic and rich history in Aurora's library as a child.

"No druids, lady?" Marcon settled down beside her, as unconcerned by his scant attire as he had been on the mountainside. She'd seen many powerful fighters over the years in the castle, but Marcon's rippling array of muscles looked more appropriate to the meticulously illustrated covers of the scandalous novels servants would sneak into castles for their noble masters than to the cramped practicality of Mara's hut.

She tore her eyes away from the complicated carving of ancient Arcane symbols around his shoulder and met his gaze. "Sorry?" *Pay attention*, Iellieth chastised herself.

"No, my apologies." He furrowed his brow. "I was simply surprised that you had not met any druids before. I thought the residents of Lis-Maen and the Hallowed Hills had traveled widely enough to make up for their small numbers."

Iellieth shook her head, not recognizing the names of any of these mysterious places.

His lips parted to clarify, but Mara interrupted. "Marcon, we have much to tell you as well. Foremost, Iellieth is not familiar with Eldura."

"Then where—"

Mara interrupted him, "It has been five thousand years since you disappeared on a mission into the mountains." Marcon stared back at Mara, incredulous, cycling through the questions about her grip on reality Iellieth had puzzled over a short time before. "These lands are called Azuria now, after a great flood that divided the city-states from one another. That was a few thousand years after the end of the War of the Champions, after the fall of Respite." The color drained from Marcon's face, and his eyes drifted beyond the confines of Mara's hut into the wide, unreachable universe of the past.

Iellieth laid her hand on his arm to communicate her own surprise at this revelation. There had to be a mistake of some kind. "He's from five thousand years ago?"

"Yes. I know this comes as a shock to both of you."

"Linolynn's founding almost goes back one thousand years, but five . . ."

"I don't know what to say," Marcon began. He stared into the distance again as though the words he needed were inscribed in tiny print on the wooden walls of Mara's hut. "What happened?"

"That is a long story, much of which has been erased. We had hoped that you might be able to tell us."

"You've been waiting for him?" Iellieth asked.

"In a sense, though the entire affair is quite complex."

"I will need some time, but if you are indeed allies as you say you are, I will endeavor to help as I can." He set his expression into one of stern determination. "So, then, where are we?"

"We are at the base of a mountain range on a continent named Caldara. Near the center of a large forest, two and a half days' travel south and west from where Iellieth found you."

Marcon considered Mara's words. "And no one uncovered me before?"

The druid pursed her lips. "That is a more complex question. Others searched for you, but your enemies hid you extremely well."

Mara's demeanor had changed. She had looked them both in the eye when she began speaking, but now she busied herself in the cabinets instead of meeting Marcon's gaze. What was she hiding?

"Is that anything to do with my amulet?"

Mara's cheeks flushed in answer, and she looked up from the mortar and pestle she had been pouring ingredients into.

"In a way." Mara studied them each in turn. She sighed deeply and her shoulders fell. "I realize that this is a lot to take in. I do not want to overwhelm you with more information. You," she said to Iellieth, "are still recovering. And you"—she nodded to Marcon—"have an entire new age to grow accustomed to."

Mara set down her supplies and walked over to the burbling kettle over the fire. "Marcon, would you go out and refresh our stores of firewood while I tend to Iellieth's arm? I'll let this steep, and it will be ready when you return." .

He nodded and rose to leave.

"We can find you more substantial clothes from one of the neighbors. It will grow chilly this evening."

"That would be most appreciated, thank you."

"And, Marcon? Just the ones that have fallen."

He grinned. "My memory is still muddied, but while I cannot recall their names or faces, I have met druids before." He opened the small wooden door and stepped outside.

🏵

Mara poured a splash of steaming water on the mixture of herbs and petals she had ground together in her bowl. "I believe it may be time for us to wrap your arm again."

"It is feeling rather sore."

The elven woman knelt beside her and placed her warm hand on Iellieth's. "I saw your reaction a short time ago. I assure you, I am not trying to trick you or Marcon."

"I did not think you were, not exactly. But I could tell that you were leaving something out."

"I am leaving out a great many things. But we must hold space for knowledge as well as for wisdom. And a necessary condition of being part of a conclave is trusting those around you."

"Part of a conclave?"

"Yes, a druid conclave." Mara peered at the punctures from the ice creature on Iellieth's forearm. "Or, in your case, being taken care of by a druid conclave."

Iellieth winced as Mara applied a molasses-like liquid to her arm, then worked to wipe it away. "My apologies. The swelling has been worse than I accounted for, and the arm is still bruised." Mara poured the remnants of the kettle's contents into a clay bowl and pulled a stack of towels from one of the bureau's drawers.

"It's important, when working with remedies, to remove any vestige of the old poultice to ensure the cut remains clean. Since we've left yours uncovered for a time, we'll go through the same cleansing process."

"A great many of the castle residents would say that is the work of holy water."

Mara smiled. "And were we of a different faith, I am sure I would agree with them. What about for you?"

"I understand that many herbs have healing properties. It is more common, among the nobility, to sterilize the wounds. That practice was passed down from the soldiers, I believe, or a portion of their ranks. They have special tinctures that the war-priests and healers use."

"This was not something you personally experienced?"

Iellieth laughed. "No, not physically. Mamaun was quite careful. But there was a woman, Marie, I knew when I was very young—it seems I had more scrapes and falls then—who would craft cures for me from the sea. The water burned, but our wounds healed quickly and never became infected."

"She sounds like a wise herbalist. Those who are adept at their practice are diligent to learn their environment. A cure in one place can wear a mask that hides poison in another." Mara dried the remnants of the claw marks and dabbed the healing poultice onto Iellieth's skin. The wound felt cooler the moment the mixture touched her.

"In the castle gardens, we grew a few herbs, but I never had the chance to study their uses."

"And why was that?"

"I don't know that I could say exactly. I learned of the historical meanings and significance of the flowers, and the arborist taught me to care for the trees. But the herbs, as far as I understood, were for scent, decoration, and flavor. Any used for healing were kept in their own greenhouses."

Mara wrapped a clean bandage around Iellieth's arm. She made each turn slowly so the binding would hold. "Many years ago, in my parents' lifetime, it would have been forbidden for one to study the natural herbs and remedies. The world was a wilder place then, traversed by wandering, willful spirits. Interference with the natural order risked inviting powerful forces, beyond the influence of mortals.

"People like the members of my conclave were driven away. Most druidic history follows a similar narrative pattern. Such is the way of things. We settled here, and our community grew. The seasons changed many times over, and the minds of those beyond our borders shifted as well." Mara finished wrapping the bandage and secured it, tucking the end gently into the folds around Iellieth's arm.

"They wanted access to our 'magic,' as they called it. This is an imprecise description of what we bring to the world. For the most part, we practice ancient wisdoms handed down across the ages. Our leaders told them no. They imagined hordes of travelers damaging our home in search of a miraculous cure and turning to violence should we be unable to help.

"Even now I had to seek the blessing of the elders to tend to your wounds and frostbite. Being rescued by the saudad as you were, they were unlikely to refuse."

"It's hard for me to believe that they rescued me. Until a short time ago, I did not know whether or not they were real. But Mara, how did they know where I was?"

"I wondered when we might return to the complicated questions."

The light crunch of Marcon's footsteps outside announced his return before he called from the other side of the closed flap, "Where would you like these, Mistress Druid?"

Mara's light laugh danced across her hut. "By the door is fine for the present." She tucked the shawl she'd lent Iellieth back around her patient's shoulders. "Come back in," she told him. "Your tea is ready."

Marcon gave Iellieth a quick smile as he stepped back into the cabin and asked after her arm. Mara brought tea over for the two of them and remained standing with her own cup. "The weather is so pleasant today," she observed. "I thought the three of us might take a short walk."

"I would be glad to see more of the woods," Iellieth said. "I have never been this far east before."

"Movement would benefit your circulation as well, lady," Marcon said. "I know that was one of the concerns initially, that your extremities had grown too cold."

"Initially? By whom?"

Mara spoke over Iellieth's questioning. "I am going to step out for a brief moment to see about heartier clothing for you, Marcon. I cannot see how you're not shivering. And, while I'm gone, Iellieth, I laid out your things behind the divider. Would you help her up and into her jacket?" she asked Marcon. "We've just affixed the bandages."

He assented, and Mara slipped through the leather door flap. His stare lengthened again when they were alone, but he helped her to extract herself from the blankets and furs.

"Marcon," she began tentatively, "could you hear our conversation earlier? Before I called to you? Or when they found me?" Despite the roaring fire, the room was chilly beyond the confines of the furs. Behind the silver screen, Iellieth pulled off the shift and dug through her bag for warmer, more practical clothing.

"I did not mean to pry, lady. But yes, I have heard much of the events transpiring around you in the last few days."

The long span of time elapsed underground helped to explain Marcon's unique accent, and the low rumble of his voice still sent chills down the base of her spine. "Do you think we're safe here?" She stuck her head around the divider to meet his eyes.

"I do, at least for the present. There is much that I do not understand. The first instances I overheard were on the mountain. I was in a well-appointed room, decorated in reds and golds. From there I emerged to stand between you and the giant a second time." He exhaled in frustration. Iellieth carefully tied her leather breeches, her fingers stiff from days of disuse, and Marcon continued.

"After I failed you a second time, I returned to the chamber. I tried to call for you, I cried out to Ignis, but no answer came. It began to darken, to grow cold. I heard your fading heartbeat. These markings, beneath my skin, they glowed red. Burned. I returned to the agony from . . . from just before you found me. From thousands of years ago, it seems." The grief in his voice clutched Iellieth's heart.

"Over my own pain, my echoes roaring in my ears, I heard a soft scratching sound, and then a gasp. The room seemed to move, up, though my balance and the furnishings remained unthreatened. 'I cannot believe it,' the voice said, 'you will be alright, I promise.'" Marcon changed his own accent to mimic what he had heard, heavily stressing the *t*'s and shading the *w* to a *v*.

"The voice called others over. They seemed to know who you were, had been searching for you, and wanted to take you somewhere to recover. There was a second woman's voice. She said something over you, a prayer of healing. The darkness faded. Your heartbeat steadied. The runes calmed. And the even sound of your breath returned. From what I can tell, they've been tending to you for two or three days."

"But I don't understand. Where is this room?"

"I think it must be located inside your amulet, lady."

Iellieth stepped out from behind the divider, back in her leather pants and corset, the jacket draped over her arm. Marcon's expression returned to the indecipherable one he'd had shortly after they met, but it quickly passed.

"I don't see how you would fit," Iellieth said. She lifted the amulet to show him. Marcon shrugged and moved forward to help her into her coat.

"My hunch," he said, "is that we will learn more in due course. But for now"—Marcon smiled and held a bare elbow gallantly out toward her—"shall we step outside and meet these people who know so much about us while we know so little about them?"

"I would appreciate a breath of fresh air." She took his arm, and they made for the door. A weight lifted from deep inside her chest with a shifting sense of the order of the world. Something, she knew, was finally about to change.

CHAPTER 8

Hooves thundered down the dirt path at the edge of the forest. A ripple passed over the druids: they would have news of the elders.

"They look frightened," Fenrys said, sniffing the air.

"And none of the elders have returned with them," Ingrid added. She swept back her long blonde hair, a nervous habit. Her eyebrows contracted as she stared at the rangers.

Genevieve bit her lower lip. It was time for her to meet Mariellen for training, but there would be too many distractions as the rangers delivered their news. They could take their daily trip into the forest after they'd left.

She walked away from her friends and searched for Mariellen's hickory braids amid the huddles of whispering druids around the conclave. Her teacher was there, at the edge of their village, with Sheffield and the rangers. Genevieve darted in and out of the small gatherings and waited beside one of the outer cabins.

Mariellen's hand was over her mouth, her eyes wide,

and Sheffield nodded gravely. Something had happened in the city.

"This is why I haven't been able to see them." Genevieve jumped as Constance appeared beside her without warning.

"Mariellen said you'd been looking for them in the waters."

"That I have, girl."

"Has that ever happened before? What does it portend?"

"That they're dead, or worse. I told everyone a few days ago, but they don't listen to me. Need some wanderers to tell them what they witnessed with their own eyes without doing a thing to stop it."

Genevieve wrapped her arms around her waist. Just last week, she and Mariellen had practiced the deep breathing necessary for accessing deeper, more powerful magic. She couldn't slow her mind for long enough to tap into it. Even the most basic spells that came easily to her peers were difficult for her.

Constance was watching her, head tilted sideways.

"What is it?"

"There's a curious sign over you. Best be careful."

Genevieve shuddered after the seer walked away. Most in their conclave dismissed her pronouncements, but Mariellen took them seriously, so she did too.

Sheffield nodded to the rangers, and they rode away, heading north further into the mountains. They normally stayed with the druids for a few days in their travels. That they continued on had to mean something significant. But what?

Her two mentors and the other *su-varran* gathered the conclave together in the village center. She hadn't been alone in her alarm at the rangers' departure. Jacqueline muttered to herself and grew a flower garland unconsciously while sparks kept flying out of Beason's fingertips.

Leha raised her arms overhead and motioned for silence. "Please," she called in Druidic. Even the trees stilled. Dark brown streaks stretched down her face, tears having carved their own pattern in her varran markings. "Our allies bring grave tidings from the city. It is worse than we had feared."

Another wave of distress crested over the community. Leha waited with her hands pressed together at her chest. "The Council of Andel-ce Hevra allowed the elders to defend our community against the farmers' baseless charges of our conclave bewitching their animals and poisoning their crops, but they were unwilling to open their ears to hear and understand our story. Rather than let them depart in peace"—Leha took a deep breath—"they marched them from the council chambers to the city's prisons." Their temporary leader suppressed a sob and bit her lower lip. Genevieve's hands were shaking, and cries of grief and dismay flickered around the gathering.

"We are, all of us, too young to remember the city's practices in the eras past, but it seems they have recovered access to darkstones." A collective gasp. The stones from before the flood that hampered one's access to the natural world. "One of the rangers saw their cages, fortified with the stones. She said that each elder was taken to an individual stone cell."

If they were each locked away, alone, they would never be able to free themselves from the darkstones' power. The shadow magic would eventually destroy the elders' connection to the energetic weave that bound all life together. And without that connection, they would die.

"They felt a final severing, and then they passed on," the druid tales retold through the generations across Tor'stre Vahn explained. The stories taught children to fear the anti-magic early should their persecutors return to power.

But if the stories were real, if Andel-ce Hevra had truly recovered the darkstones, none of the elders could have survived their imprisonment, alone, without the aid of another to help them cling to their magical connection.

Genevieve tightened her hold around her center. If she could only remain still, then perhaps, perhaps they might come back, surprising them all. In her heart, when she reached out for the lower branches, the strength of their community, she felt only the creaking in the upper limbs. Many around her were less subtle with their emotions. Some of her family cried, others fell to the earth. The young looked about, confused at the sudden distress they had not the perspective to comprehend.

"We should have gone with them," Ronaldo shouted.

"No!" Sheffield stood beside Leha and placed a hand on her shoulder. "We did as the elders wished. More would have been imprisoned and killed had they not taken the precautions they did." He bowed his head to Leha and stepped down.

Leha resumed her address. "Three of the twelve elders foresaw this possibility. They wished us to be able to defend ourselves should the city be once again unwilling to hear and value our people.

"In this case, they asked that our energy be put into preparations. We will speak to the forest and ask that she take us in at dawn. You should each be ready to travel to the far side of the mountains then." Leha took a ragged breath. "By the shade of Quercus and the light of Selene, we will find a new home." Her arms fell. She stared at their frightened community before she took Sheffield's hand to step down from the dais.

Once her feet returned to the earth, the conclave was allowed to move. Many couples and friends leaned on one another, tears flowing freely. Genevieve turned away from the elders' households and their overwhelming grief. It washed over her, its tide rising, threatening to engulf her entire being the longer she stood nearby.

Mariellen had stepped away from the other minor elders to look for her. "Genevieve!" Her teacher's voice reached her above the crowd. Mariellen wrapped her in a tight embrace, hands clutching at the back of her hair. "It will be alright, *si'retta*," she whispered. She cupped her hands beneath Genevieve's face and held her head up toward the light. "Sheffield and Leha will help the other su-varran speak with the forest and ask Quercus's blessing for a new home. You and I have more training to do." A sad smile spread across her mentor's features. She was trying to make the day feel more normal, to blunt the tragedy. Mariellen needed the meditation as much as she did.

MARIELLEN LED GENEVIEVE INTO THE FOREST TO SPEND a few moments communing with the spirits of the elders. "They will guide and protect us on our travels," she said. Her mentor laid her fingers against her throat to calm its quaver. "And they will lead us through the great forest."

Genevieve tried to sense their presence, to ask for guidance in these few days before she officially joined her community, but she felt nothing. She kept her concerns at their silence to herself as she and Mariellen returned to the cabin to pack their belongings while Sheffield and the other su-varran beseeched the forest for safe passage and oversaw the community's preparations.

Mariellen had built a small fire beside their cabin to warm bread and vegetable broth for their evening meal. She rose to embrace Sheffield, and he wrapped a comforting arm around Genevieve. "How did you find our forest today, my dear?" He smiled at her as though nothing were amiss, the way he'd greeted her each day of her druid training thus far.

"The forest does not speak to me the way she does to you." Genevieve moved a clod of dirt to the side with her worn leather foot wrap and rolled it back toward herself. Sheffield watched her in silence, waiting for her to speak.

"But something else has been bothering me today." Curls of dark orange licked at the fire's depths. "Why did the city imprison the varran? They were innocent. Our people were the ones who were attacked without cause."

"I don't think that we—"

"She has a right to know, Mari."

His partner bit her lip but nodded.

"Genevieve, the elders traveled to the city to answer the charges against our practices. Andel-ce Hevra has long had a religious circle of its own, in Haven, outside of the city walls. It is their ancient seat, one the priests took over for themselves long ago. They do as they wish there, and the city's leaders support them."

Mariellen clutched her locket, a golden acorn carved into the outside, and muttered a prayer.

Sheffield continued, "The city's official doctrine holds that no gods save those who are represented in Haven can be worshipped on the continent. Their power does not extend far enough to influence Nortelon or any on the western side of the mountains, but those who are near the city, like us, are considered under its jurisdiction.

"When we first heard reports about the farmers attacking our members on the roads, we thought they were after our land. We believe something else is at stake now. The city guards who ventured here to demand an audience with the elders said that our neighbors claimed we had put curses on their crops and bewitched their herds. We explained that the city's growing demands placed unsustainable expectations on the farmers and their lands. The elders offered to help, but the guards scoffed at them."

The color heightened on Sheffield's cheeks, and Genevieve felt heat rising to her own face as well.

"Our varran were tried on charges of heresy, practicing dark magic, and treason." Sheffield rested his elbows on his knees and ran a hand through his unruly brown hair before he could continue. His voice was hoarse. "They were each found guilty. We will not see them again." The pool of tears at the base of his eyes found a counterpart in hers. The conclave would never survive without the wisdom and guidance of their elders.

❦

A SCREAM PIERCED THE DARKNESS. THE SCENT OF ASH ON the air. Mariellen and Sheffield were still sleeping, and Genevieve crawled over to shake them awake. Mariellen's eyes were wide in fear, Sheffield's jaw set. "Keep a lookout," he whispered.

Genevieve crouched in the cabin's doorway as they grabbed their packs from the far corner and hurried toward her. Shapes moved in the undulating darkness outside. Thick clouds of smoke obscured all but their closest neighbors.

Snarling echoed from one of the nearby cabins. It couldn't be an animal. They maintained a close relationship with the forest's inhabitants.

With a crackling roar, the wooden shingles of their roof caught fire. "We must go now," she hissed to Mariellen and Sheffield and rolled outside. Genevieve shrank into the base of their cabin, back pressed against the wooden shelter she had called home for the last three moons. The smoke caught in her throat and burned, but she wrapped her cloak around her face to muffle her coughs and protect her lungs.

One step at a time, she crept to the cabin's edge. Two soft sets of footfalls behind her and a rapid glance confirmed that her companions had made it out of the blazing cabin. She exhaled; heat gathered around her cloak.

Genevieve leaned around the corner. Screams flew, disembodied, from all directions. The entire outer ring of their village burned, and the fire was working its way inward. Like a nightmare phoenix, the flames leapt from the roof of their cabin and landed on their neighbor in the next ring. They fell like delicate rain at first but soon crescendoed into a fiery deluge. The homes beyond their own and those by the forest had already been engulfed.

Sheffield crept up beside Genevieve and supported Mariellen, who stared, uncomprehendingly, at the inferno that had been their community. "Hold on to me," he instructed. His warm brown eyes were fiercely determined. She clasped his forearm. "I'll lead us out."

Over her left shoulder, deeper inside their village,

silhouettes appeared out of the smoke. Genevieve's breath caught in her throat as she watched members of her community fight the flames to find their way out of the fires. Beason conjured a wall of water that she sent crashing over homes. On the other side, vines sprouted from Ronaldo's fingertips to smother the flames. "Ewan'il, Quercus, *aiya'ne*. Aiya'ne!" Constance shouted prayers to the heart spirit of the woods and great father oak. She tossed herbs into the air and waved her hands in front of the flames.

"Selene, *pier na, pier na, bellis si'ra!*" Mariellen, on Sheffield's other side, pled with their mother goddess. "Genevieve, it's not working." Her teacher looked at her and then down at her hands and stumbled forward. "I can do nothing."

"Leave it for now, we must—" Sheffield cried out in pain as a flaming arrow broke through the plumes and lodged into his shoulder. He screamed and pulled away from the two of them as his leather jacket ignited, his back wreathed in rapid flames.

Genevieve's instincts took over, and she propelled herself backward, away from the flames. But Mariellen was braver. She yelped, her hands blackened as she tried to remove her partner from the flaming coat. Sheffield continued to scream and writhe in pain.

Genevieve picked herself up from the ground. They needed help. A hulking form leapt from the shadows with a snarl and shoved her to the side. She spun to avoid the burning remnants of their neighbor's home and fell heavily to the ground, landing flat on her back. Breath vanished from her chest.

Her mind commanded her body to move, but nothing responded. She had to get away. Sheffield's screams stopped. Panic howled in her ears. Where was the creature? She couldn't run toward it. It was—

The figure stepped back into view, black against the plumes of gray, lit brilliantly orange with glowing embers of red at the ends of his fur. A werewolf.

Run. A surge of breath filled her lungs. Genevieve sprang up from her elbows to push herself away. It took two monstrous steps forward; wolf paws perilously balanced massive shoulders and a dripping red maw. The oldest members of their conclave told of a cursed tribe to the far north, jealous of the druids' harmony and power, but they'd not been seen for generations.

In all the tales, the hybrids suffered a state of derangement, driven out of their minds by their curse and a relentless desire to spread it.

But this werewolf was in perfect control. He stood in front of Genevieve and looked down at her. His saliva dripped onto the singed fabric of her leggings and ran down her scraped knee.

The world around her slowed. One of the wolf paws pressed into the top of her foot. The claws drove through skin to strike bone. His weight buckled her leg to the side, and she screamed as the tendons twisted. He snarled and bent forward. A hairy knee pressed around the slight curve of her hip. Genevieve began to sob and looked away. *You're not here. You're not here. You're not* . . . The creature growled again. Clawed hands pinned her forearms to the ground and shoved them over her head.

Get out. Get out. She couldn't break her arms free from his grasp. Small rocks scratched against her arms as she struggled. The werewolf's knees pinned her thighs to the earth. She opened her mouth to scream again, but her voice froze in her throat at the look in his eye. Hunger. Determination. Desire for power and dominance.

The werewolf kept his dark gaze trained on her. Her stomach convulsed as he brushed the hair away from the base of her neck. The werewolf pulled back the top of her tunic and cloak, exposing her collarbone and shoulder. The seams in her nightshirt ripped one by one, with a light pop for each stitch.

He paused as he lowered his face toward her neck, snarling words she couldn't understand. But the mocking, threatening tone was clear. She jerked her arms again, but it only served to drive his claws deeper. Genevieve's oxygen came in heaving sobs, and she willed the ground to envelop and protect her, but, as in her training, no natural force came to her aid.

The hungry glow in his eyes told her that with his every move, he wanted to be sure she understood and would know each moment of this ordeal of being infected. Her body shuddered but could not move, horrified, cold.

The snarling smile stretched further, and he uttered a few more syllables before he lowered his head to her skin. She felt the cold edges of his teeth scrape lightly across her neck as he ran his tongue from the base of her throat over her collarbone. With an expression between a chuckle and a growl, the creature widened his fangs and inhaled her scent before he drove his teeth into her shoulder. Her body convulsed. The fangs sank deeper into the muscles as he bit down harder. Venom coursed through her veins.

The world roared. A place of screams. Pain. It wasn't until the shock as his teeth left her skin that Genevieve recognized her own screams amid the echoes in her ears. Her vision went dark as the poison seized her body. Her head struck the ground as she convulsed again and again.

A STICKY WEIGHT PRESSED AGAINST THE SIDE OF HER neck. She had to turn. Part of her shirt pulled free from the bloody mess of her neck and back as she rolled over. Her stomach heaved. The retching sapped her of strength, and her empty stomach tumbled over and over again. It had to stop. They would hear.

Glowing embers provided the sole source of light across the ruined druid community as thick smoke obscured the night sky overhead. Shadowy figures stalked the settlement. Their misshapen legs and long-muzzled faces swayed in and out of the flaming remains of her home. Lying unmoving, spirits extinguished by the flames, the dark silhouettes of bodies, huddled together, littered the ground. A short distance away, two familiar forms draped over each other. The corpses of Sheffield and Mariellen, arms wrapped around one another.

Genevieve covered her mouth with her left hand; she couldn't move her right arm. She stifled the cry. They were gone.

She couldn't stay here.

But there was nowhere to go. They had no other home. Save the forest. *The forest.* Inside, the gods might come to her aid. The lands they had tended might be willing, in turn, to care for her. Even if the forest could only provide a shelter, while the werewolves remained, it would be enough.

She crawled slowly, her right arm dragging along the ground. A cry from the village's smoldering remains. She stopped. Others were still alive. On the far side of the camp. A wet *thunk* silenced the cry. She waited. There was no reprisal. She had to go.

It would be possible to return after they left. Others might be in the forest. They could find a way to cure her infection or prevent it from taking hold. If she could only get beyond the outer rim of ashes. The forest would keep her safe.

Genevieve closed her eyes as she crawled past other bodies, burnt beyond recognition. One bore a charred horseshoe pin on the remains of their chest. The brooches marked the druids' scouts, a position of honor. She suppressed the bile that rose in her throat at the smell.

Suddenly, through the heavy plumes of smoke, a second figure appeared. Not a werewolf. A woman, her body covered in gray tattoos and glowing paint, with an antler crown on her head and a longbow draped across her back.

The woman placed a long, gray-brown finger over her lips as she looked down at Genevieve and glided past.

Snarls from her right grew louder. Genevieve shook her head at the woman's back. She couldn't go that way. The werewolves would see them.

A hulking body balanced on wolf's legs stepped out of the smoke. Strained tendons protruded across the creature's form, and its muzzle dripped, either saliva or blood.

Her muscles tensed as the woman's voice rang out over the fire. She stood between the werewolf and Genevieve. "Had enough bloodletting, have you?" she said in Druidic. Her voice was low, melodic, the sound of a fading memory. Long indigo braids pooled over her shoulders and chest.

The werewolf snarled a response. They couldn't have spoken the druids' tongue. But the woman somehow understood the hybrid growls. She laughed at him. "That will not do at all, beast. Be gone. You cannot continue any further."

He growled again. The woman traced the delicate

feathers that hung down from the thick braid beside her high, pointed ear.

She should keep crawling while he was distracted.

The one who stood between her and the monster reached behind her head and withdrew two curved silver blades from beneath her long hair. The metal whispered as it left its bindings. The twin scimitars, the phases of the moons engraved on their surface, hummed with energy.

"So be it," the woman said.

The werewolf sprang forward, and her rescuer spun, a swirl of singing blades, bent low on one knee. Two more whispers, like leaves in early autumn, then three wet *thuds*. The upper half of the werewolf's head splatted near Genevieve. The free-flowing blood sizzled in the ashes of a cabin, and she sprang away from it in horror.

The woman exhaled into the gathered fingertips of each of her hands, and tiny balls of fire appeared. She dropped them onto the other two parts of the severed body as she passed. She knelt beside Genevieve and placed her hand on the side of her face. Her touch was cool and as gentle as a breeze. The lilac eyes were mesmerizing. "My name is Yvayne, Genevieve. Go forward with our people's blessing. The forest will care for you. Another waits for you inside, near the heart."

Genevieve nodded but couldn't move. How had this woman arrived to help her?

"You must go, Genevieve. Leave this behind."

Her raging nerves calmed with the woman's voice. This was the next step forward. Genevieve pushed herself up to standing, and the first tingles of feeling returned to her right arm. The woman caught her as she stumbled. Genevieve rolled her shoulder and freed her skin from the binding of her own blood. *To the forest.*

The trembling along her limbs and across her insides ceased. She crept forward. Each step nearer to the forest brought an increased sense of calm. *Don't look at the bodies.* She would be safe. The woman had said so.

> *Find our lady in the stars, who waits to give*
> *you rest*
> *The oneness, our great reward, to Astralei be*
> *blessed.*

Genevieve murmured the prayer to the soul guardian as she tiptoed forward. The woman faded in and out beside her, but the sense of her presence remained. The stars glowed brightly overhead. The smoke only choked her village—the space outside it was clear. A pillar of the fire's aftermath rose into the heavens, taking the souls of her family to Astralei.

A tendril of moonlight uncurled in a path that wound through the forest ahead. The moondust of Selene.

The woman's spirit dissipated when Genevieve reached the edge of the trees. The forest beckoned her inside. She stepped through the still wall of leaves.

YVAYNE PULLED HERSELF OUT OF THE VISION, ARMS shaking. *That was reckless.* But what choice had she? The cries of her people, flaring at once. How many more would they lose? This was only the beginning.

It now fell to her to inform the Caldaran community of their sister tribe's fate. Should she tell them that the were-wolves from the northern highlands were the ones behind the attack? The more enemies they knew were on the move and mounted against them, the more cautious they would be. She needed them to have the wisdom to take the longer view, to risk harboring Iellieth for now until the girl grew stronger, until she learned to embrace the magic that had been hers since birth.

The enemy had moved against them even faster than Yvayne had thought they would, and on the wrong continent. What was she missing?

But she had to tell them something. If Lucien and the werewolves had decided it was time to act, staying silent would be akin to taking part in their death sentence. There had to be a way to buy more time. Iellieth could travel nearby, within Mara's protective reach but not directly inside the colony. Distance from the centralized druidic magic of the Vagarveil would shield her from Lucien's gaze for a while longer. But the moment the girl began to grow in her power, Lucien would know. He would come for her as soon as he was able. It was his mistress's command.

Yvayne stepped away from her casting circle and looked down at the feathered focus in her hand. A young saudad woman had made it for her long ago. Though she had hoped to avoid traveling to the Vagarveil Wood, Mara would need help convincing them to take the right path forward. She would deliver her full warning in person.

She stepped back into her tree, high in the Frostmaw Mountains, to find the jasper stone whose twin Mara held. The channel between them allowed the two women to speak with one another across long distances. *Protect her. Prepare. I will come to you soon. Our enemies are on the move.*

CHAPTER 9

"Teodric? Teodric," a rich alto voice called him from the deep. He groaned.

A strong hand gripped his shoulder and shook him. Blinking away a sticky haze, he could see the outline of Kriega's head before him. "What're you—"

"Admiral needs to see you on deck." She wrapped her hand around his back and lifted him to a sitting position.

"What happened? I just saw you. What day is it?"

"Three days past our attack on the orcs."

"Three days?"

"You had a sea sickness. Something about their settlement—it affected several of the crew, but you're alright now."

"And the admiral needs to see me? Why?"

Kriega ran her tongue over her thick upper lip and around the corner of one of her protruding canines. "She made me keep it a secret."

A flood of warning rampaged through his system. *Danger.*

"There's nothing to worry about. She needs your help with something."

Teodric sighed deeply. "Very well. Thank you, Kriega. I'll gather myself and be up shortly."

He changed into a fresh shirt and vest and combed his hair back and tied it into a knot. After a swig of water and with boot buckles fastened, he made his way above decks.

"My sweet musician, good morning." The admiral sauntered over, golden sword sheathed at her side, and kissed him, half on the cheek and half on his mouth. Syleste's lips tingled, bursts of energy that flashed across his skin. He stepped back, surprised.

She winked, pleased with herself. "We're so relieved you've made a full recovery, my dear."

On instinct, Teodric scanned the deck for Ambrose, but there was no sign of the navigator. Was Ambrose in some sort of danger? Syleste stared back at him, eyebrow raised, waiting. "Sorry, Admiral. I am simply taken aback by your kindness and your concern for my"—what had Kriega called it?—"illness. The first mate said you wished to speak with me?"

Her ruby lips spread over perfect white teeth. "I have some exciting news for you." She wrapped an arm around his waist and walked him over to the port side of the ship. The heels and toes of her boots clipped against the deck's polished wood, each sending a ripple of the captain's presence out to her crew. "Tell me, Teodric, what do you see on our far horizon?"

He squinted at the land mass ahead of them, so small as to barely be visible. "I am not certain from this distance, Admiral." She preferred to be the one in charge, and this test was a different sort of game than one that involved his knowledge of Azuria's western lands.

Syleste withdrew a golden telescope from a hook on her belt and twirled it in her fingers before she handed it to him. "Here." She pressed her body against his. They hadn't been sexually intimate for more than a year. Was he supposed to not be aware of that? Or be smitten with her all over again? She did like to think of herself as irresistible and, at first, that was usually true. "Look again." Her whisper tickled the inside of his ear.

It would be safer to play along for now. He glanced down at her with a half-smile and a low chuckle in his throat. She'd liked that before.

With a flourish, he unspooled the telescope and pointed it at the mass of land. The port city of Nortelon unfurled before him. His blood ran cold. She'd done something to his mother, and here he was playing along with her sick game and waiting for the reveal. A few ships floated at the docks, two of her own and a scattering of merchant vessels. "It seems we're sailing for Nortelon, Admiral."

"Very good." She twirled her fingers through a loose strand of hair at the nape of his neck. "And why might we be approaching Nortelon?"

"I haven't the faintest idea, Admiral." He turned back to her, a purr in his voice. Please don't say it's for Aurelia. Don't mention her at all.

"Look in the harbor for a golden ship."

He'd noticed it the first time, one of the two with her flag. Was it Steinvas's ship? The *Dread Ascari*, something like that? "I see her, Admiral. She's beautiful."

"Hmh." Syleste waited for him to turn back to her and gripped his chin between the sharp nails of her thumb and pointer finger. She drew his head closer to hers. "It's yours." Her eyes flashed, delighted with her surprise.

It had to be a trick. "I-I don't know what to say, Admiral. Of all the sailors you have to choose from . . ." Was she waiting to divulge something more?

"I will graciously see this doubt as your own precious modesty and not a questioning of my judgment or methods."

Teodric widened his eyes and mixed fear and alarm in his expression. "Beautiful Admiral, forgive me. I am simply"—what was she looking for?—"amazed at your generosity in selecting someone such as myself."

"You have served me"—her eyes glinted at the double meaning—"quite well in the past. I should like to afford you the opportunity to do so again."

"It would be my pleasure."

TEODRIC CURLED UP ON HIS COT BELOW DECKS. A captain. But why had she chosen him? It could still be a trap. Syleste had pulled similar tricks before. He searched back through the stories in his memory. The closer he peered, the foggier it became. A holdover from the sickness. Nothing more.

They would arrive in Nortelon at dawn the next day. "Mother, I've been made a captain of my own ship," he would say.

"That's very nice, dear. Can we return to Linolynn now? Your father is waiting for us."

Should he tell her again that he had spent two fruitless years searching for his father? Or should he allow his mother her fantasy, that one day Frederick Adhemar would return to her, safe and sound?

"Please, sir, if you could just spare a moment of your

time. I'm looking for a human man with dark brown hair. He's—"

"I see four right there. He one of them?"

"No, he's my father. He's missing."

"How long."

"Two years."

"Heh. He's dead. Or he found hisself a new family. Either way, time to say good-bye."

Over and over again, in Nortelon, Andel-ce Hevra, small cities along the coast, even Invae Alinor, he'd asked after his father's disappearance. Joining Syleste's ship had been driven by financial necessity, but she and her crew traveled widely. If anyone was able to find him or knew someone who had seen him, her web of influence was his best bet.

These memories came flooding back as he prepared to see his mother once again. He'd tried to explain Frederick's disappearance, but she refused to understand. "I'm sure he's held up at court. Probably too busy in Thyles Thamor—you know how the elves are."

"We've no record of the *Merry Maid*'s arrival in Invae Alinor at this or any other time," the elven dock master had sneered at him. "Perhaps you should look at one of the human ports. We've little to offer you here."

"He was an ambassador, from Linolynn. He came to speak with your leaders and form a diplomatic relationship as well as to ask for help on behalf of the government of Nortelon."

"Well, he didn't arrive in port. What more would you like me to say?"

Teodric shook his head, trying to put the memories in the back of his mind. They didn't help and only served to cause further pain.

He'd need to select a crew after they arrived in Nortelon, though the admiral would place several of her own people on board as well. Hopefully Ambrose would be well enough by then to join him. He would make for an exceptional first mate, though he would demur and say he preferred being a navigator.

Teodric pulled out his mirror and razor. He kept the hair on top of his head and down toward his neck long and wore it slicked back on land, tied up at sea. The sides were still short enough from his close trim a few weeks before, but he'd need to clean up his facial hair before he saw his mother again. A short mustache and goatee with a slight stubble. The look of a merchant sailor.

❧

A RED SUN ROSE AS THEY FLOATED INTO PORT. "A fitting omen," Syleste always said. She loved the foretelling of blood upon her arrival. "Teodric, Kriega, accompany me aboard my other ship. We've a promotion to undertake."

Kriega set her jaw as usual; her forearm muscles rippled as she uncrossed her arms and pushed herself off her leaning spot on the railing. Was Syleste calling her for backup? Or was she the true recipient of the captain's position? With her involvement with the admiral, she wouldn't want to serve anywhere except for the *Dominion*.

He had taken extra care with his clothing that morning, adding a satin vest and feathered hat. After his neighbors fell asleep, he sharpened his rapier in case he needed to defend himself at some point in the day. If fortunes turned, he wasn't simply going to wait for Syleste to dispatch him.

"What happened to Steinvas, Admiral?" Teodric asked as he walked just behind her to the gangplank.

"Nothing yet." She grinned. Teodric's blood ran cold. What was she planning to do? A red sky indeed.

The admiral strode confidently down the dock and completely ignored the dock master, who nearly squealed when he saw her. Kriega gave him a short nod, and the man logged the ship's arrival. Depending on the trip, at times the *Dominion* was officially there and at other times, despite all evidence to the contrary, it was not.

The group made their way swiftly to where the *Dread Ascari* was docked.

"Admiral," the first mate, Quellan, called from the deck. "You've caught us by a bit of surprise this morning."

"I find that hard to believe as we've been visible on the horizon for any who've been looking."

"As far as I'm concerned, you're always just on the horizon. With your fleet, beauty, and might, you've the hold on it all."

Syleste gave the middle-aged man a half-smile. She enjoyed flattery, but fear marred the elegance of Quellan's delivery.

The man disappeared as they reached the bottom of the gangplank, and he and Steinvas, a burly half-elf, stood and waited for the boarding party at the mast. All on deck did their best to look busy as Syleste scrutinized them. Those who hadn't sailed with her before were well enough aware of her reputation.

"Steinvas, thank you for having us aboard."

"My pleasure, Admiral."

"And how goes your mission? I was surprised to find you in Nortelon as we've already searched here."

The captain froze. "Yes, Admiral, we have. My crew

and I, we stopped for supplies. W-we were on our way to meet you at the island."

"But I am not returning to the island for some time."

A pallor seeped beneath his tan, sea-worn skin. "I-I'm sorry, Admiral. My mistake. We couldn't find the"—Steinvas looked at Teodric, then back to Syleste—"the item you are searching for, and morale was low. We lost a few to the centaurs, and there were rumors."

Syleste held up her hand, and the captain practically swallowed his tongue. "Kneel, Captain."

"A-Admiral, please, we'll find it."

"Quellan, you as well."

He shook as he knelt beside the half-elf.

"Kriega, what do we do to those who disobey us?"

"A trial by sea and a charge of mutiny. If they're lucky."

"And if they are not."

"The blood eagle is a favorite of mine, Admiral."

Steinvas trembled. Teodric had never seen the torture performed, but from his reaction, the condemned captain had. He sobbed and bit his lip so fiercely to quiet himself that beads of blood formed where his lips met.

"What is the punishment for mutiny, Teodric?"

"Death, Admiral." Why did she have to be one of the predators who played with her food?

"Very good. Do it." Her low voice purred the execution command.

Steinvas shook, the tendons in his arms taut as he gripped his hands together and tried to hold them still. "Please, Admiral."

She hissed at the begging half-elf and looked at Teodric. "Now."

The groveling man turned to him, tears falling from his brown eyes. What stories leaked away there, things only

Steinvas would know? His own versions of the people he had loved and loathed, the identities of each person he'd known cut short by the extinguishing of this one life, limiting thereafter who they could be in another's eyes. "Please," he whispered.

His mother had said something similar, hands clasped together, almost bowing at the feet of Duke Amastacia as they were expelled from the castle, sent on a "diplomatic mission" across the sea without an end date to their service on the document signed by the king himself.

Bile rose from his stomach up to his throat. It was because of him that the duke had acted against his family. He'd done nothing but try to free Iellieth, the woman he . . . Teodric mentally shook off the thought of her. How many people had this man killed in his service to Syleste? How many crew members in cold blood, for only the whiff of dissatisfaction with their captain, or to take a greater portion of the allotted ten percent of the treasure?

The shaking man's eyebrows knit together. Teodric contemplated mercy. What Steinvas's life could be like if he were allowed to live. Teodric dying in his stead, in Syleste's blind rage at disobedience.

Just as he'd learned in his first weeks on the ship, he drew his rapier quickly across Steinvas's throat. Blood shot forward. Syleste laughed. And the man crumpled to the ground.

"Kriega."

The half-orc stepped forward, her braids caught in the wind. She clutched either side of Quellan's face. The faintest of whimpers and a sickening snap as she twisted. His body went limp, and she dropped him to the ground.

Syleste's eyes danced at the sea of crimson that poured forth from the man who had previously held the position he was ascending to. "Next time, Teodric, no hesitation. Or that will be you." She grinned. "Now, Captain, kneel." She glanced down at the pool of blood that dribbled around the wooden bottoms of their shoes and lapped against the shaggy hair of the deceased first mate.

Teodric forced the bile down, thinking of his mother's nightmares, her deep confusion after his father disappeared somewhere in the wilderness of the Realms. He bent his knee into the warm, sticky liquid. It seeped into the suede fabric of his breeches.

With her own golden sword, Syleste imitated the royals all over Azuria and swore Teodric into her service, appointed to the rank of captain. "Kriega will be your first mate," she said as he rose. The half-orc glowered at him and rolled her shoulders back as the admiral eyed her.

He bowed his head. "You are most generous, Admiral. We will serve you well."

"I expect no less." She pursed her lips. "Tomorrow, we'll commission a new name for your ship. Find someone to clean this up, and you're free to take your leave."

Syleste snapped her fingers, and the officers save himself and Kriega filed off the ship and onto the dock below.

"Kriega, if you would be so kind." Teodric indicated the slain man whose blood ran down the front of his shin. He suppressed his shudder till she turned to shout at some of the crew to dispatch the bodies.

His first two duties as captain executed, he disembarked from his ship, whistling a sea shanty as he walked up the docks and toward the center of town. He stopped at a pub just before the high street for an ale to dull the morning's activity and then strode on toward his mother's home.

CHAPTER 10

Yvayne scowled at the younger druid, reminding herself that Mara wasn't to blame for her conclave's short-sightedness. "It is imperative the council accepts her as one of their own. I know they're frightened, but it is the only way to keep her safe."

"Yvayne, I recognize that the need is great, but I fear you ask too much. I faced enough resistance with your arrival at first, until they understood who you are. It is only within the last few decades that they acclimated to the presence of the saudad in our midst."

"Lucien will be searching for her in the coming weeks, perhaps even days. It is not a matter of if, but when. Marcon may be able to help her to some extent, but with the weakened connection between the planes, he cannot protect her for long."

"But why will you not speak to the council yourself? They would listen to you."

"The danger to you all increases the longer I remain here. Were I to try to explain what has happened, their

concerns would only grow. You do not need me for this."
She moved away from Mara, but the elven woman seized
her hand.

"But what if we do? What if we can't prepare her in
time?"

"Then we are doomed before we've begun." Yvayne
yanked her hand free of Mara's grasp and strode down the
narrow woodland path.

"That cannot be your answer," Mara shouted at her
back.

She stopped. Fear and frustration pulsed at the center
of her being.

She turned, and her eyes met Mara's, a battlefield of
conflicting concerns. The question came down to whether
or not their conclave would be willing to risk its illusion of
safety and anonymity to enable a new chance for the wider
world. And the only way for that to happen was for Mara
to take the weight onto her own shoulders.

"At least meet her," Mara pleaded. "She deserves that
much from you."

Yvayne sighed. "Do you think that I don't want to?
After all this time? But any contact with me poses great
risk to you both. She cannot depend on me for protection." No one else could. Not again.

"I'm not asking you for that. It can be as brief as you
like."

"A few moments this afternoon, nothing more."
Perhaps Mara was right. They shouldn't operate solely
from a place of fear. Her final sight of Fhaona, trapped in
the jaws of shadow beasts and dragged toward her death,
swam over the image of the druid in front of her. Yvayne
pushed the vision from her mind.

Mara sensed her weakening resolve and continued, "One day, perhaps sooner than we would like, she will need to find you on her own. I sense it. Let her know whom she should be looking for."

Yvayne sighed. "Very well, I will stay, but only for a short while. Bring her to me when she's ready." She smiled to ensure her friend knew she wasn't upset. "You've been spending too much time with the saudad, you know."

Mara laughed. "That may be. Perhaps a glimmer of the sight, or a breath of what it might be like to have it, has worn off on me. But they don't bring us ill tidings of the wider world for nothing. What you said to us before came true. Azuria is changing."

"Sais lea-t-an, an't le sai." Such is the way of the seasons of the world.

۞

IELLIETH STEPPED OUT OF MARA'S HUT INTO A CLEARING at the edge of the Vagarveil Wood, relishing the crisp air after several days pinned beneath furs. Mara's home sat alongside several other small structures that faced the center of the village, each embraced by the surrounding forest. Through the dense vegetation, side paths led off into the woods, possibly to other parts of the druid conclave.

Mara was coming up a path; her expression brightened when she saw Iellieth and Marcon, and she hurried over. "It may take some explaining as to how only one outsider arrived and two are here now, but I will do what I can. But please"—she indicated a winding dirt trail behind her hut —"we have much to discuss."

Across the glade, a young woman with curly black hair peered at Iellieth. Their eyes met before she went to follow Mara, and the girl's white teeth flashed brightly against her gold-toned skin. Iellieth returned the smile; it was a nicer greeting than she would have received from anyone in Io Keep save her closest friends. The girl slipped away into the forest and out of sight.

"Mara, is what you were saying true? Marcon is from five thousand years ago?" Iellieth meant to wait for the elf to begin speaking first, but the trees' thick covering unfettered the questions darting across her mind.

"It is true." With Mara leading, Iellieth couldn't see her face to capture any undercurrents amid her serious tone.

"But how is that possible? How has he survived for so long? What happened to—" She stopped herself from the second half of the question and turned to Marcon.

"To everyone I knew?" he said for her.

Mara bowed her head.

"If it will set your mind at ease, lady, most of them died before I arrived in that cave. The last several on the treacherous mountain paths leading to it. We were desperate. It was meant to be an ambush that would turn the tides. It was, in its own way. We were operating on false information."

"But how are you, hmm, does it bother you, to be so far in the future?"

"I have had a few days to wonder about our location. It makes logical sense that we are removed from my own time. It was far too peaceful here."

"Peaceful?"

"I come from a time of war, lady. Spread far and wide, it touched everyone. Places like this community"—he gestured back down the path—"save for those extremely removed from the central powers, were nearly nonexistent. They couldn't have survived."

"It seems that you already know, so I will not delay telling you," Mara began, "that we lost the War of the Champions. Most of your allies died in the final days of battle, as you thought. They separated the champions from one another, though a narrow few survived."

"Are there others, like me, who have awoken?"

Mara's brow contracted, and she lowered her eyes. "I am not sure."

Strain pulled at Marcon's stoic expression. His lips tightened. Just at the moment of reawakening, coming back to life, he lost everyone he had ever known.

Iellieth turned to Mara. "You said there were things we needed to discuss before we met with the council?" A new subject would give Marcon a small respite to think over the weighty news.

"Yes, Iellieth, thank you. There is someone who wants to meet you, someone advanced in the druidic ways and order. She has a few questions for you." Mara led them through the woods for several more minutes in silence.

The trees around them were ancient and almost pulsated with the wisdom and gravitas of their years. Even the largest, oldest trees in the Io Keep arboretum were saplings compared to these giants. There was a special bond between them from all the time they'd spent growing together.

But that couldn't be. She was getting lost in old stories because of her proximity to Mara and the other druids. The woods recalled memories of the faery tales she and Mamaun had read together at Aurora.

The trees thinned out, and they arrived in a second clearing. Unlike the previous one, this larger meadow did not hold any homes. For the first time in days, the warmth of the sun glowed across Iellieth's face and hair. She sighed and looked to the celestial sphere to return the sun's smile. Mara walked to the center and raised her arms out to her sides until they were level with her shoulders. She took a deep breath and let out a beautiful bird song. She folded her hands together at her chest when she'd finished and glanced at the other trail entrances, waiting for someone.

When no one appeared, Iellieth carefully interrupted her reverie. "Mara, you said this person is advanced in the druidic ways, but I don't know any of your traditions. Why would they want to meet with me?"

"Some see larger pictures of the world than many of the rest of us, and she is one such person. You should not expect a great many answers, but it is important for you to speak with her, however briefly."

The surrounding woods were silent. Without warning, a striking figure with dark blue braids emerged from the trees a short way behind them. Her skin was sepia-hued and covered in intricate, dark gray tattoos, her eyes a shockingly pure lavender. Iellieth sprang back in surprise, and Marcon's hand darted to the hilt of his sword. The light in the clearing dimmed as clouds rolled across the patch of sky overhead.

"Yvayne, you have come." Mara extended her hands to the other druid as she walked toward her. "Iellieth, Marcon, do not be afraid. Yvayne was among those who rescued you."

The woman's pale purple eyes fixed on Iellieth so fiercely she couldn't have moved if she'd wanted to. Yvayne was slight but tall and stately, made more so by the antler crown she wore above her many braids. She circled the three of them, her movements powerful and lithe. Iellieth gasped as she moved her gaze to Marcon and then to Mara. Yvayne's ears were nearly three times the size of her own.

"You're a fae," she whispered. The woman smiled and returned her attention to Iellieth. Her mouth curved still further when Marcon stepped halfway in front of her.

"Worry not, Champion of Fire." She lifted her palm toward Marcon. Her voice had a rich timbre, and the Caldaran words flowed from her tongue in a thick Elvish accent. She tossed a braid over her shoulder. "I have no intention of harming either of you. And yes, young Amastacia, I am a fae, though perhaps not in the way you have been led to understand in your stories. I am Yvayne." She bowed her head a few inches, and Iellieth returned the gesture.

Yvayne's eyes flared as they studied Iellieth's, the purple turning almost to white in a flash from within, and Iellieth tensed her back and shoulders to suppress the chill that threatened to run down her spine. A few times in the castle, she'd seen the priests and mages perform something similar when they were trying to understand an enchantment.

The indigo-haired druid's gaze shifted to her amulet. Iellieth narrowed her eyes. Why was she studying it? What was she looking for?

Yvayne met Iellieth's eyes again and released her arcane study. "Forgive me," Yvayne said. The lilac returned to her irises. "I am still trying to understand how you found your way to the peak."

It had been her amulet that reacted during the transmigration. But how had she known to look there? "Thank you, Yvayne, for finding me," Iellieth said.

"I was not alone." The purple eyes glinted. "The saudad were instrumental in your rescue—I could not have done it without them. There is one in particular who is anxious to make your acquaintance. I am glad we have met, Iellieth Amastacia." She turned her attention back to Mara. "Might we speak briefly? I cannot linger here."

"Yes, of course. Iellieth, Marcon, please excuse me."

The two women walked to the far side of the clearing, their heads bent together. "Can you understand what they're saying?" Iellieth whispered.

"I hear something every now and then, but it is not a language I speak."

"I thought at first it might be Elvish, but it's something else."

"Perhaps the language of the forest or its tenders, lady? I do not have a gift for tongues, but it sounds like what I remember of Queran. What do you make of Mara's companion?"

"I am not entirely sure. She makes me feel uneasy, but also understood. It's strange. I'm not sure how both of those things occur together."

"She has a sharp gaze, and she seemed very interested in you. But you don't know why?"

"She was studying my amulet, trying to understand it. I wonder how they found us."

Mara bowed her head to Yvayne, and the sepia-hued woman disappeared into the covering of the forest. The clouds lifted as she left, and the kiss of sunlight returned.

MARA PURSED HER LIPS ON HER WAY BACK TO THEM, AND her posture was heavier than it had been a short time before. Iellieth drummed her toes inside her boots and stretched her limbs. The soreness from the avalanche and days of unconsciousness crept back into her muscles.

"My apologies, Iellieth, Marcon. I had hoped to show you around our community this afternoon, but it's later than I'd realized, and I must attend the council meeting."

"We can come with you, if you'd like," Iellieth said. "You wanted us to speak with them?"

"I hope to have you at my side for a meeting soon enough, but I am not sure that this is the ideal occasion. There are things I must discuss with them before they will be ready for you."

"So some of the meeting today is about us?"

"That it is, *cher'a*."

"Mara—"

"I know that you both have many questions. I will do what I can to answer them but, forgive me, I must go." Mara glanced over her shoulder and started off toward the opposite side of the clearing. "Can you find your way back from here?"

"I think so."

"With certainty," Marcon answered. Iellieth grinned at his confidence. Surely someone could help them if they truly became lost.

"And after, we can talk?" Iellieth called out to her.

Mara paused. "Yes, of course. If my presence weren't imperative, I would stay with you now." Iellieth nodded. "And Marcon," she instructed, "see that she rests, please."

Clouds drifted across the leaf-framed window overhead as Mara vanished into the forested foothills.

"What did Yvayne mean when she called you a champion of fire?"

"That I am bonded to one of the elemental titans. Ignis."

"The elemental titans? Who are they?"

Marcon studied her, his confused expression cast in shadow by the dappled sunlight. "Can you tell me what you mean? You do not know them?" An edge crept into his voice, either anger or alarm.

She proceeded carefully. "I have heard of titans in stories. They're similar to giants, only bigger."

"My gods." Marcon shook his head and looked away from her. He lowered himself to sit on the ground and ran his fingers through the grass. The runes beneath his skin grew more pronounced, rising up as if through water to press themselves against his olive hands and neck.

"I'm sorry, I don't mean to upset you." She sat beside him and waited.

"It is no fault of yours, lady. I . . . I had sensed as much." He lowered his head, his thoughts still far away from their immediate surroundings. "I had forgotten what it's like, to be on my own."

"What do you mean?"

"Ignis, my titan, granted me special power in exchange for serving him. I, well . . ." He exhaled sharply. "Lady, I cannot feel his presence. That part of me is missing."

"He could come back, couldn't he? And you're not entirely alone."

"I don't know if he will return or not." He forced his face into a more neutral expression, but his eyes remained hollow; they watched an invisible, advancing desperation beyond her perception. "But you are right. We are neither of us alone." He took a deep breath and turned to her. "Shall we return to Mara's? I can tell you more as we walk, though the full story will take more time than that."

"Yes, certainly. I can't imagine how strange it must be here for you. This place with the druids is foreign to me, but only in comparison to life in the castle. If it helps, though, I'll do what I can to acquaint you with the world as it is now. I have little experience beyond Caldara, but it's a start."

"Thank you. I do need to get my bearings here before I can determine where to go next." Marcon pushed himself up and offered his hand to pull her up to stand beside him. "From what I've seen, you've handled this new environment with ease."

The clearing was still empty besides the two of them, but Iellieth whispered to prevent any unseen presence from overhearing. "What if we were to walk by the council meeting, just to see what they are like?" She smirked as the idea took shape. "If it's in another clearing like this one and Mara's, no one would know we were there, and then we'll have a better idea of what's going on before we speak to the council ourselves."

IELLIETH AND MARCON FOLLOWED MARA'S TRAIL. THE woods were so dense and full of chirping wildlife that it was difficult to hear the various offshoots of the settlement once inside the trees, but it was unlikely that the council meeting was very far away. Mara hadn't been walking quickly when she left them. The clearing they'd left behind seemed an ideal location for a gathering, with its pleasant sunlight, but it remained unclear how many druids there were who lived in the Vagarveil—perhaps a larger space was required.

"You were going to tell me about Ignis?" Iellieth asked, careful to keep her voice low.

"Yes, my apologies, lady." Marcon sighed. "You asked me if there were other titans. There are six in total, one for each of the elements." He smiled. "In my time, those the titans appointed to serve them, to enact their will and protect the balance between all forms of life, were called champions.

"A few years into my life as a soldier, shortly after I'd become a captain, I called upon the Titan of Fire to come to my aid. He answered. Ignis imbued me with power and with control over flames, and I worked to follow his directives.

"In that time as well, an age-long war was coming to a close. We were not faring well."

"But who were you fighting against?"

"Ah," he paused. "I forgot that all of our deeds were lost." Marcon studied the trees and brushed his fingers back through his short hair.

"We do not know yet if that's entirely true," Iellieth reminded him. "I come from a small, closed-off kingdom. There are many others who know a great deal more than I do. Mara seems to know who you are. And Yvayne knew."

Marcon nodded. "This world, the quiet overhead, the small populations, the calm—my life from before feels like a false memory. That events could have led us here . . . I don't yet know what to make of it." He glanced down at her. "Are you religious, lady?"

"Not particularly." Was this a strange test of how civilized they were?

"But you know someone who is?"

"Many people in Linolynn are religious. It's less common in the court."

"I hope you will tell me more about your life spent in a castle soon. I ask because in many ways, my relationship with Ignis was similar to those bound to a deity or other higher being. His power flowed through me."

This sounded dangerous but exciting. How much freedom had Marcon possessed between his own desires and those of the titan?

Marcon smiled at her scrunched expression. "It is here that the story shifts." His eyes flashed like he had a secret to reveal. "I did not answer your question as to who we were fighting. Her name was Alessandra. At one time, she, too, was a champion. But she turned from that path and betrayed her allies to ascend to godhood herself."

Marcon's face darkened. "Through the ages, her desire for power grew. That hunger is what led to the war in my time. There was so much death and destruction, as the world had not witnessed for thousands of years."

The bushes beside Iellieth rustled, interrupting her response. She held up a hand to stop Marcon behind her to see which woodland creature was crossing their path. So many questions waved in the branches of her mind, each rustling for attention. Bent slightly, as she debated which to ask first, it was only Marcon's quick reflexes that kept her on her feet as a much larger figure than she had anticipated burst forth from the undergrowth.

The young woman yelped in surprise as she and Iellieth collided, and then she froze, staring at Iellieth's face, with her hand clasped on her elbow.

"Lady, are you alright?"

"You're the girl from the mountain," the young woman exclaimed.

Iellieth released the breath she'd caught and gave Marcon a look of thanks. "I saw you earlier today, didn't I? By Mara's house."

She blushed. "Yes, that was me, this morning."

The evergreen and pale copper in the girl's eyes were even more vibrant up close with breaths of sky blue amid the hazel, accentuated by the beautiful gold of her skin.

"Do you mean Torg's Peak?" Iellieth asked. "Were you on the mountain during my rescue? There's a significant amount of that time that I don't remember."

"I should think not. You were quite frozen when we found you. And we didn't find you at all," the dark-haired young woman said to Marcon. "But I am glad that you are here now. Yvayne said it was important for us to find both of you, and here you both are even though there was only one of you in the snow." The girl studied them with open curiosity. She leaned her head in closer and squinted her eyes at the palimpsest shifting beneath Marcon's skin.

"Did Yvayne say why us being here was so important? I, well, I seem to have mis-transmigrated. Do you know anything about that as well? How it happened? Wait." Iellieth took hold of the girl's forearm. "Are you one of the saudad? Yvayne said that's who rescued us." She lightly touched the gem-colored sleeves. An ornate pattern made of gilded stitches accentuated the supple fabric.

The young woman laughed brightly. "Why yes, of course I am."

"I didn't realize." Iellieth shook her head. "In the stories, I hope you'll forgive me, we have never been sure that you and your people are real."

"You can always tell from our clothes." She grinned and looked down. The tip of a bronze ear, remarkably half-elven in size, holding a few golden rings along its length, emerged from her dark mahogany hair. Her gemstone-colored clothing stood in sharp contrast to the earth-toned leathers and cloth tunics Iellieth had seen thus far in Mara's conclave.

"I didn't want to make assumptions. Perhaps you simply wanted to look different from the other druids." They both giggled at this possibility.

"We hide inside other cultures most of the time unless we want people to know who we truly are. That's probably why the stories are incomplete." The girl's eyes brightened again, and her color rose with a sense of mischief. "I could not wait any longer to meet you even though they said that I should. I'm Persephonie." She smiled, her white teeth winking.

"I'm Iellieth, Persephonie." She couldn't help but return the warm smile. "It's such a pleasure to meet you. And this is Marcon." He bowed his head to her.

"Yes, I am very aware of who the two of you are. But come, we must hurry if we are to catch the council meeting."

"Oh, that's where we were already headed—" Persephonie grabbed Iellieth's hand and darted forward into the trees; Marcon followed close behind her.

"You aren't supposed to see this," Persephonie whispered as she ran, "but it involves you too, so I think that you deserve to watch." Her eyes glimmered in the forest's dim light, and she led them deep into the forest, far away from the carefully carved trails.

THEY SLOWED AS THEY NEARED ANOTHER CLEARING. Iellieth could hear the raised voices from afar. Many of them spoke in a rolling, mystical tongue she couldn't make out, but those who were most agitated spoke in Caldaran.

"That's my papa." Persephonie pointed to a handsome man with a bronze complexion and shiny black hair. He had dark eyes and dressed in black leather armor. He stood with his feet shoulder-width apart, arms crossed behind his back, with a few other saudad, though none were as colorfully dressed as Persephonie.

"What are they saying?" Iellieth whispered.

"You do not speak Druidic?" Persephonie's eyes widened once again.

"No, do you?"

"I speak it to some extent." She shrugged. "I always learn new things when we visit here, and my mother taught me several of the prettiest-sounding phrases. This older woman"—Persephonie pointed to a woman in pale gray leathers with a fox-fur collar—"she is saying that they have not the room for a new person to come in. They are afraid that the danger will follow." Persephonie returned her attention to the council too quickly to notice Iellieth's confusion and alarm.

Mara stepped into the center of the circle. "My friends," she said in Caldaran, "danger is upon us either way. Yvayne has just informed the elders of an attack against our sister conclave across the ocean and that the last moon druid has fallen into shadow. Would one of you like to volunteer to take her place?"

Several druids clutched their hands to their hearts or muttered over strands of beads. Mara stared at each in turn, daring anyone to speak. A few raised their eyes to hers, but most stared at the ground. "Then we have little choice, do we not?"

A slight shift across the clearing parted the ring of

people, and a young elvish man stepped forward. Iellieth inhaled sharply; she had only seen a few elves in the entirety of her lifetime, yet here were two in the same druid conclave. "There is always a choice, Mara Stoneleaf. And this is one our people cannot afford to take lightly. That time is behind us. The old prophecies represent false hopes. Our enemies have retreated—they mind their own lands and leave us to do the same with ours. It is time that we step forward into a new future and leave the old conflicts in the past."

Persephonie stiffened next to Iellieth. "He is misleading them, speaking of what they wish to be true and not what is."

He spoke again before Iellieth could answer her. "We can let the neighboring city-states know of our existence, bring them into the light of our ways. With our wisdom, our understanding, we have much to offer to them and their growing societies. And little reason to hide any longer."

Persephonie lunged forward out of the underbrush. She shoved through the ring of druids and faced off with the elf. "Have you no sense, Berivic? Have you not listened to all that we have said?"

"Persephonie—" her father began, but Mara raised her hand, asking him to wait.

"I have heard fear and doubt, to be sure," the elf replied. "We have not yet confirmed Yvayne's report. There is still every possibility that the werewolf attack was a vision that has not yet come to pass and may not ever transpire. We have long been out of touch with the druids across the sea. Their concerns are not ours. I have heard of the attacks your people have suffered on your travels, for which I am deeply grieved. But none of these are reasons for us to go back to the way things were. Not when we are so close to a new beginning. There is hope here, just beyond the woods."

"You know nothing of what we have lost!" Persephonie screamed. Though she was almost a head shorter, she stood directly against the elf, her face scowling up at his. "Your enemies awaken. They move. The werewolves slaughter any who cross their path. Those they don't kill they turn to swell their ranks."

"Those are exaggerated rumors. The mountain peoples' populations have been dwindling for some time." He glared back at her, but his hands trembled. He balled them into fists.

"My brothers barely escaped an onslaught deep in the mountains. It is a miracle they survived the attacks and made it back to warn us." Persephonie's voice broke, and she wrapped her arms around her waist and looked down. "At night, they still are plagued by the screams they left behind them."

She looked at the encircled druids and held out her hand toward her people. "We have risked much to bring you the same warning, and we ask you to do something about it. Yet you would throw the true chance at a better future away because you are frightened."

Persephonie's father stepped out of the circle and walked decisively over to his daughter. He took her in his arms and rested her head against his chest. Iellieth's heart tore with the open longing for her own father. How often had she imagined him holding her precisely in that way?

He whispered something in Persephonie's ear and then raised his head to address the gathering. "My daughter speaks true. Your decision is your own, yes, but do not take lightly Yvayne's tidings or our own. The world is shifting. You would do well to see it." He glanced in their direction and met Iellieth's eye. "Nor should you casually toss away the one whose fate might join with yours. You all would do well to honor and to help her." He lowered his eyes to her, the most delicate of bows, and returned to look upon the ring of druids.

Mara spoke into the tense silence. "Perhaps it would be best if we adjourn our meeting until tomorrow." She nodded to Persephonie's father, then to Berivic. "Shall we take the evening hours to consider our best route forward?" She stretched her lips into a smile that did not reach her eyes.

"Any who wish to speak further may meet at my hut," Berivic shouted, the anger from his initial speech returned.

Her father's arms tightened around Persephonie, and Mara's elegantly arched shoulders fell.

"Lady, I believe they are speaking of you joining their number," said Marcon.

"Persephonie's father seemed to think they were talking about me, or had been, but I can't be a druid. You have to be born into the community or chosen to join for your powers."

Marcon glanced down at her feet and smiled. Iellieth released the tree branch she had been gripping throughout the meeting and followed his gaze. Their feet were completely covered in vines that intertwined around their ankles.

He raised an eyebrow in response and bent to extract his boots from the verdant bonds. "Anyone here could have done that," she said.

After most of the conclave had gone their separate ways, Persephonie's father led Mara and Persephonie toward Marcon and Iellieth's hiding place.

"Perhaps a discussion among the five of us would be fruitful," Mara said, looking at them each intently. "I am glad you overheard that, as it will make some things easier to explain. But come, let us step away from here. I would be honored if you would all share a meal with me." She led them back to her hut as twilight claimed the woods around them.

CHAPTER 11

The five of them sat together around a fire outside Mara's hut. Mara warmed salted meat and bread over the fire. Persephonie's father, who introduced himself as Cassian, brought out a few bottles of wine. "The saudad have rules about these things," Cassian said with a wink when Iellieth expressed her surprise at the vintage.

The stress from the council meeting lingered over them. Mara and Cassian spoke in hushed tones, and Marcon contemplated the flames.

"Persephonie," Iellieth asked, "who are these enemies you spoke of at the council meeting? Are they really werewolves?"

The young saudad glanced at Mara and her father before she answered. "They are, yes. We do not know their exact location in the mountains, but they are on the move again. Have you not heard of their attacks? The news has not reached Linolynn?"

"The day I left, there was a whispered conversation I

caught pieces of. They mentioned attacks, but I don't know who they believe is responsible."

"It is likely the same forces, though it would be difficult to be sure. Who was it you heard speaking?"

"My stepfather and the head of the king's guard, Basha." Did they know yet what had happened to her? Had they sent guards out to search? "They were worried. I believe they planned to speak with the Hadvarian nobles about it upon their arrival, to see if they are aware of similar occurrences."

"Datha," Persephonie captured Cassian's attention and said something rapidly in a language Iellieth couldn't understand. "I have told him your news of the city-states' awareness. We have been waiting to see when they might be alerted to the enemy's forces."

"Is there an enemy beyond the werewolves then? Is someone leading them?"

Cassian knit his brow and watched Iellieth and his daughter, and Marcon turned from the fire to their conversation.

Mara broke the silence. "There is another enemy, Iellieth. One who will be most distressed to find you in our midst."

"But who would that be? I thought at first the elf at the meeting might have been referring to my stepfather and his officers, but even if he's been able to discover where I am, it will be a few more days before anyone he's sent for me can reach us here. I can find somewhere else to go by then."

"That is kind of you, Iellieth, but no, Berivic is reacting to something else. To grave news that's reached us from the saudad"—Mara nodded to Cassian and Persephonie— "and from across the ocean from our sister conclave."

"But I don't understand how their news is connected to this enemy." The world along the corners of her eyes pulsed in and out of clarity. She had thought that food and conversation outside around a fire, something she had only experienced as a fanciful diversion at elegant feasts and festivals, would allow her to make sense of where she was and what she was doing, but it only served to pit her body against her as she continued to recover from the mountainside.

"I . . . you do not need to worry about him for now. You're safe here."

Marcon stiffened beside her, but he relaxed the hand that had flown instinctively to where his sword hilt would have been at his side.

"While we deal with that," Mara continued, "there is something I'd like to ask for your help with. We as a people have a local dispute that we have tried to make better progress with, but they will not hear us."

"That hardly sounds like an enemy," Marcon said.

"This is the only conflict the two of you need to concern yourselves with at the moment, though I would like to discuss your stepfather with you further, Iellieth. Would anyone care for more bread?"

The yawn escaped her before she could prevent it, and Mara shook her head. "I had a feeling this might be too much."

The phantom of a piercing ice creature returned to Iellieth's limbs. "Wait, I need to understand. I'll rest easier if I know what's going on."

Mara knelt beside her and pulled the wrappings back on Iellieth's arm. "You'll need to rest regardless. I promise things will be clearer in the morning. But for now, your bandages need to be changed."

Persephonie followed Iellieth and Mara into the hut, humming happily to herself with the dregs of a glass of wine.

"Are these enemies the same that Marcon faced before, Mara? Alessandra?" She looked away, and Persephonie held her other hand as the druid removed her sodden bandages.

"In a way, yes, though it is complicated. He will tell you more about her as he's ready. We are lucky to have his perspective. But the enemies they faced were more powerful than the ones you have heard discussed today."

"I'm glad your brothers are alright, Persephonie." Iellieth met the saudad's eyes as Mara set the last of the wrappings aside. "Where were they when this happened? Has it been very long ago?"

"Thank you, Iellieth," Persephonie said. The sharp sound of the *t*'s when she spoke was charming, but shared sadness gripped Iellieth's heart when Persephonie lowered her eyes to release the tears onto her lap. "We have lost many friends recently, and I thought that Felix and Stefan were among them for a time. I was overwhelmed with joy when they came back. But now, on occasion, it is difficult for me to hold the gaze of some members of our caravan, those who have lost children or partners while my family remains whole."

"I know I've only met you and your father, but I'm sure the other saudad don't wish for you to feel that way."

Persephonie sniffed and wiped her eyes. "You are right, they would not. Datha says that I place too much pressure on myself, because I have the gift of sight. I can see dangers, when they are on the horizon, so long as they are not too obscured. But I could not clearly make out the werewolves."

Wine and fatigue began to blur Iellieth's senses. Sitting

inside a druid camp, speaking with the saudad, werewolf attacks in the mountains—she couldn't shake the sense of standing at the edge of a folktale as the lore of Azuria took shape all around her, painting a new landscape and path before her feet.

"The lycanthropes remained hidden from us as well." Mara's voice interrupted Iellieth's reverie as the druid returned from her collection of tinctures and herbs. She dipped a towel into a small bowl of water and began to blot away the remains of her previous poultice from Iellieth's arm.

Persephonie said, "I do not yet know how they kept their presence so concealed. My mother, she also has the sight. She was planning to teach me how to peer through arcane wards when I next visit her in Andel-ce Hevra."

"Your mother doesn't live with the saudad?" In the stories Iellieth had heard, the saudad prided themselves on remaining in their extended family units.

"Sometimes I forget that we have just met." Persephonie smiled at her. "My mother is not a saudad, though she lived with my people for a time when I was young, while she and my father were together. But though we travel, and roaming is part of our very being, for Esmeralda, it is not enough. She longs to be utterly free."

"When do you see her, then?" Iellieth couldn't tell if Persephonie admired this quality of her mother's or if it made her sad. Perhaps a mix of both.

"I stay with her for a month or two each year. Or almost every year. There was one very hard winter in the city when I was small. It made her worried to have responsibility for me. Datha is very kind and says that he will take me to see her whenever I wish, but I know that she needs plenty of time on her own."

Iellieth squeezed Persephonie's hand. "My mother is distant too, though I see her almost every day. But I think that she's the opposite, afraid of freedom. Or she doesn't trust herself. She lets my stepfather bend her to his will and refuses to stand up to him"—Iellieth's voice grew quiet—"even to protect me."

Persephonie's features scrunched together as she contemplated this. She surprised both Iellieth and Mara as she wrapped her arms around Iellieth and pulled her closer, just as Mara prepared to apply her healing dressing. "We will find our own way then. But Mara will help us."

The druid laughed as the twinned smiles turned toward her. "That I will. For the present, though, I need my patient to hold still so her arm can heal."

The saudad giggled. "I am sorry, Mara." She released Iellieth and settled into a more comfortable position on the scattered pillows and furs. "I will tell you a story while you work that is dear to my people: The Lost Circle of Orison." Persephonie's accent grew deeper the longer she spoke, and soon Iellieth found herself drifting off to the mystical tales of the saudad, the legends she had studied in the castle come to life in a forest far beyond its walls.

IELLIETH WOKE WITH THE FIRST RAYS OF SUNLIGHT THE next morning, the soft breathing of her new friends filling Mara's intimate home. Cassian rested against the wall, his armored leather coat undone and his sword and sheath on the ground beside him. A mass of dark, auburn-brown curls hid Persephonie's face amid the pillow and blankets. Mara's shoulder rose and fell evenly on her other side.

Marcon wasn't among the sleeping forms. A cool

breeze drifted over to her from a fold in the hut's door flap as he stepped out into the crisp morning air. Iellieth wrapped herself in Mara's green shawl, found her shoes, and followed him outside.

"I hope I didn't wake you, lady," he said as she emerged.

"No, I am used to rising early."

"A mandate in your castle?"

"More a personal preference. If I waited, less of the day was mine to do with as I wished. But if I woke with the sun, I could spend some time outside in the gardens before I had to attend to other duties."

"And what did those usually involve?"

"Much of it was still of my own choosing." She settled beside him on one of the log benches placed around Mara's outdoor fire pit. "I often worked with languages and translation. My friend and teacher, Katarina, is a Celestial scholar. I assisted her with some of her projects."

"Is that a common pursuit for many?"

"Not as far as I am aware. Katarina is unique." She grinned at the swell of memories and found Katarina's gorgeous blonde hair in the golden glow of sunlight at the treetops. "She saw me as more than a young noble-woman, awaiting the fate dictated by my family. That would have been singular enough. But I knew from the time we spent together that she genuinely cared about me too."

"You are not close with your family?"

Iellieth chuckled. "No, I am not."

"I have wondered why you did not feel a more pressing need to return to them. In my experience, most people worry about those they have left behind."

"Was that the case for you as well?"

"I was an orphan, so there was less for me to worry about."

"I'm sorry." She lowered her eyes.

"There is no cause for you to be, but thank you." Marcon reached over and pulled the edge of her shawl tighter around her shoulder and over her crossed arms to prevent the wind from catching it. "Our conversation did not continue long after you went to sleep last night."

"What did you make of what they said?"

"I would like to know who this enemy Mara spoke of is. And why they are interested in you."

"I have been thinking about that too. There are people who . . ." How should she phrase it? "There are a few individuals that I would prefer to never see again." But an unknown being who wished her harm? It made little sense, which amplified the queasy unease at the base of her stomach. "I've no idea who this would be. Or why they would wish to harm this community because I am staying here."

"Is it possible that it goes the other way? That they do not want you to be with the community, and your presence here places you in danger?"

"I hadn't thought of it that way." Why had he made that connection? A piece of her heart shifted internally, settled into place. His guess was close to the truth, whatever it was. "My stepfather would not want me to be here." Or Lord Stravinske. The brief peace Marcon's insight had brought was crushed in a wave as her insides rolled. This misadventure had provided such a narrow escape. "Or anyone working with him," she added.

"Do you consider him to be an enemy of yours, lady?"

"Yes," she whispered. "There was one time before, when he knew something I thought would be impossible. We were so careful." Her tear-stained memory of being dragged away from Teodric as he lay broken, unmoving, on the castle floor, flooded her senses. The glint in the duke's eye as she sprinted into the main ballroom of the Hadvarian palace after Lord Stravinske's assault, her wheezing breath barely contained. His cruel smile on countless occasions.

Iellieth studied the patterns in the layered dirt across her doe-brown boots while Marcon waited for her to continue. "Teodric, one of the other nobles in the castle, my close friend, he tried to help me escape once before. We had to rush our plans, but we had been so diligent about keeping them a secret. In spite of all of that, my stepfather's guards, they knew exactly where we were going to be."

She'd heard Teodric's ribs break when they slammed him into a wall and rammed a fist into his side. She fought to free herself from their grasp, but they were too strong. They lifted her off the ground, and one clamped his hand around her mouth. Her face was bruised for days afterward. They held her and made her watch while they beat him, until he lay on the ground, unconscious.

Iellieth blinked away the tears. She hadn't seen or heard from him since, and she had long ago stopped looking for a ship to bring him back to her. "They stopped us." She couldn't hide the pain on her face from Marcon when she forced herself to look up. "And I never got to leave again, until now." Iellieth hugged her knees and turned away.

A heavy hand gently squeezed her shoulder. Marcon's eyes were filled with concern at her distress. "I am sorry, lady." He knelt in front of her to bring his eyes on level with hers. "But I swear to you, if it is within my power to prevent, you will never be trapped inside those walls again."

Iellieth sniffled and smiled at him. "Thank you," she said. "I don't know how he found out what we'd planned. But he knew."

The side of Marcon's jaw twitched. "And you are worried he will try to come here?"

"He will send someone as soon as he has an idea of where I am."

"He sounds like a right prick."

Iellieth laughed in surprise. "He is."

The runes faded in and out along Marcon's neck, pale tattoos that grew clearer with the sudden intensity of his blue eyes. "I owe you a great debt, Iellieth. You saved me, returned me to myself. I know not what these signify"—he balled his hand into a fist to stretch the runes beneath the surface—"but I will do what I can to aid you, to help you find somewhere safe from your stepfather, if that is what you wish."

Gratitude knotted in Iellieth's throat, and she blinked quickly to clear her eyes. "Thank you," she said as soon as she could trust herself to speak.

Mara's door flap flew aside as Persephonie bounded into the clearing. "*Bun ineata*, my new friends," she said happily as she hurried to sit next to Iellieth. "May I share your shawl, Iellieth? It is quite chilly here in the out of doors this morning."

Iellieth smiled as she opened the shawl and tucked her new friend inside. They huddled together, and soon thereafter, Cassian and Mara came to join them.

"So," Persephonie began, "where were we?"

Mara studied each of her guests in turn before she turned to Iellieth and Marcon. "I began to tell you last night of an issue we have been trying to handle on our own for a short time, but we've met with little success."

"You spoke of it as though you had a local enemy," Iellieth said.

"In a way we do, yes. It is fortuitous that you are here, Iellieth, as you may be the perfect person to help."

"What do you mean?"

"A few weeks ago, the mayor of Trudid, the town nearest our settlement, received a tempting offer to log the forest we all share and has hired an aggressive company to help him. We recognize that a small amount of logging, for development or modest expansion, is normal for towns, and we try to stay neutral in these situations."

Mara turned to Marcon. "After the end of the War of the Champions, new cities arose, and the cities that survived the war increased in size. Our people warned them of the possible consequences of these swollen populations but, much as we are today, they were ignored at best, persecuted at worst, and the city leaders were unmoving.

"The waters rose. Cities faced disaster, but still, change was refused. The final remaining community of druids disappeared along with their forest. It is said that the devastation grieved them beyond endurance, and the gods removed them from the earth."

Iellieth was aware of the Great Flood, but she hadn't heard the druids' side of the history before.

"The ocean took their place. The great cities that had grown over the two thousand years after the war disappeared, drowned beneath the waters. So many lives were lost. Entire cultures. The world could not go on as it had, and so the final remnants of Eldura were washed away and renamed Azuria, a world marked, forever, by the dividing and joining waters." Mara's expression was grave as she waited for their reaction.

Marcon stared at her, his expression torn between grief and rage. "And this is why the old names did not endure? Why our history was lost."

Mara nodded. "Yes. Save a few remnants, and in spite of Alessandra's victory, the world of Eldura was destroyed."

He looked away from her, and Cassian came to sit by his side. "Do not lose faith, my friend. A few places survived. The memory of the Realms is long, and Azuria's most ancient cities, Andel-ce Hevra and Cyrinia, they possess remnants of your time as well. But more importantly, you have returned to us, have you not? And with you, your history lives."

Iellieth smiled at Cassian's encouragement. The saudad truly were a remarkable people. "I've heard some of those stories before," she said. "Every once in a while, they appeared in mine and Katarina's research."

"Your friend is wise," Persephonie added. "Most have forgotten the great floods and their devastation."

Mara nodded. "We have a sacred duty not only to remember but to try and prevent such destruction from repeating. With this bid, the mayor and the loggers go beyond what the land will sustain. They are cutting deep into the forest, rapidly, and removing such a large portion that the trees will not be able to naturally recover.

"We have sworn, as the ancient druids did, to not bring back the forest when it has been decimated by others but to let it do its best to survive. The purpose of our magic, of our work, is to preserve and to protect, but we will not raise the trees and plants from the dead only for them to be massacred and used once again. That was one of our ancestors' mistakes, and it is one we do not intend to make twice."

Diplomacy, however much her mother and tutors had tried to teach her, did not come easily for Iellieth. "I would be more than willing to help you and the druids, Mara, but why would the mayor listen to me when he is not willing to listen to his neighbors?"

"Our informants from the town believe the bid has come from the Linolynnian Court, from the office of the king."

Iellieth's heart fell. "You want me to tell them who I am and ask them to stop."

"The conclave and I had hoped that might be possible, yes."

"If I do that, my stepfather will find out where I am. He will send soldiers after me if he has not already."

"What if there were a way for her to avoid going back to the castle?" Marcon asked. He sat up tall beside her once again. "Could you and your people offer her protection, Mara?"

The druid began to smile, and a mischievous glint returned to her eyes. "For a time."

Had Mara thought of this before? Did she want Iellieth to join them? Would that really be possible?

"Because of the other enemy you will not speak of?" Marcon regarded her sternly.

Mara's lips parted to speak, but she bit them together instead.

Marcon leaned toward her. "You must tell us, Mara. She cannot be protected from a force she does not know."

CHAPTER 12

Genevieve traversed the moonlit trail more nimbly than she'd ever moved in the forest before. Each member of her community knew the Hallowed Wood well, though, in most cases, they did not journey more than a few hours toward its center. Their lorekeepers rejoiced to speak of the forest's origins, what had once been the sacred burial ground of the ancient elves, lost in a great war that spanned the entire region and beyond. They mustn't tread too far for fear of disturbing the resting place of these spirits.

As they grew older, Genevieve and her peers came to recognize these stories as a way of preventing children from getting lost in the forest, which would force their minders to beseech the trees' help to find them.

But on this night, in the mystical path's silver glow, this understanding changed. As the searing memory of cries of agony faded behind her, waiting for its moment to return, the whispers of the forest spirits came alive. Each branch she brushed, every leaf that wept against the soft covering of her shoes, brought back the lorekeepers' stories.

Only the strongest of our faith seek out the forest's heart, they had said. And Yvayne, the woman who had mysteriously appeared, had assigned this sacred task to her.

Genevieve's pace slowed as the adrenaline ran its course. A catch in her shoulder from the bite and the shock of the still-wet wound spurred her on occasionally, but her feet began to drag as she ventured deeper. The only light came from the arc of moonlight on the path.

She stopped as the shapes of the tree trunks shifted around her. Images of her fallen family ricocheted across her vision. Her neck throbbed. The lycanthropy was taking over. The cool blessing of the woman's touch, her protection, was fading.

A particularly heinous throb bolted from her shoulder to her ankle, and Genevieve's body seized. She crashed to the forest floor. Her wrists slammed into a root that protruded from the shimmering path.

Only the day before, she and Mariellen had studied root structures. They'd lain on the ground, almost like she was now, and pressed their ears to the earth's supple surface. "Close your eyes and listen. Send forth your sight to the unseen tree that grows beneath the earth."

She could only catch the glimmer of a few roots nearby and not the myriad Mariellen hoped she might discern. Mariellen had been fascinated by the trees' symmetry of structure. "As above, so below," she had said. "My mentor often said that to me when she and I first studied the truth of the trees, as we are doing now."

Genevieve sat up, her body still shaking, and hugged her knees into herself. Her heart reached out for her friend and guardian, but she felt nothing in return. She never would again.

"Druids have their own place in the afterlife," she said

to the dark vegetation around her. "Astralei smiles at us when we arrive and, if we so choose, she returns us to our plane to live again. That is how we grow wiser given time."

"But what will you do without your people?" the plants around her asked. "You cannot become a druid alone."

"I am alone," she answered.

"Genevieve," a warm voice addressed her in Elvish. She jolted. The movement caused a fresh rush of pain in her shoulder, and she looked for who had spoken.

The plants' voices had to have been figments of her imagination. She was not yet advanced enough to speak with them. But this new voice felt real. "Is there someone there?"

"There is, druid daughter. Be not alarmed."

Genevieve tensed and prepared to run. "Please come out," she said. Her voice was small, broken. There was no chance of frightening them away if they meant her harm.

The brush in front of her rippled, and a stunning silver dire wolf with bronze eyes emerged from the undergrowth.

The leader of the werewolves. The most powerful among them could take on wolf form. With all her might, she pushed herself away.

"Wait," the Elvish voice urged. "Sweet child, I swear that you are safe. I have led you here, and I am here to aid you still." The lustrous path she had been following shrank from the distant turns of the forest and bled into the earth around her feet, radiating out in an incandescent circle of glittering moonlight.

"We haven't much time," the voice said. "Will you trust me? We must get you to the falls."

"But my family."

The wolf's great silver head bowed. "There is nothing more we can do for your family. But we can save you."

"Did she send you?" Genevieve stepped forward and held out her hand. The wolf moved a few paces toward her in return. Up close, a brindle of pearl and charcoal shimmered among the wolf's pale gray fur.

"Not exactly, though I know of whom you speak. Come, Genevieve. There is another revelation waiting for you deeper in the forest. She is most anxious to meet you."

The wolf stood in front of her, his face level with hers. The golden glow of his eyes was like the pleasant smile of sunset on a calm midwinter sky. He looked nothing like the mangy, evil beasts who had attacked her home. The great wolf lowered down so that she could climb onto his back.

"Who are you?" The fur was warm and soft. She laid her head against the back of his neck, exhausted.

"Sariel. We have a long night ahead of us. Ophelia is waiting for you."

❦

THE SCALE OF THE TREES, FROM PETAL AND LEAF TO trunk, swelled the closer they came to the center of the forest. At the end of the second day, Genevieve's transformation began.

"Sariel, is there a faster way?" Her ribs ached; each breath was a deliberate, painful labor. It would not be long now until the werewolf's poison overwhelmed who she had been before.

"There are no shortcuts to Ophelia's glade," the worried voice answered inside her mind. Sariel was the first creature she'd met who could speak telepathically.

Would she be able to understand him when the curse took over?

Genevieve cried out as she slipped on a large root that ran across the path. When she caught herself, the bones in her hand rippled back toward her, shifted, and returned. She screamed. "It's starting. I can't prevent it."

"You must try. I have not Ophelia's magic."

She cradled her hand against her chest and ran to catch up to Sariel's light jog. Rushing risked another fall, and the lycanthropy didn't need additional reasons to try and take over her body. "Are you sure that she can help?"

He increased his speed again. Genevieve hugged her ribs and slid after him.

"She can. Ophelia is the only one in these woods who knows the old ways."

Their race continued as darkness fell. The night took on a clarity she had never before experienced. The color drained from the world, save for the grayest blues and blacks of the forest, but the light, all around her, remained. Genevieve collapsed into a tree, torn between wonder and exhaustion.

"Can we press on, then?" Sariel asked. In the moonlight, his silver fur gleamed even brighter.

"Ah!" A slash of pain up her spine pulled her head and ripped at her shoulders. A deep growl escaped her lips, and Genevieve crumpled back into herself. She sobbed through each gasp of air and clung to the rough bark.

"I can't do it. I can't, Sariel." Genevieve fell to her knees. Tears carved hot streaks down the contours of her face. She couldn't become a monster. Not after seeing what they could do.

"Listen to me." The dire wolf plodded closer.

"No. You cannot stay with me. Please. Something in

the forest will find me, and that will be the end. But what would a bite do to you?"

The copper eyes narrowed. "I will leave you a trail. Follow my marks. We'll bring Ophelia to you. But, Genevieve"—Sariel's cold, moist nose kissed beneath her chin and forced her head up—"you must continue on. I cannot bring her back to you in time otherwise. Look for the waterfall."

In a flash of brilliant silver, Sariel split away into the forest, leaving Genevieve alone. A smaller spasm quaked up her spine, and her stomach heaved. The bile burned her throat.

Was this how the predators had seen her and her family in the darkness? Each tree stood outlined against the rest, solid in their multitude, but made of fragile branches. Had she been nothing but a gray body, silhouetted by the fires, unique only in her still-beating heart and lightly singed flesh rather than—she heaved again.

Genevieve ran her hands down the rough wood of the oak that supported her. The poison found a balance with her blood. *Survive, survive, survive, survive,* her footfalls said, over and over again.

Owls passed narrowly overhead, a fox emerged from its den, and always the tree branches gently swayed as she searched the solid trunks for the violent slash Sariel left across their torsos, urging her onward. In any other circumstance, neither of them would damage the trunks in this way. After she met Ophelia, she could ask that they return and repair their trail.

HER IMAGINATION WAS PLAYING TRICKS ON HER. TWICE already in the black night, she'd thought she'd heard a waterfall. And here was the low, steady thrum again. She wouldn't be as disappointed this time when one failed to materialize.

Shades of blues darted across the purple-black of the nighttime sky as the sun exhaled her warmth across the horizon. The skin of her face prickled, itched, as hair grew down the sides of her face. The fuzzy sideburns were heartbreaking enough, but the emotional pain morphed into something physical as her cheekbones started to shift forward, melding her face into something altogether more canine. Genevieve cried out but cut her lament short for fear it would come out a howl. The transformation was nearly complete.

The air turned cooler, and soft beads of moisture fell against her skin. The first two phantom waterfalls hadn't been this convincing. Her feet were numb, but they continued to stumble on. Would Sariel and Ophelia be able to reach her in time? Would they find her crumpled body inside the vast forest? How lovely it would feel to crash into the pool of churning water at the base of the mystical waterfall, if only she could find it.

At the edge of the woods near her colony lay a small lake that was reserved for their secret initiation ceremonies. Mariellen had taken her there once in the weeks before the attacks. She had sensed Genevieve's growing exhaustion with the intensity of their training and her gnawing doubt that she would be able to officially join her people. She had tried to ignore the hollow sense that the instinct she needed wouldn't actually manifest and she would remain an outsider, forever.

In the dying embers of what had befallen them, a

superficial separation, not being chosen to be among the wielders of druidic magic, would have been better than the cruel fate forced upon her people. She had feared a less lonely path than the one now before her, but the tragedy had felt all-consuming at the time. Sariel spoke of Ophelia's old magic that might lift the curse, if such a power existed. She had been too frightened to tell him that it wasn't clear that the druids' magic resided within her.

The path curved around a dense cluster of trees. Genevieve loped around the corner and stopped short as the waterfall suddenly came into view. It stretched upward beyond the treeline. Magnificent. Surprised, she dug her swollen knuckles and their freshly grown claws into the white birch beside her. Mist rose up, sighing into the pool below and lifting to circle back. Her breath caught in her chest. A sacred space indeed.

The waterfall wasn't as broad as she'd imagined, but it fell from a great height. The plunging water gathered like a dangling scarf blowing in the wind.

Her increased heart rate activated the lycanthropic poisons rushing through her bloodstream. Her teeth shifted. Genevieve suppressed a sharp cry as her canines pushed down from the top of her mouth toward her lower lip, and the lower canines rose up and outward. She clutched her hands to either side of her face, desperate to hold her remaining bone structure in place, to prevent complete transformation. Her moan morphed into a scream as her cheekbone snapped.

She took a step forward, and the bones in her feet elongated. Her balance tipped precariously to the side as her heel became a distended ankle. Her weight shifted lower as the second foot did the same. Genevieve's back arched groundward and then curved away like a crescent moon as her spine lengthened. A few more steps, rapid, but she couldn't keep her balance on the hybrid legs. She stumbled, pitched forward. Genevieve snarled as she hit the ground.

Watching from afar, like the moment the werewolf had bitten her, she felt herself slipping away from her body.

She raised herself partway on her monstrous forearms; wiry hairs sprouted from fresh sinew and muscles.

The shimmer of moonlight through the clouds, a small smile from the goddess Selene, showed her where in the sky to angle her short muzzle. The two sister moons gazed down on her and extended their hearts in song. She had to answer.

The howl that had been building inside her erupted, both tragic and exultant.

And then a second howl answered her. She gasped. Tripped toward the water. They were coming. They had found her.

Her tall, furry ears perked up. They were still some distance away. The fastest path across the glade to them was through the water.

Genevieve step-crawled forward, more like a wounded bear than the graceful stride of the wolf, but her body answered her urgent instructions.

The cool, clear water covered the fur on her hands, then her feet and newly grown ankles. She kept going. Would she be able to swim in this new form? Her shoulders were stiffer, the socket limited. She would have to paddle.

Another howl rang out, closer. The water lapped near her shoulders. Her hips. A crash sounded from across the glade. Sariel was near. Her front right paw moved forward and found nothing underneath. She pushed back against

the water instead. Her second paw did the same. She dug
her rear claws into the pebbles that lined the bottom of
the freshwater lake and shoved off into the darker center,
beyond where she could stand. The water covered her
back, splashed onto her face. Her eyes widened, the lids
rounder. She had but a few moments left before her transformation was complete.

A light burst through the forest. Genevieve's heavy
head bobbed in and out of the water. The cold rushed into
her short snout, but the warm green light found her all
the same. The silver wolf, her guide through the forest,
leapt through the foliage on the far side of the glade. On
his back, a woman clothed in robes of moss with long,
flowing russet hair stared straight toward her, somehow
knowing precisely where she would be. The woman's eyes
were white and shone against the green-gray bark of her
skin.

Still atop Sariel, she reached forth her hand and
murmured an ancient incantation of their people. The
water around Genevieve tugged at her fur, pulled her
under. Only the faintest trickle of light penetrated the
surface. And then the woman's voice grew sharp. Echoed
all around. Rebuked the greedy pool. Genevieve's breath
seized as the water pressed against her lungs, but then her
form lifted. Bands of water encircled her, pulled her out,
gentle fingers that lifted her transformed body. Her damp
fur hung heavy, and beads of water fell in rivulets down her
arms, legs, and paws.

She trembled, floating a few inches above the water.
The woman's hand remained outstretched toward her,
white eyes rolled in the back of her head. The droplets
gathered into long willow branches and carried her toward
the shore. The powerful voice boomed to all reaches of the

glade. She spoke to the natural world with authority, issuing commands.

Genevieve's eyebrows tingled, initiating the final part of her transformation. Would her eyes turn into deep black pools as theirs had been? The air felt like dense moss beneath her toe pads. Water branches held her tight.

And then a second voice, the one she had been waiting for, in musical, accented Elvish, called out a single word.

"Run."

CHAPTER 13

Persephonie leaned toward Marcon and Mara to break the tension between them. "Iellieth can travel with us if she would like to, after she has spoken with the mayor. There is room in the wagons for both her and you, Marcon." She watched him expectantly and snuggled back under the shawl with Iellieth.

"That is kind of you, Persephonie," Mara answered, "but I am not sure that can happen."

Persephonie scowled. "Datha, what do you think?"

Cassian rose to tend the fire. "It is up to you," he said to Mara, "but if you were to ask me, I would say that you need to tell her, at least as much as you can."

Iellieth's frustration rose just like it did when her step-father and a prospective suitor or household official carried on a conversation as though she was not there. Had she still no say? But Mara was carefully considering Cassian's suggestion, and Iellieth did not wish to disrupt the work he, Persephonie, and Marcon had done on her behalf.

"Very well," Mara said with a sigh. "I can tell you only so much, for your own protection."

Marcon's eyes remained narrowed at the druid. He would weigh her every word and search for the unstated dangers, Iellieth knew. Persephonie took her hand and stared at Mara, and Iellieth did the same.

"There is a dark magician who wishes ill on those who are like me, like Persephonie, and, most especially, those who are like you." Mara's dark brown eyes fixed on Iellieth.

"Like me?"

"That is part of why you are here."

"But I am not a druid."

"Not yet." Mara's expression glinted for a moment with the spark of a plan, but she allowed it to fade. "I wanted a chance to observe you further, to try to discern your own wishes. I sense that you have already endured a great many things that have been foisted upon you without your choosing them."

There was no way to briefly explain the truth of this understatement, so Iellieth nodded instead.

"I had hoped, in the coming days, to invite you to join our community. We cannot keep you safe from this individual indefinitely, but we can for a short time."

Could this be true? Happiness and excitement pounded in her chest. She could live among the druids of the Vagarveil, learn their ways, and be part of a close-knit community?

"The council does not know all of this. They were alarmed enough at the attack on our sister colony, and we are waiting to hear from Yvayne how many survived. Cassian"—Mara glanced at him—"Yvayne, and myself have taken a great risk that endangers our conclave for the present, but it protects our future."

The layered riddles obscured her path. What was Mara trying to explain?

"But what is the danger? Who is this magician?"

"You are the danger, Iellieth." Mara froze as Marcon growled in frustration at this response. "Because you are in danger," she clarified. "Who you might become, should you choose, goes against everything this mage has been working for. He wants to destroy us, and he thinks he can do that by harming you."

"But why me?" Mara had to have her confused with someone else, or the enemy she was talking about did. The greatest threat she had ever meant to pose was to her step-father's plans for her future, and she hadn't even proved capable of that.

"It would be my preference for you to find that answer for yourself. This man, or what remains of him, will be fixated on you as soon as he realizes where you are. But as far as we know, that time is not yet here. I would ask for your help with the mayor so that I can convince the council that you should be brought into our community, whether or not you decide to take the druidic mantle upon your shoulders. Would you speak on our and the forest's behalf?"

"And in exchange, you will protect her from this sorcerer?" Marcon asked.

"Or help me find somewhere new to go? I can't go back to the castle." The plea came out more openly than Iellieth had meant.

Persephonie rubbed her hand along her back. "We will help in whatever way we can, Iellieth. Right, Datha?"

"*Así, quered.* That we will. We can stay for a few more days, to see how the cards play out." Cassian bowed his head to Iellieth, a promise.

"And whether it be the saudad and myself or the saudad and my people, I will do all in my power to set you on your way, whichever direction it is you decide to go," Mara said.

Iellieth looked at Marcon. "I have already promised to help you, lady, though I plan to learn more of this mage when we return from our dealings with the mayor. Does that title signify a general of some kind? A powerful leader?"

She grinned at his question. No mayors in the distant past, then, either. "More like a tiny king, usually picked by the people of a town."

Marcon frowned, puzzled as to why this person would pose a problem to the druids. Iellieth bit her lip and smiled. Her new friends' trust filled her with warmth. She had never performed a task of this kind before, though hopefully she could dredge up enough from her diplomacy lessons to help in the endeavor. "So what is it precisely you would like us to do in Trudid, Mara?" Iellieth asked. "Is it far from here?"

"It is a day and a half to two days' travel to Trudid from the Vagarveil. So long as you seek to aid us, the forest will likewise help you on your journey, so you need not concern yourself with wild beasts or roaming fae."

"There are fae in Caldara?" Iellieth's voice raised in her surprise.

"There are a few." Mara grinned. Her eyes were faraway, picturing fae friends. "Those that cannot disguise themselves keep to the remote places of our world."

Amazing, and she'd had no idea. Could they be walking around Linolynn, magically transformed to resemble one of the kingdom's citizens? Iellieth shook her head, returning her thoughts to the task at hand. "How will we know our way?"

"We can help you find the entrance to the path, and the trees will guide you from there," Mara explained, her smile lingering. "The head of the logging company is a terrible brute, so you will need to be on your guard. He thinks only of coin, and the mayor is not much better. There is a small chance of getting him to see reason, but you will want to speak with the head of the company as well. Perhaps between the two of them, someone will have the wisdom to consider wider-ranging repercussions."

"Do you know why they want the lumber? Why the bid came in from the court?"

"That I am not sure of, but I am certain they will tell you, given your station."

Iellieth was less sure, but saying so out loud would risk her chance at a new life beyond the castle walls with the help of a well-connected, kind group of people. Their settlement in the forest was peaceful, a home. She loved the way they had eased themselves into the woods and not forced the land to bend to their will. The harmony between the community and its space made it a pleasant, life-giving place rather than one that stifled her.

If she could perform this task successfully, they might see her as more than a noblewoman, a privileged outsider who was an imposition on their home and way of life.

"Very well then, Mara, we will take on your mission."

"This is wonderful." The druid beamed. "You and I can work together for a few days, practice some basic skills and incantations. Then I will call the council together, and we will propose our solution."

She was going to learn to cast magic! But there was still one obstacle. "What if they say no?" Her chest tightened at the thought of the council's rejection. They might see in her the same difference that had been so distasteful to the Linolynnian nobles.

Mara raised her eyebrows, and her eyes flashed as though she had been waiting for precisely this challenge. "Then we will have to prove them wrong."

◈

"IT'S NOT SO MUCH ABOUT KNOWING AS IT IS A FEELING," Mara explained after a walk together through the forest. "You can, and will, know the names of the plants. I would guess that you're familiar with many of them already. But this is about understanding the life with which you're engaging. The existence, however different yet equally valid to your own. So many are unable to tap into this other world. They only capture half of the story and are afraid to let themselves see more."

"And this more that they're meant to see, it's the life of the trees and plants around us?" Iellieth asked.

"Yes, but it runs deeper still. The spirit of water, rock, life underground, or those creatures too small to be easily perceived by our eyes—you will develop a feeling for each of them and find yourself always enveloped within a larger community." Mara stopped and regarded her. "I can feel that additional sense in you, Iellieth, just beneath the surface. You only need to let it free."

With Mathilde, the castle arborist, Iellieth had learned how to assess the health of a tree or vine. She was adamant about invasive species and went into great detail about finding early warning signs of their presence or rooting them out once they had begun to establish themselves.

Mathilde was the first person Iellieth had met who

spoke of the natural world as the living, feeling, thinking, breathing thing it so clearly was. She explained nature as a mixture: a few parts place, a few parts creature. It was life expressed in a different form, an older form, than most people, limited by their own minds and perceptions, had the ability to understand.

Mara held many of these foundational beliefs as well, and much of the history that she taught Iellieth, the druidic understanding of each species' life and story, was reminiscent of the folktales she had learned from the gardener whose lore had been passed down through generations and traced all the way back to the great flood.

On their second day of training, Persephonie joined Iellieth and Mara in one of the smaller clearings. "It's best to have room in case something goes awry," the saudad explained.

"But what would go awry?"

"Any number of things," Mara said. "When a certain friend of ours was training"—she cast her eyes over to Persephonie—"she bewitched an entire flock of birds. They stumbled after her, dazed, chirping nonsense for the rest of the day."

"I became slightly distracted." Persephonie blushed. "But we got them all back to their nests eventually, did we not?"

Iellieth laughed, picturing Persephonie followed by an adoring bird chorus. "Is that what we're practicing today, Mara?"

"Not exactly. There are unique traces of magic in each of us. Charms and shimmering illusions came easily to Persephonie when she was first learning, so that is what we practiced. Tapping into the emotion, learning to channel nature's power, her energy, is a common starting point for us all, though the individual magical effects can be as unique as the druids who cast them."

Mara directed Iellieth to stand in the center of the clearing, her feet shoulder-width apart, hands pressed together at her chest. Her mentor and Persephonie stood behind her shoulders. They practiced slow, methodical breaths as a way to open themselves up to the world around them.

"Remember what I said yesterday, Iellieth"—Mara inhaled deeply—"it's a feeling."

Iellieth breathed in the sun-warmed grass and rich earth. She retained her breath for a moment. Persephonie began her exhale in time to a soft breeze. Iellieth exhaled alongside a gentle birdsong, trilling in the forest as the bird darted from tree to tree.

Slowly, her consciousness of the two women standing beside her shifted. Others were present. Beneath her feet, especially as she inhaled, roots intertwined, the roaming tendrils sent out to one another from the encircling trees. Energy cascaded up her shins, thighs, her torso, head, and neck. Life swept down the curve of her arms, past her elbows, and back up to her fingertips.

Pppsst.

Iellieth's eyes flew open.

There, beyond the end of her nose, sparks of bright green energy danced in circles around one another. Mara and Persephonie were in front of her in an instant. Mara's eyes were cloudy with pride, and Persephonie giggled in excitement. "You did it, Iellieth," she exclaimed. "Show her the next part, Mara."

Iellieth couldn't move for fear of losing the sparks. If she even spoke or looked away, they might vanish. The whirls grew tighter, faster.

"Perfect, cher'a," Mara said. "Now, relax. You can bring them back if they go. The first time is the most difficult."

The swell of frustration her last morning in Io Keep, the anger waiting at the tips of her fingers, pots exploding, and the sudden growth of leaves came flooding back to her. This was the grounded, peaceful expression of that energy. The trees around them nodded their distant heads and smiled. She was learning.

Until dusk fell, Mara and Persephonie talked her through channeling the sparks, joining nature's rhythm, sensing the interdependent flows of energy that surrounded them. She practiced sending focused beams into precise points in the earth. She cast a flurry of sparks overhead, and they rained down, sputtering glittery motes.

To celebrate Iellieth's success—and because Persephonie couldn't bridle her enthusiasm any longer—that evening, Iellieth, Marcon, and Mara joined the saudad for a feast. Fine wine flowed freely, and they passed around toasted bread in baskets while wild boar roasted over a spit. Each member of the saudad's muster, it seemed, had learned of Iellieth's success in the field, and they all stopped by to wish her well.

Though the spells were easy for Mara and Persephonie, Iellieth was drained from the effort of maintaining such close concentration. Marcon sensed her tiredness and remained close by, ready to help her manage lengthy or excessively curious conversations.

"You are nearly as popular as Persephonie, lady," he observed with a smile. The young saudad sat beside her two brothers on the back of a neighbor's wagon, telling tale after dramatic tale of adventure and exploits from distant lands and times long forgotten.

Late in the evening, Cassian produced an instrument

Iellieth hadn't encountered before, a large twelve-stringed viol that he called a guitar. Persephonie came to join her and translated the ancient ballads of her father's rich baritone into Caldaran so she and Marcon could take part in the exchange of stories.

Before Teodric had been sent away, she and Katarina had passed a few evenings like this. He sang in a beautiful tenor, more passionate and expressive than anyone else in the court or among the musicians. Here, with the saudad, those evenings floated beyond her reach, drifting on endless ocean tides. But the experience of something shared, a common expression of what it meant to be alive —that's how Katarina always described the best songs and stories—that sense remained.

IELLIETH AND MARA PRACTICED CONJURING SPARKS THE following day as well. They returned to Mara's hut as dusk fell across the forest. Iellieth lay down in the cool grass that encircled Mara's home, and the druid leaned against the wall of her hut and slid down to sit beside her.

A short time of silence passed as the sun lowered on the horizon.

Mara opened her arms to indicate the breadth of the forest. "One day, you'll be able to sit with the ash tree and ask her to tell you her story. She will answer you in her own voice, and her neighbors will add to her tale. The saplings nearby will learn their history as she speaks, and that of the wide forest, and of each creature's place within the world tree."

"The world tree, Mara?" She was unfamiliar with this phrase.

"Ours is not the only place of life, cher'a. The lands of fae and those of shadow that you've read about, the celestial spheres you've studied, we're all arranged like the growth of a tree, dependent on one another." Mara shook her head to prevent Iellieth asking further questions.

"It will make sense in time, Iellieth. But first, we must speak with the council. You are ready."

"ABSOLUTELY NOT."

"You go too far, Mara."

"We are at risk enough already, and now you're saying she might bring soldiers?"

"No," Iellieth interrupted the stream of voices pouring their agitation on her new mentor. "I shouldn't have phrased it that way. He will only want to bring me back to Io Keep. No one here would be held responsible for my presence." The duke would never credit nature-worshippers with being powerful enough to manipulate ancient magical forces like the transmigration circles, even if that had been what transpired.

"I take it you have not had many antagonistic dealings with soldiers, have you, *Lady* Amastacia?" Berivic, the elf who had been rude to Persephonie during the previous meeting, spat out her title and sneered at her.

"I have not, but might I also assume the same holds true for you, Berivic?" She switched to Elvish to better make her point. "Do not assume by my upbringing that I know nothing of the sorrows of the world. Our experiences differ, but the misfortunes your parents and their parents faced are not yours to throw at my feet."

His retort burned in his eyes, but they both froze as the

oldest member of the druid community, Ismaer, a stooped elf with silvery skin, stood and plodded slowly forward into the center of the gathering. "Many tempers rise swiftly at this prospect, but it is not for us alone to decide. You have each pledged your lives to something larger, to the good of the world around you, the marriage of the natural and its necessary developments by creatures of all kinds.

"Something powerful was at work that sent Iellieth into our midst, and we would be unwise to so readily dismiss this force simply because it makes us afraid. Mara, Yvayne, Cassian, and Persephonie have told you what befell our kin across the Infinite Ocean. Yvayne's report of what befell Fhaona is true as well. It has been many days since I felt her life pulse moving about our woods.

"The world changes with or without us." The elderly druid turned to her. "Iellieth, Marcon, if you are still willing, we will accept your aid in this matter. Should you succeed, Iellieth, I hope you will consider joining us." A hushed tension rippled out from Ismaer at this offer, and the conclave held a collective breath. "You risk yourself for us, and we will do the same for you in return."

Iellieth's heart pounded in her chest. It truly was happening. She would have a new home.

"And what if she does not, Father?" Berivic squared his shoulders against his elder. "What if she returns without being able to guarantee a respite for the forest?"

Marcon stiffened beside her, a pillar of fury channeled toward the young elf.

Ismaer paused, and several druids whispered among one another. It was clearly unprecedented for someone to speak to their head elder in this defiant way.

"Then our community will speak together once again,"

he said finally. Ismaer looked in Iellieth's eyes and added softly, so that only those nearest to her could overhear, "But I would not bet against her." His expression was grave, weighed down by a lingering darkness she could only glimpse the edges of, but his faith in her was present and spoken all the same.

⁂

BERIVIC'S WORDS FLITTED AFTER IELLIETH THROUGHOUT the rest of the afternoon. Despite urgings otherwise by Mara and Persephonie, she could not shake the sense that he was right to doubt her.

The duke's threats after her and Teodric's escape attempt belied her assurances that her stepfather's troops would pose no threat to the druids. "One whiff of this nonsense again, and your accomplices will find banishment across the sea a great mercy they are not privy to. I will not warn you again." His vow joined together with an inner swarm of apprehension, buzzing always just behind her ears.

"Might I speak with you a moment, lady?" Marcon asked after a quiet dinner shared between the three of them. They returned to the log circle outside Mara's hut. He stoked the fire and sat beside her.

In the light of the flames, as he drew near, the palimpsest beneath his skin faded, the text less distinct.

"Marcon," she exclaimed, "your arms. Look."

He glanced down in alarm before he mulled over them in the glowing light. "I don't suppose it is likely that we will find anyone in Trudid who reads ancient texts or deciphers unknown magical symbols?"

"Your assessment is correct as far as I know. Trudid is a small town, populated by traders and farmers."

"Is it part of Linolynn as well?"

"In a way. They pay a share to the king in exchange for the promise of military protection, but they make their own laws so long as the region doesn't fall into unrest."

"That is a fortunate arrangement, on both sides."

"I think so. I'm sure not everyone enjoys the taxes, but King Arontis tries to be fair."

Marcon nodded. "I was angry, earlier, at how Berivic spoke to you. I wish I had handled it differently, though I am relieved that Ismaer spoke on your behalf. Regardless of what transpires when we're in Trudid, once we return, I will help you find safety from this enemy Mara resists speaking of."

"I had hoped she would say more about him during dinner, but she didn't want to talk about it." Mara had dismissed the subject when it arose, saying she didn't want Iellieth to worry. But the shadow of an unknown enemy loomed ever darker behind her. Iellieth shivered.

"She seemed upset after the meeting." Marcon turned his arms to study them above the fire. "It has been strange for me, to see so few people gathered in one place, for there to be no ships overhead, no immediate threats pressing in from all sides." His gaze followed the smoke on its journey to the stars. "Avoiding conflict is sensible, but it is a fallacy to believe peace will last forever."

"In recent human generations in Caldara, perhaps not in extended Elvish ones, life has been peaceful. Conflicts now and again, but not ones that span the entire continent. But which type of ships are you looking for? We are several days' ride from the coast."

"Air ships. They fly."

"They're very fast?"

Marcon laughed. "They are, but what I mean to say is that they fly above the land, through the clouds. I wish I could tell you how they worked. I had not the inclination to study them, but limited aerial attacks will make strategy easier."

"Wait, what are you strategizing?" Never mind the impossible bird ships. They must have been very small.

"That is why I asked you to come speak with me. Danger follows me, Iellieth. When Mara talked of the man hunting you, I wondered if it was truly you he was after, or if they misunderstood. Mara suggested that I stay near you and the amulet for now; she senses that we are connected in some way. And I stand by my promise to you.

"But I have been returned to life for a reason, even if I cannot feel the presence of Ignis, what once felt as natural to me as a simple breath of air. There was much I could do before that I cannot do now. It would be a poor recompense for harm to befall you again because of me. It's not something I can allow or a burden I wish for you to bear."

She had desired freedom for so long, anything to be away from the castle, her stepfather, and the constant strictures and limitations. But now, what was she supposed to do? Could the druids truly offer a place to belong? Even if they did, and the enemy was defeated or driven off, how long would she want to stay here?

"I understand, Marcon," Iellieth answered. "But you helped me too. With the ice giant, even while we've been here. I can write to Katarina and see if she knows a way to help you or a source that might be of use."

He nodded. "Will they have armor in Trudid? I asked Mara, but there is no chain mail to be found among the whole conclave. I'm no longer surprised they're overly cautious."

Iellieth laughed and watched the floating embers drift from the edges of the fire into the sapphire air. Mara ground herbs inside her hut; the mortar and pestle perfumed the atmosphere with herbs that aided sleep, part of her nightly routine. The comforting aromas of dense moss and pale purple blossoms sprinkled in dew drifted over and mingled with the smoky heat of the fire. In the woods behind the cabin, the trees cautiously whispered together so as to not disturb the grasses and leaves beneath. Marcon stoked the fire and added a few branches to ward against the falling temperature of the northern spring.

On a night like this in Io Keep, she would have been reading by candlelight, glancing occasionally at her own reflection, stark against the black window glass, alone beyond the company of her book.

❦

THE NEXT MORNING DAWNED IN LILAC AND SOFT ROSE through the leafy fingers overhead. For the first time since waking in Mara's hut a few days before, Iellieth's muscles felt limber, light. Today was the day for a new adventure.

She had overheard Trudid mentioned every now and again in conversations between her mother or stepfather and nobles whose estates bordered the southeastern portion of the Stormside Forest. Trudid provided grain, meat, and lumber to Linolynn and some of the larger estates. The others were self-sufficient, much like the principality of Red's Cross to the east.

It was incredible that to the north of the town, in the

mountain foothills, an entire druid conclave flourished in the forest near the Hadvarian border, and she'd had no idea till a few days before.

Mara's dark, tightly wound curls shone in the sunlight as she looked through an assortment of canisters and muttered to herself. A small fire crackled in the fireplace, its heat broken by breezy ripples from the early morning air. Marcon sat in the entryway, his body angled in her direction, but he watched the world outside the hut.

He smiled at her when he saw she was awake. "Good morning, lady."

Iellieth darted back from the cool air against her bare shoulders as she sat up, and Marcon secured the leather flap. He scanned the room for the shawl she continued to borrow from Mara and found it hanging on a peg near the door. With a single step, he crossed the breadth of Mara's home and knelt beside her to drape it over her shoulders.

Excitement about their upcoming travels overwhelmed the doubt and anxiety from the night before. For the second time in one week, she was going somewhere new. "What should we prepare for our trip through the forest?" she asked. Scarlett, the heroine of a novel that had been one of her favorites as a teenager, was meticulous in her preparations for any journey. She anticipated what she would find and face based on the biome and season she explored.

"It is common to have dried provisions that, with solar power and water, transform into hearty meals. There are also water purification devices, though for such a short trip, we may be fine without," said Marcon.

Iellieth and Mara stared at him in confusion. "How does the meal change in the sunlight?" Iellieth asked.

Mara pursued a different tack. "Water, if one selects a

proper stream, is pure and cool. Some of our conclave even believe it can help with adapting to the local environment. Much like familiarity with pollinators."

The castle botanist had told her something like that, but she'd only paid attention to what her flowers most needed from the bees. "I've always read about people bringing dried meats and bread and carefully foraging among the plants they found on their travels," Iellieth added.

Mara looked between the two of them and was the first to laugh. "Hopefully, with so many ideas, we can help you survive a day and a half of wilderness."

Marcon was still puzzled by their confusion, but he rose to help Mara gather supplies while Iellieth donned her leathers. She pulled back her hair in a loose, twisting braid and stepped out from behind the partition.

"You look like an adventurer to me, or you will once you have on your boots," Mara said, and Marcon gave her an approving wink.

The druid opened a small hidden drawer in her bureau and withdrew a worn leather coin pouch. "I haven't much, but, on behalf of myself and the conclave, here's a small sum for your travels." She took out a few gold coins and placed them in Iellieth's hand.

Before she discovered the duke's plot to exchange her in an advantageous marriage, Iellieth hadn't worried about obtaining wealth of any kind. Her mother's side of the family was the most prosperous in the kingdom, save the royals themselves, and all her material needs and wants were readily met. But as she and Teodric prepared to leave, her approach changed. Beyond the castle walls, she would need to provide for herself, which required coin.

"I don't want to take from your stores." Iellieth held

out her hand toward Mara's to push away the money. She had been storing gold for a few years in preparation for a final escape attempt, whenever she found an opportunity to flee from whichever cruel husband the duke had selected. It didn't amount to a great sum in noble circles, but it would allow her to survive for several weeks so long as she was careful.

"We've no need of them, cher'a," Mara said as she caught Iellieth's hand. She turned her palm face up and dropped five gold coins in her hand. "Our community doesn't use them, but it will aid you in Trudid. The mayor and the logging overseer care for nothing else."

Her mentor's earnest expression softened her objections, and Iellieth accepted the payment. "Thank you, Mara, this is generous of you. Maybe we can get the armor you were asking me about," she said to Marcon.

"For five gold, lady? Are you sure?"

"It will cost more than that if it is actually capable of protecting you," Mara said. She smiled at Iellieth. "But that will provide you with food and lodging should you need it."

"That is a more sensible plan." Iellieth bit her lip. Except for a few trips through the marketplace in the Air Ward and the elegant vendors brought into the Hadvarian palace, she had never purchased goods from merchants. Perhaps she could overhear their dealings with someone else to gauge prices and avoid being swindled.

Marcon placed the provisions he and Mara had gathered into a leather satchel that he slung easily over his shoulder, followed by his flame-emblazoned shield. He closed his eyes and took a long, slow breath as he picked up his sword and held it before him. After he bowed his head toward the hilt, he placed it into the makeshift scabbard he had fashioned from a belt borrowed from one of Mara's neighbors.

She would have preferred to not need Marcon's weapons or her own dagger on the trip. She ran her fingers over the faded marks from the ice creature's attack. The wound had healed quickly with Mara's herbs, but the skin was still tender.

"You will need to meet with one of the mayor's aides before you can have an audience with him," Mara said. "It's an unnecessary formality, but he will insist upon it."

"Thank you, Mara," Iellieth said. She was accustomed to those with political power forcing others to observe even the tiniest rules and regulations.

They stepped outside Mara's hut, and she walked with them to the faint trail cut through the woods, its small impressions visible in the undergrowth. "Be cautious, through the forest and along the road."

"We will be," Marcon said.

The path ahead radiated energy, and her emotions answered in return. So much could be starting here, now.

In the distance, the possibilities of a new life took shape. A small cabin of her own, or a hut like Mara's. Visits with the saudad and other interesting travelers. "Will you tell Persephonie good-bye for me? They're waiting till we return to go, aren't they?"

"She will insist on it, yes. I'll deliver your message directly. Cassian and I have a few more things to discuss."

Mara accompanied them on the first several minutes of their journey. "It will help the forest get to know you," she explained. She traced the edges of leaves and smiled at tiny twigs on their trail. "This creek bed that guides your path connects our home in the Vagarveil Wood with Trudid, to the southeast, and then Penshaw, if one continues several days south.

"Tendrils branch off and wind their way to Linolynn just before the edges of the forest. The creek's memory, in those places, delves beneath the ground and trickles in subterranean supplies and through the bedrock that has upheld these lands through vast and shifting eras.

"On your journey south, you'll cross a series of embankments that grow progressively calmer, with tall grasses and only a few stones. Near sunset, you'll come upon a sturdy, decisive stone, one that demanded the creek choose a new way forward. Take the eastern fork. It intersects with the main road to Trudid.

"If ever you lose the trail, the following incantation should help the forest trust and guide you back:

> *Fae and friends who light our way,*
> *through ash and birch and oaken stay*
> *Will of the willows and falling leaves*
> *grant their peace and travelers' ease*

"It sounds better in Druidic," Mara said after she caught sight of Marcon's dubious expression, "but we retained the cadence in the Caldaran translation."

Iellieth giggled and repeated the rhyme to herself a few times. "Will you teach me the Druidic version, Mara? When we return?"

"If you are keen to learn then, as I hope you will be, yes. There's one final thing before we part ways." She reached into her satchel and withdrew a small silver figurine of a raven.

"This will allow you to get in touch with anyone you need, so long as they're within a day's flight. Whisper *'nor corveau,*' and it will transform and deliver your message. Wait until it has assumed its full raven form before you begin speaking, and describe the person who's to receive your message and where it can find them. Then, after you say '*commen,*' it will match your voice for a few sentences and recite your message to the one you've sent it to."

"This figurine will transform into an actual raven?"

"Yes." Mara's expression twinkled. "I would show you now, but this will preserve the incantation should you need it. These messengers are not common in Io Keep?"

"No, unfortunately."

"We sent messages through coded sounds and magical rocks that could speak with one another across great distances," Marcon added.

Iellieth considered this. They didn't use talking rocks in Linolynn either.

Mara smiled. "Edvard will do his best to help you. He'll need a few days off after a day of flying. If you send him to me or to the castle, we can reply, but hold on to him so he can rest for two sunrises and sunsets after that."

Iellieth carefully noted Mara's directions and promised to be careful with the generous gift.

"This is where we must part, cher'a," Mara said. She stopped beside a beautiful flowering tree. The druid laid her hands on Iellieth's shoulders and kissed her on each cheek before she bowed her head deeply to Marcon. "Be well, my dear new friends. I shall look forward to your return."

"We will come back soon, Mara," Iellieth replied. She strode forward on the pressed dirt path left behind by the dry creek bed's years of undulating through the vast forest. Marcon matched step beside her.

CHAPTER 14

The dappled sunlight through the trees overhead cast a soothing green light on their downhill trail. Mara's directions were at times more ephemeral than seemed absolutely necessary, such as finding the proper turn in a creek bed based on the type and shape of a rock at the bend. But so long as they traveled south, they would find the road that intersected the forest and led to Trudid.

"Why is it they used the term 'champion'?" Iellieth asked after they were alone on their path.

"For myself and those like me?"

"Yes. Not to suggest that you aren't, of course," she added quickly. "Was it a martial competition?"

"No." Marcon smiled at the idea. "Beyond representing the titans' will, we were also warriors, though not all of our fights were martial in nature."

"And there were other champions of fire?"

"Ignis had several others who served in a similar fashion as myself, but we each had unique tasks and aptitudes. The armies of our great cities partnered alongside us, so I had a small collection of soldiers who traveled with me." He glanced away from her.

"How did they choose those soldiers?"

"For some, it was a matter of specialized training. Ignis selected others, as he did with me when I was young, and there were still more who volunteered. It was dangerous work, oftentimes even more so than for foot soldiers in the vast regiments, but the cause remained stronger rooted for those in the battalion, and that made our risks feel more worth taking."

"The battalion?"

He grinned. "The Blazing Battalion. The name sounds strange to say out loud, here"—he raised his hands toward the canopy of trees overhead—"but those men and women were important to me. We fought together, until the end." He set his jaw and looked ahead.

Iellieth laid her hand against his shoulder. "I am sorry, Marcon, about your battalion. We can speak of something else if you'd prefer."

"I may hold off on that particular story a while longer. There were other champions in those days as well, for the other titans, and there had been for thousands of years before I served."

"Really? But we don't have any now?"

"You would be much more likely to know than I am."

"Maybe, when we get back, we can ask Mara more about it?"

"I would appreciate that."

The calls of songbirds sounded in the treetops overhead, and Iellieth searched for their brightly colored plumage against the varied greens of the early spring growth. "You said something a moment ago about the cause. Can you tell me what you mean?"

"Ah, that the soldiers in the battalion had an easier time maintaining their belief in what they were doing than others, even if they placed themselves in greater danger."

"How did they manage that?"

"Well, lady, we had been fighting for hundreds of years by that point. Resources for everyone, even those removed from the conflict, were stretched thin. We had lost several cities in that last century, Beacon chief among them. They were a close ally of Respite, my home city. When people endure such hardship, for so long, against a relentless enemy who shows no mercy, who has no capacity for compassion, the collective spirit breaks.

"You saw the fear among the druids after Yvayne and the saudad spoke to them of potential threats and the loss of their allies. That was commonplace, even calm, for us. People were terrified, and they had every right to be."

The anger on Berivic's face, Persephonie's despair at the lack of care or response from those gathered, the disbelief. How could a society survive that constantly felt endangered? "I can't imagine what that must have been like," Iellieth said softly.

"When I was fighting in the war, three of the titans had recently departed, taking their power with them. Most of their champions fell, though a few endured. Ignis remained, and he helped my soldiers and I remember why we were fighting, what we were fighting for. Our belief stayed strong. That wasn't the case for everyone."

He spoke as though he'd fought for decades, but he couldn't have been older than thirty-five, Iellieth guessed. But in a time of war, perhaps they enlisted people at a very young age. "And what were you fighting for, Marcon?"

"The right answer is to protect the people of Respite, to prove faithful to Ignis, and because it was the only true and right path. But my actual reason"—he pushed his jaw forward and took a slow, deep breath—"when I first began to fight, was vengeance."

She stopped on the path, surprised. "But you don't seem very angry. What happened that drove you to seek revenge?"

"Respite was a large city, having taken in many refugees over the course of the war, and the poorest residents lived outside the protection of the city walls. We had advanced troops across Eldura, taking the fight to our enemies. As far as we were concerned, our city was well protected."

Hadvar was much larger than Linolynn and had a larger military to protect itself. Their soldiers constantly patrolled their lands, neutralizing perceived threats before they had a chance to intensify. This helped them to feel safe, while Linolynn's soldiers primarily functioned as peacekeepers tasked with protecting trade routes. She could understand how Hadvar's model would make a large city feel more secure, but she preferred Linolynn's approach.

Marcon sighed deeply, clearly still troubled by what had transpired so long ago. "Out on campaign, word reached us that Respite had been attacked by a horde of undead soldiers, a troop we had no idea existed. Impossible numbers. We returned with all haste, but it was too late. The entire outer community had been destroyed."

Iellieth's eyes grew wide in alarm. She'd never heard a credible account of undead creatures rampaging about and had always consigned those tales to storytellers' imaginations.

He spoke faster now, speeding toward his story's conclusion. "Fighting the undead brought additional cruelties. For each person our enemy slaughtered, they gained a new soldier. To lose a friend beside you was to have them turn against you in a matter of moments."

"I . . . I don't know what to say, Marcon. It sounds horrible. Gruesome. It's no wonder you wanted revenge."

"There is one element more, lady." He lowered his shoulders and head, resigned. "I told you earlier that I was an orphan. I grew up in an orchard. The husband and wife who owned it took in children like me from all across the city. I tried to reach them, but they were beyond our aid."

Marcon turned to look straight at her, his eyes blazing. "I killed the man and woman who took me in, who raised me. Their souls had already been torn from their bodies, which were left with a relentless hunger, a desire to turn all they encountered into mindless devourers just like them. The broken corpses of children were scattered among the trees." He closed his eyes and shook his head. "It was more than I could bear."

Iellieth parted her lips, but no words of comfort came to her. Marcon was too wrapped in his tale, his confession, to notice.

"I plunged my sword into the earth and cried out in my rage. I vowed to serve anyone who could help me avenge the innocent and the good, those who had done so much for me. The ones I had ultimately failed. Ignis answered me."

To have to turn on people you loved, and to lose people you thought were safe . . . what could she say in the face of such cruelty? Such suffering? "Marcon"—she laid a hand on his arm, but he had already turned back to stare down the horizon—"that's awful, what you had to endure. I'm sorry." It sounded as though he had done all he could, as had those helping him, but she didn't know how to say that in words he would accept. Every facet of his story, its scale, was beyond her experience.

His voice was little more than a whisper. "I remembered their faces, the children's bodies. Embedded them deep down. The memories became fuel and drove me on, even when the odds, the mission, seemed impossible. It's to further that vengeance that I spoke to you last night. Why I have to discover what the enemy is doing. I intend to seek out the orchestrators and bring them to justice. And this time, I will not fail."

Without warning, he strode forward on their path. She had to run to catch up with his long strides. "But this being, whoever they were, they're not here now. They can't be."

"Alessandra, the Dark Queen, still haunts these lands, be assured. She may be hidden, but she is active somewhere in this world."

He looked so certain, almost daring her to contradict him. It wasn't that she didn't believe him, but why would this god remain hidden if she was so powerful? No one in Linolynn, as far as she knew, worshipped anyone of the sort. There were goddesses of light and beauty, gods of music and literature. The only undead who roamed did so in word-of-mouth tales gleaned from the mountain communities and retold in the twilight days before the harvest. If a dark goddess was active in Caldara, she didn't seem to be interested in anyone knowing.

They traveled in silence for the rest of the morning.

And then she saw them. Faevines, the mystical ivy that, in ancient times, marked passages into the Brightlands. The colors were said to be more vibrant the nearer they were to one of the portals. Katarina had told her of a particularly colorful cluster she spied on her travels, a garnet garland twirled around opalescent and turquoise branches, with pale green moss shimmering underneath.

"Marcon, look." She pointed to the vines. "Mathilde, our gardener, wanted to grow these in the castle gardens, but they would never take to the soil, no matter what she tried." Iellieth stepped off the creek bed trail and reached forward to run her fingers over the lavender leaves. "Faevines only grow on their own. They will not take root when planted but slowly climb up and out of the soil, wherever they decide to be."

"I remember these." He stood beside her and peered at the ivy. "I cannot recall the particulars, but I believe some of the druids and fae would weave them into clothing."

"As decoration or the entirety of their clothing?"

"I believe that depended on the person."

"That sounds . . . revealing."

"It was."

Slowly, he angled his face toward her so that she could see his suppressed smirk, and she laughed. "Everything you've told me of your time thus far seems so intense, violent. It's hard to imagine someone having the time or inclination to construct a garment from vines and leaves."

"I doubt that it was a common practice. We'll add that to our questions for Mara, for when we return. Maybe that's one of the things they'll teach you when you join their community."

Iellieth narrowed her eyes at him, but her smile stayed. "I'm trying to decide whether or not you mean that as a compliment." He had been so serious all morning after he told her about Respite. "But you're forgetting, they don't want me to be part of their community."

"That one elf? Or the dissenting voices of a few others? Did you look beyond them, lady, to see the full picture?"

"Like what Ismaer said?"

"Precisely. You are right that some of them are afraid, but there were many who were silent with disapproval, and that was not directed at you." He led her back to the path.

Iellieth focused on what she remembered of the two council meetings and tried to expand her vision to include others beyond those who had garnered so much of her attention. The faces were indistinct, but she could imagine withheld disagreement with Berivic. Some would have sided with Mara and Ismaer.

Iellieth led them through a narrow part of their path as she reflected on what he had said. She dodged the branches that reached out to catch strands of her hair and wrap them around grasping leaves. "How will you find out what the dark goddess, Alessandra, is doing? Or where she is?"

"I am not sure, lady. In the past, she left her mark wherever she held sway, but there must be someone who knows of her whereabouts."

Her stomach knotted in frustration at being left out of his plan, eliminated without a question. But why did that bother her so much? She wasn't equipped to take on an ancient, evil deity, and she had no desire to fight whichever creatures would serve such a goddess. One ice monster and a rampaging giant had proved more than enough for her.

But the feeling would not relent either. Scad would have known what to say to return her to herself, but she did not.

Iellieth couldn't stop thinking about the attack on the orchard. "Marcon, do you think, if Alessandra is still out there somewhere, that she has undead forces working for her?"

"You said that you aren't aware of any having roamed Caldara in recent history?"

"Only in the stories, but most of those are folktales."

"That wouldn't make them untrue." Marcon's tone was even, a gentle reminder more than a correction. "If they were working for Alessandra, they would be so numerous as to be unavoidably recorded in both official and unofficial histories. Are there many necromancers about?"

"Necromancers? Who cast magic on the dead?"

"That is one aspect of their practice, yes. They use other dark magics and energies as well."

Iellieth shook her head. "I haven't heard of anyone like that. But if they weren't in Linolynn, or if they were kept secret, I don't know how I would have found out."

"I believe we're safe from the undead for now, then, lady." He half-smiled, but his eyes remained serious. "Alessandra may have found others to serve her, but I would set you free from that particular fear until circumstances prove otherwise."

"Thank you, Marcon, that is comforting." At least now she would know what to look out for in case the dark times Marcon had known returned.

The scent of fresh growth and the calls of birds overhead pulled her back into the brighter, safer present. A patch of wildflowers appeared from behind a large boulder at a divide in their trail. Iellieth ran forward and sank to her knees beside them. "How beautiful." She trailed her fingers beneath the perfectly petaled heads. A faint breeze picked up and turned them toward her, so slight she could barely feel it, but they responded with enthusiasm, angling their faces alongside their sisters to gaze at the sky.

"And which flowers are these?" Marcon asked, kneeling next to her.

"Most of them are species of pansies and daisies. These periwinkle ones, they used to be quite rare, though they are less so lately. King Arontis's grandmother, Josephine, loved them and forbade them to be grown in any garden in the kingdom save her own. She renamed them after herself, and the Arontis house colors are periwinkle and gold to this day. The flowers used to symbolize everlasting love. She tried to shift that to her own everlasting reign."

"That seems a totalitarian way to engage with flowers."

"It was, extremely, and it was not well received. The farmers and gardeners revolted, but subtly. They tossed the flower seeds onto the wind and replanted them in shared communal spaces. What she meant to make exclusive to herself became a symbol of camaraderie across the city-state. King Arontis saw the opportunity in this when he was still a prince, and he renamed the flower again, from the sephine to the 'olinese. It's a nickname for the city taken from the way many sailors slur the first part of the name in their speech, shortening Linolynn to 'Olynn or 'Nolynn."

The boulder that shielded the flowers from strong winds was the one that Mara had told them to look out for with "a shoulder notch, half a profile, and a willful aura." It signaled a turn to the east in their path, where the creek bed divided in twain, and they followed the new branch of the undulating trail.

"You have a great many things to say about flora for someone who grew up in a castle. Were they all in the garden you tended?"

Iellieth grinned. "Most of them were, though I doubt I could have learned all the flowers grown there. But the garden was one of my escapes. One of the places where I felt safe or could be alone in the castle."

"An escape from your family?"

"From my stepfather, at first. And his children. Later from Mamaun." The sky began its twirling dance from azure to pale tangerine and magenta above them.

"Why did you want to get away from them?"

"My stepfather, Duke Calderon Amastacia, doesn't like me. I'm a reminder of a difficult time in his marriage, to put it delicately."

"And he resents you for this?"

"It is much easier than resenting himself. He is neglectful of my mother, even now. I think my father offered for her to leave with him, or I like to believe he did, anyway. She must have said no. I was born in our estate by the sea, Aurora. The year I turned five, the duke convinced her to move back to Io Keep with him."

Marcon slowed to look for a place they might set up camp for the evening. Iellieth's legs ached from the day of walking, but she had hardly noticed before now, with the time in the open air and all the wonders of the forest around them. "Do you miss your first home? Aurora?" he asked.

"I do. Terribly." The earnestness of his question surprised her into a quick response.

After they found a place to camp, a flat bank with a

gentle slope surrounded by budding trees, Marcon built up a fire as Iellieth continued her story, relieved of some of her self-consciousness because he was occupied.

"Aurora is a full day's carriage ride down the southern coast from the castle. It's one of the oldest places in Linolynn, though it's at the far border, opposite from where we are now. The day we left, Mamaun gave me this amulet. She said Paupa had given it to her when they parted. She looked wistful when she said it, even to me as a child."

The fading sunlight winked off the golden bands as she twirled the amulet between her fingers. "This is how I found you. It's never happened before, but it flashed, and I was on a mountainside. This symbol, the three-chamber hourglass, was on the door to the cavern."

Once again the firelight seemed to calm the runes resting beneath his skin. His olive complexion shone in the warm glow. "I want to hear more about your amulet soon," Marcon said, "but for now, I would be honored to learn more about you. Please, tell me about this estate and your mother."

Iellieth spoke of Emelyee's beauty, her gorgeous golden hair, pale skin, and sapphire-blue eyes. How even now, ambassadors and nobles meeting her for the first time seemed to fall instantly in love with her. "She ignores this, of course. Propriety is key. When I was little, we would play together, and she read to me. After we moved back, she withdrew, and I was alone.

"As she left, the duke's bidding dominated my life more. At the time, I didn't understand. I thought I had done something wrong. Where was the beautiful woman I had known, who took me to the seaside? Who loved me?" Iellieth's voice splintered, and she avoided meeting

Marcon's eye. A silver-barked birch offered solace instead.

"The duke had plans for me, I found out later. It seems foolish—I don't know how I didn't see it. The last several years, there's been a parade of suitors. That's where we were going when I found you. He'd finally decided, selected someone rich, and cruel, who lives far away. They were going to make me marry him." She turned from the silvery tree to Marcon. He was watching her closely. "That's why I can't go back."

His eyes had narrowed, but the expression inside them was soft, concerned. "Then we will make sure you don't, lady. That is a terrible fate, for anyone, and you deserve something much better."

"Something like an unknown force that wants to cause me harm and threatens anyone vaguely associated with me?" She smiled so he could tell she was teasing. The simple meal they shared next to a fire by the burbling creek brought what should have been terrifying into a happier light.

Marcon laughed, "Perhaps not that exactly. I think something in between the two may suit you better."

"Hmm, that could be almost anything." Iellieth pulled out the roll of blankets Mara had given her and settled onto a soft patch in the grass. Overhead, swirls of smoke wrapped around winking stars, and the world felt at ease.

It would have taken her months to reveal what she'd said about her mother and the duke to someone she had met in Io Keep. Was it the walk through the woods, or their first meeting and having to fight to survive, together, that opened her up so much to him? He knew things about her that she had never confessed to anyone besides Teodric and Katarina.

Iellieth smiled as she thought of Scad and their late-night conversations, when he'd finished his work for the day and the rest of her family was asleep. She said even less to him, because he usually already knew. And more than the other two, he knew when she needed space to mull and to be.

When they reached Trudid, she would find a way to get word to him and Katarina that she was well. It should be close enough that she could send Edvard. Marcon could help her work out some sort of code to tell them where she was without alerting the duke. With fond thoughts of her friends, Iellieth found her way to sleep while Marcon watched the woods. She had never slept outdoors before, but the tiredness from their day's travel urged her quickly into sleep's arms. Marcon would wake her before the dawn to find some rest himself.

❧

MARCON RETURNED FROM RETRIEVING THEIR MORNING firewood somewhat breathless, and the texts embedded in his skin stood raised from the surface in angry, red burns. "What happened?" Iellieth sprang up and ran over to him. He must have encountered something in the woods, though Mara's promise that they would be protected had so far proven true.

"It's nothing, lady. Are you feeling alright?" The logs he'd carried back clattered to the ground. Marcon held her at arm's length and eyed her closely.

"Yes, I'm fine." Why did he think something had happened to her? His sword was sheathed, but he'd had ample time to use it and then clean it. "If something's in the forest, I would like to know," she said.

Marcon picked up the logs he had dropped and began to arrange them over the fire pit. "There's nothing out there you need to be concerned with."

Iellieth's teeth clamped together. Why was he lying? She sat at the edge of their fire and wrapped her arms around her knees. After she'd told him about her family, she had hoped he might be more honest with her, or understand why she needed to be included in what transpired around them.

He sighed heavily and looked at her. "I don't know what happened, lady. Something about the forest air, as I continued traveling away from camp. It was thinner, poisoned. My skin burned. I was afraid that it could be affecting you as well, and I ran back."

Already the raised lines across his skin had faded, returned to the intersecting runes a few shades lighter than his tan skin.

"Are you alright now? Why didn't you tell me? Nothing of the kind happened here."

"I'm relieved to hear it." He shook his head and returned his attention to the fire. "When I came back and saw that you were well . . ." His jaw clamped shut again; he shook his head. "I felt like a child frightened by my own imagination, but still worried that something real might be happening, to me or to you."

Marcon tried to keep his tone light, but she could tell it was an effort. "Thank you for hurrying back."

His lips lifted in a small smile.

"May I see?" Iellieth asked, crossing the circle. She pulled back the sleeve of his borrowed tunic and traced the fading runes. "I wish I could read them. I want to help. They pull at a memory, almost as though I'm in a dream. It seems like a text I should know but have forgotten."

"I have been attempting to read them as well."

She held his wrist in her hand and turned it over. The runes were more difficult to read against the lighter skin of his forearm.

"And have you found anything?"

He seemed amused at her close inspection. Iellieth blushed and let go. Her mother would be appalled at her easy manner with someone she'd just met, but he was already more trustworthy and candid than any of the suitors the duke had put in her way over the last five years.

Marcon warmed their breakfast and made them each a cup of tea to ward off the early spring chill.

One their second day of travel, the small woodland trail led them onto to a dusty dirt road just wide enough for two carriages to cross paths without having to leave the packed earth. There were deep tracks on one side of the road, but the other looked relatively untouched with scant impressions of carts and horses burdened by passengers or supplies.

Marcon emerged from the foliage first and looked both ways down the road. "We've timed this quite well, haven't we?" He smiled for this first time since before their midmorning stop.

"It seems we have. Rather good for a new traveler and a newly awakened one following Mara's directions."

"If you can follow her directions, you can go anywhere," Marcon shook his head. "I'd like to know a solid distance. Three leagues south. I can't feel the mood of the forest shift in order to know when I should bear east. One of many reasons I'm glad I have you."

"Me? What have I to do with the directions?"

"You're the one interpreting them." He grinned at her as though his meaning was completely obvious. "We've followed your instinct through this forest, lady. And now we've made it to our destination road."

It was kind of him to try to increase her confidence in their travels. But beyond enjoying their journey, she'd done nothing unusual, and she certainly couldn't sense the trees as Mara suggested. "We'll still need to figure out where exactly on the road we are, and then we can decide if we want to speak to the loggers or the mayor first."

CHAPTER 15

Teodric set his jaw as he walked past the house where they'd first lived upon their arrival to this dilapidated excuse for a city. Small gutters ran down each side of the main street, carrying filth of all sorts out to sea. The month-long voyage across the ocean had done enough to fray his mother's already fragile nerves. Her first sight and smell of Nortelon snapped them.

Or so he'd thought.

But fate had other, cruel plans waiting up its sleeves.

Frederick's disappearance drove Aurelia, forever, from her own right mind. Duke Amastacia's final victory over the Adhemar family.

Teodric scowled at the dirt path that twisted over to the market. He stopped by Smitty's flower stand to bring a gift home to his mother. "Anything pink and pretty," he told the smiling gardener. He added three extra coppers to her requested price, enough for her to buy a full meal for the husband and children she pretended not to have while she worked. He knew well enough what putting on a pleasant, flirtatious mask looked like to recognize it on another.

He approached the wood-and-plaster home, which stood on a quiet street. If he hadn't joined Syleste's band of pirates, he would have had to move his mother to a rougher side of town, with no flowers or greenery. For a woman so in love with the sunny beauty of Io Keep, who asked after her home so often, it was unthinkable.

If only Frederick could have seen it. Teodric pushed down the rising emotion at the thought of showing his father the home he'd made in his absence. Frederick knew what it was to labor for something, to apply yourself. He would have been proud.

A curvy, middle-aged woman with an armful of herbs trudged around the side of the house. She stopped at Teodric's footsteps in the gravel and looked up. Her face broke into a smile.

"You're here," she exclaimed. Nora hurried over and dropped the herbs she'd grown into a basket, and Teodric rushed to meet her at the gate. He reached over and unfastened the slide for her; she'd started having difficulties with her hands in the past few years, and any aid he could provide that would save her knuckles would be gratefully received.

She wrapped him in a tight embrace the moment he stepped off the gravel and onto the stone path that led to their home's front door. He sighed, relieved. "I was hoping I would see you before my mother spied me. How is she?" *Please don't say she's worse.*

"She's well enough, young master Teodric. Your sweet mother fares better in the spring, as I think we all do. She'd also like to see her handsome son more, and I'd like for him to tell me he's coming in, hmm? How am I to prepare for you as my lady would like if you're surprising me in the middle of the morning?"

"You know that I like to keep things interesting for you, Nora."

"That you do, lad. Here, come in. She'll be waking from her midmorning rest soon, and the two of you can speak."

Nora led Teodric into the receiving room that had also served as his father's library and office. Frederick's books still lined the walls.

The tea service sat out in the cramped kitchen, waiting for his mother to wake from her morning nap and proceed into the drawing room or perhaps out to the back garden for her refreshment.

Each day the same. Each day anticipating a new future that would never come. He paced between the two rooms while he waited, unbuttoning and rebuttoning his vest and shirtsleeves.

A soft voice cooed upstairs, and Nora, perfectly attuned to his mother's schedule and patterns, climbed up the back staircase to fetch Lady Adhemar.

He was waiting for her in the receiving room when Nora walked her downstairs.

"Teodric," Aurelia said with a sigh.

Her face lit up when she saw him, and his heart clenched. Though weak, she seemed well and happy.

His mother glanced about the room. "Dearest, where is your father? Wasn't he coming back with you today?"

He rose to take her hand from Nora's and help her into a chair. "I'm sorry, Mother, he's been delayed." The one doctor Nora had deemed suitable to tend to his mother visited the house every two weeks to check on her. After Frederick's disappearance, he advised that it would be kindest to agree with Aurelia's confusion so as not to upset her further. Teodric's stomach churned lying to her, but this was something he needed to bear to help her. She struggled and was lonely enough.

"That's too bad." She smiled. "We should see if Nora has time to cut your hair while you're here. It's getting quite long."

"You don't like it?" Light, pleasant conversations were best. There was a certain relief to the fantasy, that the biggest difficulty they faced was the length of his hair.

"I do like it, sweetheart. I only thought shorter might look more refined. It was so adorable on you as a young boy."

"That it was." He rose to take the tea tray from Nora so that she might be able to attend to her other duties while he sat with his mother. "But speaking of nice things, I picked up something for you today." He lifted the heavy blossoms from the market and placed them gently in his mother's arms. She smiled as she stared at the blooms.

"They're exquisite, Teodric. You know, they're so much like the ones they used to grow in Io Keep. And your father planted some just for me in our first years on his estate."

"I was hoping they were the same ones." Was recalling these memories beneficial for her, or would it only serve to worsen her denial? "They look beautiful in your arms, but might I fetch a vase for them?"

"Nora will be along to do that, I'm sure."

"Ah, but she's quite busy already, isn't she? I'll just fetch a vase and set them in fresh water." He selected the single crystal vase that had survived their many purges of valuable items and filled it from the pump behind the house.

"There you are, Mother." He set the vase beside her on the low table. "Now, tell me about all of your adventures these past few weeks that I've been gone." He didn't need to tell her that he had been absent for four months or that his new position as captain might increase those gaps even more. In the last three years, they'd made a life together from these brief exchanges.

Whatever Syleste's plans for him on the ocean, there should now be enough in the family coffers to care for Aurelia with or without him. Her captains didn't always live long, but they were paid well during their tenures of service. Anything to see her smile and know she was safe. That's what his father would have wanted.

AFTER HIS MOTHER HAD TURNED IN FOR THE NIGHT, Teodric retraced his steps, continuing past the flower stand to his favorite place in Nortelon, the tavern that had saved his spirit all those years ago.

Muffled applause leaked out of the sagging windows and creaking door of the Dashing Dapper Inn. The warm glow and laughter from inside invited Teodric into its loving embrace as it had five years before, when he was freshly arrived from Linolynn.

He relaxed his shoulders and straightened his scarf; Graziella, the proprietor, would be attuned to the slightest shift in his appearance or bearing. She couldn't know he was recently ill, and he preferred to keep the promotion from her for the moment too. Though he kept the details of his exploits aboard the *Dominion* from her, she didn't trust Syleste.

Strings plonked as the musicians traded the time on stage. People leaned over each other's tables and shared stories in the one pub in lower Nortelon where you didn't need a knife on your belt to feel at ease.

"There's my lad," a husky voice called out from the bar. Dorret waddled toward him, his large belly leading the way as it had his whole lucky life, as he was fond of saying.

Teodric dodged a young couple and intercepted the older man, wrapping his arms around his shoulders.

"You get taller each time we see you." Dorret thumped him on the back.

"Or you're just getting shorter." Teodric winked at him.

Dorret smiled and pointed his thumb at the kitchen door. "Zella's in the back, and she'll have a right fit if you don't head off to see her first thing. I'll never live it down."

Teodric grinned. "Well, we can't have you getting into trouble right at the beginning of the week, can we?" He patted Dorret's shoulder and wove in and out of their happy customers to find the man's partner back in the kitchens.

"I'm supposed to ask for a beautiful woman named Graziella," Teodric called as he swung open the door.

A high squeal answered him, and Graziella hurried forward. Her ancestors were half-elves and dwarves, the result of which left the tavern owner short, full-bodied, and beautiful in her kind and welcoming spirit. She had frizzy brown hair with dense spiral curls atop warm beige skin and freckles, and she always smelled of freshly made bread with the slightest hint of ale. "My darling's come home," she crooned, her mouth muffled by his silk vest as she hugged him even tighter than Dorret had.

"Did that man of mine send you in here to feed you? You're looking skinny again. That pirate witch doesn't feed you right." Graziella was one of the only people Teodric knew who openly spoke ill of Syleste.

"Well, no one feeds me so well as you, but you've got to promise not to tell Nora I said that. She'll be devastated."

"She'd be happier if you were home more often. As would your dear mother." Graziella patted the base of his ribcage and narrowed her eyebrows. He could tell she was trying to decide what to feed him first. Whatever it was would be delicious. "How is she?"

"About the same as when I was here last, which is good."

"Still no word from your father?"

A cold blade pierced Teodric's insides. The innkeeper didn't mean any harm, but he knew he'd never be able to care for Aurelia as Frederick could. "No, Zella. Nothing."

"Well, you keep your chin up. He'll find you. Have you seen August yet?"

"No, is she in this evening?"

"She's trying out a few of the new musicians, though she hasn't liked any so well since she met you."

He smiled. August had caught his eye immediately when he first arrived at the Dapper. Someone so insightful, with such a weighty presence, had been exactly what he'd needed when he was unmoored from everything he'd known. Being back in the town, that feeling of drifting had more space to breathe, to float in the seaweed-ridden shallows. It had never truly dissipated.

"I'll go find her."

"SOMETHING'S HAPPENED TO YOU RECENTLY." AUGUST'S pale, acorn-brown eyes narrowed at him. "What is it?"

"It's nice to see you too, August." Teodric set down a fresh glass of red wine for her and a crisp brown ale for himself. "Did you miss me?"

"That depends on if you've written any new songs in

your absence." She lifted the glass with a thin, delicate arm, each movement mirroring the swan's grace with which she played the viol or directed others' music.

"I have a few, but I think they'll need your help."

She smiled. "You're well beyond needing my assistance with your music, but I would love to hear it all the same." August glanced toward the stage as they both thought back to the first night she'd convinced him to play. He performed the song he'd written for Iellieth before he left Linolynn, and August had been intrigued by his music ever since.

"You looked so relieved that night, like you'd bared your soul and then found it beautiful for the first time. Why do you not feel that way now?"

August was fond of intensely personal questions and mystical statements. "You're intuiting more than is actually going on, as usual." He took a sip of ale, and she stared at him, unconvinced. "I was sick the past few days on the ship is all."

"Is that what truly happened, Teodric?" She leaned forward, eyes boring into his.

Tendrils of sickly green energy stretched across his vision, grasping fingers ready to pull him down below the depths.

Teodric pushed himself back in the booth away from her. "What are you doing?"

August drew her lips to the side. "Curious."

"What do you mean?"

"Let's leave it there for now."

"If there's something I need to know about then I'd rather—"

She reached forward and laid her pointer finger against his mouth. "You have everything you need at the present."

August closed her eyes and inhaled deeply, her way of sensing someone's approaching fate. He'd nearly laughed in her face the first time this happened, but her warnings had been well founded enough that he stopped dismissing them off-hand.

"Many changes lie before you. The impending shift you prepare to make, it will chart a path for other changes to follow. A shadow hovers over you, keeps you close. Expelling it will take a great act of will. But if you should choose to do so, you can lift its influence and pursue your own horizon."

Was she talking about Syleste and his promotion to captain? What would the other changes be? The hard wood of the booth dug into his shoulder blades as he continued to lean away from her.

August's eyebrows knit together, and she winced as though in pain. "It will be dangerous. You risk much in its achievement. But should you succeed, you will return to yourself in a way you had not previously believed possible." She opened her eyes and sat back, dazed.

Teodric waited for her focus to return to him and the present instead of whatever she had seen. "You're aware that many of your pronouncements are scary, right? I know that you're trying to help." Teodric shook his head. "August, I don't want to return to being the starry-eyed boy who landed here five years ago. It's true that change is on the horizon for me. Tomorrow, unless something goes terribly wrong, which it might, I'm receiving my own ship. I'll have more freedom than before. And that's a really good thing."

August sat up straighter and adjusted the thin strap of her white dress. "I tell you these things to speak wisdom to you." She clamped her teeth together and squinted at him. "When I perceive something I cannot tell you, it is because it will disrupt your path or only serve to cause you pain."

Teodric sighed. That was enough for one night. "I'll try to keep that in mind." He drained his ale and scooted out of the booth. August couldn't see that sometimes, her wisdom made things worse. "Give my apologies to Graziella and Dorret. They'll understand what happened."

Infuriatingly, she maintained her intense stare with no reaction to his implied rebuke. Facing Syleste in the morning, stepping up to become one of her captains, was already frightening enough.

CHAPTER 16

The road gently sloped downhill, and as the sun crested, the first farms that made up Trudid's outskirts appeared behind cleared lanes where the forest had been carved away. Some peeked through the trees like shy woodland creatures, rabbits caught in a dew-covered hedge. Others were bold, leaping out from the landscape like entitled castle squirrels darting across the arboretum. The paths to the homesteads wove through the trees of the Stormside Forest and opened onto plowed fields and orchards.

At a bend in the road, they encountered a farmer returning from town, walking beside her donkey with an empty cart trailing behind. The middle-aged woman avoided eye contact with them, leaning down to pat the donkey instead.

"I hate to trouble you," Iellieth said when they neared her. "But could you please help us? Have you an idea of where the loggers are located? Or how near we are to Trudid?"

The farmer's eyes darted between her and Marcon and widened in alarm when she saw his longsword.

"We don't mean anyone any harm." Iellieth raised her palms reassuringly.

"You're nearer the camp, though it's still a ways off." She slung her thumb further down the road behind her. "You'll make it by dusk, I'd say. And they can send you on to Trudid from there."

"Thank you, ma'am," Iellieth said. "We're much obliged."

The woman frowned, like the donkey had suddenly emitted a foul odor. They waited for her to move first and then passed her, neither party looking at the other.

"Dusk isn't too bad, is it?" she asked Marcon after the woman had faded into the woods behind them.

"I had hoped we might be closer than that, but so long as you're not in a rush, neither am I." He began to say something else, but stopped himself with a quick sideways glance at her.

He spoke again after a few moments had passed. "I have been thinking during our travels today about what lies before us. And with those questions, I reflected on what has been left behind."

Iellieth drew her eyebrows together, unsure of what he meant.

Marcon sighed. "You see, lady, I had an ally, Quindythias. He would know the next steps for us to take in this new time. From what Mara said, I believe he may have suffered a fate identical to mine. Quindythias had his quirks"—Marcon grinned and shook his head—"but he was as loyal a friend as any could ask for. He would search for me the moment he discovered I was in danger. And I must do the same for him."

"Do you know where he might be? In the mountains?"

"I think it unlikely they would have buried him there unless they'd had no other choice. In the past, I would have asked for Ignis to guide me, but such is the nature of fire."

"What do you mean?"

"The intensity of the flame is what drew me to Ignis when I swore vengeance before. Fire consumes. Its work is swift. It does not wait or rest. Through a failure on my part, I resisted those qualities. As a result, those I cared for, whom I had sworn to protect, perished."

"I don't think it's fair for you to lay that blame entirely on your own shoulders. Surely there were other factors at play, and a powerful enemy subtle enough to route your forces?"

"You think there's nothing we could have done." An edge crept into his voice.

Iellieth shook her head. "No, that's not what I meant." How could she explain without him feeling personally attacked? She only wanted to help. "Regardless of the placement of yourself and your regiment, others must have been out of place as well, for the attack to happen."

Marcon's jaw tightened, and he twitched his head to the side. "It was a difficult time. I thought I had done more to let it go. I am sorry." He still looked upset, his brow furrowed, but he was trying to make amends.

"I wanted to clarify my concern about remaining close by," Marcon began. "I fear attracting dangerous enemies to you. But there is something else, something about you that you cannot yet see. It drew Persephonie to you and, I suspect, Yvayne as well. At first, I believed, misguidedly, that it was because you had awakened me that you'd made a powerful enemy. But I would not be quick to dismiss your place in the wider scale of things."

He paused on the path and regarded her. "Quindythias was always more skilled than I at putting together disparate pieces. In addition to helping me uncover Alessandra and her servants, I hope, if it is possible to find him or what happened to him, that he might be able to help you too."

❧

IT TOOK THE REST OF THE AFTERNOON AND THE EARLY evening to arrive at the logging camp. The dirt path that sliced through the wood was well worn from the workers' trips from the road. A stump-lined walk that carved deeper into the ancient roots of the Stormside Forest marked both sides of their trail.

The white-and-tan pattern of tents appeared through the thinned forest just before dusk. They were spread across a cleared field marred by the skeletal remains of root structures and undergrowth. "It resembles a soldiers' camp," Marcon observed.

In the eastern section, one tent stood taller and larger than the rest, placed behind a gathering area with long tables and benches.

As they passed through the camp, the chatter among the loggers paused while they stared after her and Marcon. When the nobles left the castle to go into the city of Linolynn, outside of the Air Ward in particular, they were met with fanfare if it was an organized celebration or something akin to this if it was not. The duke called it a mix of scorn and awe. It looked more like confusion, watching someone who was out of place.

A few of the men and women squinted at her clothes, and others whispered about Marcon's tattoos. She prevented herself from turning to see what he thought of the camp. Best to seem at ease.

Iellieth stepped into the empty area between the tables and the large tent. Only a few people gathered in the common space, and their conversations halted at her approach. She continued past them and approached the two loggers stationed at the tent's entrance. They weren't armed as guards, but their erect posture suggested they provided additional security. The man on the left glanced at her nervously and lowered his gaze, but his partner crossed his arms and stepped forward.

She hadn't seen someone of orcish descent since the winter festival at the end of the previous year. Though some half-orcs were part of Linolynn's navy and others sailed in and out of the city on merchant vessels, their population remained low, similar to half-elves or any others of nonhuman bloodlines.

The man had a protruding lower jaw and burly fore-arms. He glanced at her but saved his glare for sizing up Marcon. They stared at one another, and the seconds stretched on. Was she supposed to state their purpose?

The guard waited for her to open her mouth and begin to speak before he interrupted. "What is it you want?" he growled.

"We would like to request a meeting with Turdoch, please," Iellieth said. She needed to avoid that quaver in her voice in future interactions. She wasn't frightened. Only uncomfortable.

"He's busy." His voice was gruff, bordering on rude. Marcon stiffened beside her, a warning.

"We'd like to make an appointment, then, when he's next available. When might that be?"

Marcon feigned brushing his cloak to the side, and his fingertips rested on the hilt of his sword.

The guard ground his teeth, furious at the threat. He exhaled in frustration and took a menacing step toward Marcon. In a flash, Marcon pulled her behind him and assumed a ready stance.

"Send them in," a voice called from the tent.

Iellieth smiled kindly at the nervous guard and avoided looking at the aggressive one. She laid a hand on Marcon's shoulder. It was far from an ideal start, but the man had invited them in. The half-orcish guard's angry glare burned at the back of her neck as they stepped inside.

A pale green half-orc sat behind a desk covered in maps and ledgers. He stood as they entered, palms resting flat on the edge of the desk. He was several inches taller than Marcon, nearly seven feet, and broad-chested. He wore a white linen shirt with the sleeves rolled up and an open leather vest. "Let's have it then." He gestured to the two wooden chairs in front of his desk and sat down.

The man leaned back and observed them closely. Marcon held the back of Iellieth's chair for her as she sat. The meeting had taken such a negative turn already. She'd need to be very persuasive to have a hope of convincing him to see their side.

"You are Master Turdoch, in charge of the Greenfell Logging Company?" Iellieth asked.

"I am. And who might you be?"

"Iellieth, and Marcon." She gestured beside her to Marcon, who gave a slight nod.

"What is it that you want then, Iellieth?"

"I have come to ask about the possible overextension of your logging company's reach into the forest."

"Have you now? And why might you be interested in that?"

"I speak on behalf of some of the nearby residents. They are concerned about the forest being able to recover from such extensive cutting."

"That seems mighty presumptuous of you. Which residents are we speaking of in particular?" He raised an eyebrow; he already knew the answer.

"On behalf of the druids."

"I figured that. You're the third they've sent to interrupt me and my work." He glared at her. "I'll say the same as I've said before. We haven't touched their part of the forest and don't intend to. It's long past a time when it was their business to instruct others on how best to tend their lands. This forest doesn't belong solely to them."

How could she make him see that the druids were trying to preserve the good of everyone in the surrounding area? She needed a different angle.

"They were hoping you had changed your mind out of care and consideration for those working for you." Turdoch's expression darkened. She'd hit upon a nerve. "The men and women under your employ depend on you for their livelihoods. If you continue felling the forest at this rate, it will be destroyed to the detriment of future generations. Your people will be put out of work."

The half-orc scowled at her. "I know my responsibilities very well."

"Then why are you disregarding the greater good for profit?"

Turdoch stood up slowly and leaned over his desk toward her. "My job is to make sure those that work for me can feed their families. We travel and are far from home, and they may be the only one making money in their household. I explained to the mayor that this rate of cutting the forest was too fast and would damage it, but he ordered that we press on anyway. I've had to expand my company to keep up with the demand coming from the king of Linolynn himself. Says it's an emergency." He crossed his arms over his chest and stood to his full height.

"Now I've a duty, and I suspect you do too. But I'll not stand for some stranger to come to my camp, insult me, and accuse me of not knowing or caring about what I'm doing or those I'm doing it for. I'll ask you to leave now, and I won't ask twice."

Iellieth, rooted to her seat, stared back at Turdoch. This was a disaster. What could she say now? The half-orc raised his arm and pointed to the doorway. He shifted his gaze to glare at Marcon, sizing up a potential opponent.

Marcon stared back, poised to step in front of her or seize his sword. They had to go. If it came to blows, he'd never hear them. She stood and walked to the tent entrance. Iellieth turned back to Turdoch. "I'm very sorry for making assumptions about you and your motivations. That was wrong of me."

Turdoch's expression remained unchanged. She left the tent, Marcon behind her.

The table on the opposite side of the gathering area was unoccupied. She sat lightly on its bench on the far side, ready to be told to move. "Marcon, what do we do now?" What was she going to tell Mara? If the head of the logging company wouldn't listen to her, why should she expect the mayor to be any different?

Marcon squared his shoulders toward the tent. The nervous guard approached them. "Excuse me," the man said, his voice soft and scratchy. "I hope that you will pardon me, miss and sir, I do apologize for interrupting, but, well, would you be in need of somewhere to stay tonight?"

She hadn't even thought of that. "Yes, it appears that we might." Where would they keep visitors' quarters or paid rooms among the tents?

"Can't trust the forest in the dark." He shook his head, alarmed at the thought. "We've a spare tent, recently vacant, if you'd like. It was my friend's. He's from Linolynn too."

"How did you know that I'm from Linolynn?"

"Your accent, miss. Smith spoke just like you, though perhaps not so posh."

Iellieth smiled at him. "That's very generous of you. We would be extremely grateful. I am Iellieth, and this is Marcon."

The man nodded to them. "My name is Flick. The tent is right over here, miss, if you'll follow me."

CHAPTER 17

Half of the loggers had turned in for the night as Iellieth and Marcon followed Flick to the unoccupied tent.

"What happened to your friend?" Iellieth asked. "Is he alright?"

"Not a logging accident or anything of the kind, miss," he explained. "Being from Linolynn, like you, he was called back with the reserves."

"The reserves? What do you mean?"

"The king's expanded his navy and batch of foot soldiers. Smith left two days ago. They're preparing for war." Flick quickly built a fire in the ring before the tent.

"War?" That couldn't be possible. Who would they be fighting, unless Linolynn had been attacked? Did others mis-transmigrate as she had? "War with whom?"

"Hadvar. There're rumors all over the country. King came back early from their festival absolutely furious. That's why we've had to increase production even more than we had before. Need more ships than he'd first thought."

Iellieth stared into the freshly laid fire and ignored Marcon's inquiring looks. He asked Flick a few more questions to cover up her rudeness. Linolynn couldn't be going to war with Hadvar. Their northern neighbors were endlessly more powerful. At sea, they stood a chance, but over land, it would be a slaughter. What had happened that would drive King Arontis to such a step?

Maybe Flick was mistaken, and there was a trick involved somehow, another reason the lumber was being requested with such haste. A hollow ache settled in the pit of Iellieth's stomach, and she could only pick at the food Marcon prepared for her despite their long walk to the camp earlier that day.

"You seemed shocked by his news, lady. Why?"

"Linolynn is a peaceful nation. And King Arontis is wise. He would not imperil the forest and the people of Trudid on purpose, and he certainly wouldn't send Linolynn's troops on such a foolhardy mission. Maybe he doesn't know about the lumber."

"Everyone we've spoken to has said their orders come from the king. But you think he's unaware of what's being demanded in his name?"

"I think my stepfather may be saying the orders are coming from the king but sending them himself."

"Why would he do that?"

"I have been trying to understand what he could gain. He doesn't do anything without that consideration, and he's the king's closest adviser and has been for many years. There isn't much oversight for his work because Arontis trusts him. And Hadvar's extremely wealthy."

"And is Linolynn's a powerful military force?"

"Only at sea. We'd be no match for them in a battle over land."

"The people leaders choose to keep close by their side say much about their own character and intentions for those under their power. How do you hold Arontis to be a good king when he is so influenced by your stepfather?"

"He's always been kind to me, though I've only seen him a few times. And my mother respects him. My stepfather loathes me, but he thinks what he does helps Linolynn. The city-state itself is wealthier under his influence, though he would never answer to the well-being of the people in the face of these changes. My sense is that the Air Ward, the wealthier district around the castle, has benefitted from his assistance of the king more than the Earth or Water Wards. Their residents aren't as well off as those who live close to Io Keep."

"However cruel he's been to you, then, you do not think your stepfather would resort to such extreme measures? Risking the lives of thousands of soldiers?"

"The queen of Hadvar is a collected, intelligent ruler. Conniving, even. She imprisons many beneath her city to work in the mines, and much of Hadvar's trade is suspect. My stepfather, despite his shrewd mind for money, is careful to toe the line of the law, and he usually thinks about both long- and short-term gains. Something must have happened at the Festival of Renewal. It's an extreme insult to turn to a course of war when one is meant to be promising another year of trade, diplomacy, and partnership."

Iellieth bit her lower lip, pondering. "Is it possible Flick's friend was mistaken?" Who would be more likely to declare war? Resorting to military conflict seemed a rash and winless choice for both sides. "Even if there was a disagreement among the leaders, I don't see . . ." She frowned. "What if Hadvar declared war against us?"

Her heart sped up. Linolynnian forces advancing on Hadvar would be its own form of recklessness, but Hadvarian forces advancing on the city? The people would be slaughtered as Marcon had described, only by living soldiers rather than hordes of undead. Linolynn had been built for beauty, not for might.

Marcon laid a comforting hand on her arm. "We don't know enough yet to determine what's happening either way. In Trudid, the mayor is sure to know, is he not?"

"I believe so, yes."

"You're worried for your people, lady, as is right for you to be. But let us wait till we've spoken to others and been able to confirm this report. Calling up forces could be a precautionary measure rather than a response to an immediate threat."

Flames burning around the city gates, turning the pale gray stone black. People screaming in the streets, fleeing in terror. These were scenes from her books, not for inside Linolynn's walls. "I don't want us to be at war."

"I know that you don't." Marcon squeezed her arm, reassuring her. "If your king is the ruler you say he is, neither does he."

❦

FLICK STOPPED BY THEIR TENT THE NEXT MORNING before he traveled into the woods with the other loggers. He directed them to the nearest route to Trudid, a shortcut that would shave two hours from their journey.

"What if we followed the loggers instead and tried to speak with Turdoch one more time?" Iellieth asked after Flick bid them farewell.

"I don't think it would do any harm, and it could help

matters," Marcon said. "He seems the kind of man to appreciate persistence."

"Do you think he'll be more willing to listen to us this time? If I approach it differently?"

"It is certainly possible, lady."

"I should have been more cautious before. Mara's been so kind to me. She doesn't seem the kind of person to hold a prejudice against someone, but I hadn't adequately considered her feelings toward loggers."

They packed their belongings and followed the workers, who were trickling down a path into the Stormside Forest.

"When I was little, Mamaun told me legends of the tree protectors—forest spirits and ancient, walking trees who would enact the will of the woods. She was curious about elves and the old stories when she was younger—that's how she knew so many tales. My grandmother forbade her from studying them, so she read in secret." The early morning breeze stirred the leaves around them. Iellieth paused on the path and closed her eyes. Before their move, she and Mamaun would play games in the forest behind Aurora, reenacting the ancient stories her mother read to her each afternoon.

Iellieth opened her eyes and relocated herself in the present, inside a northern branch of the same forest. "The one thing she was adamant about with my stepfather, when we were back in Io Keep, was that I be able to study what I wished so long as I also dedicated myself to the subjects they selected."

"And what did you choose to explore?"

"Languages and cultures first. Katarina and I love to read, and her brother Aravar would bring back novels and stories from the far reaches of Caldara for us. She used to travel, but she prefers to stay in Io Keep now. They granted me a personal section of the castle gardens as well. I wonder who's tending it now." Surely Mathilde had found someone she thought was worthy of the task.

"Do you miss your home?"

"You're asking because I sound nostalgic?"

Marcon nodded. "That is part of it, yes."

Her recent good-byes tugged on her heart. "I miss Katarina and Scad. I haven't many friends in the castle. That tends to happen when you grow up an outcast."

"Or an orphan." He smiled. "But here you are, well on your way to finding a new home with the druids."

"I have been scared to allow myself to hope for that. They could easily change their minds, or Mara could be overruled in the council."

"Mara doesn't seem the type to easily take no for an answer."

Iellieth laughed. "No, I'm sure you're right. Then neither will we."

Her happiness at this thought was cut short by the sounds of the logging ahead of them. Axes thudded into the trunks of ancient trees. What began as grunts of protest as the blades struck thick layers of bark amplified into screams of pain as the axes cut deeper into the heartwood.

Iellieth stumbled, nauseated by the cries, and clung to one of the smaller trees that had survived the purge of its elders. The sapling's fear trembled into her fingertips.

She laid her forehead against the tree and whispered to calm it. "You're alright. I'm not going to hurt you. We're trying to stop them."

The sapling quivered as another tree howled in agony at the sharp teeth gouging into her sides.

"Lady?" Marcon grasped her elbow, trying to support her.

Iellieth wrapped her arm around her stomach, the other still holding the frightened tree. "Marcon, I can hear them." His brow creased. "I can hear the trees as they're dying."

His expression reflected her horror. "Should we go? Do you still want to try to speak to Turdoch?"

"Yes, we must." Iellieth plugged her ears and moved back onto the path. She couldn't tell if the muted cries she still heard were echoes from the clearing or her memory.

Once inside the logging area, Iellieth stayed as far as she could from the active sites. At the center of the clearing, Turdoch stood on a wooden platform. He turned in slow circles, keeping a close eye on the work, barked orders now and again, and sent runners out to the various teams.

Turdoch noticed their approach and observed them curiously, especially Iellieth's hunched, ear-shielding walk. But even with her ears stopped, she couldn't drown out the sudden explosion of screams, of both trees and people, on the opposite side of the clearing. The half-orc vaulted over the platform railing and landed, already running, ten feet below. A large oak was falling differently than they'd intended, into the clearing, and workers scattered beneath her splayed branches.

Marcon sprang forward the moment Turdoch landed. He shouted instructions over his shoulder, but they were lost in the chaos.

The overseer flung himself forward and shoved two men out of the way as the tree crashed to the ground. The branches rebounded after they struck the earth, and Turdoch disappeared beneath them.

Her companion was swift and arrived at Turdoch's side only moments after the tree collapsed on him. "Lie still," Marcon ordered. The frightened workers stared at him, unmoving. Marcon shoved past the arm-sized appendages of the thick branch and wrapped his arms around where the branch met the trunk.

He looked up at Iellieth and inclined his head to where Turdoch lay. "Get someone to help you, and stabilize the branches against him. His back cannot move." Marcon directed a few others to help him with the ends of the branch.

Iellieth nodded. She jogged over to a woman who had been running toward the site just ahead of her. "Will you help me?"

"Aye." The woman set to rolling up her sleeves, and Iellieth knelt beside Turdoch.

The limb had crushed his arm, and he was bleeding heavily. His face was covered in scratches, and blood dripped from a cut across the side of his head. "Why're you here?" he grumbled as his eyes tried to focus on Iellieth.

"I owed you a better apology."

"Heh, you've come just in time."

The other logger held tight to Turdoch's shoulders and braced his head against her leg. "Hold his arms, and pin his left thigh," she instructed Iellieth.

He groaned as she complied. Marcon counted off, and the half-orc yelled again as the branches lifted. The pieces that had pierced into his skin ripped out, and more blood spurted from the new wounds. Dark snowflakes sprinkled across the edges of Iellieth's vision.

"YOU'RE NOT THE MOST HELPFUL ASSISTANT, ARE YOU?" Turdoch's voice boomed beside her, and Iellieth slowly opened her eyes.

Marcon knelt on her other side and held a cold cloth against her forehead. "Are you alright, lady?" He watched her closely, worried.

"I haven't seen blood do that before." Her head spun again.

"Easy there." Marcon's gravelly voice was grounding.

She smiled weakly at him.

"Don't think about it."

She blinked slowly. Marcon's blue eyes were pretty.

"This one says that you've come to bother me again." Turdoch's gruff voice interrupted her assessment. Strips of white gauze stretched across the half-orc's brow, and his arm rested in a sling.

"Have you a camp doctor, or a medic from Trudid?" Iellieth looked around at the collection of loggers for the person who had seen to Turdoch's injuries. Mercifully, in the excitement, the saws and axes had stopped. The clearing was calm.

"Someone's been to fetch her, but we were spared the rush with your fellow here." Turdoch nodded at Marcon and winced as the movement tugged against his stitches.

"I didn't realize you were a medic too." Had that been a normal job for military leaders in ancient times? Once or twice she'd overhead Stormguard Basha instructing teams in preparation for emergency care situations, but he would not have been the person she would have selected to hold a small needle and stitch someone back together.

"It was a surprise aptitude of mine that I had a few opportunities to exercise," Marcon said. "There weren't always healers to spare, and my team was more mobile so long as I and a few others could take care of moderate wounds." He flipped the cloth on her head. The coolness soothed her senses enough for her to sit up.

"Maybe we can avoid telling the druids about me being squeamish so they don't have extra reasons to think I don't fit."

"Your secret is safe with me, lady." He knelt in front of her, waiting to make sure she hadn't risen too quickly.

"Will the other two men be alright?"

Marcon nodded. "Turdoch pushed them far enough to be out of any real danger. One's scraped up, but he'll mend just fine."

"That was very brave of you"—Iellieth turned back to the half-orc—"to throw yourself in the way of the tree to save them."

"I look after those in my charge."

"I can see that." She took a deep breath. "I wanted to apologize again for how I spoke to you yesterday. I made assumptions that were unfounded and unfair. It's clear that you care about the people who work for you."

Turdoch squinted at her, suspicious, and waited.

"About the forest . . ."

He raised an eyebrow.

"I understand that you know what you're doing. You wouldn't be delving in so quickly or so far without explicit orders to do so."

"True. What of it?"

"If the mayor were to change his mind and make the logging less of an emergency, or if the king's timetable shifted, would that cause hardship for you and your team? Would the loss of work be difficult?" Iellieth strove to keep her tone even and calm. She didn't want Turdoch to hear a reprisal of her accusations from the night before.

"We're asking questions now instead of making demands?"

"Yes. I'm trying." The trees whispered to one another and swayed gently overhead.

The corner of Turdoch's mouth twitched. "Alright then. To answer your question, no. We'd be alright. Plenty of work's hereabouts, and slower cutting means we could return later instead of watching it dwindle and leaving naught but scraps for those who come after."

"Then we'll go speak to the mayor," Iellieth said. Relief flowed through her. She'd be able to keep her promise to the little tree after all. "And we'll send word, if he's willing to listen."

"Best of luck to you, then. I'm not sure as it'll do any good." Turdoch shrugged and shook his head.

"It may not. But you heard us out." And that hadn't seemed very possible the evening before. She smiled. Maybe there were more surprises where the mayor was concerned.

"That I did, but I was predisposed to your side. Flendon won't be."

CHAPTER 18

Genevieve dug her paws into the spongy surface of the air and struggled toward her rescuers. Sariel bounded to the edge of the water in a single leap, and the woman on his back continued her missive to the forest around her. The tug of the water's willow branches grew stronger, faster, and she flew over the pool.

Ophelia's white eyes were still rolled in the back of her head, and Genevieve pummeled toward them faster and faster. She was going to collide with Sariel. The great wolf's eyes widened. Ophelia shot her hand forward, nearly striking Genevieve in the muzzle, and she fell to the ground. *Ooph*. The impact knocked her breath away, and small stones bruised her back, all along her curved spine.

In a billow of mossy robes, the druid woman alighted from Sariel's back and stood over Genevieve. She carried a long, gnarled staff in her hand. A faint evergreen glow hovered over the woman's head, and her eyes rolled forward, milky blue.

With a sharp cry, Ophelia slung her staff behind her

head and struck Genevieve across the chest. She barked in pain. Why?

Her lungs filled with air, and a ready anger flowed through her bloodstream. This woman was no ally. Only one of the two of them could live. Genevieve sprang to her feet, and fresh venom flooded her mouth. This woman would know her pain before her eyes forever closed.

She knelt back on her haunches, and the woman readied the staff for another blow. Genevieve was ready this time. Ophelia swung, and Genevieve caught the end of the staff in her mouth and bit down.

Her enemy smiled. Light erupted from the staff and blew her backward into a tree. *"Hala'vai!"* Ophelia pointed her hand at the tree and balled it into a fist. The branches slung forward and encircled Genevieve's wrists and ankles before they grew upward to wrap her arms and legs against the bark.

This woman would pay. Genevieve growled in her fury.

Ophelia swung her staff again at Genevieve's head, but she stopped short. It rested just at the end of her nose. She bit out again, and another branch whipped down and grabbed her beneath her jaw. She couldn't breathe. Her thick saliva gurgled in the back of her throat.

"This is what it means to lose control, girl. You cannot recognize friend from foe. Your body is overwhelmed by rage and fear."

Defending herself was the only way she could survive. The druid had no idea what she was saying.

"I cannot help you unless you can learn to fight it. The cursed blood of the lycanthropes is strong. Who are you?"

Genevieve growled again. "The last of my pack." Her voice was unrecognizable, a series of yips and a low bark.

"Try again. Who are you?"

She was losing air. Genevieve struggled against her bindings. Mariellen had cast a similar spell with her in the woods. It entangled an enemy to give you time to flee or, if you were strong enough, to question them.

Wait. *Mariellen. The attack.* Genevieve shut her eyes and tried to rid herself of her monstrous form. The alluring darkness, the sense of protection, they weren't true to who she was. Her brow snapped, shrank back. She screamed in pain. Her teeth receded, and her nose returned to its rightful place.

Another crack. The vines tugged against her and held her in place as her ribcage receded, returned to her human frame.

"We must choose to return to who we are." Ophelia kept the end of the staff pointed toward her. Tiny wisps of pale green light and the soothing scent of sage lifted from it and drifted over to her. They embedded in her elongated body hair and burned. The sage covered the stench of singed fur. Genevieve winced. Another snap as her knee twisted back to its original angle. Her vision darkened.

"You must stay, girl."

Genevieve squinted her eyes shut. She could endure this. She could be herself again.

The beads of light sizzled as they touched her skin, warming into her muscles, helping her relax.

"Sariel, it's time."

The dire wolf plodded forward and came to stand at Ophelia's side. He hadn't spoken since he'd asked her to run to them. The sides of his eyes crinkled, staring at her. A soft whimper left his throat. He wanted to remind her she wasn't alone.

Genevieve watched Ophelia feel along Sariel's side; her fingers slipped easily through his silver fur. She pulled on a leather strap slung over his back and dug into the satchel at its end, withdrawing a small glass canister.

Genevieve panted, her body back to itself, the few remaining shreds of her clothing hanging from the vines. What had Ophelia prepared? The anger burbled at the back of her mind, ready to rush forward at the slightest provocation.

The druid placed her staff on the ground and felt her way forward. Her face came to rest a few inches from Genevieve's, which was raised up by the tree to match Ophelia's height.

"Are you ready to take the next steps forward, girl?"

Genevieve's stomach tingled in fear and anticipation. Ophelia didn't look ready to heal her. The hybrid wolf still stalked inside, only temporarily beaten back. What would Mariellen have told her to say? Or Sheffield? Genevieve's eyes clouded over with tears. She could almost see their broken bodies huddled over one another, ashes rising into the orange-and-smoke sky.

"I am ready, Varra."

Ophelia smiled again, and the wrinkles around her eyes deepened. "Good."

The druid twirled a long gray finger over the glass jar in her hand. The wooden lid slowly unspooled and plinked to the ground. She dipped her thumb into the liquid and drew it out, the pad covered in thick, dark green paint. Ophelia traced her thumb down the center of Genevieve's forehead and over her nose. "We bind thee to the earth."

And across her left cheekbone. "We bind thee to the air."

Then her right. "We bind thee to the water."

And down the center of her lips and the edge of her chin. "We bind thee to the fire."

Ophelia dipped her thumb again and drew it below each of Genevieve's collarbones, connecting her to both light and darkness. She wet her pointer finger in the paint and traced from the base of her ribs to the end of her pelvis. "We bind thee to the lycan."

"Wait, no," Genevieve exclaimed.

Ophelia shut her eyes but continued her work. She outlined Genevieve's upper and lower arms, the same with her legs. "The light of Enidia guide you, the presence of Selene sustain you. In the marriage of Fenrir and Luna, may you find peace, may you find purpose."

Ophelia froze, her entire body rigid, and her eyes rolled back in her head once again. In a deep, guttural voice, deeper even than her alto speech, she recited:

> Another walks beside the sea,
> your reflection, counterpart, sister.
> The third waits in mountains, no longer free,
> still others, long-awaited, roaming, passing
> through winter.

Ophelia shook her head, the enchantment passed. Sariel stared at her, his golden eyes unblinking. "You need to free her from the tree. She must step into the pool."

"Sariel, what just happened?" Genevieve asked.

Ophelia still looked dazed.

"We will speak of it soon, Genevieve. Ophelia, ask the tree to let her go."

Ophelia nodded slowly, and Sariel padded forward to stand beneath Genevieve. The vines relented, and she gently collapsed against him. "Come, I will help you."

She pushed herself up, her legs shaking beneath her. "What will happen after I step into the pool?"

"You will join an ancient, long-forgotten sect of our people." Ophelia leaned upon her staff, still struggling to slow her breathing. She raised a hand to her forehead and placed her thumb on her temple and middle finger between her eyebrows. "A time of suffering still lies ahead, child, though you will find the answers you seek."

"But which sect, Varra? Am I still a werewolf?"

Ophelia turned her milky eyes to Genevieve. It was unclear if she could see her or not. "A werewolf you shall always be unless you and your counterpart uncover the cure."

Genevieve gasped. "No." Her voice broke. That's not how it was supposed to be.

"However"—Ophelia held out a shaking hand—"you are a werewolf as has not walked these lands for a long age. Are you willing to follow a new destiny, or are you not?"

"If I step into the water, I'll become a druid?"

"You are and always have been, child. But we have not had a druid of your kind in the living memory of most who currently draw breath across Azuria." Ophelia smiled at her and laid a hand against her heart. "Most, but not all."

❦

THE CREATURE STALKED TOWARD HER OUT OF A THICK fog. Blood dripped from its snarling teeth. In the distance, Mariellen screamed. The werewolf locked her in its gaze. She couldn't help Mariellen, couldn't get past the creature. It lunged forward, teeth bared.

Genevieve woke with a start. Ophelia sat, silhouetted by verdant sunlight, at the entrance to her cave hidden deep inside the Hallowed Wood near the Cienne Mountains. Sariel had carried her here from the waterfall, and she'd spent the last several days recovering from her body's rapid transition in and out of werewolf form.

"Azuria's first humans were lycan," Ophelia observed as though they were in the middle of a conversation rather than speaking for the first time that day. She hummed to herself and trailed the thin fingers of her right hand through the air in front of her. Genevieve had yet to receive a clear answer from the lone druid elder about what she meant when she said Genevieve was a different type of werewolf than those who had destroyed her home and her family.

"What's that, Ophelia?" Genevieve groaned as she sat up. Her entire body still felt swollen, tugged in the wrong directions. Would each transformation be this painful? She rubbed her arms, thankful to find skin beneath her palms once more.

"Werewolves. The first humans in Azuria were were-wolves, though not like you, and not like those you met."

This was a story she hadn't heard before. "Then they were cured?"

Ophelia chuckled. "No, child. They would say that then they were cursed and lost their powers."

"But lycanthropy is the curse." She crouched to avoid hitting her head on the cave ceiling and went to sit beside Ophelia. The old druid had a beautiful home in the forest. Young trees heavy with bright green leaves and springy moss lined the rocky mound that made up Ophelia's settlement. It stood twenty feet above the earth below. A small mountain spring of crisp, clear water waited at the base of the hill, and colorful birds sang in the branches of the ancient trees that surrounded Ophelia's thicket.

"That is how many see things now, though the limitations of their vision condemn them to walk blindly through the world. Forgotten stories, imaginative limitations—these widespread sicknesses have stifled the memory of who we once were. Like their ancestors before them, most have little sense of who they were meant to be. The latent beast within you, child, soothed now to be unbounded by the moon, she remembers what even your parents forgot."

Ophelia delighted to speak in riddles, a fitting characteristic of a woman who clothed herself in robes made of moss. Genevieve had found success thus far in selecting a single thread and tugging on it. If she held fast, she gleaned another morsel of understanding. "So if the first humans lost their powers, what happened?"

"As the planes divided, long ago, the magical weave that holds all in balance began to unravel. The threads were stretched. Humans found room within themselves to create distance from the more ancient races, the older ways of being. They carved away what many would now call the 'animal' within." Ophelia's milky eyes gazed at the world outside. She smiled at the happy chatter of the red-tailed squirrels that clambered from tree to tree.

"Is that what you called the 'beast' within me?" Genevieve asked.

"It is, child, though I would not call you a beast, in whatever form you took, any more than I would Sariel." As if on cue, the silver wolf plodded out of the woods below, his fur bright against the damp moss.

"So I can control it?"

Ophelia tilted her head to the side as a soft breeze fluttered past them and into the cave mouth. "No, Genevieve, you can embrace it."

"Won't I still be contagious? I could infect other people." She closed her eyes against the intruding memory of the beast that had clamped down on her shoulder, the terrifying control that had glinted in his eyes.

"It will fall to you to make your peace within and try and find the primal heart beneath the generations who have pushed it away."

Genevieve sighed. Her conclave had not seen wildness as the ultimate good like Ophelia did. There was union, but with it, harmony, not chaos. "My people did not see the world that way." They'd been innocent, peaceful. A flash of rage caused the hairs on her arms to stand up. A growl erupted from the center of her being, causing her to jump.

The gray-green woman across from her smirked. "You are learning already. Good."

Ophelia was planning something. Deliberately pushing her in certain directions toward an as-yet unknown purpose. How could she balance between herself and an inner werewolf?

The druid reached out for her and laid a hand on Genevieve's shoulder. "There are things in this world we can control and others we cannot. I do not have the power to remove your lycanthropy. There were druids like you, in times long forgotten, who took on the curse to better understand it and what the wolf might tell us about the world. You must follow your own path, but trust the one who paces within you. She also longs to be free."

❦

"But, Sariel, why does she live alone? Why not take up her place within a community? If she had been there to help us, what might have happened?"

The great wolf looked out on the still pond below

Ophelia's cave. The faintest whispers of wind fluttered past them, tracing tendrils of cold across Genevieve's bare feet.

"She was expelled from her last community for beliefs that did not align with theirs. She spoke of coming truths, dangers on the horizon, that they wanted to ignore."

A different voice cut across Sariel's. "Not everyone wants to hear that ancient evils are reawakening."

Genevieve flinched at Ophelia's unexpected arrival.

The druid laid her hand on Genevieve's head and turned her face to the wind. It lifted stray pieces of her rich brown hair, brightened by strands of gray. "The woman you spoke of, who rescued you from the fires of your village, is an old friend of mine."

"Did she tell you I was coming?"

"I foresaw it, but she has also been waiting for this time." Had they both known of the impending attack? Leha had mentioned that some of the elders had foreseen disaster before they left for Andel-ce Hevra. Ophelia continued, "I thought that she would have appeared to us by now. I sense clouds on the horizon—something keeps her from reaching out for you. This is why, child, I believe it may be time for you to go to her."

Ophelia's balance tilted as Genevieve lifted her head up in surprise. "For me to go where?" She'd only just arrived here, and she still had little understanding of her lycanthropy and druidic magic.

"I have the power to restore from the brink of death, child, but this is not a gift you need. The one who will help you is in Caldara. You must board a ship to find her."

"But I can't go all the way to Caldara." No one in her conclave had ever crossed the Infinite Ocean.

"Ah, but you must try. The werewolves there grow restless. We haven't much time."

"But how will I get to Caldara? Why can I not stay with you?"

Sariel's voice interrupted her swirling thoughts. "Ophelia will disguise herself and her home in the coming months while the werewolf tribe is on the move through these mountains. She must be alone to do this. But I will take you to the outskirts of Andel-ce Hevra, and from there you can find a ship that will carry you across the ocean."

"I don't want to face more werewolves," Genevieve whispered. Sariel rubbed his warm, furry head against her hair. "I keep seeing them destroy my family."

Ophelia laid her hand against her heart and bowed her head. "It will never leave you, child. I am sorry."

They sat in silence as the forest wildlife chittered above them, unaware of the wild cascade of emotions at war in the young werewolf druid below. Ophelia raised her head and opened her eyes. She squinted as though she watched events unfolding in the distance. "This evening, child, you will begin your journey to Andel-ce Hevra. You will find the ship that will take you where you need to go."

No. She had sworn to never set foot in that city, among the murderers who had killed her conclave's elders. "Varra, you cannot ask this of me. Choose something else. I will go to Nortelon."

Ophelia's hand clamped down on Genevieve's shoulder. She winced in pain. Her skin had yet to fully heal from the werewolf's bite despite Ophelia's careful ministrations.

"Do not think I send you lightly," she whispered. "I know what they did." Ophelia released her. "Your path is your own. I speak only from what I can see." She brushed the top of Genevieve's hair with her palm and rose slowly to her feet before returning to her cave.

Genevieve balled her hands in her hair. The wolf inside her howled with rage against the situation. If she should enter the city and find those responsible, she might show them what they'd done to her people.

"Genevieve," Sariel's voice called her back. Though he could speak clearly in her mind, she hoped he couldn't hear her thoughts. "Will you trust her? Will you allow me to help you find the way?"

She owed Sariel her life, just as she did Yvayne and Ophelia. Though together they weren't a conclave, they were all she had left. "I'm sorry, Sariel. Yes, I will."

The golden eyes grinned. "Good. I have much to show you, little wolf."

Yvayne cast dried sage and moss into the still waters of her wooden bowl and whispered Ophelia's name. She'd felt the druid's spirit calling to her and knew her mind was ill at ease. The girl had been able to reach her in time, and Yvayne had felt the return of the lycan magic herself.

"Ophelia," she called into the water, disturbing its smooth surface. Though her old friend could perceive the barest outline of objects in her surroundings, Yvayne's face appearing in her seer's bowl would be too subtle for the other druid to see.

"I have been waiting for you, but you have not appeared." Ophelia's expression was troubled.

"I told you, I must stay here. Mara may need my help.

And Iellieth, the one I spoke to you about, is still in grave danger."

"It is time for Genevieve to move on. I am sending her to a ship."

Yvayne swore under her breath. "Are you sending her to me?" She leaned closer to the water's surface to try to read Ophelia's murky expression. Lucien's forces were better prepared and far more numerous than their intelligence had led them to believe. It was foolish for those in positions of relative safety to deliberately step toward danger.

"In a way." Her old friend smiled.

"What did you see? Why will you not train her yourself?"

"You know that I no longer practice that part of our beliefs."

Yvayne suppressed a sigh of frustration. "You initiated that girl in a few moments and revived lycan magic into the world. Don't pretend that you limit yourself and what you can do."

Ophelia's smile rippled in the waters of her bowl. "Why do you remain in hiding, Yvayne?"

"Lucien found Fhaona within days of her arriving outside my door. She'd been safely in hiding or on the run for years before then. I cannot believe that it was a coincidence." Sadness and anger tugged her back and forth. How did Ophelia so quickly have this effect on her?

"Nor will you believe that it was her time."

Ophelia had whispered the words, yet they grated nonetheless. Yvayne refused to place her hope in fate the way Ophelia insisted on trusting it. When had it worked in their favor before? "No, Ophelia, I cannot."

The druid in the bowl closed her eyes and laid her

fingers against her temples. "Genevieve will not make it to you, Yvayne. At least not for some time."

"Are you sending her to her death?" Yvayne's sudden fury nearly pulled her through the enchanted waters to the other side where she could confront Ophelia face-to-face.

"No!" Her friend looked shocked at the accusation. "She will travel with Sariel. The road is being laid out before her."

So Ophelia had seen a path for Genevieve, one that led toward Yvayne but veered away before the young druid reached her. She was a guiding star, not the destination. "Ophelia, who are you sending her to?"

The gray-green skin wrinkled once again as Ophelia smiled, pleased with her mystery. "That, we shall have to see." Her reflection faded away from the water's surface, and Yvayne was left with her own sepia skin and pale purple eyes staring back at her. The image grinned. In spite of their world teetering on the brink, Ophelia remained true to who she had always been. Perhaps the next time they spoke, she might unveil her prophetic plan.

CHAPTER 19

The town of Trudid was quite small, and its crowded, narrow streets were difficult to navigate amid the townspeople going about midday errands and visits. Iellieth took in as much of the commerce as she could, delighted with the rare opportunity to see what most would consider to be commonplace interactions: people purchasing candles and soaps, haggling over fresh produce, or ordering horseshoes from the blacksmith.

"Are you sure this is the right place, lady?"

"What do you mean? We passed the sign on the way in, marking the town."

Marcon scowled as a horse clomped past. "Not even separate lanes for equine and foot travelers."

"What were you expecting?"

"Some semblance of civilization, for one." He shook his head at a woman offering glass jar candles and scanned a row of plain wooden buildings. "Perhaps a more developed location than that of the druids."

"I like the Vagarveil Wood."

"It's beautiful," he said quickly. "I enjoy it too. But they don't pretend to be a planned town when they're actually —" Marcon stopped short when he observed a shopkeeper leaning in a doorway nearby, waiting to hear the truth about his small town.

"Actually a quaint and lovely location," Iellieth finished for him. She took his elbow and led him down a side street to the left, which, she hoped, would take them toward the center of town. Finally, after a roundabout between a small dry goods store and another business she thought sold parchment but seemed to hold more quills than anything else, they emerged into the dusty, bustling town center. Across the square, two stone buildings dominated the vista, standing out from the wood and clay structures of the rest of Trudid. On the left, a swinging black sign with gold type read THE LAUGHING GIANT beside a picture of a large hand clasping a mug of ale.

The nearer side of the square held a post booth and a clothier with a green wooden sign affixed to the outside simply labeled COBBLER & TAILOR.

"Let's start there," Iellieth said.

Marcon was hesitant, searching the town square.

"What are you looking for?"

"What is Linolynn like compared to this?"

She laughed. "Much larger, though I'm going to be careful to not get your hopes up about it. Hadvar would suit you much better."

"The northern nation that you don't like, and which may or may not be at war with your country?"

Iellieth shivered. She tried to keep the conflict in the back of her mind as much as possible till they had confirmation from a second source.

"My apologies, lady." He bent to look more closely in

her eyes. "I didn't mean to worry you. So, first, supplies, and then the mayor?"

"And some fresh food," she added. "I can't eat another dried meal till at least tomorrow."

He chuckled. "Our road provisions are much less delicious than Mara's soups and fresh breads."

Their boots crunched on the light gravel as they crossed the square. The dense fabrics on display inside the shop absorbed and muffled the sounds of the town, providing an immediate sense of peace and a welcome break from the sun.

Iellieth blinked in the interior's dim light and waited for her eyes to adjust as the bell on the door tinkled shut behind them. An elderly tailor helped them to find appropriate clothing, boots, and a cloak for Marcon. The new clothes and the repairs to her own armor depleted the store of coins she'd been meticulously saving for two years, but she did her best to mask this concern from Marcon. He had modeled haggling with the tailor, shaking his head before she could accept full price and explaining afterward how to go about negotiating a fair exchange instead.

The tailor directed them to the shop of a nearby blacksmith, Sanya. Entering the shop, Iellieth was momentarily startled by her young age, no more than sixteen years, but recovered quickly. Looking around at the wares on display, she saw that any soldier in Linolynn would have been glad to bear her gear.

"So you're here to see the mayor?" Sanya asked after they had discussed the specifics of a chain mail shirt for Marcon. "Mighty testy, him."

"We heard rumors about that. Do you know what he's upset about?"

"Well, there's a lot of unrest in the town, as I'm sure

you've seen or will discover soon enough. I'd say the chief reason is because his daughter is missing."

"His daughter?" Mara hadn't mentioned anything of the sort when they left.

"Aye, a few days ago. He said she's kidnapped, but we all know she's run off with a lover." Sanya held one of her ready-made shirts of mail against Marcon's back to see if it might fit. She shook her head and muttered about his broad shoulders.

"Then why does he believe something else has happened?" Marcon asked as she returned it to the pile and searched for another.

"I think he's embarrassed." She held up another and eyed Marcon from across the room. Sanya shrugged. "Doesn't want sweet Nil'sea's reputation to be muddied, though he's the only one who would care."

"And why is that?" Iellieth glanced between Marcon and Sanya, not sure if she'd missed something.

"Well, it's his daughter, isn't it? I'm sure he's had her matched up with some young merchant since she was a few years old, when his wife died, maybe even before. He's got the town guard combing the forest trying to find her."

"No one else believes she's missing?" Marcon asked again, his voice raised slightly. The town's lack of concern for the possibly missing girl was upsetting him.

Sanya noticed his distress too and shook her head. "She's been drifting place to place all dreamy-eyed for weeks." She handed him the second shirt to try. "Just as likely she's hurt her father's pride as that she's been kidnapped with no sign of a struggle or problem."

The hauberk fit Marcon's shoulders perfectly, though it was too wide around the waist.

Sanya helped him out of the shirt. "I can make some

adjustments for you by tomorrow. If you're ever in the market for true custom work, I'll need more time."

She jotted down a few measurements and took half the payment for her labor. She added the coins to a pouch beneath the counter and nodded her thanks. "Listen," she said, "I'm close with a few of the guards in town. They keep us safe, and I do the same for them at a good price. But if you do get through to speak with the mayor, I'd pretend not to know about his daughter. He's not in a spot to handle it well, and it won't predispose him to whatever else you're wanting."

❦

THE TOWN'S STREETS HAD CALMED IN THE HOURS THEY spent placing orders with the tailor, cobbler, and blacksmith to be picked up the next day. Back in the square, the Laughing Giant, the only tavern Marcon had been willing to name as such, had emptied its lunchtime visitors. Through its large glass windows, they could see that only a few patrons remained, two playing cards at a back table and three others scattered along the bar.

Marcon opened the heavy wooden door for her and stood in the doorframe to observe the townsfolk inside. Iellieth went to find a table for the two of them opposite the bar while Marcon approached the young man behind the counter. Sunlight bathed the front half of the tavern; the scuffed wooden floors there were paler than those at the back, and Iellieth wanted to rest in the shade. After days spent in the cool, fresh air of the forest, the dust and sunshine of Trudid drained her.

She pulled back her barstool, shoulders drawing up at the screech it made against the uneven wood beneath.

Marcon leaned over the bar and spoke with a young man who filled two tankards and a pitcher of water before he handed them over the bar.

"Here you are, my lady," Marcon said as he laid them on the table. "Our energetic new friend is very excited to bring you blackberries and freshly cleaned cups."

"A new friend already?" She grinned.

"This one's not my fault. But, as he's predisposed to 'the pretty redhead' already, why don't you ask him about the mayor? With so few proper taverns in this place, he's bound to be a good source of information." Marcon settled onto his stool and tipped his glass to her.

The young man brought over a simple lunch of fruit, bread, and cheese, and a new glass tankard for Marcon. "Here you fine folks are. Nice to see you this afternoon. If I may be so bold, what is it that's brought new and"—he glanced at Marcon's hands as the runes shifted—"interesting visitors to town?"

"We've heard so much about how lovely Trudid is." Iellieth decided to start with flattery this time instead of accusations.

"About Trudid? That's a surprise." He pulled out the table's third stool and took a seat beside her.

"Why, yes—do you not find it lovely?" She glanced at Marcon to support her before she returned her attention to their bartender.

"Uh, yes, a truly nice place," Marcon said.

"Well, that is welcome news—the powers that be will be pleased. They've been trying to increase trade here, as well as visitors"—he raised his eyebrows at her—"which, if they're much like you, would be welcome to me." He grew bright red as he said this but didn't look away. "I'm Shem, by the way."

Marcon turned further away from her, obviously amused by the situation he'd created. "A pleasure to meet you, Shem. I'm Iellieth, and this is Marcon. Increasing commerce, that would certainly be nice for business. Is this your bar?"

It seemed unlikely this was the case given his age, but asking was the most polite option available. What would Mamaun say in this situation?

The boy emitted a hoarse, dry laugh in response. "Goodness, no, though that would be swell, wouldn't it? I take care of the floor. We're rather slow at the moment"— he indicated the three patrons at the bar, one of whom swayed on his wobbly stool—"so my boss stepped out to get some things before the evening crowd arrives. You folks have timed your meal well."

"Very good luck for us. I'm so curious, though, about this vision for changing the town. Who's behind that idea and moving things forward?" Iellieth leaned a few inches closer toward the bartender.

"I'm not entirely sure, to be honest. The mayor for one. But," he said, lowering his voice, "things have been rather off with him lately. I'm sure you heard about his daughter."

"We did pick up a rumor or two." Iellieth matched his whisper.

"Well, he's been quite stormy about town. Anybody can see that. Most days he stays locked in his office, though. He used to frequent the pub a few times a week, 'specially at lunch, but not so much anymore."

"We heard his daughter had been kidnapped. Is that true?" Sanya's account seemed credible, but she also guessed that the blacksmith and Shem moved in different circles.

"Not sure as I can say. I know the guards are searching for her, have been for a few days. I seen the mayor snap at a few people leaving the market—one poor lady didn't see him. Used to be he would have helped her 'stead of yelling."

"That does sound like an extreme shift." Was it equally possible that the girl was missing as that she had run away? His reaction fit either case.

The wooden door at the back of the tavern swung open, and a wide man with a dense black beard stomped inside with several bags. He looked from the bar to their table. "Shem," he barked when he found the boy happily sitting with two patrons while others sat in front of empty mugs.

Shem scrambled off his stool. "I must go." He dodged one of the other patrons on his way back to the bar.

Marcon watched the exchange between the owner and his bartender with a bemused expression on his face. "What's so funny?" Iellieth asked.

He turned back to her, shoulders relaxed. "Nothing, lady. He was not very subtle, is all."

A loud crash sounded from the kitchen as several bowls clattered to the floor. He grinned and shook his head. "Well, shall we go and attempt to speak with the mayor? I'd like to have a better idea of his daughter's disappearance."

"Yes." She hopped off her stool and scooted it carefully beneath the table. "I hope what Sanya said is true, that his daughter ran away."

"As do I, lady." Despite his lightness over lunch, she could tell he was still bothered by the other possibility. Marcon gestured for her to lead the way.

THE LATE AFTERNOON SUN CAST THE TOWN SQUARE IN A beautiful orange glow. A passerby directed them to the building that housed the mayor's office.

"Do you think we're too late?" Marcon asked. The glass windows that faced the square were dark and the door shut.

"Maybe they're in the back?" The front receiving area was narrow, and the mayor and his employees might have remained within the rear portion of the building on slower days.

Marcon approached the door and knocked three times with the side of his fist. The sound reverberated across the square. He stepped back beside Iellieth and waited. After several moments' pause, slow footsteps heel-toed across the wooden floors, and the door creaked open.

A thin, pinch-faced man stood behind the door and examined them, his nose cocked haughtily in the air. "Might I help you?" From the sound, his voice came directly from his nasal passages.

"Yes, thank you," Iellieth said. "We were hoping for an audience with the mayor."

"I am afraid that is quite impossible."

"Then might we schedule an appointment with him for tomorrow?"

"He is a very busy man. What is it that's so urgent?"

Iellieth suppressed a sigh of irritation and drew herself up in her best impression of Duchess Doromir, a kind but impatient older noblewoman. "How can we be sure that the matter concerns you?"

The man pursed his thin lips even tighter. "Very well." He pushed the door open another fraction. Marcon caught the edge and pulled it fully open. The room, lit only by a few small candles, was hardly lighter inside than it looked from outside.

The assistant settled himself behind a petite, gilded desk in a high-backed wooden chair. He opened a large tome and flipped through the pages till he arrived at the present date. Though he tried to conceal it with his arm, each day for the next week was entirely blank. Despite this, he slowly traced each column with his forefinger, moving on to the next page after his perusal was complete.

"Might I ask your name, sir? I apologize that we did not enquire it earlier." Iellieth stood behind one of the chairs positioned in front of the lavish desk and waited for him to ask her to be seated.

"Philip Eaustus, First Magistrate. And you are?" He returned to his perusal of the ledger.

"Lilith, and this is my associate, Marcon."

"Lilith. A curious name."

She simply smiled. *Saying less means more*—the constant refrain of her dim-witted manners tutor popped into her head.

"I suppose"—Philip glanced at her purse—"we might be able to squeeze you in tomorrow afternoon. These things do take at least a full day to be worked in." He poised his pen over the ledger.

Don't respond to his simpering look, Iellieth told herself. Just hand over some coins. How much would a magister in a small town expect for their bribe? She removed a single gold piece from her purse and placed it on the desk.

Philip's sideways smile widened unpleasantly, and he swept the coin off the desk and into a pouch at his side. She'd offered too much. Philip scrawled *Lilit & Marco* in an angular hand and glanced up at her to see if she would correct the error. She didn't react.

Iellieth nodded to Philip and rose, allowing Marcon to hold the door for her. "We'll let you get back to work," he said.

Marcon shut the door decidedly behind him so they wouldn't have to hear Philip's response. Once they were across the square and had turned out of sight of the narrow stone structure, he stopped. "Is that a common occurrence in this time? I will not stand for bribes and cheats."

"That's not part of my general experience, but perhaps it is for Trudid. Mara did suggest we should expect something along those lines." He continued to scowl. "We need to be here till tomorrow anyway to pick up our things. Come, let's see if they have a room back at the tavern, and I can send a note to Katarina and Scad and ask about your friend and the war."

Marcon glanced back over his shoulder at the mayor's office before he followed Iellieth across the square. "We could see if we overhear anything else regarding the mayor's daughter and what's going on in Linolynn while we're there," he said as he caught up to her.

"Precisely." She smiled. Aside from her time with the druids, Iellieth couldn't think of an evening she'd looked forward to more in recent years. The tavern would be full of people looking to relax after a day of work and spend time with their friends and acquaintances. There would be questions about why she and Marcon were traveling through Trudid, but the town was near enough to Linolynn and Red's Cross for them to be accustomed to visitors.

If they kept cards at the Laughing Giant, or if one of the people in town brought their own, she might be able to play a game of aluette and teach Marcon. Or she could practice the tarock game Persephonie had taught her. She'd lost each round before and meant to improve before playing with her friend again.

Laughter leaked out of the warmly lit pub as they approached. She'd write her message to Katarina first and then go downstairs for the evening. It would be nice to let her friend know she was alright. She hoped news of her mis-transmigration hadn't reached Katarina till the king and court returned from Hadvar so Katarina wouldn't have been worried about Iellieth for very long.

CHAPTER 20

Shem led them to a comfortable room on the second floor with a view of the street behind and a small residential area off of the town square.

Iellieth opened the window and drew out her raven figurine and placed it on the side table. Next, she withdrew parchment, ink, and quill from her bag. The room had two narrow beds, a chair at the end of each, and a small table.

"You're writing to the scholar you studied with, Katarina?" Marcon asked. He carried one of the chairs to the table for her and began inspecting the room.

"Yes, she's the most likely one I can think of who may be able to help you. And I would like for her to know I'm alright." Iellieth sat at the table and rocked back and forth between the chair's wobbly legs before she prepared her quill.

Marcon's voice rose from beneath the second bed. "I am glad you have someone you can trust, lady. But she's never said anything to you about the War of the Champions, as Mara calls it?"

Iellieth shook her head. "No, but I suspect there's much I don't know about her. She lived in many different places in Caldara with her parents, who were researchers and scholars, before she came to Io Keep. We've always had plenty to talk about. Perhaps it simply didn't come up."

"Perhaps." He rose from his search and sat on the further bed, reclined against the headboard. When he thought she wasn't watching, he drew his arm to his face and began to study the markings there. She forced herself to focus on the blank paper in front of her.

My dearest Katarina,

I hope this finds you well. My discovery in a new research area has taken me to the northern reaches of the Stormside Forest, of all places. I feel like I'm among druids and the rumored saudad here in these woods, though my primary site is closer to Trudid.

I heard the strangest rumor on my journey, that Linolynn had declared war on Hadvar rather than reaffirming their treaties and partnership as usually happens at the Festival of Renewal. Do you know what's happened?

My research has revealed a fascinating old story about champions of the titans; one I thought you might find of particular interest was called Quindythias. Have you come across any folk tales about him in your research?

The bird, Edvard, will bring your message back to me, either by beak or by ankle.

Give my best to my friend who I've left with you. And remember, if he's visiting you more often than you might like, that he means well.

Please write as soon as you can, and I shall do the same.

Arrevei,

— Lilith

Marcon stood and glanced down at her letter as she waited for the ink to dry. "Do you often go by Lilith when you're working in secret?"

"I am not often working in secret, but Katarina and I had the name planned should I ever need it. I told her I would write to her, when I tried to leave before. I hope she'll recognize the name, but she knows my hand as well as her own. So long as the duke doesn't see it first, we'll be fine."

Horses clipped through the courtyard, their riders clad in heavy metal armor. "Lady," Marcon hissed as he glanced out the window, "soldiers."

"What?" She sprang up and ducked beside him to see. There were four, with the two in front each bearing a standard. One was the golden eagle on a periwinkle cloth of the Arontis family line and the other, the black rose on silver, the Amastacia crest. Iellieth froze.

"That's them, isn't it? The symbol from your ring."

Iellieth nodded. Her fingernails pressed into her palms. She had gotten so close. But she might as well have achieved nothing.

Marcon wrapped an arm around her shoulder and pulled her away from the window. The soldiers dismounted and went around back to the stables. Shem spoke with them excitedly, the nervousness plain in his voice. They mostly ignored him.

Her hands were shaking. Marcon took hold of both her arms and sat her on the bed, kneeling in front of her. "You haven't said your name to anyone here, have you?"

"No. Not here. I did to Turdoch." The blood drained from her face. "And to Shem."

Marcon's eyes narrowed. "I doubt they'll have been to the logging camp first looking for you. And there are other reasons they might be here. We don't know yet. But I promised, you're not going back to that castle unless you decide to. I'll speak to Shem."

Iellieth nodded, but she barely heard him. What would her stepfather say if she were found alone in the company of a strange man and escorted back to Io Keep by four soldiers?

He'd hush it up and still make her marry Lord Stravinske.

"Lady!" The edge to Marcon's voice said he'd called her a few times. "Have you finished your letter?"

"I have."

"Let's send it to Katarina, and then we can find out what's going on and if we need to leave town tonight or not."

Iellieth picked up the raven from the small worn nightstand. She'd had such modest plans for the evening. How did the duke's shadow continually loom so large behind her? Iellieth shook her head, returning to the task at hand. "There's twine in my bag."

Marcon withdrew it and cut off a short piece while she rolled and sealed the letter.

"Nor corveau," Iellieth whispered. The figurine in her hand shook, and silver snow trickled down onto her palm. Wind whistled across the room with tiny sparks of green energy as the raven grew in size and turned a beady black eye to her.

Marcon handed her the letter, and she tied it to the bird's ankle. "You're looking for Katarina Starsend, a scholar in Io Keep, southwest of here, near the ocean, in the castle's western wing. She has dark brown skin, chestnut-hued eyes, and long blonde braids." The bird croaked, and Iellieth jumped.

"Do you think that means it understood?" Marcon eyed it cautiously, waiting for it to repeat the guttural call.

"It seemed that way, but I am not certain."

"Edvard, do you know who you're looking for?" The bird croaked again. "I will take that as a yes then. Alright. *Commen*." Edvard's face took on a trance-like expression, and his eyes widened. "Katarina, I mis-trans-migrated, but I'm alright. Please let me know what's going on and how you and Scad are. Don't tell my family." Edvard's head twitched, and he resumed staring at her with one eye. She walked over to the window, and he hopped onto the sill. He croaked once more and flew out into the twilight.

Looking down into the yard, Iellieth saw the soldiers leave the stable and follow Shem into the tavern. "You should go find out what they're doing," Iellieth whispered.

"Are you going to stay up here?"

"At least until we know if they're looking for me."

"I'll see what I can uncover." Marcon slipped out of the door and made his way downstairs.

Iellieth paced in his absence. She'd done what she could to alert Katarina that she was alright and begun an inquiry to learn the greater stakes. Maybe she should have sent the raven to Mara and asked for help with the soldiers. But they wouldn't be able to send anyone, especially so quickly. She couldn't return to the conclave without being able to tell them she'd saved the forest. Her bid for a new home would be over before it had begun.

There was a soft knock against their door. Iellieth ducked into a corner, and the door slid open. "Lady," Marcon called for her softly.

Hiding in the corner felt silly now. How would that have protected her from being dragged back to Io Keep?

"It seems they're here to ask Flendon about the lumber."

"So they're not looking for me?"

Marcon pulled in his lower lip and glanced out the window. "The one in the black doublet did ask if anyone had seen a young noblewoman in the area."

"Then what happened?" She shivered. They could be coming upstairs any moment.

"Shem looked at me, and I said I'd been traveling nearby and hadn't seen anyone."

"And they believed you?"

"Shem helped. 'They're always in fancy dresses, aren't they?'" Marcon perfectly imitated Shem's drawl, though at a much lower range, and Iellieth laughed. "You're safe, lady. They don't think you're here."

"Thank you." She relaxed her shoulders and took the first deep breath she'd had in over an hour. Marcon gestured to a bottle of wine and two glasses he'd procured from downstairs. "They didn't ask about you taking two cups?"

"I grabbed the second one from behind the bar when they weren't looking. It's how Quindythias would have handled the situation." Marcon grinned.

"He sounds like an interesting person to know." Scad would have done something similar. "Do you miss him a great deal?"

"I do, lady. I'm anxious to hear if your friend knows anything of him." He poured two glasses of wine and handed one to her.

"As am I. The soldiers downstairs, accompanied by one on a mission for the duke—does that show that he has a hand in the war? Trying to knock out two tasks at once by checking on the ordered lumber and searching for me?" She twisted a strand of hair between her fingers. What was she missing about the war? What could have caused it?

"I'm not sure, lady." Marcon crossed to the window in three paces and looked at the ground directly below before turning his gaze to the stables. She hadn't thought of making sure no one was listening outside.

Iellieth followed suit and went to the door, glancing down the empty hall before securing it more firmly. "He is opportunistic. And sending out a party of soldiers with the sole mission of finding me would risk a scandal or smear on the Amastacia name." She scowled. He would only pursue war if it were profitable, and she couldn't conceive of a way that attacking Hadvar would serve to enrich the kingdom's coffers and his own.

Iellieth crossed her arms over her waist and continued pacing. "We'll need to be cautious when we speak to Flendon as well. If he'll even still hear us." Mara's plan hinged on Iellieth being able to reveal who she was in hopes of changing the mayor's mind. She wanted to help the druids, but she couldn't dramatically reveal her true identity with Linolynnian soldiers waiting just outside to return her to her stepfather's clutches.

Marcon drained his cup and refilled it from the pitcher before he sat at the end of the bed. She stopped pacing when she realized he was watching her with concern. "As we're stuck up here till our shiny friends turn in for the night, lady, can you tell me more about your amulet? What you know about it at least?"

It was understandable for him to be curious. She held the pendant between her thumb and first two fingers, rotating it back and forth. "I told you before that it was my father's, left with Mamaun when they were separated."

"Yes, that you did." He smiled at her as she took a seat across from him. "I've been thinking about it a great deal on our travels and Mara's suggestion that it's somehow connected to these runes." He rubbed the pale tattoos along his forearm, searching for their secret. "Did you have any idea, before you found me, that it was magical? Has it done anything strange before?"

Iellieth stared at the ruby and the golden bands as she had on so many countless occasions for the last seventeen years. Her voice was soft when she spoke. "No, it's just been a normal necklace." She bit her lip and set it back against her chest. "When I was little, I used to pretend that my father could hear me through it. That he would be able to tell if things were really bad, and he would come to get me." She rubbed the corners of her eyes.

"Mamaun grew frustrated with me for wearing it to a ball or grand event when it didn't go with the gown she had picked out for me to wear, especially when we were among the Hadvarian court." Countless arguments about more appropriate adornments for one of their standing, the offer of elaborate necklaces and earrings laden with amethysts, emeralds, and pearls that better complemented whichever evening gown her mother had selected for the occasion.

"And why did you continue to wear it?" Marcon leaned forward and rested his elbows on his knees.

Iellieth sighed and returned her gaze to the diamond-studded sapphire of the night sky. "It made me feel closer to him. In the back of my mind, I hoped that if I wore it, and he saw me, he would know that I was his daughter."

How many elves had she studied at these events, desperate for a sign of recognition?

"But he never came to any events where you saw him?"

She shook her head and met his eyes.

Marcon smiled sadly, understanding. "He doesn't know about you, does he?"

No one had ever asked her so directly before. "I don't think so," she whispered. It was a question that had often burned in her heart. "Why do you ask?" She tried to keep her voice even.

Marcon's expression was gentle as he answered her. "Lady, if he had known, don't you think he would have tried to communicate with you?"

Iellieth blinked away the tears that swam in her eyes. The further apart she and her mother grew, the more the unknown answer to this question mattered. "I really want to believe that he would have." She could barely speak above a whisper. "It's something I've wondered about for a long time." Iellieth picked up the amulet again, tracing the hourglass. "The more . . . alone I felt, especially as I grew older, the more I wanted to be able to find him some day. I thought I'd sail to the Realms and search for him. But . . ." Had she ever been able to voice this aloud? Teodric had known how she felt, but she'd never said it. "But if he knew, and he didn't want me . . ." Iellieth shook her head and set down her glass of wine.

"What would it take for you to go to the Realms?"

She sniffed and wiped her eyes clear again. "I thought you were trying to find out what Alessandra is doing?"

Marcon lowered his head to stare at his boots before he met her eyes once more, the blue burning bright. "I am, lady. But tracing her movements, in my limited experience for this particular type of activity, is easier with long-lived cultures than it is with humans, especially closed-off humans who dispel diplomats." He winked, trying to lighten her spirits.

She smiled. "The Blazing Battalion wasn't usually delving into historical records, then?"

"Not often, no. Quindythias did, on occasion. And being an elf himself, perhaps he could provide additional assistance."

"I didn't realize your friend was an elf." Iellieth sat up straighter, even more excited to try to find this second ancient being. If only Marcon's runes contained clues for the other hiding places for champions.

She rose and stepped closer to him and took hold of his arm. The runes faded beneath her touch and became more difficult to read. "I wanted to see them again, to see if they looked familiar, but I can't make them out now."

"Wait," Marcon said. Eyebrows knitted together, he looked closely at her. "Do something for me, lady. Let go, and take a step back."

"I-I'm sorry," she said, dropping his arm and moving away. She hadn't meant anything by looking at the runes. He had studied them earlier.

"No, that's not what I meant." His brow creased further. "Watch. They move in response to you."

Iellieth stepped closer again, and the runes receded. When she touched Marcon's arm, they faded away entirely from the circle around her fingertip. "What does that mean?"

"What if you aren't wearing your amulet?"

"Are you sure you want to test it that way?" The sight of him out of breath, in pain, after he'd gone too far from the amulet's aura flared in her memory.

"It will be alright. Why don't you set it over there"—he

pointed at the table where Edvard had been—"and come back here to me." He winced the moment she took her necklace off, and the runes glared out across the entire surface of his skin.

Marcon held his jaw clamped shut as she walked closer. The runes faded slightly, but they remained more visible than they had.

"And what if you go toward the amulet?" Iellieth asked. "I'll stay here."

He crossed the room. "A similar effect, lady. It's better, but only just."

She followed him and placed the amulet back around her neck. Marcon let out a sigh of relief. Iellieth laid her hand on his arm. "I wish I'd thought of it before, but we could have sent some of the runes to Katarina to see if she recognizes any of them. Perhaps you could write some out for me? We'll record them and see?"

He rubbed his skin as the redness faded. "An excellent idea, lady. That will make it easier for you to look them over as well. They change, but I haven't yet been able to work out a pattern in the scripts. But Mara's intuition was right—it's connected to you."

Iellieth gave him a small smile and went to retrieve more parchment from her bag and the novel she'd brought with her, *Atala Ciel*, by one of her favorite Elvish authors. She couldn't focus on the familiar narrative, even as Atala began her journey through time, unbeknownst to her earliest selves.

Iellieth couldn't quiet the questions that interrupted the author's words. If she and the amulet were bound to Marcon's condition, where did that leave her? Would he be willing to stay with Mara as well?

THE NEXT DAY, THEY WAITED UNTIL THE SOLDIERS HAD left the tavern before they braved the streets of Trudid to claim Iellieth's repaired leathers and the new clothes purchased for Marcon the day before. He smiled serenely after he slipped into the chain mail shirt Sanya had adjusted to his specifications.

"Let's see if Mayor Flendon is ready for his afternoon appointments," he suggested, walking even taller today through the town's crowded roads.

"His aide is going to be upset if we show up now. Do you think he let the soldiers in?" Were they visiting Trudid because shipments weren't coming quickly enough? Iellieth shuddered at the memory of the trees' pain beneath the axes.

"I'm not sure he would have felt as though he had a choice." Marcon inclined his head toward the town square, and she followed behind him. They first checked to see that the stables behind the Laughing Giant were empty before approaching the mayor's office. The horses and their riders had left.

Further promising signs awaited them at the mayor's office. Unlike yesterday, the door to the front room was open, and they walked in to find Philip behind his desk once more.

"We've arrived for our meeting with the mayor," Iellieth said.

Philip studied Marcon closely. The aide looked less confident, and his demeanor was less haughty than it had been. A light glowed beneath the nearest door, and Iellieth could hear heavy footsteps pacing back and forth.

"You're early," he said, dismissing them.

"We've heard rumors about his daughter and wanted to see if we might be able to help." Iellieth raised her voice so that the person pacing in the other room could hear her. Sanya had suggested they not bring up the subject, but she didn't want to wait another day in Trudid at the assistant's whim. They needed to win over the mayor as quickly as possible. The footsteps stopped.

Philip's eyes narrowed. "And what is it you would be able to do?"

The door swung open, and a thin, middle-aged man with overgrown stubble leaned out of the frame. "Philip, show these visitors into my rooms."

The sallow aide sprang to his feet. "Yes, of course, sir." The door swung shut, and Philip glared back at them. "Follow me, please."

He showed them into a nicely furnished meeting room with a long wooden table and sideboard. Philip prepared three glasses of wine, and the man they'd seen before walked heavily into the room. He gestured at their chairs so they might be seated.

"I'm Mayor Flendon." He sighed and slumped in his chair and pushed back his gray-streaked brown hair. "Tell me, what is it you wish to speak with me about? You mentioned my daughter."

"I did, sir. We wanted to inquire after what had happened to her." Iellieth smiled politely. They'd need to proceed delicately to gain his trust.

"And why should I disclose that to you?"

She nodded toward Marcon. "We thought we might be of assistance in helping to recover her."

"Newcomers to my town, barely here a day, have heard rumors of my kidnapped daughter and have come to help rescue her?" The mayor shook his head. "Do you not think

I have every man in my employ searching the woods for her and have for the past week?"

"We've no doubt of your concern, Mayor Flendon," Iellieth said, "but we have a"—what was a good term for it?—"special relationship with the forest and thought we could lend an extra pair of eyes."

"Special relationship with the forest?" He spoke as though such a thing were disgusting as well as impossible. "Why is it you're in Trudid, Miss . . ."

Iellieth took a deep breath. This was the moment. "Amastacia. Lady Iellieth Amastacia." Marcon's fist tightened beside her. She raised an eyebrow at the mayor. *Your move.*

If he didn't believe her, he might still be interested in what they could do to find his daughter, and she would have an opening to present the druids' case. If he did believe her, his reaction would most likely split in one of two ways. As armed soldiers had arrived from the castle instead of a simple messenger, it seemed someone in the castle wished to assert their power to intimidate the mayor, an experience, from what she'd seen, that men accustomed to wielding power over others particularly despised. By knowing who she was, he would now have leverage over her stepfather to use to his own benefit. So long as he perceived her revelation of her identity as a sign of alliance, he might return the favor by more openly hearing the druids' requests.

On the other hand, she and Marcon risked what had been on the line all along—Flendon would inform the soldiers who she was, and they would escort her back to Io Keep. However, if Flendon would agree to delay his report in exchange for the druids' assistance locating his daughter, she and Marcon could buy the time they needed to leave Trudid and the Vagarveil Wood.

Flendon stared at her closely. "Lady Iellieth Amastacia?" He tilted his head as though waiting for her to reveal that she was joking.

"That's correct." Iellieth nodded once. Nervous energy pulsed along her body.

"The missing noblewoman from Linolynn?"

So they had been looking for her. "Yes, sir."

"Hah." Flendon laughed, in short bursts at first, which then escalated into a full belly laugh.

Iellieth glanced at Marcon. What should they do in the face of this man's sudden lunacy? Had the pressure of his missing daughter and the court's demands finally proved to be too much?

Flendon gripped the arms of his chair and leaned forward, smiling widely. "Why, how convenient for me that the missing noblewoman I was questioned about this very morning was in my midst the entire time. So now, not only am I behind schedule in fulfilling my duty to the king, I've also to send word back to the soldiers that the woman they're searching for is here in front of me. My own daughter, however, is of no import to them." He waved his hand to the side.

"I know that there are several events coinciding at one time—" Iellieth began.

His eyes shot back to hers. "Do you recognize that, now? Who are you, really?" Flendon studied her once more.

"Sir, I've just told you." Iellieth rubbed her thumbs over her fingers, trying to calm her nerves. If he would only say what he planned to do next, she and Marcon could enact one of their contingency plans.

Flendon threw his hands in the air in irritated surrender. "Fine. *Lady* Amastacia, why did you originally set foot in my city?"

"We are here on behalf of the druids, of the Vagarveil Wood. They've offered me sanctuary and, in return, I am here to speak with you about the felling of the forest."

The mayor shook his head, agitated. "I've already spoken with several of them, a mismatched collection of hermits, elves, and half-bloods"—Marcon stiffened beside her—"bidding me to think of the future with no appreciation for the position I'm in, as though that is not already a constant weight on my shoulders."

"We're not trying to negate the pressure you're under. I can speak with my stepfather—"

"Can you now, Lady Amastacia? You have some immediate sway to dismiss the goons they sent to my door to reprimand me for inadequate production?" He crumpled one of the papers on his desk in his fist and waved it in front of her. "While you're at it, in this great hour of need, have you the ability to reject Arontis's order that I sacrifice my citizens in this sudden, asinine war that he's declared?"

Iellieth sat back, frightened by his rising anger. "I-I don't know that I can tell the soldiers not to come back, but if the court only understood that the long-term survival of the forest is at risk, along with the livelihoods of the citizens of Trudid and those who make the forest their home? I'm sure they could be persuaded—"

"The time is long past that the well-being of those in Trudid has been a concern of the royal court," Mayor Flendon replied, his voice cold.

Iellieth shuddered as the chilling realization seeped through her. He was right. She'd never heard anything of the people of Trudid, only the raw materials they supplied. The residents they had met—even those with seemingly successful businesses, like Sanya and the tailor—wore threadbare clothing. They looked the way she'd overheard other noblewomen and their ladies' maids describe the farmers coming in and out of the Earth Ward.

"Maybe we can change that," she said softly. The hopelessness of the task dug in its claws. This would be a larger shift than halting the tree-cutting and stopping the war. The duke didn't listen to her about decisions for her own life. Why would he care what she thought of this small town? "If we sent word to Linolynn—"

Flendon laughed at her again and shook his head. "Unlikely."

Iellieth's shoulders tensed.

The mayor's expression twisted into a derisive smirk. "You claim to be the bastard daughter of a wealthy noble house hundreds of leagues from here? Why should I believe it? Because you wear a silver ring with a black rose and have long red hair?" Flendon balled the crumpled paper in his hand and slammed it onto the desk. "Don't think I'm unaware of your scheme. You and the soldiers likely have a division of the reward worked out." Flendon wagged his finger at her and leaned back in his chair.

"Know this, first"—he held up the accusatory finger— "that they'll cheat you out of your share. And second"—his middle finger joined the pointer—"I have a writ from the king himself and a duty to perform. Whoever you are, girl, you've no power here. I'll bear no more insults today. You may go." He swept his hand at her like he was removing dirt from the air.

Iellieth sat, rooted to her chair. That couldn't be it. If she could only convince him to listen harder, to really hear that they wanted to help him find his daughter. They weren't there as a threat or a trick.

"Now!" Flendon banged his fist on the table a second time, and Iellieth jumped.

Marcon leapt up and stepped between her and the mayor, who breathed heavily, watching him with wild eyes. She scooted back her chair and stood, smoothing out her breeches as she did so. No possible recourses presented themselves. He hadn't cared about their offer to help him. And he rightly doubted her sway over her stepfather.

There was going to be a war. A line of soldiers in silver armor, row upon row of the king's standards, gold and periwinkle, blowing in the wind. They would be mowed down by unrelenting forces from the north, horns blaring, red flags waving.

"Lady, we must go," Marcon whispered. The image wouldn't leave her mind. A hand on the small of her back directed her out of the mayor's office, through the front room, and into the sunny town square of Trudid.

She collapsed on the lowest wooden step and laid her head in her hands. "What are we going to do now?"

CHAPTER 21

I ellieth and Marcon stopped in a small clearing off the road for the night shortly before dusk. She gathered stones to create a circle for their campfire while Marcon searched for logs and kindling. With each rock, she set aside others' objections to her joining the druid conclave.

She was an outsider and didn't know the ways of the forest.

Her privileged upbringing hadn't prepared her to contribute meaningfully to the community.

A great enemy threatened her, and her proximity endangered them all.

She'd failed to protect the forest from loggers.

Beneath each of these, a single fear pulsed. *She didn't belong. She didn't belong. She didn't belong.*

"Did you find enough stones, lady?" Marcon's voice startled her. She hadn't heard him return.

"I did. It's all ready."

Iellieth helped him light the fire and tried to quiet her thoughts. Marcon watched her but said nothing. After the fire had reached a steady burn, he withdrew a bottle of wine from his pack and handed her one of the wooden cups from Mara's house.

"I didn't realize we'd brought wine along," Iellieth said.

Marcon poured the dark garnet liquid into her cup. "I learned something in my past as a soldier that I wanted to share with you."

"Oh? What is it?" She tried to keep her tone light. It wasn't Marcon's fault she had failed to help the druids.

"You can't only toast the successes. Both they and the failures deserve respect and recognition."

This wasn't a sentiment she'd heard before. "Why is that, Marcon?"

He grinned. "In my experience, lady, failures tend to outnumber wins. At other times, moments that seem like successes when they occur bring unexpected consequences. The wide world is available to you now. Toasting everything that befalls us, both the good and the bad, acknowledges that we don't always know the difference."

"Hmm, I like that. So as events come back to us, and fate spirals out from them, we don't always know where it will lead."

"Precisely."

They clinked their cups together, and Iellieth giggled at the heavy wooden *thonk* instead of a gentle chime. She took a sip. The dark berries and pepper warmed her chest, and she soon turned in for the night.

Transmigrating to a mountainside instead of a marriage sentence had worked out much better than she'd thought. And she'd misjudged Turdoch at first and found common ground with him later. Perhaps a positive outcome might arise from the mayor's rejection. But it was unlikely the druids, especially those like Berivic, would allow her in on such a narrow chance.

If only she could tell them how much she loved their organic family, that many of them had chosen one another, that they had formed a bond over time by electing to be there. She'd never witnessed anything of the kind before and likely never would again.

Krrr-eck.

Iellieth woke from her slumber as something crashed into a tree nearby. Marcon unsheathed his blade and sprang up, his silhouette a dark orange glow in the light of their fire.

"What was that?" she whispered.

"I'm not sure, lady. I'll find out."

Iellieth slid her feet into her boots and scrambled after him. Staying together and pursuing an unknown entity was far preferable to waiting alone in their campsite should something else come along.

"We've broken the wheel it seems, darling," a melodious voice in the woods ahead of them observed. Marcon held out his hand to stop their approach. The clouds shifted overhead, and soft white moonlight revealed a richly appointed covered wagon resting at a precarious angle, its front left wheel upheld by an overturned tree.

He placed his finger over his lips and moved ahead on tiptoe. Each step risked announcing their presence with the loud snap of a twig. She ducked into the undergrowth and followed.

A portly man waddled in front of the wagon, panpipes strung around his neck. Iellieth and Marcon froze as the wagon's door creaked open and an attractive young woman with light tan skin emerged from inside. She brushed a long braid over her shoulder and skipped over to her partner. He laughed when he caught sight of her and reached out to catch her around the waist.

Her hair was the same cool brown shade as the mayor's.

The man kissed her deeply before he gestured to their wagon's predicament. "It seems we've struck something, my dear. I'm not sure we can fix it in the darkness." He stepped closer to the cart, and Iellieth covered her mouth to prevent her gasp from breaking free. He had goat's feet, and his lower half was covered in fur. A satyr.

She startled the tree beside her in her attempt to remain silent, and the satyr's head flew up to glance around the clearing in her direction. He took a few steps toward them and raised the panpipes to his lips. "Darling, go back inside for a moment, please."

The girl looked about, frightened, and hurried to return inside. The tree holding the wagon shifted but held.

Beautiful music erupted into the clearing, and Iellieth froze. It called to her. She smiled at Marcon. Wasn't the moonlight pretty, in these enchanting woods? "We should go see," she whispered. Iellieth reached out for his hand.

Marcon groaned and caught her arm. Why didn't he want to meet their new friend?

"It's alright," the satyr called. "We mean you no harm so long as you extend the same to us. How many of you are there?"

"Just two," Iellieth answered. She giggled and pulled at Marcon's arm. It was rude to wait inside the trees instead of introducing oneself to someone new.

"Lady, wait," he objected. He held both of her arms, and she struggled to break free.

"It's alright, sir, miss," the satyr said as he approached.

"You're welcome here." The satyr eyed Marcon's sword and blew a foul note on his pipes.

Iellieth shook her head, her thoughts freed. Why had she been so sure that the satyr was friendly? A scimitar glinted at his side.

Iellieth pulled the dagger from her boot and stood just behind Marcon's shield arm as they had practiced. "Come no further," she ordered.

The satyr glared at her but stopped.

"Who's the young woman with you?" she asked.

He withdrew his blade, and Marcon's shoulders rose. "That's no concern of yours," the satyr grumbled.

"Is that the mayor's daughter? Have you kidnapped her?"

He growled at her and lowered his horns.

"Stop!" the young woman cried from behind the three of them. She'd run from the wagon to stand by the satyr's side and clutched his arm. "Did my father send you?"

"No," Iellieth answered. "We only heard you were missing."

"Kidnapped," Marcon added.

"Are you with her father or not?" the satyr demanded.

"Not," Iellieth said. The young woman smiled at her, relieved. "Would the two of you like a place to stay for the night? Perhaps we can fix your carriage in the morning? Your name is Nil'sea, is that right?" The girl nodded.

"Lady, I'm not sure—"

"We would love that," Nil'sea said. "This is Anorias." She laid a hand on his broad shoulder. "We'll grab a few of our things and return in a moment." The satyr followed after her, checking back over his shoulder every few steps to ensure nothing suspicious transpired.

He handled himself well in his movements—was graceful, even, for his disproportionate size. Marcon watched her close observation. "Lady, have you ever seen a satyr before?"

"No." She shook her head. "This is the first time. I'm not sure if anyone I've ever met has seen one. Well, aside from the druids and the saudad."

"They are quite elusive. We must be careful of the music he plays—that flute is enchanted."

"Is that why it's so beautiful? Or it was until the end."

"That was a charm that he used on you. It's why your behavior shifted, why you immediately trusted him. The second part was a warning, meant to scare us away. It could signal ill intent."

"Is there a way to make sure that doesn't happen again?" She didn't want to be tricked into not being herself.

"Learning to recognize the enchantment is the first step."

Iellieth nodded. She would be sure to scrutinize the satyr's music in the future. His presence with the girl in the woods revived several unanswered questions. "We need to find out which of the rumors are true. Did she run away, or did he take her?" Marcon set his jaw as he watched the couple leaving the wagon with a few blanket rolls and a wineskin. "Should we get her away from him? Return her to Trudid?" Iellieth asked.

"That is what the mayor would have us do, yes."

"But we don't know if we believe him about her not wanting to be here." The young woman's smile had looked so genuine when they saw her the first time. "Was she acting that way because she's enchanted too? She seemed . . . happy."

"I agree, lady. She did."

"Is there a way to easily tell if she's charmed or not? Could it be a prolonged enchantment?"

"Depending on how powerful he is, yes. Mara and Yvayne would have an incantation they could use to decipher it. For us, without their advanced abilities, it will be more difficult. But trust your senses, and watch closely."

"I will." She would have no part in separating two people who wanted to be together solely because of the objection of one or both of their families. It wasn't anyone else's place to decide, and she didn't mean to see it happen again.

⚘

"WE DIDN'T THINK YOU'D STILL BE SO NEAR TO Trudid," Iellieth said. "We met with your father earlier about the logging, on behalf of a local community." The girl's expression twinged at the mention of the mayor. Did that signal a special part of the enchantment or that she regretted the way she'd left home?

Iellieth searched for signs of a charm in Nil'sea's interactions with Anorias around the revived campfire, but she wasn't sure what she should be looking for. They stayed close to one another, and Nil'sea rarely looked away from him. She kept constant contact between the two of them, holding his arm or rubbing his leg as she lounged against his belly and sipped her wine.

"The logging created some trouble for us as well," Nil'sea said. "Anorias and I had been meeting in the woods each night just outside of town. The loggers complicated that as the forest around us kept disappearing, so we decided it was time to head off on our own."

She'd left a few gaps in her story, but it didn't resonate

as an outright lie. "We've been taking some out-of-the-way trails through the woods to avoid my father's guards," the girl added. "But please, will you make me a promise?"

Nil'sea leaned forward, her eyes wide in the firelight. Marcon and Anorias sat back, observing one another and the two young women.

"What promise would you like me to make?" Iellieth asked.

"Will you swear not to tell my father where I am? He refuses to understand."

Her heart tightened. She was well aware of the objections Nil'sea had likely heard regarding her rank as daughter of the mayor, the smart match she might make with someone "of her own class" and not someone beneath her.

Iellieth trailed her fingers through the grass around their fire, warmed by the blazing light. "I promise," she said. "We won't tell him."

Watching her further over the course of the evening, she saw that Nil'sea laughed easily and often, and her eyes sparkled whenever they met Anorias's. Could such a strong signal of affection be an enchantment?

Anorias rose to tend to the horses, and Marcon offered to accompany him. He bent down and squeezed Iellieth's shoulder. "We'll be just over there." He nodded to where the horses were tied a short ways away and gave her a significant look. Now was the time to be doubly sure.

Iellieth leaned over to Nil'sea, the promise of a secret to be revealed dancing in her eyes. "Now that it's just us, I must ask you something."

"Ooh, what is it?"

"How is it that you knew that you were ready to run off

with Anorias? That you wanted to travel with him and leave everything you know behind?"

"Are you asking for any reason in particular?" Nil'sea giggled. "It seems you've already taken that step yourself."

Iellieth blushed at the misunderstanding but decided to use it to her advantage. She twisted her lips to the side in a guilty smirk. "Perhaps." No reason to reveal she'd attempted something similar many years ago or to detail the nuances of her present circumstance.

"Well, I decided the moment I was sure that I wanted us to begin a new adventure together. My father forbade it —our relationship, me leaving—but I couldn't be separated from Anorias, so here I am."

"You're determined that no matter what, you want to be together."

"Yes."

Iellieth leaned in closer. "You'd rather die than be separated?"

"That is rather extreme." Nil'sea looked puzzled by the question. "But, yes, I would."

Iellieth smiled at Marcon and took his hand in hers as he and Anorias returned. "I think it's real," she whispered as she kissed him on the cheek. He froze, eyes wide.

She glanced demurely at Nil'sea, careful to keep the smile on her face.

Marcon grinned, understanding her meaning, and wrapped an arm around her waist. He pushed a lock of hair behind her ear to answer. "I think so too."

THE NEXT MORNING, IELLIETH AND MARCON HELPED Anorias extricate the wheel from the fallen tree. Iellieth laid her hand against the tree and closed her eyes. She willed it to release the wagon, as she thought Mara would have done, but nothing happened.

Marcon noticed her frustration and shook his head. "You'll learn in time." He and Anorias lifted the cart while she and Nil'sea held the tree fast. With a crack, the wheel broke free, and all but two of the spokes remained intact.

"That should be well enough to get us to the main road," Anorias declared happily. Both he and Nil'sea seemed relieved to finally be on their way, to whatever future lay before them.

Iellieth and Marcon walked a few paces ahead of the couple to give them some privacy. The horses trailed dutifully behind Anorias, pulling the wagon. He murmured to them from time to time in a mystical language she didn't know. One of the horses whinnied, and Iellieth looked back to see that it was alright. The horse cried again as a spear burst into view from the thicket beside them.

Iellieth shouted and jumped toward Marcon. Guards shoved their way out of the brambles, spears and crossbows pointed at Anorias, and surrounded the travelers.

Nil'sea locked eyes on her, mouth open and eyes constricted, disbelieving. "We didn't, I swear," Iellieth said. The girl clung to Anorias's shoulders as two guards broke away from the others and stepped menacingly in her direction. The satyr growled and raised his flute to his lips when the mayor emerged from behind a tree.

"You will go no further," Flendon said, arms crossed and glaring up at his daughter's lover. "You've got her bewitched somehow, and I won't stand for it."

The two guards seized Nil'sea and pinned her against a tree to keep her away from Anorias. A few of them watched Iellieth and Marcon, but they didn't retrain their weapons away from the satyr. At the same time, Iellieth knew that if either she or Marcon moved, the guards would shoot Anorias.

The satyr was torn between helping Nil'sea and attacking her father. She shouted at both of them to stop and begged the guards to let her go, to not hurt him, but they ignored her. The mayor looked at Marcon and Iellieth. "It seems that my time spent with you proved useful after all. Thank you."

Anorias pawed the ground and exhaled his heightened frustration at this betrayal. "Anorias, don't listen, it's not true," Iellieth shouted. Marcon stood between her and the guards behind them, blocking her from any stray arrows, hand on the hilt of his sword. He held her shoulder with the other to prevent her from running forward to help.

Mayor Flendon sneered at her defense to Anorias. "The soldiers will be along to escort you home shortly, Lady Amastacia. The runner we sent after them managed to find the trail of my daughter and this beast on his way back to town. I supposed I owe the druids a modicum of thanks after all." He smirked.

Marcon ripped his sword free at the threat against her and faced the mayor. "Do it!" Flendon shouted to his guards.

Iellieth had promised she'd never let this happen again. Not while she could prevent it. She stretched out her arm to stop Marcon and to save Anorias. Nil'sea had said she'd rather die than be parted from him, and she knew precisely how that felt.

She exhaled slowly, just as Mara had taught her.

An explosion of green energy shot from Iellieth's hand and struck the tree beside Nil'sea's head. The girl screamed and ducked into the two guards pinning her. She stared at Iellieth, paralyzed by fright and confusion.

"Notice the energy all around you," Persephonie had said each time she struggled to hit her target. "That way, you will never miss."

The tree branch she'd struck sizzled to the ground. Both Anorias and the mayor had moved toward the girl in their alarm. Perfect. She raised her hand and squinted at Nil'sea. "I asked you before and will do so again. Would you rather die than be separated from him?"

Nil'sea whimpered.

"Answer me."

"Not my daughter!" the mayor cried. He launched himself into the space between them, but a guard seized his cloak and held him back.

"It's her decision," Iellieth said, her voice low and even. Nil'sea didn't know what it was to see someone you loved beaten in front of your eyes. The best-case scenario the guards had prepared for Anorias was a quick death on the forest floor. Flendon was unpredictable enough to imagine something much worse as a lesson for the satyr.

"Say it. Yes or no." Iellieth didn't take her eyes from the shaking girl. Bright green sparks flickered between her fingers. She lowered her hand, pointed at the young woman's heart.

"I am sure," Nil'sea said. "Whatever must happen, of that I'm sure."

"What will it be, Mayor Flendon?" Iellieth asked. She drew her fingertips closer to one another, and the sparks began to swirl.

"She can go. She can go!" Flendon exclaimed. He nearly collapsed in the arms of his guard as he tried to free himself to run to his daughter. "Lower your weapons, all of you."

Iellieth grinned and stretched out her fingers, releasing the swirl of energy back into the forest. The sparks rose harmlessly up into the tree branches.

Anorias sprang toward Nil'sea the moment the arrows pointed away from him. The two holding her against the tree released her at his approach, and she ran to Anorias and embraced him. The guards backed away from the pair and waited at the edge of the trees for further instructions.

"Lady, were you truly going to hit her?" Marcon whispered. Concern knit his brow.

"I didn't need to, did I?" Iellieth said with a wry smile. He kept his eyes narrowed at her. "What did you think I'd been practicing with Mara and Persephonie each day?" The floating sparks she'd released twinkled overhead. New leaves and blossoms spiraled out of each branch they touched.

Marcon shook his head and suppressed a smile of his own. "Not that."

The mayor stood behind Anorias and waited for the satyr and his daughter to acknowledge his presence. Nil'sea leaned around her lover and, holding on to his hand, faced her father. He stumbled through an apology to both of them. Nil'sea listened politely, and the glower slowly left Anorias's face.

"Might I speak with her alone for a moment?" the mayor asked.

Before Anorias could answer, Nil'sea laid her hand on his arm. "Yes, Father. Step over here with me."

The girl's expression was cheerful, and she nodded often during her conversation with her father, careful to reassure him. After several minutes, he embraced her and let her go. Anorias took Nil'sea's hand in his, and they walked back to their wagon.

Flendon scowled in Iellieth's direction. Marcon squared his shoulders, and Iellieth stepped forward to speak with him. "Did your man inform the soldiers or not?"

"He did, but—"

Iellieth turned to Marcon. "Then we need to go."

Marcon stepped back, gesturing that she should lead the way.

"I knew they wouldn't help me," Flendon called after her. He hurried forward but stopped at a look from Marcon. "The druids, I knew they wouldn't help me with the satyr. They would never have sided against a fae creature, even if I had been in a position to stop the logging."

Iellieth balled her hands into fists. "You've no idea the damage you've done, but I'm relieved you were prevented today. Let that sit with you, and see if that changes your feelings about the orders you've received." The mayor looked down at the ground, and Iellieth continued. "There are some in the court of Linolynn who care about the people of Trudid, but there's nothing we can do inside a cage."

"I am sorry." He took another furtive step forward, and Iellieth shook her head.

"Think over our request once again. And be thoughtful toward your daughter." She stepped into the woods, Marcon's footfalls heavy and sure behind her.

Brush crashed behind them, and they both whirled around as Nil'sea launched herself forward and wrapped her arms around Iellieth's neck. "I don't know how I'll ever thank you." She released Iellieth and embraced Marcon.

"There's really no need." Iellieth smiled at her. "We're glad you're both free to do as you please now."

"I hope that you will be too," Nil'sea said.

Iellieth grinned and nodded farewell. They would see with time. Flickers of lively green rested at the tips of her fingers, ready.

CHAPTER 22

"A mbrose!" Teodric called, smiling. "I hadn't expected to see you. I thought you were ill."

The navigator glanced up at him and then looked away out over the ocean. "No, thank you, Captain, I'm alright."

"Might the two of us speak for a moment then?" Teodric placed a hand on Ambrose's shoulder and led the navigator over toward his new quarters. He kept his voice low. "I want you to know that I would have made you my first mate, if it were entirely up to me. Kriega's a capable sailor, and she leads with a strong hand, but you and I have worked closely together for some time. I trust you. And" —Teodric checked over his shoulder to ensure no one else was nearby—"to be honest, I hadn't imagined Syleste being willing to part with her."

"That took many of us by surprise, sir."

His friend was even more reserved than usual. "Come, Ambrose, be open with me. I've no wish to be in Steinvas's position. Were you terribly disappointed? Are you still willing to sail by my side?"

Ambrose finally met his gaze, but the older man still seemed ill at ease.

"Truly," Teodric said, "you may speak your mind. I'm not so heady yet as captain as to be incapable of hearing an honest critique or to learn of a friend's disappointment."

Ambrose squinted out toward the horizon. "It's not that, Teodric, er, Captain." He rubbed his thumbs over his fingers nervously. "I was merely surprised is all. That you wanted me on board."

Teodric laughed. At times he forgot Ambrose's extreme modesty. Its origins confounded him. "Surprised? Do you really think I'd undertake a journey without you? You've repaid my assistance from when you were first on board the *Dominion* ten times over. Neither of us would be standing here without the other." He lowered his voice further still. "And I believe it will take the cunning of us both to turn this new appointment and ship to our advantage. No safety under a snake's eye, eh?"

"Under what?" Ambrose's head shot up, eyes wide.

"Just an expression. I thought it was a common one?" Perhaps he was mistaken. "I thought I had picked it up in Nortelon. Regardless of its origin, so long as you're in the predator's sights, you're in danger. I"—the sun glinted off the admiral's long black hair as she walked along the dock toward his ship—"well, speak of her, and she shall appear."

Teodric motioned for Ambrose to follow him to greet Syleste by the gangplank. He called to one of the sailors to fetch Kriega from her rooms and alert her that the admiral had arrived for her inspection.

A hush fell as Syleste's boot clicked onto the deck. "Captain Adhemar, a fine crew you've assembled."

"Only the finest, Admiral, especially as they ultimately serve you and not myself."

"Good." She grinned as she looked over his collection. Syleste paused over a few who were young and beautiful, her two favorite qualities, but they proved to be just shy enough of her standards for her to resist the temptation and allow them to stay aboard his ship.

"What name have you selected for this fine addition to my fleet, Captain?"

Teodric smiled. "The *Amber Queen*, for you." He bowed his head. Flattery was one of the admiral's few weaknesses.

Syleste's eyes flashed as she took in his meaning. The golden wood of the ship's deck mirrored her own skin tone, especially beneath the pale blue sky. But the darker gold of the hull perfectly matched the vibrant center of her orange-brown eyes, precisely the shade of refined amber. "*Very* good, Captain. I am most pleased."

"I live to serve, Admiral." Teodric bowed.

At all times, Syleste exuded self-satisfaction. He appeared cowed and charmed exactly as she wished. So long as he could maintain the ruse in front of Kriega, he might be able to provide the sort of life and freedom for his crew that he himself had desperately longed for. The sea made her promise to each of them, but the powers that sailed her waters had agendas of their own.

Syleste directed him and Kriega into his cabin while Ambrose and the newly appointed officers prepared the crew to set sail. She rolled her shoulders back into the leather armchair in the corner of the expansive room. Given time, he could make something of this space.

Her eyes glittered as she looked back and forth between them. "You will both be relieved to know that I've decided to assist you through the first two days of your assignment. We'll make our way north and, once I'm assured of the excellence of my decision, you will proceed to Andel-ce Hevra. There's a very important agent of mine I'd like for you to procure."

Teodric nodded and glanced at Kriega, curious to see how she took the news. The half-orc bowed her head to Syleste's wishes.

The admiral continued. "His name is Darcy. You'll know him by his long black hair and piercing blue eyes. He's performed a great service for me, and I would like to see him rewarded. I'll need you to pick him up from the docks along the coast, outside the city, and return him to me. We've an important matter to discuss in person."

The admiral rose from her chair. "The windowed quarters, at the bow, will serve perfectly as his guest room while he's aboard. He's to receive every convenience possible, but not so much as to become self-important or spoiled. Do you understand?"

"We do, Admiral," Teodric answered. He stood at attention with his arms crossed behind his back, speaking for himself and Kriega.

"Very well." Her sharp white teeth shimmered, and she rose from her chair. "Look for my signal. We set sail at noon."

"A WORD, KRIEGA," TEODRIC SAID AFTER THE ADMIRAL had left. "I have been hoping the two of us might have a chance to speak. Please"—he indicated the chair Syleste had vacated and sat across from it.

Kriega sat, straight-backed, eyes turned to stare out over the sea. He might have been better off delaying until they were further removed from the *Dominion*. In all likelihood, Syleste had placed Kriega in this position to spy on him and wait for him to make a wrong move. "Are you pleased with the crew thus far?" A neutral question might help them establish a better rapport.

"I am, especially those I've brought on board." She continued to scowl at the end of the dock and the stretch of blue beyond.

"They seem exceedingly capable." Teodric smiled. He'd been pleasantly surprised by her selections. They were more . . . polished than he'd expected. Her associates aboard the *Dominion* were often rough-and-tumble.

"Is there something you need, Captain? I'd like to keep an eye on the crew." She turned her glare to him.

Teodric grinned, ignoring the ire in her tone. "There is, actually. And Ambrose is more than capable of keeping the crew on task without us for a short while longer. Would you like a drink?" He stood and walked over to the small bar Steinvas had kept well stocked during his tenure as captain.

She grunted in response and shook her head.

"Very well. I shall have one, if it's all the same to you." Teodric poured himself a glass of wine and sat back in his chair, one leg crossed over the other. He could affect an air of ease even if he did not feel it. "I'll stop stalling then and get straight to the point." The wine he'd selected was pleasantly fruity. He leaned toward her. "I was surprised, Kriega, when the admiral informed me that you would be my companion for this new adventure." Her expression softened, taken aback by his disclosure. Syleste wasn't one to share openly unless it furthered her own ends. Teodric continued. "You have served by her side, loyally, for the last three years, in my experience, and I believe even longer still, if others' reports are to be believed."

"Yes," she said quickly. "What of it?" Her tone was less gruff than it had been a few moments before.

How he phrased what came next was crucial. Kriega might not ever transfer her loyalty from Syleste to him, but he needed to earn as much of her trust as he was able. The safety of everyone aboard the *Queen*—himself, his crew, even her own—depended on it.

"There is another reason I was surprised to find that you would be joining my crew." Teodric met Kriega's eyes, a striking tawny brown against the moss green of her skin. "Kriega, I am well aware of your relationship with Syleste. Among other things, it created some"—deep-seated anger? Violence and aggression?—"difficulties between the two of us early on. I hope, of course, that we are past those now. The admiral grew tired of me long ago." He waved the horrors of that experience aside. "But you have remained dear to her. And knowing your romantic involvement together, I was concerned about how you would feel being on a new ship."

"You were concerned?" The edge in her voice said she didn't believe him. He'd need to tread forward carefully.

"I was." He kept his voice low with a slight scratchiness. As far as he was concerned, anyone would be better off keeping their distance from Syleste, but he doubted Kriega saw her relationship with the admiral in that way.

"Your concerns have been noted, Captain." She rose out of the chair.

"Kriega, wait, please." He followed a few steps after her but not near enough that he was within arm's reach.

She curled her hands into fists, and the muscles in her arms bulged.

"I want what's best for my crew." She had to know he meant this. "For all of my crew."

Kriega sighed and turned to look at him, biting the side of her lower lip. "That is an honorable aim, Captain. I will remember it. I've no illusions about what I am to the admiral. I hope that gives you peace of mind enough. I'll say nothing further on the subject." She nodded to him and stepped back onto the sunny deck.

Teodric tapped his foot a few times on the wooden planks and walked over to one of the windows. He drained his glass of wine. That certainly could have gone worse. Honesty, on his side, was where they would begin. Loyalty could come in time.

CHAPTER 23

Iellieth could feel Marcon's eyes watching her from across their evening's campfire. After the encounter with Flendon and his guards, they'd traveled as quietly and swiftly as possible, conscious that soldiers might be following close behind.

"What are you going to tell them, when we get back?" he asked.

"Besides the fact that our negotiations failed and my stepfather's soldiers have been tipped off about where I am?"

"Is that truly how you see it, lady?" His voice was calm, but it did nothing to soothe the irritation that prickled across her skin.

"What would you have me say instead?" She'd run through dozens of possible scenarios for her report to the conclave, but none of them resulted in anyone besides Mara wanting her to stay.

Marcon sat in silence. She hadn't meant to snap at him. Iellieth lifted her head to apologize, but he spoke again as she looked up. "You would be well within your rights to say, 'I called upon the natural world to help me enact justice, and it answered.' Or something to that effect."

Iellieth shook her head. "But that's normal for them."

The faintest hint of a smile played at the corners of his lips. "Precisely. They need to know it's normal for you too."

"They already know I can summon magic. It still doesn't mean they'll accept me." Iellieth picked up her amulet and ran her fingers over the golden bands.

Marcon kept his voice low, its deep cadence blending with the crackle of the fire. "True, but you have to give them the chance, lady. And it's not up to them to tell you that you belong. This is something you must decide for yourself."

Tears filled Iellieth's eyes. How did Marcon know what she'd been afraid of? "Thank you," she whispered.

They neared the conclave the next afternoon, and Iellieth returned to the question of their report to the druids. "Do you think we should tell them about the approaching war?" she asked. "They know about the were-wolf attacks, but they may not be aware of the larger-scale conflict that could result from them."

"I believe they should be informed, yes. But as far as your stepfather's soldiers go, I would be honored if you would leave dealing with them to me."

Iellieth turned back in surprise. "What are you going to do?"

Marcon's expression was stoic as ever. "Once we've returned and you are settled, I plan to find out the truth of Flendon's report. The soldiers being informed of your general whereabouts and them finding their way to you are two different things."

"But what about the amulet, and separation?" Even

from the other side of their room at the Laughing Giant, the runes registered his distance from her. What would happen if he went beyond what the connection would bear?

"Perhaps Mara can investigate how far I'll be able to go."

A drop of relief loosened the tension in her shoulders. At least he shared her concerns.

The two moons smiled brightly against the cerulean sky. As they walked, Iellieth rehearsed what she would say to Mara—Turdoch wasn't as greedy as she had supposed; Mayor Flendon, however, likely was, but now that he knew his daughter was well, there was a chance he might change his mind, especially if word came from the court about the war being called off—branches crunched on the path ahead. She froze. Had the soldiers beat them here?

"Who's there?" Marcon called.

Iellieth leaned her weight onto her back foot, ready to leap behind Marcon's shield or dart into the forest.

"It is me, of course." Persephonie's deep auburn-brown curls emerged from the tangle of branches ahead. She grinned, looking between the two of them. "Who were you expecting?"

"It is good that you have returned now," Persephonie said. She hurried along the path ahead of Iellieth. "There have been dark omens of late, and we will have to leave soon. I was afraid that I would not be able to see you. Datha will be very happy to hear that you are back. I would have been very cross with him if we hadn't been able to say good-bye."

"But where are you going? Why?"

Persephonie glanced about as she walked as though she was waiting for something to leap out of the woods at any moment. Had the soldiers traveled through here already?

"It will be easier if Mara explains." Persephonie led them along one of the conclave's many trails. They emerged in the clearing where the first council meeting had been held, into chaos.

All around them, druids rushed from hut to hut, carrying supplies and loading their bags onto wagons and horses. A few piles of scattered provisions waited between the homes. Every once in a while, someone took a water-skin or tool from one of the piles or left a bag of grain at another. The woods were eerily quiet, and the energy inside the clearing was fractured, nervous.

"Mara," Persephonie called out as the druid emerged from one of the huts, "I have found them. They are back."

Her mentor's usually calm demeanor was burdened. Dark circles pressed below her eyes. Mara smiled as she saw them, and a glimmer of her warm and welcoming presence returned.

Iellieth ran forward and wrapped her arms around the elf's waist. "I am so happy to see you, Mara."

The druid chuckled happily. "And I am happy to see you, cher'a. Come, there are important matters to discuss." Mara laid her arm across Iellieth's shoulders and led her, Marcon, and Persephonie into one of the communal huts.

They sat facing one another on two sets of the room's long benches. Questions darted around Iellieth's mind about the activity outside, but she waited for Mara to speak first.

"News has reached us of an impending attack on our

conclave," Mara said. Her voice was cold and unsteady. "We are making preparations now so that as many as possible can flee. A few others will remain here to ensure the rest are able to escape."

"But, Mara, who's attacking? Is it my stepfather's soldiers? Mayor Flendon said—"

"Wait, si'retta. This is the other enemy and his followers. His name is Lucien."

Lucien. Iellieth searched her memory, but she couldn't recall anyone of that name.

Mara continued, "He has sworn into his service a pack of werewolves. The saudad told us that they have attacked several mountain villages, decimating their populations. They will be here soon."

Soon? Iellieth's blood ran cold. A pack of werewolves? Where had they come from?

Persephonie spoke into the stunned silence. "There is still time for most of the conclave to leave. That is why we must go as well, Iellieth, especially now that you are back. We would not have left you and Marcon in the woods alone."

"And I'm the one they're looking for?" Iellieth couldn't speak above a whisper. Beside her, Marcon emanated an angry resolve.

"You are." Mara's brown-and-copper eyes met hers, tears brimming. "But I swear to you that we will keep you safe."

"We? What do you mean? Are you saying that some are staying behind to protect me? Mara, don't do that, please. I can go somewhere else."

"I will help her," Marcon said. He scowled as though he could already see the enemy forces threatening her.

"Depending on how much time we have, we may send

the two of you away from the rest of the conclave. But not until we adopt you as one of our own first."

The thought of fleeing through the woods, pursued by slathering werewolves, muted Mara's last sentence. If it hadn't been for Persephonie's squeal of delight, she might have missed it.

"As one of your own? Truly?" Her heart's dampened wings fluttered off the ground.

"Truly, cher'a."

"But I wasn't able to convince Mayor Flendon to stop felling the forest. Turdoch, the overseer of the logging company, he would have, but they can't disregard the mayor's orders. He would just bring in someone else. I think—" Iellieth sighed. She didn't want to, but she couldn't see another way. "I think that the best option is to go to Linolynn and speak with those giving the orders. They're originating with someone in the court."

"Were you able to find out why, cher'a?" Mara tilted her head, curious.

"They've declared war on Hadvar." Iellieth pushed her hair back away from her face. "We don't understand why, yet, but that's what we gathered. They're felling the forest to create more ships. I don't know if it's my stepfather or the king giving the orders, but Flendon doesn't feel that he's in a position to say no, even if he wanted to."

The rest of the story tumbled out—finding Anorias and Nil'sea in the woods, Flendon potentially reconsidering. "So there is some hope." As she said it, Iellieth believed it. Linolynn had nothing to gain from the war with Hadvar, and as soon as they understood that the attacks came from the werewolves, both kingdoms could direct their attention to eliminating them and Lucien.

Iellieth's eyes widened. Why hadn't she thought of this

before? If they could move quickly enough, they could bring the soldiers here before they attacked the druid conclave.

"That is a lovely thought, Iellieth." Mara smiled sadly after she revealed her plan. "But I am afraid we do not have the time."

"How close are they?" Iellieth's stomach flipped, frightened of Mara's response.

"We expect them here within a few days."

Her heart shattered. Mara was right, there wouldn't be time.

The druid took both of Iellieth's hands in hers. "For now, cher'a, you should see Persephonie off. This is not their fight. I will tell the council that you have returned. It has been decided, in your absence, that you will become one of our number." She squeezed Iellieth's fingers. "Tonight."

Iellieth's gaze flew up, sure that Mara was mistaken. "But how? I . . . I failed. I couldn't save the forest."

Mara placed her hands beneath Iellieth's jaw. "Your willingness to try was enough to win over the majority of the council. For the rest, they came to see that Lucien would have attacked us either way. They decided that before he did, it would be nice to add another to our midst. One we wish to protect."

Her mentor smiled down at her and released her face. "Tell the saudad good-bye for me"—she turned to Persephonie—"your father especially. I must prepare for tonight." The druid strode out of the tent, leaving the three of them sitting together.

Iellieth didn't know where to begin. So much had changed in the hour since their return. "I have never encountered werewolves before," she said slowly. Once more, her only point of reference was the stories she'd read.

"There were some small packs in my time, though they were not common," Marcon said. "Those who could blended into the populations in the cities. For the rest, there was not enough space in the wilds." He studied his shield and its emblem of fire.

"We first ran into them when I was very young," Persephonie said softly, a quaver in her voice. "We were in Tor'stre Vahn, a few days away from Andel-ce Hevra. My friend and I were playing in the forest. We heard growls. Before we could react, they leapt out of the trees. I screamed."

Persephonie's eyes stared off to the side, reliving the terror. "Datha, on his black horse, appeared a moment later. The horse reared and kicked the werewolf as it stalked toward me. Datha shouted and reached down. He lifted me from the ground and onto the saddle in front of him. We rode away as fast as we could."

Iellieth held her breath, waiting to hear what had happened to the other child.

"Ellyn's father was there too, but the werewolves, they got to her first." Persephonie shuddered. "They dragged her away, and he had to let her go."

"Persephonie, I'm so sorry." Iellieth reached out and clasped her arm.

"Thank you." She sniffed and laid her hand over Iellieth's before she dabbed the corners of her eyes. "The werewolves followed us, racing through the woods. Saudad horses, they are very swift. In times like those, they have to be." The note of pride in her voice brightened her tale. "The one in the lead, it reached out for me, to pull me from Datha's saddle. He stabbed the creature."

Persephonie moved her hair to the side and showed Iellieth the base of her neck where three thin scars, a few inches long, ran toward her spine. "Its claws caught me, but not its bite." She looked at the hut's dirt floor. "The hardest part is that we do not know what happened to Ellyn. If they killed her, if she became one of them. Her father, he blames himself to this day."

Marcon watched Persephonie closely. "How did your father know that you were in danger? Were there warning signs of the werewolves before their attack?"

She nodded. "Yes. Others gifted with the sight, they foresaw the werewolves' arrival. We have since studied their patterns and learned the omens. That is how we know they are coming now." Her eyes misted over as she looked at Iellieth. "I wish we could take you with us."

Iellieth moved to Persephonie's bench and embraced her friend, their hair intermingling. "As do I. But we'll see each other again. I know it."

<hr/>

THEIR FAREWELL TO THE SAUDAD WAS EMOTIONAL BUT brief. Cassian was reluctant to abandon the druids in their time of need, but his people had already experienced heavy losses at the hands of the werewolves, and he could not subject them to further conflict if it could be avoided. After they said their good-byes, Marcon walked Iellieth back to the clearing where the first council meeting had been held. A ring of torches surrounded a large gathering of druids.

"It looks like the entire conclave is here," Iellieth whispered.

"That seems fitting, does it not? To welcome one of

their own?" His smile glowed in the firelight. "You go on from here, lady. I will wait for you at Mara's hut."

"You don't want to come?" Nerves flitted in her belly.

"I believe this ceremony is for druids only." Marcon took her hand and kissed it, his lips warm on her skin. He grinned over her shoulder. "Besides, your escort has arrived."

Mara slid up to Iellieth's side, beaming. She nodded to Marcon, who bowed and turned away, walking back through the twilight to Mara's home. "Are you ready?" The druid wrapped her hands around Iellieth's elbow.

"I believe so," Iellieth said. "Though I don't know what I'm meant to do."

"The journey will guide you. Do not worry." Mara patted her arm and led her toward the outer ring of the circle.

As they approached, two rows of candles flared to life, guiding their path. The candles passed their light on to others, and, one by one, lights glowed before each member of the conclave. On the far side of the circle, a chorus chanted to the beat of a few drums. A young girl in a white shift dress waited for Iellieth and Mara at the edge of the torchlight.

The moons shone brightly overhead, the major moon nearly full, the minor a perfect crescent. The clearing sparkled with energy and possibility.

Mara released her arm with a squeeze and drifted around the first semicircle of people to the opposite side. Berivic, Ismaer, and a human woman Iellieth hadn't met came to stand beside her mentor. They joined the chanting, their outstretched hands facing the center of the circle.

The young girl waited for Iellieth to look at her before

she spoke. "You reenter as you first did." She held her arms out. Iellieth smiled down at her and, unsure of what to do next, placed her hand on top of the girl's. The young druid blinked up at her. Iellieth added her second hand to the first. The girl smiled and shook her head.

What did the little girl want her to do? Iellieth shrugged her shoulders to signal her confusion. Maybe that would encourage her to provide further clues.

The young druid nodded to the center of Iellieth's chest and tugged on her own collar. Iellieth lifted the strings around her tunic and moved to untie them. The girl nodded.

Mara's voice rose about the chants, a lifeline. The druid stood on the opposite side of the gathering with an elegant circlet of vines placed on her head, its tendrils winding through her curly hair.

"On the eve of great change, we meet together to join Iellieth Amastacia to our conclave. As she has taken our mantle onto her shoulders, setting aside other paths to align herself with ours, so do we take her onto our shoulders and welcome her into our midst." Iellieth unlaced her boots and removed her jacket at the girl's direction.

"As each of us who came of age have done, we stripped off the markings of what once was." The little girl tugged urgently on Iellieth's sleeve. She was taking too long.

The chorus hummed in the background, and the drums beat on. As quickly as she could, Iellieth slipped out of the remainder of her clothing and handed the pieces to the girl. The cool night air nipped at her skin. The child nodded once more and stepped back to the edge of the circle.

The gathered bodies faced toward the center where a pool of water had appeared.

Mara's melodic voice rose above the chanting. "Following in the footsteps of those who came before, and leading the footsteps of those who will come after, she steps into the pool." Iellieth shivered and walked toward the water, arms wrapped around her chest. "The pond holds the water from below and the stars from above. A step into the waters, Iellieth, expresses your desire to join brothers and sisters in the druidic way of life."

The pool grew larger as she approached. Mara's voice drifted to her on the breeze, and the drumbeats quieted, pounding from farther and farther away. At this rate, it would take several minutes for her to swim to Mara's present position. How was the circle so much wider than it had been before?

Iellieth pointed her toes and placed them in the water. The surface responded, welcoming her. It lapped gently over the top of her foot. As the ripples flowed outward, the voices and drumming increased in volume and others joined the cadence. Mara's voice broke into ancient druidic prayers, calling her forward. Iellieth closed her eyes as she stepped into the pool, lulled by the musicality and the water's warm embrace. She immersed her ankles, knees, hips into the pond and then submerged completely.

The chanting and drums echoed above her, but otherwise, the water was silent. A faint light on the far side of the pool beckoned. She swam toward it.

At first, this pond reminded her of the pools kept beneath Io Keep for the nobles' amusement, especially the sense of floating in a contained space. But the rippling connection to her surroundings, the sense of being a part of something greater, brought back childhood memories of playing in the ocean.

Those treasured moments teemed all around her. Her

body and heart remembered, and the sense of belonging enveloped her. For the first time in as long as she could remember, she felt whole. The water, the ceremony, filled a gap at her core, healed what had been broken. This was where she was meant to be.

Connection swelled in her like the tides, rising within before it flowed out into the world beyond. It washed over the druids who waited for her at the water's edge, poured out to the town of Trudid, rippled on to Linolynn, and bound through the currents of the Infinite Ocean. Each lifeform this energy touched shone back to her, not only the people but animals, plants, dirt, fungi, rocks. The waters that flowed down the Frostmaw Mountains joined their voices to the peaks and sang to her. They all had a place with her, and she with them. The fullness overwhelmed her, and a sob broke from her lips and bubbled to the surface, but she found herself smiling too.

Iellieth swam several more lengths forward. Her lungs began to burn as she neared the light. It floated up at her approach and dimmed once she reached the edge of its radius. She stroked closer, feet kicking behind her, and tried to catch it, but the glowing orb stayed out of reach. It faded completely as her hand broke the water's surface at the far side of the clearing, right at Mara's feet.

Breathless, Iellieth filled her lungs and took her first steps out of the water. The varied textures in the stones beneath her toes whispered to her, wished to tell her more of how they came to be. Water streamed off her body, and the light in the clearing slowly rose once again to reveal the candlelit faces of her conclave. The voices called out at full volume now, echoing back and forth against the woods around them. Mara hurried forward and wrapped her in a deerskin cloak. Her mentor laughed and hugged her before she removed the woven crown of ivy and flowers from atop her curls and placed it on Iellieth's head.

Iellieth laughed as well, elated. She felt . . . alive.

Mara held Iellieth at arm's reach, looking her over. "I am so proud of you, Iellieth," she said over the chanting. "Welcome to our family. We have been waiting for you."

Ismaer stood behind Mara with a gnarled quarterstaff. He clutched it to his chest and bowed his head. The elder reached out his hand, palm upward, indicating that Iellieth should do the same. The drumming grew even louder as the conclave's newest member took her final step.

Iellieth took Ismaer's other hand and held it to the center of her breastbone. She bowed her head over the ceremonial oak staff as druids had been doing in Caldara for the past age. A few tears fell from her cheeks as she raised back up, and he smiled at her. Ismaer raised his hands over his head and turned to all sides of the clearing. "Welcome, Iellieth Amastacia," he cried.

The conclave cheered, clapping and chanting their welcome in reply. Mara clasped Iellieth's shoulders and led her off to the side so she could dress before sharing a meal with her new community.

Celebration and feasting lasted late into the night. The rising sun would bring a time of the unknown, of fear and partings. They reveled in their night of togetherness. Iellieth left the clearing in the early hours of the morning. The wholeness she'd felt in the water kept her wrapped in its arms. Twigs and leaves crackled welcome beneath her feet as she walked back to Mara's cabin. At the edge of the smaller clearing, she bent down to a blade of grass and ran her fingers over it.

The life inside it pulsed upward, and she gasped as it responded to her touch. The blade grew up and around her finger and bloomed in a small white flower. She smiled at this new wonder and held on to it as she looked behind her at the forest and the beautiful collection of homes it held.

Iellieth unspooled her finger and glided through the darkness. Sleepiness paced the edges of her elation, ready to carry her away to a land of peaceful dreams. A burly silhouette waited for her on Mara's doorstep and rose as she approached. Marcon smiled and bent to embrace her. Much to her surprise, he lifted her into the air, laughing. "And how do you feel, lady?"

"Complete." Iellieth grinned as she said it. She knew it was true.

CHAPTER 24

Yvayne paced back and forth in the snow outside her highland treehouse. Lucien's forces were drawing nearer to the Vagarveil, she could sense it, and yet wherever she searched in the waters, whichever trees she asked, she could find no trace of them. Fhaona's crescent moon charm was cold against the palm of her hand, the metal clinging to the chill in the air.

She had promised to warn Mara if there were any sign of the pack's approach. How could an entire host of werewolves and their foul leader disappear into the forest? It would have taken an incredibly powerful shield charm to hide them from her, one she wasn't sure that even the likes of Lucien could muster.

Unless—she continued her pacing—unless they weren't in the Stormside Forest at all. Had Lucien found a portal near the druids' encampment? If he had, they wouldn't need days to reach the camp.

They could appear at any moment.

Yvayne sprinted inside and down the entry hall to a small central chamber at the heart of the tree trunk. She had to warn Mara. Though they remained vigilant in patrolling the forest for such passageways, a week might pass between a portal's appearance and its discovery, and a few more days still before its destruction.

Opening a door from the Shadowlands to the prime plane was an incredible feat, but not entirely beyond Lucien's capabilities. She would have felt his intrusion into the forest, however. Any unnatural entry left its mark. But a portal appearing of its own accord was more likely than the lich and his two hundred werewolves simply disappearing from their raids across the Frostmaws. Yvayne cursed under her breath, furious that she hadn't realized this sooner.

She rubbed the jasper stone between her palms. Yvayne closed her eyes and focused on her message, embedding it into the rock. "Mara, they may have found a portal. You need to leave. Now."

She waited for a sign that the druid had heard her. Nothing. She groaned and began to prepare the seeing herbs instead. Her search for the werewolves over the past several days had depleted her stores. The spell wouldn't be ready until the afternoon. "Please let it be enough," she whispered.

ANXIOUS VOICES AND THE CRASH OF WOODEN CRATES woke Iellieth with a start the next morning. Outside Mara's hut, the druids resumed their frantic preparations. They would begin their retreat from the Vagarveil Wood in a few hours. Mara's voice burbled beneath the chaos, a steady stream of calm and encouragement. Marcon sat at the hut's door, watching silently.

"Do you think it's a mistake for them to be leaving?" Iellieth asked.

Marcon turned to her, lips drawn in a narrow line. "There are tactical disadvantages to retreating, especially in waves as they've determined to."

She waited for him to say more, but he returned his gaze outside. Iellieth wrapped a blanket around her shoulders and went to sit beside him. They were talking about her community now, something she belonged to. Perhaps that was why he held back. "What would you have them do instead?"

He sighed and looked down at his crossed hands. "It depends on their goals."

She scooted closer and leaned against his shoulder. "What would their plan of separating from one another best achieve, then? As opposed to something else?"

His low voice grated as he spoke. "Survival, lady." He met her eyes. "I don't wish to alarm you or to be critical of your new family. There's still a glow about you from your ceremony last night." The corners of his lips lifted in a slight smile.

Iellieth nodded. "Thank you for saying that, Marcon." She turned to watch the druids loading wagons. "I just want to understand." His answer, survival, tugged at a pit in her stomach.

Mara hurried toward them from across the clearing. "Si'retta, good morning." Her eyes still shimmered with pride from the evening before. "An idea struck me during last night's festivities. I'd like to try something before the two of you leave with the second wave."

Iellieth pursed her lips. "Are you coming with us in that one? We can remain with a later group to be sure that we're together. I still—"

Mara waved her hand, dismissing Iellieth's concerns. "There is much left to be determined, but all of it can wait a short while longer. Come, both of you. It's time we understood your amulet."

The druid strode off into the woods. Marcon glanced at Iellieth as Mara disappeared behind the trees.

"I guess we should go after her?" Iellieth said. She grabbed her jacket from the peg and slipped into her shoes before they hurried to catch up to Mara.

She led them behind her hut into the denser part of the forest. "Just inside here," she said. Her hand rested on a silver birch tree covered in vines. Iellieth stood beside her mentor and peered through the covering. The ivy wound around a tight cluster of trees with a small space in the center, marked by a circle of soft yellow petals.

Mara held up one of the strands of ivy for Iellieth to climb beneath. She worked her way through the vertical maze, careful not to disturb Mara's setup. As she crouched beneath one strand, another would wrap around her shoulder or ankle.

At first, this sensation of being constantly seized made her feel trapped. There'd be no easy way out should they need one. But then Mara began to sing to the vines, and they awakened. They caressed her skin as they guided her through, trailing strands of her hair among the tiny leaves.

Marcon's expressions of frustration behind her quieted as the enchanted area began to aid their windings through it.

Iellieth sighed as she stepped into the small clearing. The closeness she'd felt beneath the water, it was here too.

Mara grinned at both of them as she completed her path through the vines. "Welcome." She held out her hands to either side, indicating the forest's inclusion in her message. The leaves overhead rustled against one another, echoing Mara's greeting with green whispers. Marcon ran his hand over the ivy, walking in a slow circle around the inner perimeter.

"Iellieth, you'll assist me with this first part." Mara handed her a length of hempen rope woven together with the same vines that surrounded the tiny clearing. "Now, Marcon"—he came to stand across from Mara as she directed—"you'll take my hands, cross at the wrist. There you go." She nodded at him and turned back to Iellieth. "Cher'a, you'll wrap the rope around our hands, passing across both of our palms, and then come stand behind me."

This was the first time Iellieth had seen Mara, or anyone for that matter, performing this sort of magic. How would it help them to understand the amulet? Marcon kept glancing at the murmuring leaves overhead. Iellieth squeezed his wrist as she wrapped the rope around his hands, trying to ease his worry.

"Are we ready?" Mara asked. Iellieth and Marcon both agreed. The druid closed her eyes and began her prayer. "Spirits of the Vagarveil—" The melody of her chant lifted Iellieth's heart and carried her along, a leaf floating down a stream. When she focused on the words and syllables, she struck a rock, jarring her journey. But as she relaxed into the cadence of the prayer, the rolling rhythm of the Druidic language and verses, flickers of sunlight brushed over her leaf, buoyed by the gentle current.

"Father Oak, in your ancient wisdom . . . from deep beneath the Stormside, buried away in ancient roots . . . Mother Moon, Selene, grant a gentle shimmer of truth . . ."

The prayer continued as the sunlight brightened overhead. Marcon inhaled deeply, matching the patterned breathing of Mara's meditation. Waves of energy drifted off of the two of them, and the branches above swayed in time. Iellieth kept her hands on top of theirs as each flow of energy crested and splashed across the circle.

Suddenly, Mara's chanting stopped. She gasped as she emerged from her prayer and gripped Marcon's hands. "You are in grave danger."

Marcon frowned, his brow knit together, as Mara continued, shaking her head. "Your condition, the binding to the amulet, is not permanent. It can be undone. But you cannot be separated far from it until this occurs." Mara took a deep breath, inhaling clarity from the natural world around them. "There is more."

Iellieth stepped over to Marcon's side and wrapped her hand around his arm. They'd known about the connection already, but being bound, trapped, to the amulet and together? How? Would he have no choice but to follow wherever she decided to go?

"Great potential lies on the path ahead of you," Mara said, "and great peril as well. I saw a bright, glowing fire, but it did not consume." The druid shuddered. "But there were other instances, of trees burning, the woods washed away beneath the flame. In these"—Mara shut her eyes—"she was there." She met Marcon's eyes, her gaze wide in horror. "Alessandra."

Marcon's jaw muscle clenched.

Iellieth laid her other hand on his back. "But how is that connected to the amulet, Mara?"

"It was she who bound you, wasn't it?" Mara stared at him, understanding dawning on her expression. "She was the one who trapped you beneath that mountain."

Marcon nodded, his features tense. "Her servants did."

"Is she the one connecting you to me?" Iellieth couldn't keep the hurt and fear out of her voice. There had to be a mistake. Her father would never have given Mamaun something so dark and dangerous.

"No," Marcon answered quickly and turned to her. He began unwrapping his hands from the rope and vines. "Whatever you and your amulet are, lady, you stand against her. She would have left me there, fractured, alone, forever."

Mara spoke hurriedly. "My sense, from the vision, is that the amulet connects your body to your sentience. I believe that's why I saw the fire. Your soul didn't travel to Astralei, which is how you've come back. The amulet, when Iellieth wears it, tethers you here. Holds you in place."

"And so without it?" Iellieth turned to Mara.

"You return to frozen crystal," the druid whispered.

Marcon's shoulders fell, and he dropped the rope onto the ground. "Thank you, Mara. I will bear that in mind." He turned away from them, stepped over the coiled rope. The vines woven between the trees lifted to allow him to step out of the circle.

"Wait! Marcon, wait," Iellieth called after him, scrambling forward. The vines didn't drift away for her exit as they had for his, and she became entangled trying to follow after him. "Mara, help me, call them off!" Iellieth pulled against the maze of ivy as it wrapped around her limbs.

The druid stood behind her, also unencumbered by the vines. "The circle doesn't believe it's time for you to leave."

"Why does it get to decide? I need to talk to him."

"To say what, exactly?"

"That we can figure it out, a way to undo it."

"It's an incredibly powerful enchantment, Iellieth. However strongly you wish, it will not be enough."

Iellieth stopped struggling against the vines and turned to stare at her mentor. "Mara, all I've wanted since I left is a way to be free. But I don't want to be alone. I'm incredibly thankful to have joined you and your people, but Marcon needs help too."

"And what is it that you desire now, Iellieth?" Mara carefully uncoiled a strand of ivy from Iellieth's wrist.

Anger swelled in her chest. This really wasn't the time. She tugged again, but the vines held her tighter. She groaned and held still, surrendering herself to Mara's question. "When all I wanted was to be free . . . that was in reaction to the duke, to the power he held over me. But now I want so much more. I want to understand where I belong in this world. At one time, I thought that answer would be simple. I can see now that it isn't. But beyond that, I don't know enough to be sure."

Mara smiled at her and lifted a few more vines, freeing her hands and feet. "You've taken the first step, then, cher'a. When we recognize that we don't know, we can begin to find out."

Iellieth pulled her arm free from one of the thicker strands. "All I've told him was that I wanted to get away from the castle and find somewhere that will accept me. He's left because he wants me to be able to do that." She pushed a loop of another vine off her thigh and wriggled her knee and ankle out of its grasp.

"He's not wrong to see those two realities as opposing forces." The druid's voice was slow and even.

Iellieth's frustration rose in reaction to Mara's calm. There would be time for this conversation later, once they were all three on their way out of the Vagarveil Wood. She shouted as another vine slipped over her once-freed hand: "But I don't want him to turn back into a statue!"

Her voice broke, and she clung to a vine that refused to release her. "He's trying to find someone, and I can go with him. I can help."

"And where will you go, cher'a?"

The final clinging vine fell off the branch it hung from overhead, and Iellieth yanked her hand free. Panting, she rubbed her wrist. She could feel the answer drifting toward her, riding on the breeze. "Yvayne." The name was sweet on her tongue, and her swirling emotions stilled. That's where they would go. "She knew who he was and where he was from. Or when." Iellieth glared at the vines, waiting to see if they were going to ensnare her again. "She can help us discover where we need to go, and you and I can keep training while she helps him."

Mara looked away from her, back into the circle between the trees. "I think that is a wise path, Iellieth."

She was leaving something out again. "Mara, what is it?"

Her mentor shook her head. "It's nothing, cher'a. Go and find him. It's time to leave." Iellieth took a step forward, but Mara caught her hand. "It will be a long journey. Not here"—she waved her hands over the ground and then laid them on Iellieth's heart—"but here."

❧

"MARCON," IELLIETH YELLED, DUCKING BENEATH THE long arms of the pines. "Marcon?" The amulet glowed warm against her chest as she raced over the foothills away from the colony. Energy from the forest swirled around her to aid her search. She redirected its flow back to the trees as she ran, leaving a trail of delicate white blossoms at the base of their trunks so she and Marcon could find their way back to the conclave.

"Marcon?" She climbed onto a pile of rocks that looked out over the woodland. The forest stretched as far as she could see. He could be anywhere.

Iellieth ran her fingers over the amulet's familiar points and curves. "Help me find him," she whispered. A light pulsed inside the ruby. She was getting closer. Iellieth scrambled over the rocks and continued down the slope. Why would he have gone this way?

She stepped to the edge of a sharp ridge and peered down. A shape moved on the rocks below her, and the amulet flashed again. A lighter gray shifted against the stormcloud boulders that had fallen from the steep slope. Marcon.

Bare rock bit against her palms as she clambered down the hillside. How had he gotten down there? A sheer cliff rose twenty feet above him. "Marcon," she shouted again. He didn't move.

Not that turn. This one. Hold on to this tree. The instructions flowed over her as the forest guided her down the treacherous path. A few of the bends were so steep she lost sight of him, winding around the uneven hills on her invisible trail.

He tried to lift himself but faltered. She slid over a fallen tree and bounded between lines of erosion carved by the spring melt as it trickled down from the mountains.

Breathless, she arrived beside him, doubled over with her hands on her knees. He squinted up at her, his skin aflame with raised, welt-like runes. "Iellieth." His forehead wrinkled, and he groaned as he reached over and pulled a spherical object onto his chest. A silver helmet, with a black rose emblem at the crown. The Amastacia guard. The jawline of the helmet had been cleaved in two, and dark stains spattered the underside.

Marcon grimaced and pushed himself up to a seated position.

Iellieth knelt beside him. "Marcon, where did you go? What happened?" Relief washed over her, drowning out her questions about the helmet and why she had been left behind.

"I—" He stared up at her, dazed.

Warnings swarmed all around her, darting from tree to tree. Something wasn't right. "We need to go." She pulled beneath his arm to encourage him to stand. When he remained stationary, she wrapped both of her hands around his, insistent.

His burning skin cooled beneath her touch, and the markings faded. Marcon sighed and blinked his eyes clear. He heaved himself up to his feet, his hand wrapped around the hilt of his sword. "Iellieth," he turned to her, "there was a great force in the woods. Hundreds. The fallen soldiers, I found them over there." He pointed at a small hill a hundred yards away and shook his head. "They had been ripped apart. I . . . I knew I'd made a mistake, leaving. I tried to come back, to tell you, but I couldn't."

Ripped apart? The hairs along Iellieth's arms and the back of her neck prickled. "It's alright, Marcon. Please, we must go." She tugged on his arm to have him follow her up the hill. Iellieth shuddered. Once they were safe, she would mourn for the soldiers. Their lives had been cut short believing they were helping her.

Marcon resisted her and gestured away from the direction she'd come. "Lady, no. The lycanthropes are circling around through the forest. I saw the tail end of their ranks. It will be safer if we travel south."

She'd lost all sense of direction in her search for him. The white flowers would take her back. "Where are they going?"

"To the druids."

No. They hadn't left yet. Only the first wave had vacated, and the next wasn't supposed to leave until the following dawn. There should have been several more days still before the werewolves reached them. "We need to warn them." Iellieth's heart raced. Her conclave. She couldn't abandon them to an ambush. "I promised Mara I would find you and bring you back."

"No, the soldiers' bodies." Marcon's jaw twinged. "Lady, they're no match for this force."

"All the more reason for us to tell them."

"We'll need to run."

Iellieth narrowed her eyes. She would succeed in this service to the druids. It might not make up for the danger she'd brought to their door, but she wouldn't run and surrender them to die on her behalf. "Then we run."

CHAPTER 25

Evening fell across Ophelia's thicket. The druid had emerged from her cave shortly after delivering the news of Genevieve's impending departure to the city of her enemies, looking tired but resolved. Genevieve spent the afternoon and early evening hours alone, practicing the connection exercises Mariellen had taught her and that Ophelia had helped her hone.

The great wolf appeared behind her. She felt the weight of his paws beneath the root structure she studied. Though he said nothing, she could hear his smile.

He waited for her to thank the oak for her time and shared meditation. "Are you ready to go with me?" Sariel asked.

"Yes, though I'll need to say good-bye to Ophelia first."

"She's waiting for you inside the cave."

Genevieve took one last look at the woods blanketed in cobalt twilight. She would miss the peacefulness, the gentle scents of pine and new life, amid the press and bustle of the city. Sariel's silver fur gleamed in the pale moonlight as led the way up the rocky path to the cave entrance. Ophelia sat just inside the opening, eyes closed.

"Varra," Genevieve began, "we're leaving. I wanted to thank you and say good-bye."

Ophelia's opalescent eyes slowly fluttered open. The older woman smiled mischievously. "I know you are unenthused about your destination, but I believe you will enjoy the trip."

"What do you mean?" She'd been through these woods only a few days before. What would be particularly special this time?

"I won't spoil Sariel's surprise for you, but you must listen, child, once more before you go."

Genevieve sat in front of her new teacher and waited for her lesson.

"As you learn the ways of the wolf, you must come to know her desires. She rests at your core, has allied herself with your instincts. The inner wolf is patient and will wait for you to learn her ways. However," Ophelia paused to draw a deep breath and study Genevieve's features, "should she believe you are in danger, she will act. You must remember this."

Genevieve nodded. Ophelia had given her a similar warning before, though she didn't understand what precisely would constitute danger to her lycanthropy. She didn't think of the curse coursing through her veins as an inner wolf companion, as Ophelia so often referred to it. "You're saying that, even if I don't mean to, I'll transform if the inner wolf thinks it will keep me safe?"

"Very good, child, yes." Ophelia's smile softened, and she took Genevieve's hand in hers. "You have provided a light for me, following a heavy loss of one who studied with me so many years ago. You provided a path out of my grief. I know your own weighs on you still." A single tear trickled down the wrinkles of Ophelia's face, darkening its shade of pale sage moss. "I will be watching over you, my child." Ophelia kissed Genevieve's knuckles and released her hand.

The weight of losing her family returned with this parting, and Genevieve sat motionless. Had Ophelia known someone from her conclave, someone that she taught, who had died when the werewolves attacked? Or was she speaking of someone else?

"Genevieve," Sariel's voice gently echoed through her mind. "It's time for us to go."

Ophelia smiled at him and closed her eyes, turning to her evening meditations. Sariel walked deeper into the cave system, his shimmering silver fur disappearing into the murky blackness untouched by the celestial light from outside.

Genevieve waited a moment longer. She bowed her head in a fond farewell to Ophelia, grateful for their time together. Without the druid and Sariel finding her, the lycanthropy would have taken over. And with her death, the last trace of her family would have vanished as well.

Her gratitude expressed, she drew herself up and hurried after Sariel. "I thought we were going to Andel-ce Hevra?" she called out to him.

"We are." Sariel's voice floated through her mind.

"Then where are you going?" They needed to travel south and east to reach the city.

The great wolf plodded out of one of the cave structure's deeper tunnels. "This way."

She swallowed a sigh of frustration and followed him. He and Ophelia were well matched in their affinity for mystery and surprise.

Luminescent mushrooms lit the back caverns of Ophelia's home to guide their way. Genevieve followed in silence for several minutes around the damp turns and sloping passageways. She prepared to tell Sariel that she had to know where they were going before she would continue any further.

But then the light ahead changed. A faint pink glow shone against the dark rocks and shifted into a warm shade of tangerine. "Sariel," Genevieve whispered, "what is that?"

The wolf stopped and waited for her to squeeze beside him. She leaned into his warm fur and peered ahead. The lights danced against the wet stones. All the hues shared by the sunset and the sunrise were there, intermingling. "This, my dear Genevieve, is a shortcut."

"A shortcut to where?"

"To my home." He turned, and his golden eyes bored into hers. "To the Brightlands."

They rounded the corner and there, at the end of the tunnel, a mirror made of liquid glass bade her to step inside. Colors rolled over one another across its shimmering surface.

The tunnel granted space enough for her and Sariel to easily stand side by side without squeezing as they approached. The portal mirrored their figures back to them. Sariel's regal head was taller than hers, his fur alight in the dancing rainbow light. Genevieve's emerald eyes shone in contrast to her beige skin and raven hair. Around her face, the streak of white hair that she'd had since birth took on the swirling colors.

A third figure appeared between her and Sariel while she meditated on the liquid sunset. Genevieve gasped. A wolf, head waist-high, with a frame much slighter than

Sariel's muscular build. It too had black hair, and rings of white fur surrounded its striking green eyes.

"Sariel . . ."

"I believe this is the wolf within that Ophelia was telling you about." He met the eyes of her reflection and tilted his head, looking down at the wolf it showed between them.

So the inner wolf was real? No additional creature stood beside her, but the figure in the portal never looked away from her.

"Would you like to meet her, Genevieve?"

"Is she really there?"

Sariel chuckled. "Step into the portal, and we will see."

Genevieve exhaled slowly. Her reflection didn't change as she approached, and the wolf didn't move. No one in the last hundred years of her conclave's history had traveled to another plane, at least not as far as she knew. Genevieve closed her eyes and stepped through the colorful liquid glass.

🐾

AND INTO A WORLD OF IMPOSSIBLE COLOR AND BEAUTY.

Before her stretched an utterly unknown landscape. Rolling azure fields cascaded into magenta cliffs. Midnight lazuli bushes with pearlescent flowers grew alongside scarlet trees with blood-red leaves. Sunset bathed the sky in deep oranges and drips of purple.

The dire wolf appeared beside her, eyes crinkled in amusement. "Sariel, what is this place?"

The smile in his voice was infectious. "Welcome, Genevieve, to the Brightlands." The warmth of the sky reflected in his bronze eyes, and they glowed darker than usual.

She still stood with one wolf rather than two. "Where is the wolf I saw in the portal? You said we were coming here to meet her."

"And so we have." He trotted forward over the blue hills, and Genevieve hurried to keep pace with him.

"But why didn't she travel through the portal with us?"

"We'll have to find her, won't we?" He stopped, glancing at her, and then lowered to the ground. "It will be faster if you come along for a ride. Would you be opposed to that?"

Genevieve shook her head and climbed onto his back.

"Hold on tight, young druid daughter." Genevieve wrapped her fingers in the long fur at Sariel's shoulders, and the dire wolf sprinted toward the distant pink cliffs. Myriad colors unspooled beneath Sariel's feet. During her first night in the forest, with lycanthropy running through her veins, her heightened senses allowed her to perceive parts of the world she would have missed before. But this, this was something else altogether.

A herd of elk, with opaline pelts that glinted in rose, lilac, and palest blue, thundered across a distant hilltop, unaware or unafraid of the dire wolf and his companion sprinting in their direction.

"Did you see that?"

Sariel laughed in answer.

Overhead, a flock of midnight blue ravens with red-tipped wings studied the two travelers before they returned to the trees. "Who exactly are your people, Sariel?"

"They are like me, Genevieve."

"Wolves?" What would an entire society of Sariels be

like? Quizzical and quiet? Was there a reason he'd left them?

"You will see very soon."

Genevieve settled into her mount and resigned herself to waiting. Foreign birdcalls rose like mist from groves of trees. Though Sariel had been carrying her for at least an hour, the sun had yet to set.

A series of caves took shape before her across the pink cliff face, but Sariel darted around them, taking her through a shaded canyon hidden inside the cliffs. The stark rock face was even more striking up close. Strata of gold and quartz glittered across their expansive heights. They captured the warm sunset light from above and glimmered, casting their brilliance on the narrow trail. They wound down and through the canyon for another hour or more until Sariel began to slow.

The path curved upward toward an overspill of the deep blue grass and bright purple flowers at the top. He plodded up, careful to keep her on his back so that the steepness of the gorge wouldn't cause her to slip off. "Come and stand beside me, Genevieve," Sariel said as they reached the edge of the grasses. They were midway up the canyon's height, and she dismounted and stood at his shoulder.

"This, druid daughter, is my home." A dark turquoise valley stretched before her eyes, and all across its surface, dire wolves and their pups roamed. Some were onyx, others copper, with feet varying shades of olive green. Flowers and vines sprouted from their coats, the botanical growths as much a part of them as their multicolored, radiant fur.

The young ones played, and their elders watched them, lounging near berry bushes. Their care for one another, their bond, was clear. It was like watching her conclave from above if they had been under some magical spell that turned them all into wolves. Genevieve looked at Sariel, at a loss for words.

His eyes glowed warmly back at her. "Would you like to meet my family?"

"I would," she said hoarsely.

They climbed down the embankment and picked their way over to the society of wolves. Many raised their heads curiously as she passed. It seemed two-legged creatures without wings were rare in this part of the Brightlands.

"The daimon have lived here for some time," Sariel explained as they walked. Tiny silver leaves had emerged from his coat. They traced delicate lines along his back and down the front of his legs. She would never have said it to him, but he looked fuzzier than he had in the forest with Ophelia.

"We were displaced after the flood and came to settle here. Traces of our stories have lived on in the legends of your homeland and across Azuria, spirits of protection, inspiration, guidance"—Sariel's eyes flashed—"but we are so much more."

Her lorekeepers had spoken of an ancient society of powerful, creative spirits. How had they failed to mention that they were wolves?

"I brought you here because I believe my people can aid you, Genevieve. You need a safe place to practice your transformations. But I hope, in time, that you can help us as well."

"Help you? How?"

Sariel looked out over his community, and her eyes followed his. His gaze rested on pups rolling over one another, young daimon racing, and stopped on a stately female wolf at the far end of the settlement, with great antlers any elk would have been proud to bear. "We would like to roam. My people are happy, but we need more space. We are too many for this area tucked away inside the Brightlands."

"But how can I help with that?" Genevieve couldn't take her eyes from the beautiful wolf with the antlers, bathed in golden light. She was supposed to cross the ocean and find Yvayne, not stay here and practice accessing an inner wolf. She still slept fitfully, plagued by questions about what had happened to her family.

Sariel seemed to read her thoughts. "I know you have many pressing responsibilities in the months ahead. My people's greatest hope, we believe, is to make a home among the elves of the Realms. When the time arises, will you help us to make our case with them?"

Only the very oldest of her community remembered a time when their conclave had open relations with the Elven Realms. They spoke of those years with reverence, recounting the stories of their elders, many of whom had learned the druidic arts from the elves. "It has been a long time since any of my people spoke with them or were called to visit," Genevieve said. "They have grown closed off." She didn't want to disappoint Sariel, but why would they listen to her?

"I understand that, Genevieve. We only ask that you try. It would start as simply as you traveling with me, claiming me as your companion. Though their rangers are now few, many still work alongside our wolf kin, keeping the darkness that closes in across their lands at bay. If they will hear us, others might as well."

"Sariel, you have done so much for me." Genevieve sighed. "I promise to give whatever help I am able." The wolf rubbed his head against her neck in thanks, and she stumbled back, surprised by the expression of affection. Genevieve caught herself and chuckled. She wrapped an arm around his neck and rested her head against his fur. Tears welled in her eyes. Nothing could fill the gaping hollow at her core where her family had been, but here was someone, an entire community, who might help her to find purpose once more. "Thank you," she whispered.

⚜

HOURS LATER, THE SUN REMAINED LOW IN THE SKY. Genevieve gave up waiting for it to set fully and returned her attention to the beautiful golden wolf she'd seen at a distance: Aspen, Sariel's mate and the leader of the daimon. "Our name descends from the word for guiding spirits," she explained. Her powerful alto voice glided through Genevieve's mind when she spoke. Flowering vines draped off her massive antlers, and the same flora trailed the ground behind her, hanging low from her tail. "What you need, Genevieve, is to make your peace with the spirit who resides within. Sariel tells me that you saw her?"

"I did, yes. Just before we stepped through the portal." She glanced at Sariel to see if she should say more. It felt strange to be the only one who spoke aloud, but she wasn't sure that she could communicate with both of them tele-pathically at once.

"If the two of you remain at odds," Aspen said to her, "your every quest will be made more difficult. But, if you can find harmony, an understanding, you will become a pack." The wolf tilted her head to the side, a smile. "Or at least a pair."

They spent the next hour practicing Genevieve's transformations into a werewolf. Whatever she tried, she couldn't find the inner spirit. Aspen led her to their den and told her to rest. They would try again after.

Genevieve arose refreshed at dawn and rushed outside to greet the pale orange sky. The two daimon joined her in the fields.

"How are you thinking of her?" Aspen asked after her third failed attempt. "What are you picturing?"

"A raven-colored wolf with emerald eyes." The wolf had seemed peaceful, calm. Nothing like the werewolves who had destroyed her conclave.

"Don't think of them," Aspen said. "I can feel your thoughts shifting, like a rotten stench on the air. Set them aside."

Genevieve tried to follow Aspen's instructions. The memories from the fires dimmed.

"Let me help you." Sariel came to stand in front of her. "Lay your fingers on my head. There you are. Now, picture the young wolf you saw."

She slid her fingers over Sariel's silver fur, careful not to disturb the tiny blossoms that had appeared since his return to the daimon. His skin was warm beneath his coat. She thought of the gemstone green eyes that had stared back at her, ones that looked just like hers.

Genevieve's pulse quickened as her inner wolf responded, scratching against invisible bindings that held her back. Her toes curled, morphing into claws. "No," she cried, bending down to clutch her feet and return them to normal.

Aspen growled behind her. "Trust. You cannot trust that which you do not know. Give her a chance."

"What if we gave her a name, Genevieve?" Sariel asked. "Would that help?"

A name would make the other form less frightening, but should the wolf feel so separate from herself? "Jade," she thought to the two daimon, "let's call her Jade."

Sariel's smile warmed her. "Jade," Genevieve called in the same way she spoke to the daimon, "Jade, might I meet you?"

A deep sigh rippled through her body as the wolf answered. Jade felt . . . unsure, as well. She was young and —Genevieve squinched her eyes shut, trying to understand—frightened. She didn't know if they were safe or what to make of these two giant wolves.

Jade conjured a picture for Genevieve. The two daimon transformed into firelit werewolves. Jade had seen her memories, or lived through them, as she had. The young wolf trembled at the thought of them being threatened by such monsters.

"These wolves are different," Genevieve thought to her inner wolf self. "They're here to help us. They won't hurt you."

A round paw pressed on the top of Genevieve's foot, asking to be let through. Genevieve exhaled slowly. She could allow that.

Jade resumed their transformation, helping Genevieve to navigate into a form somewhere between their two selves. Her fur-covered arms pressed into the turquoise grasses of the Brightlands, and two emerald eyes peered out at the pleased faces of Sariel and Aspen.

CHAPTER 26

P anic had descended upon the druid conclave by the time Iellieth and Marcon returned. Iellieth dodged a young family, their backs laden with provisions, as she searched for Mara. A stream of people fled deeper into the forest, and Iellieth dashed around them. She fell back as a horse thundered past but finally made it to the center of Mara's clearing. The druid stood on the far side, ushering people out and away from the approaching danger.

"Mara," Iellieth shouted. She and Marcon raced to the druid's side. "We need to leave, everyone, now. Marcon saw the werewolves. They're almost here." Iellieth grabbed Mara's arm, but the druid pushed her hand away.

She looked into Iellieth's eyes only for a moment. "Marcon, get her out of here." Her command was calm and even, a sharp contrast to the fear that surrounded them. Marcon inclined his head.

"No, we can't leave you." Iellieth clung to her teacher. "We can help. You don't need to stay here." Tears blurred her vision. It was her fault Lucien was coming. If anyone stayed behind, it should be her.

"Mara, they are many," Marcon said, trying to help her. "An entire company of armored werewolves." He laid a hand on Iellieth's back. She sensed his readiness to pull her away if Mara refused them again.

"We will give you as long as we can." Mara's face was grim.

"No!" Iellieth screamed. "If there are too many of them to stop, we need to run." She trembled. "Or I can stay." She was frightened but determined. Linolynn's four soldiers were sacrifice enough.

Marcon gripped her arm. "Lady, I made you a promise. It's time."

Mara nodded and placed her hand over Iellieth's. "We're holding them off for our family, cher'a, and that includes you. Now go. I've told Yvayne. She'll be waiting for you." Marcon held on to her shoulders as Mara strode away toward the approaching enemy force.

"But we can help them, Marcon." The corner of his mouth twitched as he looked down at her. "Please." Hot tears ran down her face. She couldn't leave Mara behind.

Screams echoed through the woods, and Mara ran ahead. She darted onto the path on the opposite side of the clearing that led to the central meeting area. Their enemy had arrived.

Iellieth ducked beneath Marcon's hands and slipped free of his grasp, sprinting after Mara. Two more on the druids' side could only help. Marcon's footsteps thundered behind her, but she kept just out of reach.

She flew along the narrow trail following Mara and skidded to a stop at the opening to the larger clearing.

A dark army filled the edges of the forest across from them. They growled, muzzles lifted to the sky, thick arms raised and shaking. Some even brandished dark metal swords. In the center of the clearing, Mara stood behind a line of ten other druids, but they faced hundreds. Ice blossomed inside Iellieth as she understood Mara's plan. They would never defeat this horde. All they could do was delay the onslaught and give the others a chance to escape.

Even in Linolynn's grandest parades, had she witnessed so many soldiers? Row upon row of the hybrid creatures stood shoulder-to-shoulder behind the trees. Marcon, a solid wall behind her, wrapped his arm around her waist to pull her back. But she couldn't move. "I've never seen . . ."

A ripple ran over the forest as Mara raised her hands. The trees behind Iellieth and Marcon, and those across the entire circumference of the clearing, rose with a great ripping of earth. Their roots skittered—massive tentacles, spiders' legs, snakes—and carried them toward the center of the clearing. They swarmed, shambled, drowning out the werewolves' confused cries. The trees intertwined their lowest branches, linking hands and arms against the invaders. The forest would aid the druids in their fight. It encircled them, a living fortification.

Four great oaks came to rest around Mara as the last vestige of the division between forest and copse fell away. The line of druids wrapped in a ring around the four great trees. Instead of green sparks, tongues of bright, verdant flames coursed down Mara's arms and swirled about her.

Berivic tore through the gap in the trees that had opened behind Iellieth and Marcon and into the clearing. He shouted in Druidic, the few words she could pick out a cry of readiness, and withdrew two scimitars from his sides. Mara's hands twisted around her, and the wreath of flame she'd burned into the earth grew taller, pouring off of her arms and rising waist high. Her low-voiced incantations thrummed around the clearing, magically amplified by the power of her spell.

The dark ranks shifted, ready to respond, and wood groaned all around them. "Archers," Marcon said under his breath. He withdrew his shield and thrust it in front of her, placing her between it and his body. "Lady, please, we must go." A cloud of arrows launched into the sky and fell toward the circle of druids. They sliced through the trees and thunked into the branches and trunks. A tall druid to Mara's right crumpled to his knees, three arrows sunk deep into his torso.

Her feet wouldn't move. Could she help, or buy more time for those attempting to flee? The trickles of energy in her hands swirled in confusion. Should she run or fight?

Mara raised her hands up overhead, and a row of roots erupted from the earth beneath the lycanthropes. The invading force screamed as they were ripped apart by the above-ground vines and others pulled beneath the earth's surface.

A wave of werewolves answered the tremor, their feet crushing the bodies of their fallen kin as they ran to meet the druids.

One of the werewolf commanders climbed over a pile of bodies and boulders to stand atop a newly emerged rock, broken free by Mara's spell. He pointed a bulging, fur-covered arm at Mara and raised a guttural call, growling in a harsh tongue Iellieth couldn't understand, but the message was clear. They were going to kill her.

"Mara!" Iellieth yelled and ran into the fray. Shadows

flashed in the woods as she flew past, the trees gutting the lycanthropes as they tried to flank the small collection of druids. Their bodies transformed as they fell, returned to their original human forms. Mara's eyes were unseeing, rolled in the back of her head, and she delved deeper, growing more entrenched in her spell. The circle of flames rose to her shoulders and enveloped any enemy who made it through the oaks to draw close to her.

Opposite Iellieth, on the side nearest the invading host, druids and trees continued to fall as wave upon wave of the army advanced. Streaks of light darted through the trees, striking back at the werewolves. The commanders drove them on. The entire clearing would be surrounded within moments.

"Mara!" Iellieth screamed again. She gasped as a long blade tore through the torso of Traeyl, a woman she'd met the evening before, after her initiation. The slathering creature hooked her chest with the end of its blade. Her body spun through the air and tumbled to the ground.

Berivic, also running toward Mara, jumped graceful and strong as a deer and collided with three of the lycanthropes as they lunged toward the inner circle. The impact sent them flying into the solid trunks of trees, their heads smashed open. Bloody human bodies crumpled to the ground. Others took their places and snapped at Berivic as he ran. He barely outpaced them and dove into the shelter of the trees' whirling limbs.

"Iellieth, stop!" Marcon shouted after her. He was still several paces behind her, sprinting with sword and shield bared. If she could make it inside the trees, she could save Mara, and then Marcon could guide the three of them out.

A werewolf pounced at her, and Iellieth slid beneath its

body. Steel rang behind her as Marcon cut it down. The gap where Berivic had disappeared was covered in snarling creatures. Iellieth dodged around to the left. Twigs swiped at her face and neck, but they drew back as they recognized her and allowed her inside.

Mara's circle of green flames was lower, waist high once more, and she tossed spheres of fire at the battered were-wolves who managed to make it into the rings between the trees. Iellieth held back. Was it possible for her to pull Mara away without disrupting her powerful spell?

A cry echoed across from her. Berivic and a half-elf named Vinheri stood back-to-back, tearing down attackers. A flurry of blades amid the heavy hacking of their seemingly endless enemies, the two druids could only hold them off for so long.

A werewolf tore through the leaves to her right and ran at Mara from behind. "No," Iellieth shouted and leapt toward the figure. Dark green sparks shot from her fingertips and caught the werewolf in the back of the neck. It whimpered and crashed to the ground. Iellieth ripped her dagger from her boot, backing further into the treeline. The creature pushed itself up onto four legs and stalked toward her.

Blood pounded in her ears. More were approaching. They would break through the encircling trees at any moment.

A slinging branch caught her in the back of the shoulder and Iellieth winced, stumbling forward. The werewolf growled and lowered its head, preparing to pounce. Poisonous saliva dripped from its fangs.

Iellieth's arm shook, clutching her dagger. She'd have to dodge out of the way and then fire a second stream of sparks. Her legs tensed.

A roar from behind her ripped through the trees, and Marcon slid between her and the lycanthrope. It flung its body into his shield, and Marcon met its head, the metal ringing. With a second shout, his sword erupted in flame, and he drove the blade into the base of its neck. A gout of blood spurt forth, and the werewolf's body fell limp, returning to her human form.

Marcon turned to her, his eyes blazing.

The earth across the clearing groaned as the larger trees began to fall, their roped limbs pulled to the ground. Roots ripped through dirt as they tried to embed themselves back beneath the surface. Werewolf bodies flew from the flailing branches. The trees crashed into the ground, crying out as they fell. The beasts had breached the defensive wall.

A wave of arrows found its way through the remaining branches. "Marcon!" Iellieth cried, pointing. She hunched by his side, both of them covered by his shield.

A gurgle and thump beside them. Berivic had fallen beneath the rain of arrows, ten paces away.

Mara shouted, her fire circle failing, only a hot bed of coals protecting her. Three wolves stalked around her, waiting for their opportunity to strike. She blasted two at once. The balls of green flame exploded against their muzzles, reducing their flesh to ash. They howled in pain as they died.

Both of Iellieth's hands shot toward her mentor as the third wolf leapt at her back. She caught its shoulder with a thick ray of green energy and knocked it away from its target. The werewolf fell against the coals, its coat immediately erupting in bright green flames.

"Mara!" Iellieth cried and ran forward. The druid's eyes

flashed at her, the same green as her fire had been. Iellieth froze, held by her mentor's spell.

"We cannot lose you now, cher'a, or it will be over before it's even begun. Find Yvayne. Go."

Iellieth resisted the magic that held her. Tears prickled at the corners of her eyes. Marcon's sword sang behind her, beating back attackers. Mara couldn't do this. She wasn't ready for the end. She needed her.

A single tear ran down Mara's bronze cheek. "I'm so proud of you, cher'a." She pressed her hands together and bowed her head to Iellieth and then turned away. The spell broke, and Iellieth fell onto the ground. The druid shouted once more, a new spell, and stomped her foot. Another great rumbling. Werewolves continued to pour into the circle, the dam of ancient trees utterly destroyed.

The earth between Mara and Iellieth split. The hybrid wolves screamed as they fell to their deaths. Iellieth scrambled up and away from the divide. Mara kept one hand spread wide behind her, increasing the gap between Iellieth and the horde. She was giving her the chance to run.

Iellieth dashed to Marcon's side. He blocked a werewolf's bite with his shield, and she stabbed it in the eye. The squelching noise turned her stomach. She ripped the dagger out, squinting so as not to see the blade.

A cold wind blew on the back of her neck. Her body shivered. She turned back. A robed figure walked slowly through the divide in the trees. The werewolves beside him stopped, waiting. His cloak rippled behind him, and shadows pooled beneath his long fingers, forming dark clouds that drifted over the churned earth.

Space tunneled between them as the mage locked eyes on Iellieth. All other movement, all other life around her faded. Darkness fell along the edges of her vision. She could see nothing but the sickly pale, yellow-green mage, the two of them alone in this moment of abyss.

His mouth twisted sideways in a smirk. "It's been so long." His voice sighed out all around him, a smoky baritone that might once have been seductive were it not so tainted and decayed. The mage tilted his head slowly, the grin in his eyes brightening. "Good-bye." His eyes flashed, a soiled yellow, and threw Iellieth back.

The robed figure raised his arm to shoulder height, pointing at the center of her chest as she scrambled up and away. "Kill her," he growled.

The werewolves nearby howled and raced toward her and Marcon. "Go." She spun and sprinted for the mountain foothills.

Mara's voice filled the space behind them, and spheres of flame rained from the sky and struck their pursuers. Iellieth turned and blasted another werewolf with a narrowed beam of energy. The trees screamed in agony, the smell of oil and smoke heavy on the air as the werewolves set them ablaze.

Iellieth choked back a sob. Marcon panted as they fled, gripping his side where claw marks had slashed through his coat of mail.

IELLIETH GUIDED MARCON THROUGH THE FOREST, following the path the trees laid out for her. Werewolves teemed in the woods behind them, gathering in packs before they made their second strike. She'd led them away from the direction the rest of the conclave had gone, hoping to avoid further loss of life.

They reached the foothills, where the forest thickened. "Obscure our steps, protect our passage," she whispered to the trees, unsure if they could heed her wishes or not. She squeezed below her ribs as her lungs cramped. Her final sight of Mara, standing alone across from the dark-robed mage, surrounded by werewolves on all sides, clung to the edge of her vision.

"We must climb, lady," Marcon advised between rapid breaths. "It will be harder for their archers to hit us if we have the aid of the slope." She nodded, too winded to speak, and guided them through the hills at the steepest angle she could manage.

In the distance, a final blast. From the center of the conclave's home, where Mara had been, the trees rippled outward as they fell. Each reached out for its neighbor, holding on to one another as they tried to endure the end. Their lament washed over Iellieth, striking her heart, as it reverberated across the forest, root to root and branch to branch. She fell to her knees.

Browns and greens swirled around her. Death nipped at their heels. "Iellieth." Marcon's voice lifted her from the fog, his arm pulling her up from the ground.

"She's gone." Iellieth wheezed. "I can feel it. Gone." Her breath came too rapidly, flying in and out, shallow, faster and faster. She turned, wide-eyed, to Marcon.

His brow furrowed as he watched her. He took hold of both her wrists and raised her arms overhead. She groaned as her lungs seized and then expanded, oxygen rushing in. "Lady, Mara did this for you." His voice was urgent. "We must not waste it."

He was right. But each step away from Mara felt like a betrayal.

Branches snapped in the hills below them as the werewolves advanced, tracking them through the forest. "We must find Yvayne," Iellieth said. Mara's final instruction.

"Lead on, lady. I'll shield us."

A werewolf's broken cry below. They'd been spotted. Any hope of their escape now depended on the forest's aid.

THE OAK'S GNARLED BARK BIT INTO YVAYNE'S PALMS. As steady as a heartbeat, the tree absorbed messages from those around it, passing through root and branch. She pressed her forehead against its trunk, listening, begging the news to change.

Why had she left them alone?

Yvayne tore herself away from the tree, sprinting back through the snow to her treehouse. The water. It would show her what transpired in the valley below.

She crumbled the herbs she'd prepared that morning in her hands and sprinkled them over the top of the bowl. "Vagarveil Wood, grant me to see."

The crushed leaves floated to the bowl's edges, and a once familiar valley came into view beneath the ripples.

Trees splayed out of patches of ground where they didn't belong. Dirt and debris coated formerly grassy surfaces. The forest had helped them. She whispered to the water and guided the vision around the trees. Werewolves vaulted over one another as they sprinted deeper into the woods, their eyes wild with bloodlust. One tore into the body of a fallen druid. The beast's snout dripped with blood.

Yvayne shook. The images rippled beneath her breath as she urged the sight, faster, around the remains of the druids' clearing, where now a displaced wood spread. Where was Mara?

There. She sensed her, the druid's energetic pull, calling the forest's life force to herself, much as Yvayne had done when she tried to rescue Fhaona. But at this scale?

Her friend didn't plan to survive.

Yvayne's lips pressed together, contorted. She couldn't bear to see it. Not again. The vision stopped, and Yvayne squeezed her eyes shut, teardrops disturbing the water's surface.

But she owed it to her friend to bear witness to her final moments. She had to understand. "Take me to her," she asked the spirits, and they rode the waves of energy arcing around the trees, flocking to the druid's side.

Yvayne's breath caught at the sight of her friend. Mara was bent nearly in half, holding herself up with one hand on her knee. Cruel black arrows stood out from the arch of her back, and dark stains pooled along her green and copper garments.

He was there, across from her, hovering off the ground beside the bodies of his fallen werewolves. Lucien. His eyes glinted, and he hurled a comet of necrotic energy at Mara, meant to agonize and destroy. She batted it away, her body wracked by the effort. Why wasn't she casting anything back?

Mara glanced over her shoulder, her lips working to hold the edges of a spell. She was delaying them, then, holding out as long as she could.

Yvayne whispered to the water, searched its surface, frantic for the rubied glow of Iellieth's hair. Blood seeped into the earth all around the clearing, bright in fresh wounds, rust in those that had died in earlier waves. She wasn't there. She'd gotten away. Mara was holding on so that Iellieth could escape.

A wave of arrows burst from Lucien's pack of were-wolves, and Yvayne's eyes clenched shut, blocking out the carnage. She peeked, a sigh of relief as Mara rose, and a flurry of leaves rushed upward in a great torrent and blocked the arrows. Her friend had moments left, nothing more. Yvayne panted, watching. She hadn't the power to stop them, not from here.

But she could help.

She chanted the strengthening spell over the water, calling further life to Mara from the surrounding wood-land. The druid had bet her life on Iellieth's escape, but together, they could achieve something more.

The corners of Mara's lips lifted. She could feel Yvayne's enchantment. A tear glinted in her eye. She knew she was no longer alone. Mara rose to her full height, her shoulders straight despite her wounds. Lucien laughed across the clearing and waved his hands in a circle around one another, conjuring a death curse. Mara closed her eyes, her spell prepared. It was time.

Lucien threw both of his arms overhead. Thunder echoed across the valley, and a dark cloud gathered above Mara. Blood dripped from the sky, and flashes of black necrotic energy struck the earth beneath.

Mara raised her head, grinned. She thrust both her hands forward, and a current of brilliant green struck Lucien in the chest. He stumbled back, clutching at the hole carved through the core of his being. His breath rattled, and his body crumpled to the ground.

A final blast of shimmering black streaked down and struck Mara. The druid fell.

The torrent of energy they'd conjured together ricocheted across the valley, obliterating the nearest wave of Lucien's forces. It shoved Yvayne backward, throwing her against the wall of her inner chamber. She ran back as the vision faded. Mara's body lay at the center of her woodland home. The few trees overhead stood still.

CHAPTER 27

The werewolves continued their pursuit as Iellieth and Marcon sprinted toward the mountains. They darted in and out of trees and over ridges, climbing higher into the Frostmaws.

Iellieth collapsed shortly before dusk. Orange light glinted through the trees, on the verge of fading to crimson before it disappeared and left them alone in the darkness. She clutched the cramp in her side, on her knees in the grass. "Marcon"—she panted—"I can't." Each breath was agony, and the muscles in her legs burned.

Marcon breathed heavily beside her but remained standing straight. "Take a moment, lady. I'll check our perimeter." He walked to the end of the ridge, shield at his side, to search the trees below for their pursuers.

"I don't see them," he said as he returned, "but we cannot linger." Iellieth nodded and crawled over to the rock face behind them. She sat back against it and drank deeply from their store of water. The woods had led them to a rocky outcropping, the stone cold against her back.

Mineral-rich water trickled down the boulders, and moss grew in the moist patches between them.

A faint howl, caught on the wind, whistled through the trees. "Marcon," Iellieth said under her breath. She used the rocks to push herself up. Her thighs and calves strained. "They're coming." The wind grew fiercer, howls calling from multiple directions. They would be surrounded.

Iellieth turned her thoughts inward and sought out the forest's energy to replenish the well inside her. Keeping her distance from the werewolves and dealing with them one at a time would be her best chance. The ground shook beneath her, roots responding to her energetic need.

Marcon readied himself beside her, sword in hand. "I don't know that I can summon the fire as I did earlier, lady." He shook his head, studying his sword closely. "For a moment, I felt the heat of Ignis once more, flowing through me." He traced the flame engraved into the hilt. "I had begun to think we were forever separated, that he would not answer me in this new time."

He smiled faintly at the symbol and then returned his attention to the woods surrounding their small cliff. His sword had sliced easily through the werewolves earlier that day, the brilliant flames matching the passion of their wielder.

A branch snapped in the shallow ravine below them. "They're here," Iellieth whispered, shaking. Earlier that morning, she'd imagined an orderly retreat through the woods, not a desperate sprint. Her neck and shoulders ached from the constant tension of glancing over her shoulders, anticipating a werewolf flying out of the underbrush at any moment to seize her by the throat.

Five lumbering lycanthropes stalked out of the woods,

lowering onto all fours once they were clear of the trees. They fanned out. Saliva dripped onto the moist ground. Three angled themselves at Marcon. Two faced her.

Iellieth's heart clambered in her chest, and she squeezed the dagger hilt tighter, flexing her knuckles. She wriggled the fingers of her left hand over the earth, unleashing her magic to flow freely.

"Eina, sh'ea yalei." Iellieth lowered her voice and called to the roots beneath her feet as Mara had taught her. Orbs of green light sparked between her fingers and floated along the ground.

Her spell was the signal they'd been waiting for. The two nearest her sprinted forward.

No roots rose from the earth.

Iellieth took a step back. The rock pressed hard against her shoulders. There was nowhere to go. Marcon called out beside her and ran forward, sword and shield ready to meet his foes. *"Eina, sh'ea yalei,"* Iellieth urged. She pushed another wave of energy out from herself, clenching the dagger. She'd felt the roots before. The werewolves pounded closer, eyes glinting in the low evening light. The orbs she'd released were nearly upon them. *Now.*

Two sets of grasping vines sprang from the earth's surface. They wriggled and slurped as they sought out their targets. Rubble crackled over the rocks.

The first werewolf yelped as a vine wrapped around his forelegs and flipped him onto his back.

The vines caught the second werewolf around the neck and tugged it back. The creature choked, clawing at the vines, slicing its own neck in its desperation to be free. Yellow eyes glinted at Iellieth, and the werewolf's body contorted. The lycanthrope convulsed, and its shape crumpled, bones crunching in on themselves as the werewolf transformed back into his smaller human frame. The roots yanked at the man's neck once more. It snapped, wet, deep, and he fell limp.

Iellieth spun around to aid Marcon. He battled two of the werewolves, forcing them back toward the woods, but the third had climbed up the jutting rocks, preparing to attack him from above. Iellieth pointed her palms at the creature, calling forth the ancient life within the rocks. Vines exploded from the boulders. Rock splintered. The werewolf crashed down with the rockslide, bones crunching as his heavy body tumbled.

Marcon gained the advantage over one of the two remaining werewolves. As the first retreated from the rock fall, Marcon's blade sliced through the other's skull. He threw himself backward to avoid the tumbling rocks. Iellieth caught his shoulder and steadied him against the shaking wall.

The final werewolf glowered at her and charged.

Iellieth slammed her fist into the ground. The roots answered. They sprang up beneath its feet and ensnared the werewolf. Marcon lunged forward and sliced its throat, dodging its snapping jaws.

Her vision swayed, and she tipped sideways, falling hard onto the rocky surface. "We must focus, channel our energy," Mara had told her over and over again. "We cannot guide the natural world to aid us without lending it some of our own power and consciousness."

Iellieth opened her eyes slowly. The blood of five human bodies darkened the rocks around her, their faces contorted in pain. Marcon's boots crunched on pebbles as he ran back to her, blood still dripping from his sword.

"I had to make sure they were dead," he said as her eyes widened, staring at the blade. "The first one you caught was still alive, but only just." Marcon knelt and helped her to sit up.

"What did I do?" Iellieth asked. Her knee pounded beneath her leather breeches. She must have struck it when she fell.

Marcon sat beside her. "You saved me, lady. And yourself."

Her hands trembled. She'd wanted their enemies to die. But so close to their bodies, resting only a few feet away . . . she'd caused this horror.

Marcon grasped her shoulder so she would look away from the corpses. "They would have done far worse to us, lady. And you did not ask to be attacked." He helped her to her feet and held out their waterskin. "The forest will take care of the bodies. We need to continue on, far enough for them to lose our scent."

Iellieth picked her way carefully through the forest. Her knee was swelling, and each step forward was a battle of wills between herself and her sore muscles. Her head swam from the heavy expenditure of magic. The earth had answered her call. Each tree she passed reminded her, helped to steady her on their way. They remained ever-present as night descended.

A brook coursed through the forest ahead of them. Iellieth sighed and sank beside its burbling waters. She splashed the cool water onto her face, and the droplets spoke of the mountains they had traversed on their path to her.

Her insides calmed, soothed by the creek. The creatures they'd fought had killed her fellow druids. They'd murdered her teacher without cause. But she couldn't entirely shake how, in death, they'd looked like ordinary men.

Moonlight glinted off the water and shimmered over their skin. Once she'd caught her breath and cleansed the dirt and blood from her hands, Marcon talked her through tending to wounds and creating bandages. Three deep gashes ran down his side from one of the were-wolves' paws, and his arm had been sliced by an arrow. The runes tattooed across his skin rippled over muscles and glowed faintly in the moonlight. Those nearest his wounds stood raised from the surface of his skin, glaring and red. As Iellieth dug through their bag for a store of bandages, a small jar rolled out and came to rest by Marcon's boot.

He caught it and turned the jar carefully in his fingers. "Mara's tincture," he said softly, smiling. "She taught me the recipe, though I haven't been able to find one of the herbs." He met her eyes. "She wanted to make sure I could create more, should you need it." He looked down at the burbling brook. "Or if she were unable to make it for you."

Iellieth's heart swelled, a wave of grief rising, cresting, crashing. "She said she was proud of me." She brushed away the tears and wiped her running nose. "But I haven't done anything for her to be proud of yet."

Marcon leaned forward and laid a hand on her ankle. "I wish I knew a way to help you see how that isn't true. What about the spells you conjured back there?" He nodded in the direction they'd come. "Were those not the workings of a mighty druid?"

Iellieth shook her head. "I don't know what I would have done had there been more." She hugged her knees into her chest. "Mara also taught me an incantation for healing, but I don't think I can summon anything more today." She hadn't been able to stop shivering since the final spell that had nearly knocked her unconscious. "She told me you only have so much energy each day, and then it must be replenished."

"I'd not have you waste it on me, lady." Marcon finished securing his bandages and slipped back into his linen shirt. "Had either of us been bitten, I might ask you to try."

She couldn't return his smile at this one bright side to their predicament. The creek continued on through the vast reaches of the Stormside Forest. Eventually, it would find its way to the ocean.

Marcon held a blanket out to her. "Get some rest, lady."

Iellieth nodded and laid her head on a mossy rock. The stars twinkled brightly. Sadness swelled in her chest again, and she closed her eyes against their cheery glittering.

She woke once in the night as Marcon moved them across the creek to a sheltered cove upstream. He carried her through the water to disguise their tracks, only stepping on the bank when the creek pooled too deep for him to see the bottom. He mumbled a prayer as he walked. The language was low and scratchy, but it set her at ease, and she turned her face toward his voice.

In the morning, Edvard sat beside them, a letter tied to his ankle.

᭒᭒᭒

"Marcon," Iellieth said, shaking his shoulder. "Our bird."

She scooted over and knelt beside the raven. *"Nor corveau."* Iellieth spoke its word of wakening, and Edvard's eyes opened.

Katarina's voice lilted perfectly from the raven's

mouth. Iellieth had never heard her so frightened. "Iellieth, I am relieved you're alright. We've been so worried. Are you coming back soon? Are you safe? Something's happened. They declared war, and Scad—"

The message stopped. The earth tilted sideways. What had happened to Scad? Her hands wouldn't stop shaking, and she couldn't grasp the twine. Marcon laid a hand on her shoulder before he leaned forward to untie the letter from the bird's ankle.

Katarina's usually clear hand had hastily scrawled the second half of her message. Was she in danger too?

Scad's disappeared. Your mother is frantic. Please come back.

The fear from their flight the day before returned to engulf her. Marcon wordlessly took the letter from her trembling hand and read it over.

Iellieth couldn't speak. Her lips quivered. Life without Scad . . . this was all her fault. What could have happened to him? "What if he left trying to look for me? What if the werewolves found him and—" She lowered her head and clamped her hands around her mouth, suppressing the sobs that shook her shoulders.

"Iellieth," Marcon said after her initial shock had ebbed, "he couldn't have made it this far. And the werewolves were coming from the opposite direction, from the mountains. Where would he have gone to look for you?"

She shook her head, unsure. *Think.* She pushed her hair back and looked at Marcon. "Hadvar." She exhaled, confident her hunch was correct. "He would have gone to Hadvar. He wouldn't have believed the duke that something had happened to me before I got there. And I'm not sure anyone could have seen what happened with the mistransmigration."

Marcon was right: Scad would have been safe from

the werewolves. But he wouldn't know anything of the coming war. What if he were caught on the wrong side? Iellieth wrapped her arms around herself, fingers clenched into fists. "I should have sent them word sooner." How could she have been so selfish? Why had she assumed Scad wouldn't go searching for her on his own? She laid her forehead on her raised knees.

Recounting what she should have done differently wasn't going to help Scad. Marcon walked back to her, their container of water dripping after he'd refilled it.

"We need to find Yvayne," Iellieth said. "She can help me, can teach me what—" She swallowed, pushing the wave of grief down. There would be time for mourning later. "What Mara and I didn't have time for." She brushed the remaining tears and salt from her cheeks and rose. "She may be able to help us find Quindythias too." And perhaps Scad as well.

Marcon grinned and glanced away. "I hope so, lady." He met her gaze, slowly. "Do you know how to find her?"

"No." Iellieth bit her lip. "Somewhere in the mountains."

"Then we're getting closer," Marcon said.

Iellieth chuckled. It was the lightest she'd felt since he'd disappeared the day before. "That's true, we are." Where would Yvayne reside in the vast reaches of the Frostmaw Mountains?

Marcon walked beside her as they trekked through the woods. "Away from the wolves and toward Yvayne," she chanted over and over again to the trees. They emitted ripples of energy in response, guiding her path.

They stopped for a rest before noon, the air around them already colder as they climbed to higher altitudes.

The sharp range of the Frostmaws towered above them like jagged teeth, spanning both sides of the horizon.

"Lady, might I say something?" Marcon rubbed his jaw. "I wanted to explain why"—he looked away down the southern range—"why I left you yesterday."

He turned back to her, arms crossed over his chest. "Staying with me makes you a target, Iellieth, more so than you already are. If we can find a way to break the bonds, as Mara talked about, I would like to do so. But regardless, I'll not take for granted that the amulet binds me to you, that you and it are responsible for keeping me alive."

"But I—"

He shook his head, stopping her. "Lady, if our enemies were to discover that in harming you, they would destroy me as well"—Marcon sighed deeply—"it's not a risk I'm willing for you to take."

"But it isn't your decision alone." He was trying to shut her out again, thinking he was protecting her. But she had chosen this.

"No, it is not." Marcon reached out for her hand and grasped it in his. "I will not leave without you again. I promise."

CHAPTER 28

Golden light shone through the trees as they continued to climb. Iellieth glanced over her shoulder, searching the forest for the dark swarm of the werewolf pack. The trees swayed in a slight breeze. She sighed. Thus far, their steps remained hidden.

A figure stepped out from a cluster of birches ahead, backlit by the afternoon sun.

Marcon shouted, and steel hissed as he withdrew his blade. Energy flowed to the tips of Iellieth's fingers, ready to face whatever enemy now presented itself to them.

The silhouette stepped closer. What Iellieth had taken to be branches were antlers in a crown of flora. A longbow crossed the figure's back, and the sunlight glinted off her silver tattoos and the hoops laced through her long fae ears.

"Yvayne?" Iellieth called.

Two steps closer, and the druid's pale purple eyes emerged against her sepia skin. Midnight blue braids pooled over her shoulders.

Iellieth rushed forward, relief coursing through her

veins. "You found us." She halted within arm's reach of the fae. How did Yvayne greet others? She would have embraced Mara, but that seemed unfitting for the powerful being before her. The fae's eyes glittered as though she could hear Iellieth's indecision.

Marcon stomped up the hill, his grumbling clearer as he climbed. ". . . unnecessary surprise, sneaking up on us when we're expecting werewolves." He stood by Iellieth's side and nodded to the druid. "Yvayne."

"Champion of Fire." Her full lips lifted in a self-satisfied grin. "Iellieth." Yvayne extended her hand, palm facing outward. Iellieth mirrored her, pressing her palms and fingers against Yvayne's. Her hand cooled at the druid's touch, and her pulse slowed. Truly, now, they would be safe.

"You have done well to survive," Yvayne said, looking at each of them in turn. "I will take you to a secure location in the mountains. Come." She turned and strode away.

Iellieth met Marcon's eye. He looked as surprised and confused as she felt at the druid's sudden appearance. If Yvayne knew to come and find them, did she also know what had happened to the conclave? To Mara? Iellieth ran to catch up to her long-legged strides.

Yvayne stood in front of a large oak tree, trailing her hands over the bark and whispering to it in Druidic. With a low groan, a crack splintered up the bark, carving a line along the gnarled vertical ridges. The druid laid her palms flat on either side of the splintered trunk. "Aiya'ne, si'retta di Quercus," she chanted.

The crack widened as it climbed toward the oak's branches. Yvayne continued her prayer, head bowed, hands pressing against the bark until the jagged chasm in the trunk was as wide as her shoulders. Inside, instead of heartwood or spirals of growth, a gray archway appeared, with mist swirling down from the tip of the lancet arch.

The fog reached the earth and pooled over Iellieth's boots, rippling past her ankles. Her tensed muscles began to unwind as familiar herbs curled through her senses—the warmth of rosemary and thyme, with a pinch of juniper's spice.

"You first, Iellieth," Yvayne said. Her right arm swung into the mist and disappeared below her elbow, consumed by the thickening fog.

Iellieth jumped back.

"It's quite alright," Yvayne said. She pulled her arm back, and it emerged, whole. Her tattoos glowed brighter in the shimmering light from the archway, ancient Druidic script curling around patterns of vines and branches.

"Marcon and I need to stay together, for the amulet," Iellieth said. The stomach-churning pull of transmigration weighed against the pit of her stomach. She couldn't risk arriving in the wrong place, alone, and forcing Marcon to return to his statue form.

"Very well, together then," Yvayne waved Marcon forward.

He squinted up at the archway. "I've seen something like this, long ago."

"It's time," Yvayne's voice was short, ordering her forward.

Iellieth wrapped her arm around Marcon's waist, and he held on to her shoulder. "Ready, lady?" He looked down at her.

She nodded in answer and stepped through.

THE LOW THRUM OF TREESONG, THE ARBORETUM IN THE early throes of a storm rolling off the sea, elder trees groaning as they swayed with the wind. Another step. The scents changed: fresh pine, sap, the biting wet of snow. The mist swirled forward, eddied, pooled. Iellieth's foot followed, and crunched, ankle-deep, in snow.

"Oh!" she exclaimed. A light flurry drifted down over her hair and onto the exposed skin of her face. She pulled her jacket tighter and took another step forward into the clearing ahead. A fire pit rested at the center of a semi-circle of ancient trees—smooth-skinned beech, sprawling pine, shimmering birch—rounded out by the largest oak tree Iellieth had ever seen. Its towering trunk disappeared into the low-hanging snow clouds. An elegant doorway stood in the center of the tree, and a stained-glass window glimmered from a second story.

"Are you alright, lady?" Marcon studied their sudden new environment and opened his palms to the snowflakes.

"Yes, just"—she waited for a better word to float down and land on her tongue—"surprised, I guess. Where are we?"

Another dash of juniper, and the mist floated back over their feet. A third set of crunching steps joined theirs in the snow. "My home, Iellieth. Please"—Yvayne indicated the massive oak—"we can speak more inside."

The double wooden doors creaked open as she approached, leading into a wide hall. Fireflies, the same golden color that had silhouetted Yvayne's appearance, flickered along the passage, lighting the way. The floor was dense moss, the walls delicately curving wood, as though an acre of forest had pressed trunk to trunk to form a hallway. The entry led into a comfortable sitting room with mossy stumps scattered around the spherical chamber, the wooden walls curving up overhead. A tree stretched tall on the opposite side of the hallway, glowing stairs rather than branches sprouting in a spiral from its trunk.

Iellieth gazed upward into the impossible heights of Yvayne's home. The druid chuckled beside her. "I'm glad you like it."

Yvayne left the two of them for a moment and returned with steaming mugs made of glazed clay. "You are both tired. Drink."

Iellieth inhaled the fresh mint of the tea and took a sip. The warm liquid coated the back of her throat and blossomed out into her extremities. The rooted heat absorbed the soreness from her muscles. She sank onto one of the low stumps.

"How?" Marcon rested his hand on his wounded side as he looked from the tea to Yvayne. He set the mug down on the stump beside Iellieth and removed the bandage from his arm. The deep slice from the arrow knitted together as they watched, and his skin returned to its warm olive glow.

"The waters here have healing properties." Yvayne smiled at them. She waved her hand over the earth, and a long, flattened log appeared across from Marcon and Iellieth. Flowers sprang up along its surface. Yvayne sat, one leg tucked beneath her, the other extended over the floral growth.

"I saw the final moments of what transpired in the conclave." Her face hardened, the seriousness of their plight settling over all of them. "Because of the brave actions of Mara and those helping her, the rest of the community was able to escape."

So Mara's plan had worked. Iellieth pressed her lips

together. She stared down at her hands, waiting until she could trust herself to speak.

"What of Lucien and the werewolves?" Marcon asked, his voice matter-of-fact.

"Mara's final act sent Lucien back to the Shadowlands. The werewolves that remain will continue to roam the forests, but without their leader, the pack will be less effective."

"Is Lucien gone, then?" Iellieth sat up. *Please say yes.*

"No." Yvayne shook her head. "But it will take him time to recover and return. This is an opportunity we will need to use to our advantage."

"Will we mount a counterattack?" Marcon asked.

Mara had sent her here for answers and to continue her training. Would they go after the werewolves instead?

"At present, no. We have other matters to attend to first."

Iellieth waited to see if Yvayne planned to say more before she spoke. "Then what will we do?"

The lilac eyes turned to her. "I would like for you to tell me, Iellieth. What is on your heart for the path that lies ahead?"

⚜

YVAYNE AWOKE IELLIETH EARLY THE NEXT MORNING FOR their first scouting mission. They emerged, bundled in furs, from the tree into the brisk mountain air, breath condensing in tiny clouds against the snowy surroundings. Yvayne instructed Iellieth to search for animal tracks with her intuition as well as her senses.

One of her childhood literary heroes, Daphne, had done something similar, using animal tracks to help her find suitable places of shelter, food, and water as she roamed the wilds. Ultimately, the heroine joined a pack of wolves and adapted to their lifestyle, forever solidifying herself in Iellieth's admiration.

In addition to Iellieth performing the trail-hunting rather than reading about it, Yvayne asked her to go one step further. She should not only seek to understand where bears or elk might be going and why, but to try to see the world through their eyes.

As the light rose, Iellieth crouched beside a large boulder, sending her thoughts out into the surrounding forest to see if she might be able to discern any animal habitats nearby.

Yvayne knelt beside her. "You do well to ask the forest to aid you." The druid closed her eyes and inhaled deeply. "I believe you've found a rabbit warren, just on the other side of those trees." She indicated the thin pines ahead.

Iellieth released the breath she'd been holding. "I sensed something nearby, a few creatures in a home together, but I couldn't tell who they were. I didn't want to accidentally startle a mother bear with her cubs."

Yvayne grinned. "No, that would be best avoided." She rose. "Come take a walk with me. Let us speak of what weighs on your mind."

Was she referring to Mara's death? Scad's disappearance? The growing war between Linolynn and Hadvar? "What do you—"

"Mara and I, and many others, have waited for you for some time, Iellieth. Living in reduced numbers as we do, there are fewer druids with your unique potential. In the days before we met, I . . . failed at protecting the other. I was too busy looking ahead and did not see the truth in front of my eyes."

Which other druid was she talking about? Someone in the colony in Tor'stre Vahn? Had she traveled through one of the misty doors to arrive there as well? "Yvayne, I'm sorry, I don't know who you mean. Mara and I"—Iellieth's breath faltered—"we had a limited amount of time to discuss it. She and Cassian both made me feel like I could do something special." Berivic's anger at the council meeting came flaring back. Not everyone had been anxious to admit her into their community. "But I never understood why, or what it was."

Yvayne turned and held out a thin golden necklace with a crescent moon pendant. The chain dangled down toward the snow. Ripples of energy caught on the wind and flickered past, tugging at Iellieth's hair.

The charm was simple, only a few inches in length, but it called to her anyway. She couldn't take her eyes from it. The faint voices of animals lifted on the wind: a wolf's howl, the chitter of squirrels, the croak of a raven.

Yvayne held the necklace out toward her. Iellieth hesitated. What was this magic pooling around her? The roots beneath her feet pulsed, leaves in the trees hissed against one another. She touched the center of the crescent with her pointer finger, and the life around them stilled. Slowly, she lifted the necklace from Yvayne's hand, the links shifting one by one. She slid the chain over her head and let it hang down her neck. She pulled her hair through, and the golden crescent-moon pendant reached below her ribcage, framing her amulet with its slender chain.

"This necklace belonged to her." Yvayne's voice was low, her purple eyes misty and bright as they met Iellieth's. "Fhaona. She left it behind for you." Yvayne sniffed, the tip of her nose turned a darker gray by the cold air.

The shape of the rabbit's warren was clear to her now,

the burrows curving beneath the earth. An owl slept inside his tree fifty yards to the east. She held the pendant, a perfect curve in her palm.

"All druids can adapt their forms, Iellieth, depending on their connection to the natural world and personal preferences." Yvayne raised her eyes and ran her fingers along her three-pronged antlers. "But there was an ancient sect of druids who were shapeshifters. Their entire bodies could transform. They wouldn't simply bear the headdress of an elk but become an elk themselves."

A few legends she and Katarina had read spoke of shapeshifters, but they usually morphed their form into that of another person rather than an animal. The strength of the elk, the weight of mighty antlers, settled onto Iellieth's shoulders. Powerful hooves struck the surface of the earth, running and climbing. The wind lifted her hair, and she shivered.

Yvayne watched her closely. "I thought so." She gave Iellieth a small smile. "These druids, even more than the rest of our kind, were hunted, rooted out for their power. It came to be that only one or two lived among us at any given time." Yvayne's voice fell to a whisper. "Fhaona passed the honor on to you, Iellieth."

"But why me?" Why would this other, more experienced druid have trusted her legacy, this special responsibility, to someone she'd never met?

"Those of us who know what to look for sensed you when you were born."

Iellieth froze on the path that led back to Yvayne's tree. "But how?"

The druid stared at her and shook her head. "Wrong question, si'retta. The true one is *why*. You signaled the dawn of a new age, another chance."

Questions flurried around her, falling with the snow. "A chance for what?"

"For Azuria."

⚜

IELLIETH FOLLOWED YVAYNE BACK TO HER TREE IN silence, weighing what she'd been told. She explained the new mysteries to Marcon over another cup of the druid's magical tea.

Yvayne settled beside them, legs extended down the log she'd called to the surface their first day here. She waved her fingers behind her head, and two branches grew and arched toward one another. The druid scooted, rolled her shoulders, and leaned against the backrest. She sighed, staring up at the inner depths of her home tree.

Iellieth waited, sure the druid had wished to speak, but she remained silent.

"Might I explain further, Iellieth?" Yvayne finally said.

"Yes, that would help. The more I think about it, the more questions I have."

Yvayne leaned forward and drew her hand over the mossy floor. A floating spectre of the cloaked figure Iellieth had seen, the one who had ordered her death, appeared beneath the druid's fingertips. Yvayne swept her hand over his head, and the scene changed. An elven woman ran between the ghostly shimmers of trees, the horrifying figure floating after her. The woman fell, and Iellieth's stomach tightened. The figure waved his hands, and two tigers suddenly appeared from beneath the moss. They latched on to the woman and dragged her beneath the spongy surface. A crescent moon appeared briefly among the smoky shapes and then trickled away.

Yvayne's voice was low, strained. "Lucien killed the last druid like you, Iellieth. He has been hunting them through the ages, driven first by anger and revenge, now by greed. He has lived on, since Marcon's time, from the souls of others. He devours them, preventing their journey to the afterlife or to their rebirth, and feeds on them to sustain his own life."

"From my time?" Marcon asked, eyes narrowed. "I have no recollection of an enemy such as this."

Yvayne shook her head. "There are reasons for that, Champion of Fire." She turned away from him and back to the place where the elf had disappeared into the moss. "He was a hidden enemy at the time."

Iellieth had missed something. The sense fluttered behind her ear. Something Yvayne had said, or not said. "Yvayne, why anger and revenge?"

The druid's lavender irises burned with an emotion Iellieth couldn't identify. "There was one druid in particular he wished to harm. She was incredibly powerful. A phoenix. His enmity with our people began with her."

A phoenix? Yvayne peered at her, searching for something. "Yvayne—" Iellieth began.

"Si'retta?"

A piece of the puzzle fit into place. "You were there, weren't you? Before. You saw Marcon's time, what Mara called the War of the Champions?"

Marcon spun around. "Is that true?" he demanded, his breath shallow.

Yvayne pulled her lips between her teeth and looked at the moss once more before she nodded slowly. "It is." She met Marcon's questioning eyes. "I was in hiding at the time. That is why you and I never met. But I heard tales of you and your heroic deeds. You were an emblem for many."

Marcon sat back, stunned.

Iellieth crawled forward and sat between the two of them, her hand resting on Marcon's knee. "Then you know who else we've come to ask you about, don't you? Quindythias?"

"A great champion of the elves." Yvayne smiled. "Yes, si'retta. I know of him."

Marcon rubbed the back of his head and cleared his throat. Emotions played in quick succession across his face. "Do you know where he is? Has someone found him?"

Iellieth inhaled sharply, waiting for the answer.

"Yes"—the druid smiled—"and no, not yet."

"HE'S BEEN BENEATH IO KEEP THIS ENTIRE TIME?" Iellieth could hardly believe Yvayne's revelation.

"He has, si'retta. It took a lengthy study between me and another of our allies to uncover his hiding place. After we found out he was so near to you, there were times when we worried you might awaken him accidentally, before it was time."

There were too many promising trails calling for Iellieth to follow. "Why didn't my amulet lead me there? Why haven't I sensed him before?"

Marcon leaned toward Yvayne, waiting to hear her response.

"We've no idea how deeply Quindythias is buried beneath the castle or the state of his keeping room. The maker of your amulet, Iellieth, was very careful, very precise. This is why you found Marcon first. She was drawn to the fire."

Had this maker been a champion of fire as well? And had her father known, when he left the amulet with Mamaun, what it could do? Had he been aware of its ties to ancient warriors? To the druids?

Marcon, energized by Yvayne's news, spent the afternoon in her library, a towering room that reached one hundred feet up through the trunk of the tree, lit by a glowing root structure that curved upward in a spiral staircase. Tiny wood sprites flitted back and forth to aid his search among the ancient tomes.

Iellieth sat with Yvayne on the library's ground floor. She balanced one of the wood faeries in each of her hands, marveling at their large sparkling eyes and curious twig bodies.

"You mentioned another ally who helped with your research?" Iellieth asked. She sifted through what Yvayne had told them that afternoon. How much had the fae learned and seen over her extended lifetime?

"Yes, si'retta. I have been thinking of him a great deal of late. Tomorrow, you and Marcon will make your way back to Io Keep to find Quindythias. Then, the three of you together should visit my old friend. If anyone in Caldara knows how to free the champions from the runes that bind them, it would be him."

Had Yvayne known the nature of the runes this entire time? Did her tattoos perform something similar? "How did you—"

Yvayne answered her question before she could finish asking it. "Marcon has spoken to me of his concerns about the danger his connection to the amulet poses to you. He is right to worry. And that threat will only increase when you carry the bonds of two souls with you."

She hadn't considered that Quindythias would be covered in the binding runes as well or what his connection to her amulet might mean. She could ponder that matter later. "Who is it we should seek out, Varra? Where are they?"

The druid smiled. "I believe he may be familiar to you. Make for Red's Cross after you have retrieved Quindythias from Linolynn."

Her stepfather admired the industry and growth of Red's Cross, but she had never visited the city. "And who should we seek out while we are there?"

"Red, of course." Yvayne's eyes brightened. "The city's founder. He has made great use of his people's prolonged memory. A profoundly curious and industrious mind."

"Is he an elf?"

Yvayne shook her head. "A gnome."

Iellieth's eyes widened. Katarina had lived among a community of gnomes for a time. Their extensive libraries were helpful in her research, and she spoke of those years with great fondness. Soon, Iellieth would have a similar opportunity.

◈

THAT EVENING, YVAYNE AND IELLIETH RETURNED TO the snow to continue Iellieth's training. "It's time to test these powers of yours, si'retta," Yvayne said. "And then you return to the beginning."

She and Katarina had discussed something similar as they studied the transmigration circles before she left Io Keep. What was it? Had Katarina said that circles, especially for the ancients, represented not only completeness and renewal but also new paths forward?

The freshly fallen snow crunched beneath their feet and shimmered on branches all around her. "Tell me, Iellieth," Yvayne said, "are there any forms of life, especially animals or plants, that stand out to you, that capture your imagination?"

An owl hooted nearby, and the roots wriggled their greetings beneath her feet. A howl caught on the wind and ran up Iellieth's spine. She shivered. "Wolves." Iellieth met Yvayne's eyes. "They always have. It began in stories when I was small, but they have stayed with me since."

The druid nodded. "And why do you think that is, si'retta?"

"Mamaun and I read together when I was young, and then after we moved to the castle, it became a form of solace for me." Iellieth brushed the melting snowflakes from her cheeks. "Many of the books described magic and tales of adventurers. But there was one set I read over and over again, even as I grew too old for them. In the story, a young girl ran away from her family. After several days alone, she joined a pack of wolves. They took care of her and . . . she belonged with them. They were a family."

Yvayne tilted her face up to the falling snow. "The wolf is a beautiful and fascinating creature, si'retta. You have chosen well." She waved her hand; a majestic wolf took shape between them, made of smoke and mist. Snowflakes swirled through its ephemeral form. "Much like our people, wolves have been vilified by places that call themselves civil, by those who destroy that which unites order and the wilds."

She had asked Mamaun countless questions about wolves after she discovered the figurine on the grounds at

Aurora, wanting to know more about them. She pictured the alabaster likeness in Scad's calloused hand, and her chest tightened.

The misty wolf Yvayne had created shrank, its form shifting and dividing into an entire pack who raised their foggy noses toward the moons overhead in a silent howl. "Every member of the pack has a role, and they are each necessary to the others. They know, intuitively, that they are stronger together." Yvayne looked at her, eyebrows raised. "There are some who travel alone, but they are the exception."

Each foggy wolf plodded forward until the pack surrounded Iellieth's feet. "Alright, si'retta, it is time."

Time? For what? Should she try to create a wolf from the mist?

"Grasp your necklace, Iellieth. Feel their energy." Yvayne's eyes flashed. "And transform."

Iellieth stood staring at Yvayne. How was she supposed to know how to transform into a wolf? She bit back her questions and did as Yvayne instructed. Iellieth clasped the crescent moon that had been passed down to her in her left hand. She closed her eyes, shutting out the snowscape, her mystical new mentor, and thought of Daphne, the girl from her stories, and the wolves who ran beside her. Paws pressed into the snow around her, waiting.

Her senses sharpened, ears perking up to catch even the faintest sound nearby. Yvayne's shallow breaths, the owl's wings on the wind as it sought its prey, a bunny's rapid heartbeat as it hid at the base of a tree. She inhaled. The dampness of snow gathered from mountains farther to the north drifted down toward them. The druid's warm, sagey musk. Pine. The traces of roses she'd grown in the castle gardens on her own skin.

Iellieth opened her eyes and squeezed her toes in the snow. The clawed tips of her paws answered her, softly crunching. Flakes rested against the fur along her back and in the bushier hair of her tail. She swished it back and forth and caught more snowflakes. Her heart surged in her chest, ready to run. Beside her, the misty wolf, large and singular once again, lowered his head. Yvayne smiled down at her and nodded. "Go."

Iellieth took off through the trees, racing around silver trunks, in and out of splashes of moonlight. She bounded over snowdrifts, her foggy companion racing beside her. Midway down the mountain she turned, powder cascading beneath her feet, and she charged uphill back to Yvayne, sides heaving. Her ears twitched, attuned to the quiet wood.

The druid knelt to be on eye level with her. "Now, search your heart again, and return to yourself."

Iellieth's wolf eyes closed, and she tried to follow Yvayne's instructions. She opened her eyes. Yvayne shook her head.

She set aside the elation. What if she couldn't transform back? She closed her eyes and exhaled warm, wet air from her snout. Iellieth shot upward, returned to herself, and swayed on her feet.

Yvayne caught her arm, chuckling. "Very good, si'retta. Come, let us return." The druid led them back through the snow, Iellieth's head reeling with her transformation. Yvayne stopped her in front of the door to her treehouse. "It seems to me that you have already begun to find your pack, Iellieth Amastacia. But where will you roam?" She placed her chilled hand on the side of Iellieth's face and stared into her eyes before she bowed her head and stepped inside.

Iellieth and Marcon set out down the mountain the next morning, Yvayne's farewell heavy on Iellieth's heart. "I will be watching over you." She laid her hands on Iellieth's shoulders as Mara had done after she joined the conclave. "Save your transformations for times of great need, si'retta. The spirits will answer you."

Yvayne clasped Marcon's hand in hers. "Until we meet again, Champion of Fire." She pressed her hands together at her chest and bowed to them. Iellieth did the same. Yvayne smiled, lowered her arms, and watched them go.

CHAPTER 29

enevieve and Jade grew closer as the days passed. She learned to listen to the wolf's rapid assessments of other creatures and of their surroundings. As pink stormclouds filled the sky, Jade helped her to find shelter beneath a grove of violet trees, knowing they wouldn't have time to return to the daimons' caves before the storm. Jade showed Genevieve their full wolf form, should they need to blend into a wild environment, and Genevieve made space inside of her human form for Jade to feel welcome and comfortable.

By the end of their first week, Genevieve could change her form at will, and she and Jade remained in near-constant communication with one another, a language of scents, pictures, and impressions. The time came for Genevieve to return to the task set to her by Ophelia, to make her way to Andel-ce Hevra. Sariel bid an affectionate good-bye to Aspen, and he traveled with Genevieve and Jade, in their wolf form, bounding over the color-soaked fields of the Brightlands, to a portal that would lead them to the outskirts of the city.

"We will be ready for you, when your path returns you to us," Sariel said, head bowed. Jade and Genevieve nuzzled against him, the bright scent of his small white flowers mingling in their fur.

"I will never forget what you've done for me," Genevieve thought to Sariel. "I'll come back as soon as I'm able."

Sariel smiled. "You have new lands to cross first, but it will not be as long as you now assume."

Jade's ears perked up, happy to learn that they might soon return to the daimon, where she felt at home.

The portal Sariel had found was made of a white stone archway, covered in thick moss. The scent of rain lay heavy on the air beyond the portal. "This will take you to a ruin reclaimed by the forest, beyond the outskirts of the city. From there, you can find your way to the gates that will lead you inside."

Genevieve pressed back into her human form, securing her cloak around her shoulders. "Thank you, Sariel," she whispered. She wrapped her arms around his furry neck, breathing in the soothing scent of his fur.

"Good hunting, little wolf," Sariel's voice said.

Genevieve took a deep breath and stepped through the portal.

Rain lashed through the thin trees that had taken root along the ruin's foundation. Genevieve tucked her hair against the base of her neck and drew her hood up over her head.

Jade growled inside her chest, sharply attuned to the nerves darting through Genevieve's body. Saplings and young oak dotted the woodland hillsides. The new growth was healthy, but the trees were not yet old enough to offer shelter or protection. Genevieve jumped as a pair of squirrels darted past, chittering and bounding over one another on their way through the trees. Two days before, she had seen a similar pair, magenta with tinges of violet, a coloring appropriate to the personalities of all squirrels, she had observed to Jade. Rain lashed down on them as they trudged through the forest. Beyond the embrace of the Brightlands and her adopted pack, Genevieve headed east, to the outskirts of Andel-ce Hevra.

❧

GENEVIEVE'S STOMACH DROPPED AS SHE LOOKED OUT over the sprawling city from the edge of the sparse forest. Tan bricks, worn smooth by the dusty summer winds, surrounded a great lake of stone and iron. Black silhouettes of ancient temples created voids across the pre-dawn sky, monuments to the accepted religions of which her family wasn't a part. Once she stepped beyond the trees, there would be nothing separating her from the city's hordes and guards. Would they know her heritage on sight?

She made her way down the final foothills into the labyrinth of huts and fragile dwellings that surrounded the metropolis. The small homes leaned against one another, giving the impression that if a single beam fell out of place, the entire community would collapse. Thick puddles gathered between the shelters, and cloth roofs dripped onto those who clustered beneath.

Groans echoed down the narrow corridors. On the opposite side, the heavy cough of long-term sickness rang out. So many, in so small a space. Genevieve pulled the edges of her cloak tighter and searched through the maze for a path that would open onto the city.

Shortly before Arrinia's light was to peek over the horizon, she found it. The tenements gave way to a broad, flattened path. Ten people could have stood in a line with their arms outspread and still barely span end to end. Sloping white walls led her gaze up and away from those sheltered outside the city to the enormous gates that stood between her and entry.

An intricate casement made of black iron wove in tendrils up the archway and stretched across its breadth. Every few feet, spikes clawed outward, disguised in the metal pattern, but a warning to unwanted intruders nonetheless. Behind the interlocking bars, two doors, each made of a single piece of wood nearly thirty feet wide and fifty feet high, stood shut tight against the outside world.

The trees that had been sacrificed to make them had to have come from the forest's heart. Even to the north, near her colony, trees of such size were a near-impossibility. What were they trying to keep out?

Along the parapets, the pacing of tall spears and the occasional plume of a red feather marked the movements of guards. Remembering Sariel's instructions, Genevieve ducked back into the tangle of tents and leaning structures outside the city walls to await the gate's opening after sunrise. Jade paced inside her chest, senses attuned for the slightest provocation from their environment.

When the first eyelashes of daylight appeared across the sky, the world around her came to life. Entire families emerged from the small shelters. Some greeted their neighbors as though they were old friends. Others scowled at their surroundings and rubbed their eyes, their hearts still clinging to their dreams. A few people stared at her, especially when she stood still, but so long as she kept walking through the rows, no one paid her any special attention.

Visitors to her conclave were always met with warmth and curiosity. Mariellen was fond of saying that the friendliness was a guise for greater study, to encourage the newcomers to feel at ease so the colony might grow to understand them more. Genevieve knew this was true, but the kindness was genuine all the same. What must it be like to awaken each day and see so many unfamiliar faces? The farther from home you traveled, the more strangers you would encounter.

Across the shelters, people donned strange cloaks and started toward the gates. Rather than draping them around their shoulders, they pulled the garments on over their heads, and the material fell over their chests and backs. Almost every garment bore a decoration of some kind. One held the picture of a sparrow. Another, a blue flower nestled among oak leaves. What might they signify?

Others outside the city walls slunk into jackets and strapped on boots before they too joined the throng gathered outside the gates. Genevieve followed their lead and became part of the crowd. She huddled near a smiling family, the parents close in age to Mariellen and Sheffield. Their young child squawked at the cold morning air, and the baby's older siblings rushed about their parents' feet.

More pikes joined the vigil along the top of the gate, and murmurs spread among those gathered outside. What was causing the soldiers to increase their presence? If they turned on the people, she could flee through the tents till she could safely return to the forest. Jade pressed against her toes, ready to hasten their journey.

Once her heartbeat slowed, she understood that the

whispers were only of anticipation. They were preparing to open the gates.

The throng of people surged forward, whisking Genevieve along in their hurry to press past the city walls and mingle with those fortunate enough to dwell inside Andel-ce Hevra.

Ophelia had said that if she could simply get inside the city, she could either ask for help or find a sign that would guide her to the river. From there, she could step onto a barge that would take her to the coast, where ships harbored on the Infinite Ocean.

It took a few tries for Genevieve to locate someone interested in helping her, but, with Jade's keen sense for friends and foes, eventually a young woman standing outside a bakery pointed the way to the river.

She would never have found the river that ran through the city's web of streets on her own. It was cleverly disguised, churning under stone walkways or eddying across several designated paths. Much of the water, she learned, ran underground. The city had rerouted small trickles of it and used these as a way of providing water to the households spread across its vast territory. Many of these trails ran overhead in interconnected troughs made of thin stone, and some of them cascaded into fountains around which people gathered to drink or to fill buckets of water.

The water lent its inherent energy to these places. People talked and laughed while they waited for their turn to drink their fill or to splash the cool liquid over dirty faces and hands. In these brief flashes of camaraderie, Genevieve felt a pang of home.

Other parts of the river carried packages and barrels through the city. They floated independently, and guards walked along the causeways and supervised men and women with long poles that helped the cargo along as it traveled.

Near one such site, Genevieve watched a woman in a bandana negotiate several large barrels trapped at a bend in the river. A spirit called to her.

Genevieve spun around, searching. Jade pointed. *There.*

A dagger she would have known anywhere. In an age long past, her conclave's ancestors had crafted the hilt from the pale horn of the great mountain goats and carved the blade from bone. The sacred object, meant to be wielded by the head elder of her conclave, rested at the side of a thin man with dark, stringy hair and pale, sallow skin. He carefully observed the street around him, fiercely blue eyes glinting before he darted into an alleyway between the buildings.

Jade growled, hackles raised.

The dagger called to her again. Genevieve pushed aside the swell of her grief. How would this man have come to possess the dagger after the varrans' deaths? And why?

She and Jade crossed the bridge to follow him.

CHAPTER 30

T he fourth day of their travel brought Iellieth and Marcon down through the Frostmaw Mountains and back into the Stormside Forest. Yvayne had outlined a direct route to Linolynn that would allow them to avoid the ruins of the druid conclave and the patrols surrounding Trudid. Iellieth spoke with the forest as they passed through, ensuring that no werewolves stalked nearby.

The stream they followed led to an open field along the forest's borders, one that had not yet been claimed as farmland. Iellieth stepped out from the wood's cover and knelt beside the crisp mountain runoff to tighten her boots.

"Lady Amastacia," a voice called from across the field. Iellieth froze. The soldiers couldn't have found them, not now. They were only three days out from Linolynn, and she had hoped to enter unnoticed. Without her stepfather knowing, she would sneak beneath the castle to search for Quindythias and, if possible, find out what was causing the war. "Lady Amastacia," the voice yelled again.

"Run," Iellieth hissed to Marcon. They could lose the soldiers in the trees. She sprang to her feet and sprinted back into the forest. Further shouts reverberated behind her as the troops charged through the woods. Trees and plants cried out, damaged by the crushing feet and dashing limbs.

"Agh," Marcon yelled as an arrow pierced his calf. Two others pinged off his shield. They must have thought he had abducted her or held her captive against her will.

"Let me help you." Iellieth slipped beneath his arm to counterbalance the weight from his injured leg. He adjusted his shield to cover her, and another arrow pierced into his shoulder.

Marcon shouted in pain. "I'll find you," he groaned. "Use the spell Yvayne taught you, and hide in the woods."

Teodric's cries ricocheted through her memory, his blood splattered across the guards' fists. "No." She set her jaw. No more running. It was time she faced the shadow of her stepfather head on. "I need you to trust me." She had to convince them to spare Marcon, at least long enough for her to get him back to the castle.

His voice was strained. "With my life, lady."

"Alright, stop here." She squeezed his waist and slid back beneath his arm, stepping in front of him with her arms raised.

Pang. Marcon's shield flew in front of her and blocked an arrow that would have struck her straight in the chest. The soldier who had fired it stopped short, eyes wide. Another late arrow pierced Marcon's arm.

"Stop!" Iellieth screamed.

A second voice joined hers, echoing the command. The captain ran forward, fist raised in the air, halting his company.

"This man is with me," Iellieth shouted. A grunt of pain behind her as Marcon removed the newest arrow and tossed it onto the ground. "We will go back to the castle with you," she told the captain. It was he who had spotted her in the field. "But no further harm will befall this man. Do you understand?"

The troop of soldiers had edged closer to her and Marcon, crossbows raised. They were surrounded on three sides, and he was in no condition to run any further.

The captain signaled, and five soldiers stepped forward from the ranks, brandishing longswords. The leader stood twenty feet away from Iellieth. Anxious sparks waited at her fingertips. "My lady, you do not know what you're saying. Is this the man responsible for your disappearance? A Hadvarian in disguise?"

Angry grumbles passed over the ring of soldiers at the accusation.

"No!" She needed to try something else, fast. "He's been helping me, trying to aid me in my return to the castle." Then why had they run? "Take off your helmet," she ordered.

"Lady Amastacia . . ."

"Captain, remove your helmet. Do not make me ask again." Linolynn's law placed nobles in a position of power over the military, a holdover from a time when King Arontis's grandfather became convinced he would be slaughtered in a military coup. If she could take advantage of this now, it might be enough to save Marcon and get them back to the castle. "I refuse to leave with an officer I do not know."

Private forces inside the castle walls were an exception to this rule, and the duke's most loyal thugs wouldn't have listened to her under any circumstances, however dire. But these men wore Linolynn's livery and the periwinkle and gold of the king. They might listen.

The young man removed his helmet. His blonde hair clung to his scalp, wet with sweat from the sprint through the trees. "Captain Hutcheon, Lady Amastacia." He bowed, and the rest of the company followed suit after he rose.

Iellieth put on her best noblewoman's smile and curtsied to the soldiers. The sign of respect felt awkward in pants and boots, but she maintained her most regal demeanor, as her mother would have done.

"Do you truly wish to go with them, lady?" Marcon whispered into her ear.

The captain strode forward. "We will escort you safely back to Linolynn, your ladyship."

"I wish for us both to live long enough to revise our plan and then find Quindythias. Trust me," she whispered back.

"That's close enough," Marcon growled at the captain. The young man halted, surprised, but then glared at Marcon.

"Tie his hands," the captain shouted.

"Is that truly necessary?" Iellieth stepped forward. If they could only take her at her word.

"Hers as well."

Iellieth whirled around and laid her hand on Marcon's arm. "Elenai." A warm lavender glow seeped from her fingers into his arm. The arrow fell from his back in a shower of white sparks, and the two soldiers nearest her hesitated, staring.

The captain barked his order again, and the soldiers sprang forward and clipped Marcon's hands behind his back in metal links. His eyes flashed as a soldier approached her with a rope, and he struggled against the two that held his arms, flinging one of them to the side.

"Stop, please, it's alright," she begged. However angry he was at their change in circumstances, their safest bet was to return peaceably to the castle. Basha would help her. Any law that protected prisoners, of any rank, ceased if they resisted.

Marcon held still at the look on her face. His jaw twitched, but he stopped struggling. Two more soldiers came and grabbed his arms, holding him fast. The captain stepped forward, his hand out toward the soldier with the rope. "May I, my lady?"

Iellieth bowed her head and turned, her arms wrapped behind her back.

"Loosely in front is fine, Lady Amastacia."

Iellieth sighed, smiling at the guard. "Thank you, Captain." She held her wrists out on top of one another. The young man removed his gauntlets and gloves. He made a show of finding the smoothest part of the rope and wrapping it carefully around her wrists before he tied it in a knot.

"Your mother has been most worried about you, Lady Amastacia. She's sent as many of our ranks as can be spared to search for you. We had begun to despair."

This was unexpected. Her lips parted, ready to speak, but no words came.

"She'll be relieved to see you returned safe and well." The captain glared at Marcon again but grinned at her as he secured the knot. "Narvis." One of the five soldiers holding longswords stepped forward. "Take four men and ride ahead. We'll set the duchess's mind at ease." The soldier nodded, gestured to four others on the end, and they strode back through the woods.

The troop marched them out of the forest and to their herd of warhorses. They loaded Iellieth and Marcon into the supplies cart, the captain apologizing to Iellieth about the less than auspicious travel arrangement. She assured him that it would serve them very well, and the company began their return journey to Linolynn.

◈◈◈

THE CART LANDED HEAVILY ON ONE SIDE AS IT ROLLED down a rise in the field, jarring Iellieth and Marcon. He grumbled and adjusted his shoulders, clearly uncomfortable from his hands being bound behind his back for several hours.

"Linolynn is a beautiful city," Iellieth said, hoping to turn his mind to something besides their current predicament. "The castle sits at the top of a cliff and shines in the sun. The first royal family of Linolynn named it Io Keep for an ancient Caldaran deity of the moon, inspired by the pale rock and glass they used to construct it. The keep below, that makes up the core of the castle, is thousands of years old." She raised her eyebrows, and he nodded. That's where they would find Quindythias.

By midmorning their second day, the rolling fields flattened enough for them to spot the city's silhouette on the horizon. The soldiers murmured happily. The mood of the company had grown lighter the farther they traveled from the Hadvarian border, but Iellieth couldn't escape the grip of her stepfather's shadow. At one time, it would have filled her with joy to ride over fields she had only glimpsed from behind panes of glass, but now? It would take so little for her to be back under his control. Even with her newfound power and Marcon's aid, would it be enough?

She pulled her arms against her stomach and hunched forward, avoiding the castle's glimmer in the distance.

"Is something wrong, lady?" Marcon asked, leaning toward her.

"It's just that—" Iellieth cleared her throat—"that I've never viewed the city from this vantage point before." She glanced up at him and clasped her hands together. This time would be different. It had to be.

As their road wound through nobles' fields and generously portioned farmsteads, the elegant buildings of the Air Ward and the small homes and shops of the Earth Ward appeared against the hillside below the keep.

"It is very pretty," Marcon said. "Smaller than I would have anticipated, but you warned me that might be the case."

Iellieth grinned. "A few of the other city-states are much larger, especially those that survived the floods."

The road sloped down toward a central gate in the stone walls that surrounded the Earth and Water Wards. They'd pass through a second, taller wall to be allowed entry into the Air Ward. Merchants and travelers glared as the guards at the gate pushed them to the side, making way for the soldiers' procession.

An argument ensued when Captain Hutcheon revealed who he was bringing back into the city. He was anxious to ensure that the Duke and Duchess Amastacia knew who to thank for the safe return of their daughter, and he grew suspicious of the gate captain, sure that she wished to share in a triumph that belonged to him and his unit alone.

"I doubt they'll thank you for returning her bound and in a cart full of boxes, especially after the rumors start as to why she was paraded in this state through the wards," the gate captain said, eyeing Iellieth and her unkempt appearance. Had the soldiers been less worried that she would run away the night before, she would have taken more time washing away the accumulated dirt from her travels, but she hadn't had a moment alone since the captain found her.

Lucinda would be horrified by the layers of dirt and dust embedded in Iellieth's leathers and the knots through her hair. Her half-sister had been upset enough to see her return from planting one morning with flecks of soil clinging to damp knees—this would be far beyond her capacity to endure. Iellieth pressed a finger to her lips to suppress her grin. The duke's reaction would be less enjoyable, another lecture on their responsibility as Amastacias and how she had yet again fallen short of that prestigious heritage. But her mother? The captain kept telling her how worried the duchess had been, which was hard enough to believe. Would Mamaun actually express that concern when she saw Iellieth again?

While they argued among themselves, a carriage arrived, sent down from the castle by Hutcheon's advance party who spotted his approach. With a smirk of self-satisfaction, the young man transferred Iellieth and Marcon into the coach. He led the procession up through the winding streets of Linolynn to return her to Io Keep.

CHAPTER 31

"**S**tand aside, stand aside." A familiar voice rang out across the entry courtyard as Stormguard Basha shoved his way through the assembled troops. "Where is she?" The dwarf peered among the ranks, eyes finally alighting on the carriage that held Marcon and Iellieth.

"Where've you been?" He stomped forward and yanked the door open, waving aside the guard stationed next to it. "By the gods, Ellie, what've they got you bound for?" Basha guided Iellieth out of the carriage, squinted at Marcon, and then resumed his shouting at the freshly arrived soldiers. "Who's responsible for this?"

The captain sprang forward, stammering apologies and trying to explain the circumstances in which he had found Iellieth and her captor in the woods. Basha roared and threw himself toward the carriage.

"No, no, he's been helping me!" Iellieth seized the dwarf's sleeve with her still-bound hands. "Stormguard, I swear."

"Humph," Basha grunted. "Alright, bring him out

then."

Hutcheon and one of his men reached inside and pulled Marcon out into the sunlit courtyard.

"You've been aiding her?" Basha squinted up at Marcon, assessing his trustworthiness.

"I have, sir." Marcon's low voice rumbled across the stone cobbles.

Basha looked from his captain to Marcon and back. "Well, don't just stand there," Basha snapped. "Let the lady free, and her associate as well."

"But, sir—"

"What danger do you suppose one man poses to an entire company, eh? We've enough assembled here to overpower him twenty times over." Hutcheon frowned at Marcon, dubious of Basha's assessment but eager to follow his commander's orders.

"Alright, alright, off with the rest of you now," Basha said, waving them away. He held out his arm toward the castle gates, indicating that Iellieth and Marcon should proceed ahead of him. "Your mother's been to see me every day since you disappeared, and I'll not be held responsible for her worrying a moment longer."

"I'll be sure my family knows who to thank for locating me," Iellieth said quickly to Captain Hutcheon. The bloody helmet Marcon had found in the woods flared in her memory, its wearer and his companions slain by Lucien's werewolves. Basha would help her find out who they were when the time was right.

Another familiar voice echoed in the corridor ahead, hurrying toward Iellieth. "Excuse me, excuse me." Scad's mother, Celia, navigated through the guards and castle servants, standing on tiptoe to try and find Iellieth in the crowd at the gates.

"Celia," Iellieth called, hand raised overhead.

Scad's mother rushed forward and clutched Iellieth's arm, peering anxiously behind her at Basha and Marcon. "Is he with you?"

Iellieth had never seen Celia in such a frantic state. Dark circles bloomed beneath her eyes, and her usually tanned skin was pale, her lips strained. "Celia." Iellieth held on to her elbows, trying to calm her. She led her over to the side, away from the crowded entryway. "I don't know where he is, I'm sorry. He's not with me. But I'm going to help you find him."

It was possible Scad had left a note in her room. He would never have deliberately caused his mother this amount of worry, but where could he have gone? "Can you tell me anything more? When did you last see him?" *Please, some sort of clue.*

Celia sobbed, her hands gripping Iellieth's sleeves for support. "He's missing. He disappeared the same day you did. I've been hoping all this time he had run away with you. They told me it wasn't possible, but I—" Her voice broke again, and she fell against Iellieth's shoulder, crying.

Basha patted Celia's back, trying to comfort her.

Celia pulled out a handkerchief and wiped her eyes. The smallest flicker of hope lit her dark brown irises. "Have you heard from him at all? Do you know anything?"

Iellieth shook her head, restraining her own distress as she realized that she would have to disappoint Celia further. "I'm sorry, Celia. I only heard a few days ago that he was missing. I-we'll do everything we can to find him."

Once she had a chance to explain that it was were-wolves and not Hadvar responsible for the attacks, they could call off the war and make their peace. Then both kingdoms could work together to root out the remaining werewolves, and Scad could return from Hadvar. That had to be where he had gone.

"Thank you." Celia embraced Iellieth. "I'm relieved you're well and have come back to us. It's been . . . difficult, with the other children vanished also, for anyone to listen to me. But I know you'll be able to find my boy." She smiled faintly and squeezed Iellieth's hand, excusing herself to return to the castle kitchens.

Iellieth leaned back against the cold stone wall, trying to gather her thoughts. "Basha, what children was she talking about? Did someone else mis-transmigrate?"

The stormguard looked down, shaking his head. "No, she's referring to something else. They've been disappearing for a few weeks now. A couple from the castle and ten or twelve from the Air Ward, that we know of so far."

So many. "And no one knows where they've gone?"

"No trace that we can find so far," Basha said. He sighed. "My troops will continue searching. We're trying to keep panic down. There's worry enough about the war as it is."

Iellieth followed Basha through the more crowded hallways and toward the Amastacia wing, Marcon close by her side. "Basha," Iellieth began once they were alone in the corridors, "I don't know how much you can tell me, but why is there going to be a war with Hadvar? We heard about it while we were gone, along with the werewolf attacks in the mountains and—"

"Werewolves?" The dwarf turned to her, surprised. "Hmm. We hadn't heard that specifically. Did Hadvar release them?"

"No, that's not what I meant." Why would Hadvar have unleashed werewolves on those dwelling in the mountains? Even more of their subjects than Linolynn's lived in the remote communities. "It's the werewolves attacking the villages, a large pack, not Hadvar."

"We've had reports for some time now of troubles in the mountains. That's part of why Lord Nassarq came back from Nocturne—wasn't safe for him to stay up there without enough soldiers to protect him and the household if things turned. But while there've been whiffs of war, the king made it official just after we lost you. It seems the Hadvarian queen crossed King Arontis during the trip. I've never seen him so angry. He gave the command to send out troops, and it's my duty to follow. We're making ready to march soon."

What could the queen have possibly said that would have driven Arontis to such an extreme course of action? Iellieth couldn't voice how hopeless a battle over land with Hadvar would be; Basha would have been deeply hurt, and he had enough to contend with as it was. Even if it had been Lucien and his werewolves who started the war, or the threat of it, they weren't the ones pushing it forward. So who was?

⚜

IELLIETH TURNED THE QUESTIONS BASHA'S NEWS HAD raised over and over in her mind as they neared her family's corridors. Her feet retraced the steps they'd taken countless times before and, much sooner than she'd anticipated, the black doors of the Amastacia wing stood solidly before her.

She took a step back, bumping into Marcon behind her. Basha rapped twice on the door, and it swung open, the duke's steward ready to escort them inside.

Iellieth paused beside Basha, hoping to tell him that

she would seek him out later with more details about the werewolves. Someone in Io Keep needed to know.

The steward cleared his throat.

"I just need a moment to—"

"Surely your long disappearance has been time enough," a cold voice interrupted her. Chills ran down Iellieth's spine. Duke Calderon Amastacia glowered at her from the center of the receiving hall, flicking his eyes over Marcon before returning to her once more. "Follow me," he ordered and strode across to his office.

Anything she said to Basha now, the steward would repeat. She'd find her moment later. Basha's worried eyes watched her file in after her stepfather, and the steward clicked the door shut behind them.

"Take a seat," the duke ordered, barely glancing up from the papers on his polished, dark cherry desk to look at Iellieth and her companion.

Iellieth sat in the single chair across from his desk, and Marcon stood with his back against the wall behind her.

"I hope you are pleased with the dramatic nature of your reentry." The duke's upper lip curled as he took in her dirty armor and disheveled appearance. "It is unbecoming for one of our family's station but"—he smirked—"you have long thwarted that, haven't you?"

Iellieth stared back at him in silence, the most effective way she'd found of coping with her stepfather. Marcon's anger pulsed throughout the room, growing more insistent as the interview continued.

Calderon leaned back in his chair. "Tell me, Iellieth, what precisely is the nature of your relationship with this man behind you?"

She kept her face as devoid of expression as she could

make it. He wanted to embarrass and frighten her. That time had passed.

"Are you grown suddenly deaf as well as obstinate in your absence?" He slouched forward, squeezing the edges of his desk. "After the absurd expense of trying to find your hiding place, wherever it is you've been, your bride price ruined by your roaming around alone with—" he waved his hand dismissively at the champion.

Marcon growled in response.

"I haven't time for this," the duke continued. He slammed the ledger in front of him shut. "After all the work I went to, begging Lord Stravinske to reconsider after your nonsense." He narrowed his eyes, his lips curling into a snide grin. "Had I known, years ago—"

"Calderon," the duchess called sharply, interrupting his insults. The duke's head twisted over to his wife in the doorway, and Iellieth spun around in her chair. Her mother looked pale. Several long golden curls had sprung loose from her normally immaculate coif and hung loosely around her neck. "I would like to speak with her."

"I will be done with her in a moment, Emelyee. I—"

"No," Mamaun snapped. "I will speak with her now." The duchess stepped inside the room, holding her hand out to indicate which way Iellieth and Marcon should proceed. "Marcon, was it?" She glanced at him, her voice calm and polite.

Marcon bowed to her. "Marcon Colabra, Your Grace."

Mamaun smiled briefly before her lips returned to their tense line. "A pleasure. Please allow me to show you to one of our guest rooms. Iellieth, you'll come with me as well."

Iellieth rose and followed her mother, careful not to glance back at Calderon's reddening features. The aura of his frustration soothed her enough. His eyes bored into her back as she left, but she followed her mother, head held high. When was the last time she had seen Mamaun contradict him?

The duchess turned gracefully on her heel and glided down the corridor. She said nothing as they stepped into the side hall that led to the Amastacias' many bedroom suites. After a few paces, Mamaun stopped abruptly. She looked back at Iellieth, wringing her hands.

Iellieth stepped forward. "Mamaun, are you—"

A small, strangled cry, fingers pressed to her lips, and then Mamaun embraced her, holding Iellieth against her chest, fingers clutched at the back of her head. "My sweet girl, I've been so worried about you." Mamaun stroked the messy tangle of braids tied at the base of Iellieth's neck.

Words caught in her throat, and she returned her mother's embrace. Her early years in Io Keep settled around them: the duchess soothing her as she sat in her mother's lap sharing a cup of tea after the other children mocked her pointy ears or excluded her from their games.

"I'm sorry," Iellieth finally managed after several moments had passed. Should she have sent Mamaun word faster? She shooed the thought away and clutched this expression of affection tightly, adding it to her small store of such treasures.

The duchess straightened and pressed her fingertips against the corners of her eyes. "If you'll follow me, please," she said to Marcon, turning once more down the hall.

Marcon stared after her for several steps before he began to follow. When he glanced down at Iellieth, he was beaming.

She returned his smile. Her mother's response to her return was beyond anything she had dreamed possible.

Emelyee showed Marcon to his room, a few doors down the hall from Iellieth's, and explained that a servant would be along shortly to see to his needs. The duchess then followed Iellieth to her room, where the familiar circle of windows greeted her with warm sunlight. Mamaun sat on the chaise and patted the space beside her, gripping Iellieth's hand in hers when she sat down.

Her mother gazed out the windows and rubbed her thumb over the back of Iellieth's hand before she spoke. "Iellieth, what happened? Where have you been?" Her voice was soft, and her eyes creased with worry.

"I'm alright, Mamaun. I . . ." How could she best explain? "I got mis-transmigrated on our way to Hadvar."

"Mis-transmigrated? Did someone pull you away from us? Can such things happen? I felt you, slipping away from me. And then when we arrived—" Her mother shut her eyes tight. She must have been frightened and confused to transmigrate across the continent with one of her children having disappeared along the way. "How did this happen? Where did it take you?"

Should she explain about the amulet? No, Mamaun would be angry with her father for giving her something so dangerous. "It took me to the mountains, to Torg's Peak. I found Marcon there, and a group of travelers helped us and took us to a druid conclave nearby."

"A druid conclave?" Her mother squinted at her and brushed a few of Iellieth's stray hairs back into order. "How far away were you in the mountains? Why did you not return here earlier? With the war—" Emelyee shook her head. "Calderon has been doing all he can to talk the king out of this foolish and aggressive path. He's been very distressed by his weakened influence of late. I'm sure that's why he spoke to you that way just now. But no matter." Mamaun smiled as though the situation was entirely resolved. "At least you're here and safe now."

Bridget entered with a tray of sandwiches and tea. Her eyes lit up when she saw Iellieth, but the duchess dismissed her.

If there was ever a time to be open with her mother, this had to be it. "Mamaun, I know you want to defend him, but I feel you must know why I didn't return sooner." She bit her lip and paused to see if the duchess took her meaning. "After Katarina told me Scad was missing, though, I had to come back."

Her mother's teacup clattered on its saucer. "Katarina? How did she speak with you?" Mamaun's lips shrank back into their angry line. "I visited her several times, asking about you. And to think—"

"I asked her not to say anything to you," Iellieth whispered. She pressed her fingernails into her forearm. She couldn't lose her nerve now.

"What?" Her mother's breaths trembled, and she stared at Iellieth.

She proceeded cautiously. "I sent word to Katarina about what had happened. I-I asked her not to say anything to you because I didn't want the duke to know where I was."

Mamaun sprang up and away from Iellieth, skirts swishing as she hurried across the floor to the windows, arms tight around her waist.

"I didn't want him to find me and force me to return to Hadvar to get married."

Her mother whirled around, her dark blue eyes bright as color flared on her cheeks. "You told a translator that you were alive and well and instructed her not to pass on the same courtesy to your family? Do you have any idea—"

"Do you honestly blame me?" Iellieth bolted upright. Unbelievable. How long had it taken for things to return to the way they had been? "Can you truly not understand?" Her voice rose as she teetered dangerously between yelling and tears.

Her mother's face froze, but now that she'd started, Iellieth couldn't stop. "If you hadn't been so determined to turn a blind eye to what he was doing, to the endless parade of suitors he threatened me with, settling, deliberately, on the cruelest one." Iellieth shuddered at the memory of Lord Stravinske's assault. "A monster. They both are. And it didn't matter to you. It still doesn't matter to you."

Mamaun was breathing quickly, shaking.

Iellieth lowered her voice. "Why should I have thought that just because I disappeared suddenly, it would be different? Wasn't that what you wanted anyway?"

Her mother's eyes blurred, and she jolted away from Iellieth, heels clicking on the stone as she rushed for the door and slammed it behind her.

Iellieth shivered. She stumbled back and sank onto the chaise, burying her head against her knees. The one chance she'd had in ten years to connect with her mother, she'd ruined as quickly as it had appeared.

An hour passed as a thunderstorm gathered outside. The latch to her door slid open. Footsteps approached. A solid form sat on the sofa beside her and wrapped an arm around her shoulders. Iellieth turned and buried her head in Marcon's chest. "I can't stay here," she mumbled.

"You don't have to, lady." He patted her back.

"We should find Quindythias. Tonight."

CHAPTER 32

Teodric took the stairs from below decks two at a time and strode to Ambrose's side. "What's going on? David said you needed to speak with me straightaway?"

"Yes, Captain." Ambrose kept his eyes trained on the *Dominion*, waiting for further semaphore signals. "We've received an order about the merchant ship Curt spotted from the crow's nest."

Teodric nodded. He drummed his fingers against his pant leg, waiting for Ambrose to answer. The navigator drifted through the world at his own speed. "And what of it?" he asked when he couldn't linger any longer.

"Admiral wishes us to seize them and bring the plunder and survivors aboard the *Dominion*."

Teodric sighed. "Very well, thank you, Ambrose. Have you informed Kriega?"

"Not yet, sir."

"Please do so and ask her to ready a boarding party. I'll convene with both of you shortly." Ambrose bowed his head and went to find the first mate.

If the other ship had timed their voyage differently, ahead or behind by a few more hours, they could have avoided this. With such a specific retrieval mission to the ports outside Andel-ce Hevra, Syleste wouldn't have minded if they met her on her island with the requested passenger and no additional plunder. That very afternoon, she had been planning to split off from their northern course. But as she was nearby and never missed an opportunity to enrich her store of goods and people, the smaller vessel couldn't be allowed to peacefully sail away. "Ten percent to my captains," she'd said to him with a wink two days prior.

Teodric crossed the deck to his cabin to finalize their preparations.

৩৯৫

AT TEODRIC'S ORDER, THE *AMBER QUEEN* PULLED alongside the smaller vessel. They'd signaled their surrender the moment his ship and the *Dominion* raised Syleste's flag: a coiled green dragon crushing a carrack. Ambrose commanded the rowers below, and Kriega's boarding party stood poised beneath the mast. It was unlikely they were heavily armored, but he didn't want to take any undue risks this early in his tenure as captain. Kriega stomped up and down the deck, barking orders.

"Shall I step aboard, or shall you, Captain?" she asked as he approached her. The late afternoon sun glinted off her teeth.

"Let's go together," he said. "Ambrose can watch the ship while the admiral sorts through the vessel's holdings."

"She'll be pleased to have acquired a new target so early in her voyage. You follow orders well, Captain."

"Thank you, Kriega." Teodric smiled, pretending not to notice her mocking tone. His father would have been aboard a ship similar to the *Vervain* when it was lost at sea or whatever had become of it. Syleste had sworn that she hadn't encountered him. He desperately wanted to believe her. Teodric knew what his father's fate would have been had they run across the *Dominion*; those aboard the *Vervain* would soon find out.

Kriega handed him the rope to swing across with the first wave. She would follow with the second. The salty sea wind rippled his hair as he flew, rapier drawn, and landed on the *Vervain*'s deck.

The takeover went smoothly and swiftly. Syleste followed them aboard after all the crew had been gathered at the mast. She cut the captain's throat as Kriega oversaw the division of the cargo. Teodric kept a sharp eye on his crew but distanced himself from the admiral and her malice as best he could. He was relieved not to find many passengers aboard. Syleste had little patience for those who couldn't sail. She alternated between leaving them on a plundered, abandoned ship to fend for themselves or tossing them into the waters.

With the slaughter of the captain, a few others of the *Vervain*'s crew resisted and met a speedy end at Syleste's rapier. The blood glimmered along the blade and dripped freely onto the deck of the ship. The trial was nearly over, their plunder divided and dispatched, when Syleste caught sight of an attractive young woman hidden behind several other crew members. The girl was shaking as Syleste seized her by the hair and dragged her forward.

"My new captain, what would you say to an addition to your crew?" Syleste laid her free hand against the girl's waist.

The admiral smirked at his anxious study of the young woman. Even after all his work at wearing a mask whenever he interacted with her, she could effortlessly read his mind. She toyed with the girl further, caressing her side and neck, waiting to see which of them would break first.

React. Do something, Teodric begged the young woman. Syleste wanted a show and surrender. On his travels, he'd heard of magic that allowed one to speak into the mind of another. How greatly he desired that ability now.

Syleste laid her head on the girl's shoulder and turned her eyes toward her fair-skinned face, drinking in the young woman's fright as she whimpered.

It was almost enough. He steeled himself. If he could stay unmoving, emotionless, she might relent. Her sharp fingernails dug into the girl's neck, drawing blood. A strangled cry broke from the young woman's lips.

"Say enough, Teodric," the sing-song voice had said as Syleste tormented him, her breath hot against his ear. "Say enough or there will be more." He'd screamed as her knife dug into his chest, even louder, damaging his throat, when they doused his bleeding body in saltwater, carving the constellations of scars that covered his chest and back. And what she'd had done to him on the island—no. This humiliation was something someone could recover from. Other tortures were not.

The admiral locked her eyes on him when the girl screamed. He gave her the smallest glint of amusement, not knowing if it would assuage Syleste's desire to see those under her power echoing her corruption. Playing his part now would protect his crew in the future.

Syleste chuckled. "Very good, Teodric. I thought you might need some company for your first mission." The admiral unlaced the collar at the base of the girl's neck and pulled the fabric looser across her chest. "I hope she'll do well."

The girl's bleeding throat convulsed, her limbs shaking. Teodric focused his eyes on the bottom of her jaw. *A few moments longer, and you'll be free.*

The pirate queen shoved her captive toward him, and she stumbled forward into Teodric's arms. He caught her and grasped her shoulder and elbow, holding tighter than he would have under other circumstances, but he needed to maintain his façade and not arouse the admiral's suspicion.

"Teodric," Syleste called over her shoulder as she walked away from the carnage strewn across the deck of the smaller ship, "I don't give gifts without expecting something in return."

He raised an eyebrow and smirked in response.

"I'll try and make it a redhead next time." Syleste smiled cruelly, and Teodric's blood ran cold. The admiral stepped onto her boat laden with plunder from the *Vervain* and snapped at her crew, signaling them to row her back to the *Dominion*.

"Your generosity is greatly appreciated, Admiral," he finally managed. "We shall make haste on our successful return."

The grin that haunted his nightmares flared once more. "See that you do."

Teodric gestured for the girl to climb up the ladder his crew had lowered. She did, slowly, and Kriega escorted her to his cabin as he climbed up behind her. He inclined his head to Kriega and stepped into his quarters, the solid click echoing in the room as the door shut behind him.

The girl bolted to the opposite side of the room and crumpled into one of the corners, breaths shaking as she glared at him and waited to see what would happen to her next.

He stayed with his back pressed against the door, hands held forward at his waist. "Words cannot express how sorry I am about what happened. I promise that you are safe here. No one will—" The door jolted against his back and pushed him forward. A high-pitched, angry voice grumbled on the other side.

Teodric jumped to the side as the door to his cabin flew open. A short, gray-blue goblin scowled up at him, silhouetted by the late afternoon sunlight. "If the captain insists on having food brought to him for himself and his guest, he might at least avoid barring the door."

The young woman's eyes were wide, staring at the ship's chef.

"Keever, my good man, my apologies. I didn't realize you would be arriving so quickly."

"The first mate insisted, so here I am." Keever stomped into the room. He carried a silver tray over to the young woman, who pressed herself even tighter against the wall.

Keever held out the tray, and the girl shook her head. "What, you want something else?" The goblin set the tray on the ground and flicked his fingers at it. A roasted chicken and beans appeared where a cut of beef had been before. "Still no?"

"Master Keever is our incredible cook," Teodric explained, trying to help set the girl at ease.

She looked back and forth between them.

"He was seeking . . . independence from his former

home, and the two of us struck up a beneficial arrangement." He'd saved the goblin's life after Keever angered the head of his community. He brought him aboard the *Dominion* and now the *Amber Queen*.

"Captain Teodric is lucky to have me," Keever explained. The goblin stared at the cowering young woman, lips scrunching together as she continued to watch him and not the food "Fine." He flicked his fingers forward again, and the area in front of her filled with soups, meats, and loaves of bread. "I'm going back where it's safe." Keever glared at Teodric on his way out and slammed the door behind him.

"He doesn't like being above decks." Teodric shrugged. "His people lived underground, so he prefers being as low in the ship as he can. I'll, umm . . ." He cast around for something more he might say to her but, finding nothing, returned to his place by the door. "I'll just leave you to—"

"Can he really create anything? Just like that?" The woman mimicked Keever's finger motion.

"It's remarkable, isn't it?" Teodric smiled, relieved she had recovered enough to speak.

"You're not like her, are you? The pirate with the long dark hair and the dragon flag?"

Teodric shook his head. "No. I try very hard not to be."

"Then why do you sail for her?"

"Following a choice spurred on by desperation, I've yet to find a way out." August had believed he would at some point. That's what she was trying to tell him when he left.

"I'm Athena," she said.

"Teodric." He tucked his arm around his waist and bowed. "Welcome aboard the *Amber Queen*."

❀

TEODRIC PULLED OUT HIS LUTE AND TOOK A SEAT BELOW the quarterdeck. Two days more, and they would reach Andel-ce Hevra's northern port. "Friends and sailors," he called, "a well-won evening's celebration." Hearty cheers echoed down the deck. "To the *Queen* and her crew!"

The sailors took up the toast, clinking mugs together. "The *Queen* and her crew!" Though the first part of their voyage had been compromised by Syleste's greed, here, for the first time, he and his sailors were free. As captain, he could set a new standard for their life at sea.

Celebrations had been few and far between aboard the *Dominion*, another tradition he intended to break. Morale was crucial to smooth sailing, and a crew who elected to serve under their captain, rather than one bent to service out of fear, was a crew well worth having and working for.

All those who could be spared from duty drank and laughed, enjoying the smooth waters and an evening of relaxation and amusement. As the hours passed, crewmates rotated in and out, playing music and singing alongside their captain while a few others danced nearby.

When he was unaccompanied, he played the sea shanties unique to the Caldaran coast where he'd grown up. Few of these songs had crossed to the other side of the Infinite Ocean, a fact that had shocked him when he first arrived in Nortelon.

As dusk stretched across the horizon and bathed the *Queen* in pale gold, a song he'd written while still in Caldara floated back to him, asking to be played. He resisted its siren call, playing a popular ballad instead, but the song refused to relent.

Roses and drying, autumn leaves danced through his senses despite being at sea in the spring. The scents of that last night, before they were separated, when he'd performed the song he wrote for her, the one that refused to relent, always drifting back.

A sudden presence beside him startled his reverie; an off-key twang interrupted the song's chorus. Athena sat beside him. His hands easily found their way back to the melody and continued strumming.

"Which song were you just playing?" she asked when he met her eyes.

"One I wrote several years ago." The salty sea breeze rustled through his hair. A burst of shouting and laughter echoed down the deck as players revealed their hands at cards.

"Was the girl in it someone you knew?"

"She was." He smiled at Athena. The version of himself who had written that song could never have imagined any of this: sailing, captaining a crew, losing those he loved. He'd taken so much for granted then, wrapped in more immediate troubles, ignorant of the storm brewing on the horizon.

Athena leaned back in her chair and crossed her feet at the ankles. "What happened to her?"

The silkiness of a dark red tendril of hair curled between his fingers. Laughter frolicked behind bright green eyes. Teodric shook his head. "I'm sure I couldn't say. If things went as planned for her, she's somewhere in Caldara, married to a wealthy nobleman." His fingers strummed the individual notes of the final chord. Minor with a hint of sweetness.

"And if things didn't go as planned?"

A shadow fell across his memory. Syleste gloating. A terrible fate. He strummed the chord again. "Ultimately, she would meet the same unhappy ending any of the rest of us fear, I suppose."

Athena frowned and turned away.

He stopped playing and reached out toward her. "No, Athena, wait. I'm sorry. I didn't intend to sound so callous." She had found her place as part of his crew, a hard-working, sharp addition interested in aiding Ambrose when she wasn't stationed elsewhere. "I know you lost people who were dear to you a few short days ago."

"Like you lost her?" Athena raised an eyebrow.

Teodric bowed his head. "She was the first, yes. I lost others, after." The ocean lapped serenely against the sides of the ship, her gentleness hiding the countless bodies that floated in her wake.

"I wanted to thank you for bringing me aboard and for helping me find pleasant quarters." She smiled and played with the end of her scarf, which was fluttering in the breeze. "Everyone on my last ship snored terribly. It's quieter here, for the most part. And listening to you play tonight has helped."

Teodric gestured to his crew, leaning against the ship's railings or drinking side by side at tables brought up from the hull. "You are surrounded by people with stories similar to yours, Athena. I don't know if that's any consolation or not. Out here, on the open ocean, none of us emerge unscathed."

She nodded. "Most of the songs would like us to believe otherwise, wouldn't they? Tales of daring . . . or survival." She raised her glass. "I hope the woman in your song found an ending that suited her, as you say, Captain."

"So do I," Teodric said, raising his own mug of ale to

hers and taking a deep swig. "And may we all be so lucky in fate's chosen paths." His fingers wandered up the neck of his lute, finding their transition chord and embarking on a new song. But the siren's melody continued on, calling softly, softly, as he drifted on the sea.

CHAPTER 33

The hidden servants' entrance to Iellieth's room shook. Marcon leapt up from the couch, hand at his sword hilt. "Scad," Iellieth whispered. She hadn't found any clues to his whereabouts in her room, and her mother had kept her distance, sending Bridget with a tray of food when it was time for the evening meal.

Iellieth ran to the door, fumbled with the latch, and flung it open.

A head of thin blonde braids and a glowing smile met her on the other side.

"Katarina!" Iellieth cried. She seized her friend's hand and pulled her into the room. Katarina laughed, happy to follow.

"Marcon, this is Katarina, who you've heard so much about."

"A pleasure—"

"I'm so glad you're back," Katarina spoke over Marcon's greeting. "And who is this?"

It was the happiest she'd felt since her wolf transformation that night with Yvayne. Iellieth summarized her and

Marcon's adventures to Katarina, explaining that he was the reason she had asked about the War of the Champions.

Katarina's attention was rapt as Marcon told her about his friend and some of their exploits together. "It's extremely fortunate that your letter came when it did," Katarina said. She pulled a sheaf of notes from her satchel and laid them out across Iellieth's desk. Several of the documents were covered in runes, many of which resembled Marcon's tattooed markings.

"Katarina," Iellieth began, "are these—"

"Nonsense," the scholar answered. Iellieth and Marcon both looked up at her in confusion. "They're complete nonsense. Unless"—she raised her eyebrows, smiling—"you're able to break through their enchantment, which, because of your friend's long and unusual name, I was."

"Is this something you do normally?" Iellieth had never seen Katarina enchanting or de-enchanting documents during their research before.

"It's not something I've had much cause to do during my residence here, but now that I know what to look for, that may change. However, we haven't much time. I can explain in more detail as we go." She turned to Iellieth. "Am I to understand that your plan is to awaken this other champion from the distant past?"

"Yes," Iellieth said. All of these years working with Katarina, and she'd had no idea. "Since you've been looking into it further, do you think you might come with us?"

"I believe you may need me as a guide," Katarina said. She shuffled a few of the papers around and held out a yellowed parchment, half-covered in glyphs.

"I certainly can't read this." Iellieth shook her head and

handed the page to Marcon to see if he recognized any of the writing.

"This one has been difficult," Katarina explained. "I cannot break all the way through the enchantment, but I've had some assistance in the catacombs in your absence. I nearly have the route memorized, though I keep this with me in case something goes awry, but I believe we've found who you're looking for."

Had they really found Quindythias's burial place based on a few altered documents hidden away in the Scriptorium? How many were involved in the search? "Katarina, will we have trouble with guards? Are there more patrols now, because of the war?" If they'd been granting the scholar time and space below the keep because they thought what she was searching for was tied to her research, perhaps they might grant access to Iellieth and Marcon as well.

"The guards are more concentrated in certain areas," Katarina said. "But that doesn't necessarily mean they'll be patrolling the places we'd like to go. Plus, I've brought some supplies that might help." Her dark brown eyes sparkled as she withdrew a silver thread from her satchel. "I will need a short while to prepare, but that should give our other helper time to extract himself from his duties so he can meet us."

"Our other helper?" Iellieth asked.

The scholar grinned. "Stormguard Basha had a feeling you would be up to something tonight. He's taking a break from his extra patrols to search for the missing children to come and aid you. From your reception here earlier, it seemed he didn't think you would be staying long."

Iellieth sighed. "No, I don't plan to. What is it that you're preparing?"

Katarina looked up from muttering over her piece of thread. "It's a simple shield charm that should help us escape notice."

"Why did you never tell me before that you could cast magic?" Had she simply missed the signs?

The scholar laughed. "We're all entitled to a few secrets, aren't we?"

"It would seem so." Iellieth still had a few surprises of her own to share, and she had no idea what to expect when they awakened Quindythias.

Katarina instructed them to each tie one of the magic strings around their ankle so that their journey through the hidden passageways might go undetected. "Can you guide us into the basement of the castle from here?" she asked Iellieth after she was sure the spell was working properly.

"Yes, I haven't been down there in some time, but I remember the way." It was rare that she had a reason to explore the castle's lower levels, especially the tunnels that led deep underground. Keeping them away from the primary passages would make navigating to the catacombs more difficult, but she would be able to find her way.

Once most of the castle had turned in for the night, Iellieth led them through the Amastacias' hidden passageways and out into the tunnels that ran behind the walls across the keep. Small torches lit the narrow passages, and they tiptoed in and out of the fires' glow as they wound deeper.

On the southern side of the castle, near the Jorgan wing, the tunnels split in a turn Iellieth couldn't remember having encountered before. The passage straight ahead seemed more promising than turning right. Surely she would have recalled turning off one branch of tunnels into another.

A white stone glimmered on the floor of the side corridor. What was it? "Wait here," Iellieth whispered. She crept down the other passage.

"Lady," Marcon called after her.

Iellieth's stomach froze. It couldn't be. She bent and lifted the cold alabaster figure from the ground and ran her finger along the ridges of its carved fur. "It's my wolf." A chilling wind blew toward her from the passage ahead. She stepped back.

Marcon was at her side. "What is it, lady?"

Iellieth crouched in the low-ceilinged passageway, staring down at the wolf figurine. "Scad had this, the day I left. It's been mine since I was a child. He thought we would never see each other again." Her lips scrunched together as the fear for her friend and what had happened to him threatened to overwhelm her. "How did it get here?" There were no other clues or signs of disturbance. Why would he have been here?

Something wasn't right. The wind whistled toward her again, a wet cold that clung to her skin.

"He wouldn't have just dropped this," Iellieth said. "He knows how important it is to me."

"Iellieth," Katarina called from the main route, "we must keep going. We'll miss Basha, and we need his help to make it through."

Was Scad somewhere down that passage? Why would he have come this way? Even if he'd been fleeing the castle, he would have chosen another route. It didn't make sense.

Scad's parting words wrapped around her shoulders. *There's more for you than what they've planned, Ellie. You'll see.* If she went to find him now, assuming she could, she would be making the same sorts of choices she always had. Staying small, protecting herself and those she loved. But from what she'd seen in the woods, that wasn't enough. How long would it be until the werewolves regrouped? What if they turned their sights on Linolynn?

I love you too, Ellie. Be careful.

Iellieth took a shuddering breath and met Marcon's eyes. "Let's go find Quindythias."

◈

THE TUNNELS FINALLY LET OUT INTO THE ANCIENT catacombs beneath Io Keep, many of which served as a sewer system for the castle.

Katarina took over for Iellieth and directed them to their meeting point with Basha. Iellieth shivered, thinking about the side passage. Scad couldn't be down there. She shook her head and looked around the stone chamber for a task that might take her mind off the strange chill. The foul air that filtered up from the sewers pressed heavily against her senses, lying low in the room. The portals to Yvayne's home had possessed such a reassuring smell.

"Oh!" Iellieth glanced down in surprise as tiny jasmine blossoms sprouted from her fingers, manifesting from her excess nervous energy. Their sharp scent pushed back the stench of the sewers. If she could knit them together, as a mask of some sort, their journey below would be far less odious.

She wiggled her fingers over one another, encouraging the strands of flowers to interlock. Tiny roses appeared alongside the small jasmine blossoms, and she created a square that would fit over her mouth with strands that could wrap over her ears. For Marcon, she chose thyme and cinnamon, and juniper and lemongrass for Katarina. The flowery masks weren't powerful enough to entirely eliminate the smell of putrefaction coming from their surroundings, but they helped.

Basha emerged from a separate passage as Iellieth put the finishing touches on Katarina's mask. "Ellie, good to see you." He clasped her forearm. Her hand barely spanned half of his burly arm, but she gripped tightly nonetheless. Basha indicated the two soldiers behind him. "These are Marshall and Hawkins, two of my finest. They've been helping me since Mistress Katarina informed us that our castle might have a few secrets hidden in her depths."

The scholar's eyes crinkled behind her floral mask. "Some of the runes you and I examined before you left kept tugging at me. I knew they were significant, but I couldn't place where I'd seen them before. After your bird paid me a visit—an incredible creature, by the way—I shared my findings with Basha. We found the statue a few days later." Katarina shrugged as though she found it insignificant that she and Basha had found an elf who had been imprisoned beneath Io Keep for five thousand years.

At some point in the future, Katarina would need to explain these enchantments to her in case she came across them again. She still couldn't understand why the historians of Io Keep would have wanted to cover up the record of where Quindythias was located, unless the document had been manipulated even before they found it.

"We may need that sword of yours, Marcon," Basha said, eyeing Marcon's blade. "I'd rather we didn't, but vile creatures prowl these tunnels." The dwarf's face twisted in disgust. They must have come across something truly vicious for Basha to react so strongly.

"I'll follow after you, lady," Marcon said as they filed out with Basha and his men in the lead. "I don't want anything sneaking up and catching us unawares."

Their path led them into the sewers. Basha's soldiers walked expertly along the edge of the sludge, keeping their boots and cloaks dry. Iellieth did her best to place her feet precisely where Katarina stepped, but she still slipped twice, Marcon catching her by the elbow to prevent her from sliding too far. She tried to ignore the wet squelch of her boots as they continued along the careful trail ahead.

After the first hour in the sewers, Marshall directed them through a few narrow passageways. Water rushed up ahead, reaching a crescendo the closer they came. They emerged in a wide tunnel, at least twenty feet across at its center, where three waterways converged and made their way out through a fourth, larger tunnel.

"We're nearly there now," Katarina called back to Iellieth.

Marcon stood at her side as Marshall stepped into the rushing water, submerged nearly up to his hips. At high tide, seawater filtered through the waterways beneath the keep, causing higher water levels and a swift current. The inundation ahead would be well over Basha's waist and near her own. Iellieth grimaced and pulled her mask tighter. The dwarf signaled that Hawkins should proceed ahead.

A shout rang out as Marshall disappeared beneath the surface of the water, arms flailing. The light in the cavern dimmed as his torch extinguished. Basha yelled and thrust his torch into Katarina's arms, plunging into the churning waters.

Marcon ran forward, and Iellieth cast an orb of green light between her fingers, brightening the waterway. The muscles in her shoulders wound tighter as she waited to see what would emerge from the depths. Marcon ripped his sword from its sheath, peering out into the water before he jumped down to follow Basha.

The center of the chamber gurgled, and a domed figure emerged from the water, sewage clinging to its sickly green skin. Tentacles whipped out from under the surface, striking at Marcon, Basha, and Hawkins.

Marshall's head splashed out of the water for a moment; he was screaming in horror, his arms beating against the current and creature in his desperation to escape. Iellieth twisted her hands and split the orb into two. She pitched the smaller ball at the creature, a burst of bright green as she struck true. An array of mouths rippled across its skin, emitting piercing cries.

Marcon sliced through a tentacle that had encircled his arm, leaving puckered boils in its wake. A thicker appendage wrapped around Basha's waist, and he hacked at its stalk, trying to cut himself free. Black blood pooled in the water.

Hawkins strode ahead, struggling against the tide to reach Marshall, dodging the tentacles' grasp above and below the water. Beside Iellieth, Katarina chanted to the torch, motes of firelight splitting off and flinging themselves at the creature. Each sizzling strike elicited a high-pitched scream.

Marshall clamped on to Hawkins's arm. He might be saved.

A flurry of tentacles exploded from the creature and sucked the soldier into the monster's torso. "No!" Hawkins shouted. He ran headlong at the creature, slashing at its writhing form.

For a moment, it seemed as though Marshall had freed

himself from the creature's grasp. His face appeared along its side, locked in a silent, agonizing scream. Iellieth screamed as well as his skin ripped away from his skull, his wide-open mouth the only recognizable feature as it stretched across the creature's body, sliding toward Hawkins.

Iellieth threw a second green orb at the face, determined to spare Hawkins the sight of Marshall's horrible death. Another tentacle wrapped around Hawkins's arm, pulling the shoulder out of socket as it tried to absorb his body as well. Basha cried out for his men as he slashed at another tentacle, nearly within arm's reach of Hawkins. The soldier shouted again as the tentacles encircled his waist; there was a deep snap as his leg was broken, and the creature dragged him beneath the water.

She wasn't going to allow it to seize the stormguard or to torture Hawkins as it had his partner. Streaks of bright green energy burst from Iellieth's fingers, piercing through the creature's flesh. It screamed as she burned away its corruption, writhing and slithering toward her, tumbling over itself in the water. Iellieth shouted against the effort, her magic draining quickly. She had to destroy it before it could cause further harm.

The creature's form exploded, casting rotted plant matter and goo across the chamber. Marcon yelled as he flung one of the pieces off his neck, a deep welt rising immediately from where it had made contact with his skin. Hawkins's body floated, facedown, on top of the water.

CHAPTER 34

Marcon and Basha carried the soldier's body out of the water and over to the tunnel opening opposite. Iellieth reached out for Katarina's hand, shaking, and they stepped into the deadly waters and made their way across. On the other side, they rounded a corner, emerging into a passage marked by little more than a trickle.

Basha leaned against the tunnel wall, head hanging low. "We've lost a few down here in the last few weeks. Most we haven't been able to recover. I stopped sending them on individual assignments—too many disappearances in the catacombs trying to find the children." The storm-guard shook his head. "I'd no idea we were up against something like that. Ellie, if you hadn't . . . whatever it was you did, thank you. I didn't realize you had powers of that sort."

"They're new," Iellieth said softly.

Marcon arranged the soldier's limbs and positioned him against the wall. From a distance, he might simply be sleeping.

Iellieth walked over to him and laid a hand on his arm, the other on Basha. She closed her eyes. "Elenai." Life-giving energy drifted from her fingers over to them, their wounds glowing pale blue as her magic mended the burns and boils from the foul creature. The passageway smelled of soft spring rain.

"Thank you, lady," Marcon said. He gave her a small smile and glanced back at Hawkins's body. "Here." He bent down and untied the silver thread from his ankle and carefully draped it around the soldier's neck. "So his rest will go undisturbed until we return."

Katarina nodded and knelt in front of Hawkins, murmuring quietly to renew the enchantment as she tied the thread in a loose knot.

The four of them filed down the tunnel toward Quindythias's burial place. Basha's path led them away from the sewers, back into the maze of the catacombs. They wound down curving cobbled passages and stairs carved out of the stone, the air growing colder as they descended.

"Very nearly there," Katarina said as they carefully picked their way around a pile of boulders. "There was a cave-in some time ago. Basha and his men were generous enough to trust my hunch and help me remove the obstacles. The reward was well worth it, even more so now."

Piles of boulders and discarded stone littered the hall-ways ahead. "My crews worked night and day, clearing this passage," Basha explained.

Marcon stared straight ahead as they walked. Was he worried about what state Quindythias was in? He hadn't had time to examine the chamber where he was buried, though he must be wondering how similar Quindythias's burial place would be. "Katarina, was there a giant in the room where you found him?"

She couldn't imagine how they would have gotten such a large being through these narrow passageways, but they could have built the walkways up around Quindythias afterward. That room, above Marcon with the frescoes, it might have been in use long after his imprisonment.

"There was another stone figure," Katarina said. "Very curious placement. I believe it was meant to function as a guardian of some kind. It was damaged in the cave-ins. We lined the pieces up around the outer wall."

"And Quindythias?" Marcon said quickly. "Was he harmed?"

"No, no, I didn't mean to alarm you. The crystalline figure in the center of the chamber is still intact."

Marcon sighed. "Thank you, Katarina."

"Right around this corner," Basha called from up ahead.

"Excuse me, lady." Marcon laid a hand on her shoulder and ran to catch up with Basha to be reunited with his friend.

"You found him in a similar state?" Katarina asked.

"Yes, I did. It's where my amulet took me." Iellieth stroked her necklace. The ruby was faintly warm beneath her fingertips.

Katarina smiled at her. "It really hasn't been the same here without you. But come, show me this new magic you've found."

Iellieth took Katarina's hand and jogged ahead, into Quindythias's holding cavern.

Broken chunks of the giant's stone body encircled the room. Some of the pieces were unrecognizable from the rubble they had passed on their way to the chamber, but she could distinguish several body parts amid the piles. A massive foot rested near the right-hand wall, as though it had been caught midstride on its way across the chamber. On the opposite side, the giant's chest had been split in half and laid end to end beside one of its arms. Each section was more than twice as long as she was tall.

Marcon stood face-to-face with a crystalline and stone statue in the center of the room, raised on a dais. He gazed at his friend, relief and pain at war with one another across his features. What must they have been through together, in that ancient time of conflict?

"Will you give us just a moment, please?" Iellieth whispered to Basha and Katarina. Would Quindythias awaken as soon as she drew closer? What precisely had her amulet done that brought Marcon back?

Iellieth waited at the bottom of the dais. "Are you ready, Marcon?"

"Yes, lady, I am." He moved to stand behind the statue, resting his hands on his friend's shoulders. "What do we need to do now?"

The figure's pointed elf ears stood out from the tightly wound curls that clung close to his scalp. His crystal form was a vibrant aquamarine as opposed to the garnet and ruby of Marcon's statue. The muscles along his shoulders and arms strained, his hands and legs trapped by a rocky encasement, as though the sculptor had been interrupted in completing her work. His mouth stood open, shouting, his eyes squinted shut. He must have been in great pain when they trapped him in the crystal.

How was she going to wake him up? The runes

surrounding Marcon had begun to react as she walked toward them. The stone around Quindythias was also covered in embedded runes, but no light flickered beneath them.

"Lady?" Marcon said, concerned.

"I—"

Katarina's torch sputtered, the flames calling out to her. Of course.

"You said that Quindythias was a champion of air?"

"Yes. Chosen by Atamos, his titan."

"Perfect." Iellieth grinned. "Basha, Katarina," she called, "the giant is going to wake up in just a moment."

Basha strutted toward the head, his broadsword held out toward the giant's nose.

Iellieth closed her eyes and began chanting one of the Druidic prayers Mara had taught her, beseeching the spirits of the air to come to her aid, to bring forth wind in still places. She asked the atmosphere in the underground chamber to churn, to dance around herself and those inside. A cool breeze picked up around her, blowing centuries-old dust across the ancient stonework.

She opened her eyes as the winds kissed her cheeks.

The runes beneath their feet glowed in dark sapphire, lightening to aquamarine, filling and shimmering across the floor and onto Quindythias's body. Bright beams of light broke through the stone holding his legs and hands as chunks of rock fell away. The blue light traveled up the statue, intensifying as it rose.

The crystal form began to twist, rock exploded, and a piercing scream shot across the cavern as the blue light flashed from Quindythias's awakened body.

"Quindythias," Marcon cried. He wrapped his arms around his friend's chest, holding him upright.

The elf's breaths came rapidly. He stared at Iellieth, Basha, and Katarina in turn, finally turning to look at Marcon's head beside his as he found his feet. "Marcon?" he whispered. "How?"

With a roar, the stone giant returned to life, its ancient signal activated. Its cry of rage morphed into one of pain, shouting as its separated flesh rejuvenated only to die again. Blood poured forth from the disjointed pieces of its body, pooling across the round stone chamber.

"Ugh!" Katarina shouted and ran toward Iellieth on the dais. Basha brandished his sword at the dying figure. It stilled, its face twisted in a grimace of pain. The dwarf splashed toward them, his boots two inches deep in blood that slowly dribbled out to the edges of the chamber.

"I certainly seem to have returned at a dramatic moment," Quindythias observed. He steadied himself and patted Marcon's shoulder, taking in his surroundings. "You've no idea how good it is to see you," he said.

Marcon smiled. "Nor you."

"And who are these lovelies?" Quindythias asked, turning to Iellieth and Katarina. "To be frank, I would have expected a larger force coming to my rescue, but what we lack in numbers we make up for in beauty, eh?" He smiled brilliantly and bowed. "Quindythias Dark-strider, but as you're here, I suppose you already know that."

Iellieth bit her lips together, holding back the urge to giggle at this auspicious moment. She had been expecting someone more like Marcon. Katarina, beside her, stared at Quindythias, brow creased.

Marcon cleared his throat, grinning. "Quindythias, this is Lady Iellieth Amastacia, Katarina Starsend, and Stormguard Basha." They each smiled and bowed their heads to him in turn.

"Charmed, I'm sure. Now, where precisely are we? The last I remember . . ." Quindythias's eyes widened. "My gods." He shook his head, staring off toward the side of the chamber, as Marcon had done when they were first at Mara's.

"Quindythias," Iellieth said, "you're a ways in the future. And as far as we know, for now, your old enemies are"—she glanced at Marcon for the right words—"less active than they had been." She pulled Mara's green shawl from her bag and draped it around his bare shoulders. His body was covered in tattoos, like Marcon's, though the runes were a tawnier brown against his walnut-toned skin. Flecks of brilliant bronze flickered in his dark amber eyes.

"What do you mean, 'in the future'?" Quindythias squinted at her. "You seem rather familiar. Do I? . . . No, sorry. Marcon, where are we?" He turned back to his friend.

"What Iellieth says is true, Quindythias," Marcon said. "Five thousand years have passed since we were imprisoned."

"Five thousand years?" Quindythias frowned. "Then where are we?"

"Azuria," Iellieth said, smiling at him as she led the way down the dais. "Underneath a castle in the kingdom of Linolynn."

CHAPTER 35

The man with the long, dark hair disappeared around an alley corner ahead of them. Jade pushed urgently against Genevieve's senses, begging to be put back in control. The wolf sensed danger as well as prey, and her instincts howled.

"Not yet," Genevieve told her. "Guide me, but you cannot be seen." They crept forward, carefully following the scent the man had left on clothes hung out to dry. He smelled of metal and smokey incense.

They took three turns and a set of stairs that led to a darker part of the city. Genevieve gave Jade further control of her senses, scared they would lose the man's trail otherwise.

His tracks crept underneath a bridge and stopped. A twenty-foot-wide canal guided a foot and a half of dirty water serenely out to sea. He must have crossed to the multistory building on the other side.

No one approached from either direction, and the windows of the tall building opposite her were too dark to perceive any shadowy figures watching her from the rounded windows. Genevieve tugged the tops of her boots up and splashed into the water.

Wet footprints tracked into the tall, seemingly deserted building but disappeared over the threshold. Dust and the tang of blood covered over all other scents in the rooms. How had he avoided leaving a trail through the dust that coated the floor on the lowest level?

A heavy object thumped above them. Genevieve jolted, and Jade nearly burst out of their form. Scraping, a quick struggle, and then stillness returned. The metallic scent of blood grew heavier on the air.

A gentle pull on Genevieve's heart. Grief. Anger. She dragged her foot and stepped forward, knowing instinctively that through the doorway on the far side of the room, a set of stairs led up to the next floor.

Her pulse quickened. Jade growled. Another tug on her heart. A flash of memories of her conclave, burning sage, crushed herbs, fresh-caught kindling atop a bonfire. Their most sacred ceremonies. The dagger was calling her.

Jade growled again, momentarily pressing her feet against Genevieve's, the tendons expanding. Genevieve stumbled backward, off-balance. She fell against the outside of the building, panting.

Shoes clicked toward them from the room they'd just vacated. Genevieve covered her mouth and ducked around the corner. The dark-haired man slid out of the building and walked along the canal. He knelt by the water beneath the bridge and dipped the dagger in. A trickle of red lightened to pink and faded entirely as it meandered past Genevieve's hiding place.

The man climbed up the stone wall beside the canal. Genevieve darted under the bridge just before he could walk past her, heading to the river docks. She counted under her breath, giving him time to join one of the thin throngs in this part of the city.

Genevieve wrapped her hands around the smooth stones and pulled herself up onto the street above. They wouldn't lose him this time.

The larger buildings fell away behind them, the gray and white marble of the ancient city casting its shadow on this less developed portion of its expanse. The road they were on joined with a few others. Fine carriages whisked past; beggars crouched in alleyways.

A line of trees led out of the shadow and to a collection of boats. They floated in a perfectly symmetrical lake fed by the river, awaiting passengers. The figure stepped aboard one and strode to the front. Genevieve followed, keeping her head down as one of the dockhands helped her over the walkway and onto the bobbing barge.

The boat carried them downriver toward the city's harbor and the wide expanses of the Infinite Ocean. A few ships sat bobbing in the wharf, but one stood out from the rest. The ship looked as though it had been crafted from golden wood in the fading sunlight, floating a few hundred yards beyond where the river poured into the sea.

Sailors strode confidently up and down the river docks, sure of their purpose and destination.

The sallow man squinted at each in turn, and Genevieve followed his gaze. It landed upon a handsome young man in a pale blue coat with silver buttons who watched the arrivals expectantly. He had tan skin and cool-toned brown hair pulled back in a knot behind his head, the sides shaved.

One of the barge captains helped her off the raft and asked once more if she needed any assistance finding her way aboard a vessel, but she assured him she could barter passage, careful to express her gratitude at his kind offer.

The man with the dagger approached the younger man he'd been studying, holding out his hand in greeting. The river's roar dampened their speech beyond even Jade's keen hearing. The man who had been waiting on the docks gave the one she'd been following a dashing smile and a short bow and gestured down the wooden plank path to the ships floating in the harbor.

She'd need to be careful now. Jade paced, shoulder blades slicing close to one another. They'd need to be clever as well as calm if they were to gain passage on a ship.

Genevieve let a few sailors and their cargo step between herself and her quarry. She followed them down the docks and felt the air change as the fresh river water gave way to the salt of the sea. Beyond the gentle lapping of the bay, white-tipped waves rose and fell, crashing and churning back upon themselves. Caldara lay more than a month's sail to the east, but the dagger refused to release its pull. She had to know how this man had come upon a treasured artifact of her family.

The two Genevieve and Jade were trailing walked down the docks to one of the longer piers where the pale golden ship awaited her crew. The ship's name was carved along her side, the *Amber Queen*. Genevieve doffed her hood and rolled her shoulders back. Somehow, she'd find her way aboard. Of this, she was certain.

CHAPTER 36

"Y ou and I have been statues for the last five thousand years? And we're here now because she has a magical necklace?" Quindythias asked, his voice echoing down the tunnel. Marcon explained their situation as Basha guided them through the catacombs, but Quindythias remained incredulous.

"Yes," Marcon answered.

"But next," Iellieth added, "we're going to find someone who may be able to help free you from the runes and being bound to the necklace." He might feel more at ease if he understood what they were trying to accomplish.

Quindythias poked the layered texts that covered his skin. "I actually don't mind some of these. Could be an interesting aesthetic, though at present it's overly cluttered. What do you think?" He spun around to Katarina.

"I am more interested in what they say, and why," the scholar answered. "Many of them are not scripts I've encountered before. Though I do agree with you, it is a curious effect."

"And thus far, there's little to no trace of Alessandra or her servants?"

Marcon nodded. "As far as we can tell, that's correct."

"Then why have we woken up now? Why not before?" Quindythias scowled.

"Well, we've been hoping you might help us figure that out," Iellieth said. She had assumed that he would be happier to be awake. And returning at a time when the lands were free of the rule of an evil goddess seemed more positive than he seemed ready to acknowledge.

But Marcon believed that Quindythias would be the one to help them put the pieces together, and the elf certainly asked enough questions to start that process. Her companion's bearing was taller, happier, and he looked as though he might smile at any moment.

Marcon turned Hawkins's body over to Basha after carrying him through the sewers and back to the chamber where they'd met the dwarf earlier. "I'll take him from here," the stormguard said. He turned to Katarina "Can you lead them out?"

She nodded. "Yes, I will."

"Good." Basha narrowed his eyes at Marcon and Quindythias before he spoke to Iellieth. "If they don't take good care of you, I'll know it. And I expect you to send us word that you're well."

"I'll do that," Iellieth said, touched by his concern.

"If your stepfather demands that you be brought back once he learns you're missing again, it's not in my power to counter those orders. But I will see to the eyes at the gate being redirected elsewhere in the early hours this morning so the three of you have a chance to leave. I hope that's enough."

"We are in your debt, Stormguard," Marcon said.

"Heh. Well, I'll see that you get a chance to repay it then." Basha shook hands with Marcon and Quindythias and hugged Iellieth tightly. "This war will move apace soon enough, miss. See that you're well out of the way when it does."

"I will, Basha." She raised her eyebrows. "It would be easier if I understood what had caused it. Please, why is the king so keen to go to war with Hadvar?"

The dwarf scowled. "Reason and safety are unrelated in this case, Ellie, and I won't be convinced otherwise. King Arontis has his reasons, and that should be enough for us all." Basha nodded farewell before he heaved Hawkins's body onto his shoulder and stalked down the passageway back into the castle proper. Katarina led them out through another set of winding tunnels while Quindythias asked her detailed questions about her research. Her friend delighted in answering them.

None of the passageways contained the biting chill or oppressive air she'd experienced when she found Scad's figurine. Perhaps he'd also escaped by this route, making his way to Hadvar in search of her. After they spoke with Red, she would find out.

Marcon brought up the rear as he had on the way into the catacombs, protecting them from any unknown forces sneaking up from the depths beneath the castle.

The ringing of a blacksmith's hammer echoed down the passage ahead of them, and early morning light filtered through the tunnel's barred entry.

"Welcome to the Earth Ward," Katarina said, smiling with her hands outstretched. She whispered an incantation to the iron bars, and they creaked to the side, allowing the party to pass through and into the dawn. "One final touch before you go. *Lev'ay*." Katarina waved her fingers in front of each of them. The filth from the sewers flaked off their clothing, disappearing as it fell to the ground.

"Thank you." Quindythias bowed. "We're now fit for this"—he glanced around—"village, and we will be less offensive to ourselves as well."

Iellieth laughed, the brightness above ground lifting her spirits. "This is a city, Quindythias."

His lips pursed, trying to decipher if she was speaking seriously or not.

Marcon patted him on the back, rippling the oversized tunic he'd lent Quindythias. "Much has changed, my friend. But I'm glad to have you by my side once more."

The weeks that had passed blurred as Iellieth stood beside Katarina, preparing to say good-bye again. "Keep an eye out for Edvard," Iellieth said. "We'll let you know once we've reached Red's Cross."

"I will." Katarina grinned at the three of them. "If I find any more revised records, you'll be the first to know."

Marcon nodded, and Quindythias bent to kiss her hand. "My own history is full of gallant tales, so anything you find that says otherwise, know that it's farce." The elf winked and turned away, walking with Marcon to investigate the sleepy Linolynn streets.

Iellieth shook her head. Katarina had charmed yet another acquaintance. "Do you come by that naturally, or is it the result of enchantments?"

Katarina smirked. "Naturally. Unless they have an important text or resource I desperately want, and then I've perhaps used a charm or two." Her friend's expression turned more serious. "Do be cautious, Iellieth. The altered documents were powerfully enchanted. Though I found enough to locate Quindythias, I still wasn't able to break all the way through. Whatever did that to them, and binds them to you . . ." She frowned.

"I'll be careful, Katarina. Can you do one other thing for me? Will you—" Iellieth sighed. She wasn't leaving things as they ought to be. "Will you find my mother and tell her that I, hmm, that I'm sorry for what I said to her?" She looked down, recalling the way Mamaun had run out of her room.

"Yes, of course."

An idea struck, an act that might say more than she knew how to voice at present. Iellieth hurried over to a patch of grass beside the road, rubbing her fingers over it as she requested its aid. The blades shivered, and a bloom and stalk slowly grew out of the earth, forming a perfect black rose bud in her hand. Iellieth whispered her thanks, and the stem freed itself from the ground. "Here"—she handed the rose out to Katarina—"will you give her this too?"

Katarina's fingers paused as they brushed hers and she took the rose. Her friend smiled. "Yes, I will."

Marcon and Quindythias strolled back from the block they'd been circling, pointing out curiosities to one another.

Iellieth said a final good-bye to Katarina and went to join them. She added her voice to Marcon's assertion that there were not ships that flew over the ground in this time. Quindythias struggled to accept this reality. "We'll have to walk everywhere," he exclaimed, throwing his hands up in despair. "And don't say that riding horses will make up for it." He narrowed his eyes at Iellieth. "It's really not the same." He sighed, growing wistful. "Not the same."

She couldn't suppress the giggle this time.

Iᴇʟʟɪᴇᴛʜ ɢᴜɪᴅᴇᴅ Mᴀʀᴄᴏɴ ᴀɴᴅ Qᴜɪɴᴅʏᴛʜɪᴀꜱ ᴛʜʀᴏᴜɢʜ Linolynn's quiet streets a few blocks off of the main roads. How much of this would be left if no one could prevent the war with Hadvar, and the queen's forces advanced all the way to the city? Would the young families they passed —sleeping soundly, eating breakfast, bidding one another fond farewells for the day—be forced to flee, picking their way through side streets to protect themselves from the press of bodies on the thoroughfares?

She shook her head and set those dark thoughts aside. A new phase of their journey was opening up before her. What would this learned friend of Yvayne's have to tell them about her amulet and how it anchored Marcon and Quindythias to her? What would she need to do in order to set them free?

Several weeks ago, she'd longed for a similar exit from the city, although then, she had imagined herself leaving alone. This actuality was much better, with Marcon at her side and Quindythias, found, added to their midst. Yvayne would say their pack had swelled by one. Iellieth smiled to herself and stood taller as they neared the city gates. Her new mentor's final question still remained to be answered. Where would they roam?

Sparks flickered at her fingertips. Their real journey had only just begun.

EPILOGUE

Yvayne inhaled deeply, the sun-warmed dirt and drying leaves of the devastated conclave filling her nostrils. But something else caught on the air. A liveliness, sharp. Pure oxygen in early spring. She followed the trail a few steps farther, her feet taking her southwest, toward Linolynn and the scent dredged up from the recesses of her memory.

The druid smiled. So Iellieth had done it, reawakened the champion of air. Thousands of years prior, in his lifetime before, she'd seen the elf's mischievous smile from afar. Marcon had been farther away on the battlefield, beyond her sight. In those last few weeks, leading up to the end of their age, so much had gone wrong. Perhaps this time, their efforts might be enough. Perhaps they could prevail.

"Do you believe that Lucien is working for the dark deity, Alessandra?" Mara had asked her as Cassian and Persephonie laid Iellieth's unconscious form out in the druid's hut, covering her with furs.

"I do, Mara, but I can't prove it. We'd suspected as

much before. That was part of his fall and subsequent quest for revenge."

"Are you going to tell her?"

Yvayne had breathed deeply then, as she did again now, enjoying the lively spice on the breeze. "When the time is right, but not yet," she whispered. Iellieth must be frightened enough knowing what hunted her. What help would it be to strengthen her fear by revealing the larger pieces in play, the dark game Alessandra had designed thousands of years before? No, this was knowledge she alone would bear.

Yvayne ambled over to a strand of fallen ash trees, murmuring to them, helping them find their roots and return to the earth that they might live once more. Beyond them was the circle of razed oaks she had seen, sharing in Mara's final moments. Their branches stretched over her friend, protecting her body from the ravages of the scattered werewolves.

A circle of white earth surrounded Mara, the life energy seeped from the ground around her. Yvayne carefully moved the limbs aside and arranged the druid's body in a peaceful repose. In spite of the turmoil of her final moments, her face was serene.

Yvayne knelt to move Mara's hand onto her chest. A searing jolt struck her palm, and she yanked her arm back. Mara's emerald ring glowed. The druid had embedded something, a memory or a message, into the gemstone.

She whispered a word of awakening to the ring. Its center swirled, and the stone glowed brighter.

Mara's clear voice rang out across the ruined clearing. "A wise druid once told me, 'From ashes we rise.' I didn't believe her. I couldn't see how we would be stronger for having failed or fallen, a part of our people forever gone.

Maybe one day my soul will return, and you can teach me that truth over again. But until then, watch over her for me. She'll be more powerful than you or I can yet tell. Don't give up hope, Yvayne. And don't blame yourself for lingering after the rest of us are gone. It is your nature to stay, to be here as we circle back and try, again, to find the better path."

Yvayne sank down to the earth, head bowed to receive her friend's final words. She slid Mara's ring onto her finger, a way of having her near.

Darkness stirred to the south, the threat of blood and war brewing in Linolynn. Whatever forces fanned the flames of conflict, they would need to be ready to meet.

Two had left her conclave, and two more had joined. Such was the way of the seasons. Yvayne rose. Alessandra wasn't waiting, and neither would she. Scattered allies remained from the ages past. It was time she found them again. She whispered a final incantation to the forest, and the trees set about interring the protector of the Vagarveil Wood.

Yvayne brushed the long branches aside as she climbed. It was time for old friends to be awakened.

THE STORY OF HOW IT ALL BEGAN

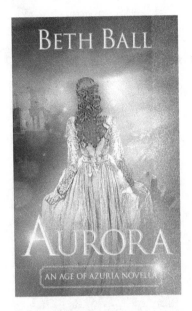

Dorric Themear has experienced the giddy flutterings of new love before. But not like this. Behind the sapphire eyes of Lady Emelyee Amastacia lies a long-awaited destiny that neither of them can sense or stop.

However, forces darker than Emelyee's husband are prepared to stand in their way.

Ridel, one of Lucien's most trusted servants, is less than enthused about her assignment to watch the lovers. If only her master had been visionary enough to see that a child cannot result if the parents are dead. She'll do her best to comply with his orders to watch and to wait—at least for now.

High in the Frostmaw Mountains, Yvayne has seen the signs of a turning of the age before. Perhaps this time, with the proper intervention, she and the druids can make a play for Azuria after all.

Visit bethballbooks.com/join to get a free copy of *Aurora*, the prequel novella for the *Age of Azuria* series and find out where Iellieth's story truly began!

THE ADVENTURE CONTINUES!

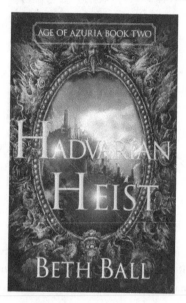

The lives of your friends are bound to your own — can you do what it takes to free them and ensure the survival of your world? In *Hadvarian Heist*, book two of the *Age of Azuria* high fantasy series, Iellieth, Teodric, Genevieve, Persephonie, and Briseras must summon the strength to withstand the pull of the darkness surrounding them, a tide whose time, whose destruction, has finally come.

Available now!

ABOUT THE AUTHOR

When she's not writing fantasy fiction, Beth Ball is a tabletop RPG designer and a literary scholar. Her academic work focuses on contemporary novels that encourage readers to find agency and empowerment in their approach to nature and their impact on the natural world, and her TTRPG adventures incorporate lots of druids.

You can find her and more stories set in Azuria at bethballbooks.com.

twitter.com/GroveGuardian

instagram.com/bethballauthor

CPSIA information can be obtained
at www.ICGtesting.com
Printed in the USA
FSHW022115090221
78446FS